a pain in the neck – and there's no chance him joining Georgie in the land of Nod. You just cannot seem to switch off. He stares wide-eyed at dawn sneaking in through the window, wondering deeply deeply where him and Georgie are going, whether he'll ever get famous, whether he'll ever get to sleep, where the Cat in the Hat went. He yanks the green sweater down from his forehead, then strides about the room feeling irritated, kicking the empty sweety wrappers round and round the carpet. The flat's a mess, and being on LSD it's quite hard to remember how it happened to get like that. All Bobby clearly remembers is twirling round with Georgie, her drunk on cheapo vodka, him tripping his numbskull off. Twirling twirling twirling. Whirling curtains. At one point they'd been dancing so much Bobby's hunger came back unexpectedly and he had to make pills-on-toast for himself in the kitchen. Here's the recipe for pills-on-toast: *2 crushed ecstasy pills, 1 slice of toast (butter optional)*. Yawn! Smoke-rings loop-the-loop past like dreamy spectacles. Where did that whole twenty-deck disappear to? Bobby considers going across the road for more fags, but the prospect of being taunted by scallywags while still slightly tripping feels daunting, and in any case he hasn't got any money. His last pound coin went on a paintbrush yesterday from Jarreds, and Johnnie from upstairs sorted him two blotters and two ecstasies on tick, and the idea was this: get wrecked and paint one two three four (or more) masterpieces. Hallucinogens are perfect for that nutty, colourful art no one can explain, but now Bobby feels ⟨...⟩ doing anything, and now the ⟨...⟩ff. He looks at Georgie breath-

2

ing louder and louder on the settee, her eyelashes pressed shut like wee Venus flytraps, and with maximum effort he starts gathering his acrylics together. Georgie's his Muse, and there's tons of Georgie canvases strewn around the flat in various poses and multicolours – the best ones, like 'Stripy Socks' (45x35cm) and 'Georgie Girl' (50x50cm), are hung above the telly in lime green and pastelly blue. Bobby the Artist crawls about the floor for a scrap of A1, then wallops bright pink across it with a six-inch DIY brush, slopping it everywhere. He ruins the carpet. Then he goes through to the bedroom to huff some Lynx Africa, spraying it into one of the dirtier argyle sweaters: the red one hasn't been washed for a bit. Smothering his face in the deodorant and sucking it all cold into his lungs, after three seconds Bobby feels a bit spacey again and floats back through to the living space, the colours in his head nice and bright again for a short while. He crosslegs himself in front of Georgie, suddenly spewing up eyelashes and blue hair-bands and fuchsia blocks all across the paper. Georgie's dressed in a blue and white sailor's outfit – often she plays up to her Muse status, her and Bobby the Artist flouncing around town in stupid attire and usually only to buy a new oil pastel or a jam-jar from Lidl. Now and then they get abusive comments from nobodies with buzzcuts, but they're well loved in Peach House and on the estate – Bobby's a bit like a doggy, quite dozy and partial to falling in love with everybody; Georgie's more like an apprehensive kitten: she loves to have fun, but it's got to be with the right person. She's often seen gawping at the sweety counter in the newsagent across Longlands

Road, with her disco-ball eyes. Bobby the Artist chucks a jelly-babies bag out from under his bum, adding a bit of wacky detail to Georgie's face – spiky mascara, chewy lips, and a thought-bubble coming out of her head with a mermaid in it. There was quite an oceanic feel to the trip tonight – swimming in the carpet, imagining the doorbells were seagulls, etc. etc. – and he blames it on Georgie's sailor gear. He continues doing the Lynx while he paints, but after a while you get immune to it and Bobby finally feels the tiredness slip over him. He's so shattered. It seems like such an effort just to mix a decent phthalo turquoise, and his hand doesn't have that usual fluidity or purposefulness – in fact Georgie looks more like a blob with eyes. Bobby the Artist screams inside – coming down off acid is such a disappointing feeling. How awful it is to float back to a grey, drab world when you've just seen happy rainbow Munchkin land. It's frustrating, and Bobby tosses 'Blob with Eyes' (58x81cm) to one side, his head hurting from all the annoyance and wretched thinking. Georgie pipes up now and then with the odd snore, and Bobby wonders what they get out of each other anyway – all Georgie does is go to work, come home moody, nibble a few sweets and fall to sleep, though she does look good in a ballerina costume. All Bobby does is splash a bit of paint around in an argyle sweater getting mortalled. But all that negative thinking is a killer – Bobby doesn't believe in being sad, he wants everyone to get on with each other (and off their heads), and the temptation's miles too strong to phone up Johnnie and score more white doves. Some of Bobby's best work comes from an MDMA-fuelled binge, all colourful and smiley and demented, although he does sometimes end up making love to the canvases. Bobby the Artist stands by the window, gazing at occasional shiny toy cars whizzing past way down there, dialling up Johnnie's mobile, but he stands there for a whole two minutes and Johnnie doesn't answer. Johnnie feels it go off in his Admiral bottoms, but he reckons it's probably his girlfriend Ellen and in any case he's got his eye on some youths over there with quite a flashy mobile and all. It's freezing out in the morning light, and Johnnie whacks up his collar as he darts across Kedward Avenue and squares up to the lads. 'Give us that, you daft cunts,' he woofs, nodding at the fancy Siemens. After Johnnie got kicked off the dole five months back, he got self-employed as a full-time thief and professional let-down. In his younger years Johnnie used to march around the estate slapping anyone who looked at him and, like a lot of the lads in his year, he was the Hardest Lad in His Year. But he's not especially macho or psychotic or unstable — in fact since he met Ellen he's calmed down slightly, and for example he loves painting pap paintings with Bobby or fixing Alan Blunt the Cunt's creaky door or helping his Nanna do the shop every Thursday. It's just a shitty state of affairs that everyone needs money. The lads look at him with their best don't-fuck-with-me (please) faces, but they can both tell they might be in for a pasting. 'Do youse wanna get battered or what?' he enquires. The lads don't, really. Johnnie roughs them up anyhow, pushing the two kids round the block, giving them little kiddy-slaps now and then for his own entertainment. Strangely, Johnnie hopes they turn on him – giving him an excuse to pull out all his best moves – but the boys are sort of fannies and they just stand around looking a bit gutted. After a while Johnnie takes the flashy phone and £7.18 off the lads, then sprints off back down Kedward. At four in the morning there's hardly going to be a copper about, but now and then they do patrol Cargo Fleet Lane so Johnnie makes a beeline straight for Peach House. He's buzzing – thievery still gives him that burst of satisfaction, plus the sevenish quid should keep Ellen happy for sevenish minutes, say if they get a pizza or something later on. Johnnie grins, glancing up at the tower – it used to be dog muck and Sugar Puff colour but in the 2000s the council tarted up all five of the blocks, and in this particular instant Peach House looks very gorgeous, like pink and yellow ice cream on top of a raspberry ripple sunrise. Instead of stalling for the lift, Johnnie darts up the stairway past 2C's knackered fridge waiting to go to the fridge graveyard, and he dodges a binbag here, there and everywhere. There's an odd sock on floor three. There's half-eaten chips on floor three and a half. When Johnnie gets to floor four he's greeted by a crazy person hurling a crazy painting down the stairwell in total disgust. 'Now then, Bobby,' he smiles, 'what you up to?' Bobby the Artist blinks quite wildish at Johnnie, all dishevelled in his green/red-trim jumper and gurning. 'Ha ha, oh how's it going? I'm pissed off like, can't fucking paint again, can I . . .' Scratching his veiny neck, Johnnie slants his head at the crumpled 'Blob with Eyes' (58x81cm) landing halfway down the staircase. Still wet, Georgie lies there on the sofa on the ocean on the paper on the step. 'As if!' Johnnie says with his eyebrows, 'it's fucking mint. God, is that Georgie? She looks dead relaxed. I like it, me.' One thing Johnnie misses in his life is relaxation. Having a hundred pills tucked in the vitamin tin and various other Class As playing hide-and-seek about the flat makes for an unsettled young man. Plus having no income means he's constantly thinking about the next steal and the next one and the next one – Johnnie gave up robbing his parents three weeks back after he nabbed £30 for the teddy-bear acid, and all the profits had to go on rent and even then it didn't stop the bailiffs coming round but Johnnie didn't open the door to them and eventually paid them off a week later after kneecapping a youngster who owed £70 ticky. On top of that, he's stressed about Ellen – they've been together about seven months, and he loves her to death, but he's completely plagued with jealousy. If she hasn't phoned for a day or two he instantly conjures up an image of her fucking one of the scummy rats she hangs around with. If they're at a party, Ellen can't talk to another boy without Johnnie getting the hump. He trusts her, but part of what attracted him to Ellen in the first place was the nymphomania and her general brassy, come-hither attitude. If he ever caught her shagging someone else, that cunt on the other side of her cunt would be absolutely fucked. That's why when Johnnie sees a portrait of Georgie all sleepy and content on a pink background, his heart expands into a big juicy strawberry. 'Can I get a picture of it?' he asks, leaning the painting upright, getting a bit of sticky acrylic on his fingers. 'I just twocked this mobile,' he goes on, unleashing the Siemens. 'It's got a camera and

7

that.' Bobby the Artist smiles while Johnnie figures how to work it, but even so the painting's totally dead to him. He believes in spontaneity, madness, pure psychic automatism, childish colours and sloppy brushstrokes, but this one's just a mess. He sighs while Johnnie snaps the disaster, although it is always nice to receive a compliment. There were these people in the 1940s who called themselves CoBrA and they believed in painting with that total abandon like a little child, but of course you do run the risk of making a massive boo-boo. 'You don't need a new phone, by any chance?' Johnnie asks, scarpering the rest of the way up the stairs. Bobby the Artist shakes his mad brown mop-top. He stands silently for a bit weighing up the prospect of forcing sleep or saying fuck it and carrying on working, and in the fuzzy dawn he figures the most rock-and-roll option would be, 'Johnnie, you couldn't sort me another couple doves on tick, could you?' Johnnie feigns a look of you-fucking-bastard, but he loves Bobby the Artist and it's been a pretty fruitful night in terms of wheeling and dealing, and he just smiles and tosses over a few left-over halves and crumby bits from his tracky-top pocket. Bobby grins and stuffs his face with the doves, although he soon realises his mouth's like sandpaper and the pills won't actually go down the chute, so he fumbles into the flat and into the kitchen and has to tapwater them down a few goes. But it's worth it – almost straight away the placebo effect of putting ecstasy between your lips perks him up, and despite the clock saying 5.31 Bobby decides he might go wake Georgie up and try to paint her properly. Georgie's not happy. She's been working all day behind the sweety

8

counter at Bhs, and the vodka and sheer shatteredness of it all had her in one of those black-holey bottomless sleeps. She was dreaming of fairgrounds and carousels, not mermaids, imagining her and Bobby riding plastic horses high above the housing estate like a scruffier Mary Poppins. Bobby the Artist grabs her by the shoulders and gives her a little shake, but it's like being dragged from dream into reality through a mile of gravel or a thornbush. Her massive eyelashes part, and she glares up at Bobby with gigantic throbbing peepers. 'What?' she snaps. Bobby the Artist smiles blissfully, the love-doves already sending a sparkle in one or two veins, and he answers, 'Sorry, pet, it's just I scored more pills off Johnnie and, like . . . do you wanna do some poses for me? Painting and that?' If there's one thing that annoys Georgie, it's her boyfriend getting over-excited about a teeny-weeny tablet. She hates them – what does it say about your life if you keep having to gloss it in druggy lovey-doveyness? Georgie's perfectly happy with her life as it is, even though it was murder at work that afternoon. Mr Hawkson, her boss, keeps scolding her just because she's easy-going and cheerful on the counter. These kids of about age eleven came in around dinner-break and, even though they were clearly pilfering the milk-bottles and fizzy cherries and scoffing them on the sly, Georgie thought it was nice to see them enjoying themselves. The cherries were a fine choice. Hawkson could see it all unfolding from his hands-on-hips stance over by Womenswear, and he marched over and gave Georgie a bollocking. He's a prick – he's in his forties and apparently he's got a 'partner', but he still enjoys perving on Georgie in

the terrible stripey blouse. He'll never fire her –
Hawkson's never seen anyone over twenty so enthusi-
astic about sweets before in his life. For Georgie sweets
are her only vice – she's grown out of listing her top
ten confectionery each month (the last instalment had
rhubarb and custards knock white jazzies off the top
spot), but much of the mess around 4E looks like a U-
bomb hit a Haribo factory. She flings a few empty
wrappers out from her bum-crack and elbows,
although it sounds like the Smarties packet has something left in it so she munches those fellows for a bit.
'Bobby, I'm knackered,' she moans, her brain pulsing
and threatening to run out of her nose, ears and
mouth, like something from those manky manga films
Bobby used to watch. It was his cousin from Eston
who made him watch all the video nasties, and Bobby
remembers vividly screaming and squeezing his face
down the back of the sofa and bad-dreaming after seeing *Driller Killer* and *Hellraiser* aged nine and three-
quarters. That bit where the man's face gets stretched
and ripped off by hooks had him in tears for two
weeks. Funny, though, how *Un Chien Andalou* doesn't
have the same aaargh-factor (that insane Buñuel/Dalí
film with split eyeballs and severed hands, and nuns),
since it's really a horror film too, but Salvador Dalí's an
artist, you see, and Clive Barker's just a sicko. Shivering,
Bobby the Artist props one of his ready-stretched canvases against the coffee table (not that they drink coffee any more – Bobby had a horrible experience neck-
ing loads of espressos while on the Billy Whizz, finding
himself fidgeting and spasming for approximately
forty-eight hours), and gives Georgie the puppy-dog

eyes. Or the ecstasy eyes. Whenever Bobby needs canvases making, he snorts an amphetamine mountain over the course of a day, coming down in the evening surrounded by perfectly stretched frames and with blisters on his fingers. Such a hard-working drug! Bobby leaps and puts Galaxie 500 on moderately high volume, the guitars feeling particularly swoopy-loopy this daybreak. He starts to feel the smudgy rush of ecstasy spread through him; the perfect feeling for painting your girlfriend, he thinks. Sometimes he doesn't even realise he's irritating her. Georgie just sits there, not really fussed about posing, but the Smarties are a bonus. Lots of blue ones and all. She watches her boyfriend through slitted eyes, all those tell-tale signs of a man coming up such as manic eyeballs, can't-keep-stillness, and his jowls getting more and more demented. Bobby's feeling brilliant – he washes a brush, then sketches Georgie really large and cute and sailorish in a tiny fuchsia boat. He blocks her in with fleshy pink and navy blue, putting love-hearts in her eyes, then he rolls around the carpet laughing at it. '*Voilà!*' he slobbers. Georgie's not impressed – all she got woken up for was a five-minute splasharound, not some highly considered jaw-dropping *coup de grâce*. Speaking of jaws, by seven o'clock Bobby's is all over the place. And Georgie's still knackered. At least she hasn't got work today – she thinks about slithering next door to go to bed, but Bobby the Artist keeps jabbering on in the swing of his druggy buzz. 'Aww, Georgie, you're gorgeous. I don't want to be a dickhead and that, you know, like all sloppy and that, but God you were made for painting. You know Modigliani? Well I feel like that, you know; getting wrecked and just painting all these birds and that . . . not that I knock around with other girls like, don't worry . . . I just mean you're mint . . . like . . .' he blabs, frothing a bit at the mouth. At the moment he feels utter wonder and contentment sitting with Georgie, like nothing else matters to him in the big wide world, but as it always does when he finally comes down around ten o'clock (and Georgie's long gone, a sailor-sized lump in the bed next-door), he wishes she was more outgoing and would swallow drugs with him instead of just sweeties. It's totally depressing falling back to earth for the umpteenth time. Bump. Bobby the Artist sits on his own on the pink couch, still wired, but now the white morning outside just makes him queasy. He scours the carpet for any sort of intoxicant (Nescafé would do), but there's not even any Smarties left. 'Grrrr!' he says in his head. Unfortunately it's time to call it a day. Sniffing, Bobby pops through to the cool bedroom and changes into his kangaroo pyjamas, as is tradition after every long-haul inner flight. Speaking of which, he dribbles himself onto the edge of the bed and puts on Primal Scream's own beautiful 'Inner Flight', and the comfort's exhausting. Georgie makes a little gurgle as the song kicks in, and it's actually in the same key. She rolls over but doesn't wake up, and for five minutes Bobby just enjoys being there with her and the song, and he strokes her stray pinky shoulder poking out from the bronze bedcover. An eensy-weensy part of him wants to rouse Georgie again and have ravenous sex with her, but he doesn't want to push it. In any case, she looks so holy and adorable all wrapped up, it's nice enough just to be sat in her presence. But sleep's still off the cards for Bobby for at least a couple more hours, and he just concretes himself to the duvet and stares at morning stretching until then. Georgie, unaware he's there, has sprawled herself across seventy-nine per cent of the bed but Bobby still feels happy perched precariously on the frame edge. He lets his mind wander, eyes closed, where quite a few trippy pictures still hang on the backs of his eyelids. Faint multicolour boxes unfold and repeat and repeat and repeat and repeat and repeat and repeat, and it keeps him entertained for a bit before bedtime. Little spirographs rise and fall, easing Bobby the Artist into slumber with their soft swirly twirls. For a second he thinks he sees his face on the Haribo kid's body, and all of a sudden he wonders what it'd be like to be famous – he'd rather see his face on *Frieze* magazine, mind you. Imagine going to all those posh parties and sniffing all the free drugs! He dreams of getting a £1,000-a-day coke habit. But the opportunity seems so far away when you're holed up on the fourth floor of some tower block no one's even heard of, overlooking bumpy tarmac and unhappy little shops, though if Jean-Michel Basquiat could come out of a garbage can with rubbish paintings and still get famous then so could he. Basquiat's his big influence, just like smack was for Jean-Michel. There's this painting, 'Bombero', of Jean's girlfriend giving him a thump and, although Georgie would never lay a finger on him, Bobby can kind of relate to it. Georgie kicks Bobby in the face every time she goes to bed early in a strop. Every time she scolds Bobby for having too much of a good time. Every time she goes to work.

Every time she frowns. From day one they've been perfectly happy together, though Bobby sort of thought she could be weaned onto drugs or at least have her arm twisted once or twice. Georgie's dad's been clocking-on at BASF for twenty-five years (they gave him a stereo to celebrate), and it's his daft influence making her think you have to work so you can survive so you can die sometime later on. Bobby the Artist's ethic is: do what you want and enjoy it or else! But saying that, it's not really that much fun sitting next to a corpse at noon o'clock with nothing to do. With the teeniest dots of energy still left in his system there's the teeniest window of opportunity to carry on painting, but Bobby's head's got a rock in it instead of a brain and soon sleep takes over. He ends up squashed on the remainder of the mattress like a broken Sticklebrick. The instant relief of deep slumbers drops him straight into the same hole as Georgie, but just as he begins to snore the front door goes blam-blam-BLAM and he's spatten back out again. Poor Bobby the Artist. He rolls off the edge of the double bed, rubs his mop-top to and fro for a bit, then staggers sadly to the door as the next blam-blam-BLAM begins. Although he was only asleep for a millisecond it feels as if he's been brought out of a coma, and he can only offer extreme hostility to the Express Pizza boy standing there in the corridor. 'What?' Bobby the Artist snaps. The pizza boy wobbles a bit, dressed in his dingy olive-green company T-shirt and holding out the 12" box like a riot shield. 'Americano,' he mumbles, offering it. 'What?' Bobby the Artist snaps. 'Americano,' the pizza boy repeats, feeling all shitty. Bobby doesn't mean to be a dickhead, but after a night gurning his chops off the last thing he wants is a fucking pizza crust to chew on. Bobby's about to slam the door in the pizza boy's mush, but then he remembers all those parties and sit-ins round Johnnie and Ellen's and the two of them always munching Americano pizzas, and he goes, 'You want 5E not 4E. See you later then.' As the door slaps shut, the Express boy pushes his bottom lip out then pushes on up the stairs. He hates his crap delivery job, especially when you get sent to weird tower blocks in the centre of dodgy estates, and people can be so rude sometimes. He passed his driving test first-go at age seventeen and got the job at Express at eighteen, and at first it was quite fun hurtling round town scoffing free Hawaiians, but the novelty wore off when he started getting lots of abuse, and when he started getting the spare-tyre belly. It's heart-wrenching trying to get money off stubborn cunts, usually hard-case lads at a party who grab the pizza then tell you to fuck off in various ways. Then you get back to the kitchens and Mr Ashram clips you round the head and grumbles and you feel like dog poo-poo. The Express boy sighs, stepping gingerly down the vinyl corridor as he searches for 5E. What he really wants to be is a fighter-plane pilot. Squinting in the fluorescent white light, he knocks three times on the correct door then holds out the pizza, bracing himself for more abuse. And he couldn't have knocked at a worse time – Johnnie and Ellen are in the bedroom having completely awful sex. As a rule their sex is typically shite with neither of them reaching orgasm, but this particular session reaches an all-time low. After getting in from pilfering phones and suchlike, Johnnie slept next to Ellen till midday then drank some flat White Ace and ordered the Americano on the promise of a quickie with his girlfriend. But it's a longie – Ellen managed to get him hard, stripping down to dandelion knickers and stroking her nails down his balls, but she was unable to get any sort of wetness going herself what with Johnnie's pathetic attempts at stabbing his fingers into her fanny, and when he swapped fingers for knob he might as well have been shagging a hole in the road. And thirty-seven minutes later it's not any more enjoyable for either of them. The front door suddenly goes blam-blam-BLAM, and Johnnie and Ellen prise themselves apart with equal parts relief and exasperation. Ellen drops back on the covers with an all-red minge while Johnnie yanks on his Boro FC dressing-gown and stamps through the flat like the Incredible Sulk. 'What?' he snaps, opening the door to the Express boy. He'd forgotten all about the Americano. The 'quickie' should've been over ages ago, leaving Johnnie and Ellen in a warmish trance ready to gobble down some dinner. The pizza boy winces, then sucks in a little breath and mumbles, 'Americano?' Johnnie just yanks the 12" box off him, tosses the door shut and leaves the Express boy with a good old-fashioned, 'Fuck off.' He stomps his bare feet across the dog-eared carpet, growling to himself as he hops back into bed, then him and Ellen eat the pizza in painful silence. Ellen's tucked under the duvet again with a few undergarments back on, and she crunches her teeth softly with a face like sour cream. Useless prick. The most annoying part is she loves Johnnie as a person (he looks after her, he's funny, he lets her live at the flat, he owns drugs . . .), but sex to her is the most wonderful part of a relationship and it feels like getting raped every time he's with her. With other lads it used to be lovely after a good fuck just to lie all tangled up chatting nonsense, but after a session with Johnnie she just wants to die. Often Ellen sucks him off in the beginning in the hope of him coming quickly and then not being in the mood for full-on sex. It kills him. Johnnie's sexual prowess is based largely on hardcore pornography, where butch men gang-bang vulnerable ladies, and where foreplay means sticking your hand up the cunt or getting a skull-fuck, and every episode ends in the man gobbing hot white filth in the girl's mush. It's strange how any hetero man's worst nightmare would be having a hard cock shoved up his arse, and yet their ultimate fantasy would be shoving theirs up a lady's. Admittedly, Johnnie has been able to make past girlfriends orgasm but those were the dominant types, riding his cock into all the right places. On one occasion, with this girl Sharon, he accidentally found the clitoris. Johnnie wonders if Ellen's just fucked so many lads she's become picky and pernickety about how she likes it, but there go them jealous thoughts again. Johnnie screws his face up, finishing the chewy Americano, feeling absolutely tortured. He wonders what it is about sex with Ellen that just doesn't hit the spot – the girls in the pornos all scream like cheery monsters! Maybe their bits don't fit together properly, or maybe they're just unlucky. The sex did get off to a crap start: Johnnie and Ellen first shagged each other on a Saturday back in January, and Johnnie remembers waking up that morning with the shits after a bad Hot Shot Parmo. Him and his boys had been on a bit of a binge the night before, hammering the ecstasy and cheapo Cassini, oh and a Parmesan. Today Johnnie doesn't really take pills after suffering a wee bit of depression, but back in January he could nail ten in a night and still drive the Nissan Sunny home without much bother, and buzz off his tits. So anyway, the day after this binge he had severe diarrhoea, and spent most of the morning sat on the lav in his family home somewhere down Ormesby. It was definitely the Parmo – his matey Bello warned him it was a bit on the old side, but Johnnie was pissed and he hadn't come up yet and he hadn't eaten owt. You could smell the sloppy chicken in the bottom of the toilet bowl. It was disgusting, but once he flushed it away the bathroom didn't stink so much and Johnnie started feeling better right away. He first noticed Ellen at the Jobcentre in a miniskirt and amber Puma top: she signed on at 10.33, Johnnie signed on at 10.36. After a few fortnights of shyness, they got talking and now and then Johnnie would bump into her wandering around town with her mates and a load of shopping bags. One night at the Purple Onion they had a kiss and a grope, and the week after that at the dole she got his number and, just as Johnnie was cleaning his bottom, she vibrated in his trousers. 'Beep-beep!' said the phone. Ellen was wanting to meet him at Aruba that night, not so much a date but just checking he'd be out and whether or not his dole came through on time. There'd been problems with the payments going through over Christmas, what with staff shortages and p-p-p-paperwork, but that morning checking her balance at Halifax Ellen had a crisp £176.14 and she wanted to go out and get pissed and perhaps shag that charming, pale boy she'd found at the Jobcentre Plus. Ellen's attractive according to most men and despicable according to most girls (dripping toffee hair, too skinny, cream foundation acne, and a good arse even in her jogging bottoms), the type of girl who fucks a lad until she gets fucked about then fucks off to the next one, but she always seems happy. Johnnie hadn't had sex for four months so he said yes he'd meet up with her, and he rallied up a few of his less-favourite mates, and they all got pissed and supercharged in Spensley's before heading under the flyover to Aruba. The club had the bluey glitzy look of an aquarium but instead of fishies was full of skinhead lads in horizontal-stripe sweatshirts trying to pull, and noodle-haired girls looking sour in minimum clothes. Johnnie was pretty embarrassed meeting Ellen in a place like that – he used to go a lot when he was sixteen or seventeen, except back then it was the Royal Exchange and he used to exchange spit with girls without much hassle. His loudmouth patter gets him most things he wants out of life, despite him being rather ugly. And sure enough, by eleven o'clock he'd hooked up with Ellen and the two of them were bantering happily about each other and taking the mickey out of strangers while they sat together on the space-age settees. Johnnie liked to think of himself as a perceptive person, and he could clock all the signs of a prospective shag on the cards: Ellen's leg crossed in his direction, occasional stroking of the knee, over-the-top laughter at anything he said, snogs with more and more tongue.

Oh and her asking him, 'Fancy a shag then tonight?' The exhilaration knocked out Johnnie's ribcage, heart beating the bass-drum at beats-per-minute, and the temptation was quite high to start nailing her there and then but luckily he refrained. Instead, Johnnie just kept a tight hold on her, and when Ellen went off to powder her nose or maybe have a piss he surreptitiously hid his rock-hard knob up his jean waistband and wandered off to Bello to perhaps get a pill. Bello was in charge of the ecstasy that night, and Johnnie found him dancing like a red windmill in the middle of the sunken dancefloor, occasionally fondling girlies' hips and bums and getting slapped but not giving a shit, just carrying on in a mad Hackett world of his own. Bello was more than happy to give Johnnie a SmileyFace. 'Yes mate, there you go,' he said. It wasn't really like Johnnie to go gurning a few nights on the trot (after all, the problem with being a pillhead while trying to punt hundreds of the fellows is you can eat all your profits), but he felt so wiped-out from the night before and wanted so much to have stamina for Ellen in bed, it seemed like the thing to do. But in the end it wasn't stamina that let him down. The pill started to glow inside him like a pearl, the modest happy rush stacking on top of the five or six pills still vaguely rolling around his system from Friday, and the kisses with Ellen began to get more rampant if a bit drier what with his craggy ecstasy-mouth. Ellen didn't seem to notice – she was getting more and more pissed, and in any case there was a chance she'd dropped a pill and all and just not let on to Johnnie. It was round about 1.09am things started to get dodgy. In some people pills create awful farts and you can get a sort of laxative effect, and what with all the sex excitement Johnnie had forgotten completely about the Hot Shot Parmo and the severe diarrhoea. Ellen was getting randy and she pulled Johnnie onto the dancefloor for a bit of a grind, and occasionally while shoobeedooing Johnnie let off a string of terrible pumps but the club was so packed the blame could easily be brushed off onto someone else. Ellen continued kissing him and smiling and jutting her hips out at dreamy angles, all the while Johnnie feeling bubbles up his bum and a sloppy turtle-head waking up from hibernation in his undies. With every fart he had to simultaneously clamp down his pelvic-floor muscles, resulting in the poo-poo travelling uncontrollably up and down his rectum like he was bumming himself. It was sort of obvious that at one point something had to give. In between the eleventh and twelfth bar of DJ Alligator's 'Lollipop', there was another rumble in Johnnie's sphincter then a big fart and suddenly he began to notice his boxer shorts caking together. His bum-hairs felt all claggy and the hole stung slightly. For a bit Johnnie tried to keep dancing and following Ellen's footsteps, but even in the ecstasy joyousness he felt all the colour dribble from his face when he realised he'd soiled himself. He panicked, still gurning but with all his little pink dots of pleasure turning brown with paranoia, and quickly went to Ellen, 'Just going to the bog. Don't talk to anyone else.' He fluttered to the bathroom with his trainers in cement, all nervous as he pushed himself into a cubicle and checked his M&S boxers for disaster. The whole crotch was plastered with thick furry brown crap. His cubicle didn't have a lock and, wedging the flimsy door shut with a bony elbow, Johnnie realised there wasn't much he could do to salvage them. He tried to give his arse a little wipe, but the paper just came away light brown flaky and smelly, and it'd probably take half an hour and some industrial-strength detergent to get himself completely clean. The time was already 1.28 and he didn't want to lose Ellen. So Johnnie pulled up the crusty EmAndEsses and went strolling back into the nightclub with his head held high and his bum-crack in tatters. The crystally little light-fixtures were spotlamps in his eyes and he found Ellen quite easily in the cold, emptying-out club. She was smoking a long dirty Marlboro in the corner with a bunch of strangers. She was still pleased to see him, and the two of them bounced back onto the dance-floor to the beat of the last few drums. Johnnie felt a bit self-conscious with the pill fading off and his knickers in a twist, but he didn't want to appear a killjoy so he kept throwing the Travolta moves and the big-fish-little-fishes with quite a bit of conviction. It was painful. Eventually it got to quarter to two and the club was all dead inside, bevvy carcasses and smashed glass snoring on the flooring, and Ellen took Johnnie by the hand and dragged him into the rushing gales of the street outside. She could tell he wasn't quite himself, but there was no way he was going home without her. In terms of men, Ellen also always got what she wanted – she didn't consider herself to be particularly stunning or highly sexed, but boys did tend to circle around her like swarms of bees. Perhaps she gave off a scent (was it CK Be that night?), or perhaps it was the miniskirts. Her and Johnnie jumped in the back of a black taxi, her pulling the skirt down to cover her botty, then they yelled the name of Johnnie's estate and the taxi shot off. They snogged each other rushing past the faulty CNE sign and the cubist Workers' Union, and the town was a spider's web of streaky lamp-posts what with the taxi going so fast. Roads scooped under flyovers and dead shopping arcades like spoons through ice cream. The taxi got to Peach House within fifteen minutes and the fare cost £4.50. Though Johnnie hadn't been selling any pills that night he still had money to pay the driver – on ecstasy you tend not to need that many alcoholic drinks, instead guzzling tapwater and passing the time dawdling around hugging everyone. Johnnie and Ellen were still quite lovey-wuvvy as they stepped between the pillars with the two boulders on top, but occasionally Johnnie flinched when her hand went to grab his bum-cheek. He had to make excuses when they got into 5E and nip to the toilet, straight away ripping off his Lee's and unpeeling the boxer shorts. It was quite obvious Ellen was going to shag him, which left Johnnie in a bit of a conundrum. The M&Ss were fairly suave, and it seemed worth running the shower and trying to squeeze the shit out of them while undressing and feeling like a daft cunt. He didn't want to leave Ellen waiting too long, especially since he lived in the flat alone and the floor was exploded with Super Tennents and ashtrays and porny pictures and vomity plates and cheese trainers and pillbags and shit CDs and torched carpet. He pulled a gigantic sad face in the mirror then got on with the wash. Naked, he popped his arse under the shower-flow, all the while checking out his knob-size and giving that a rinse and all. His dick was looking particularly shrivelled, poking around in the nightmarish bathroom light, but he expected that was due to the complete shittiness of the situation. His bum-fluff was totally matted, and to get most of the crap off he had to dig in with his nails. It was disgusting. The bottom of the bath looked like a muddy worm had crawled across it and died. Aaaaaaaaargh! His fingers smelt like fishy poo-poo, and the boxers were stained rusty orange. Johnnie sighed, then had a tiny gurn to himself and decided to cut his losses – the M&S pants went flying out the window like a beautiful brown kite. There was no more time to mess about. Johnnie dried his arsehole on the towel turning beige and beiger, and he frowned bushy cater-pillars putting back on his clothes. It was getting on for half-past two as he strolled into the living room look-ing quite bedraggled and he wondered if Ellen would really wish to shag such a tragic person. But sure enough she smiled and took his hand, and Johnnie led her out of the bombsite and into his boudoir. Johnnie's bedroom was red and white stripes with posters of Juninho and John Hendrie and Ravanelli on top, and although his sheets were a crumply mountain the room wasn't particularly mucky. Ellen was feisty and sat straight on top of the peak, and when she started unzipping Johnnie she didn't think it was strange he had no pants on. Johnnie felt a bit awkward (and maybe a wee bit paranoid off the pills), and he worried Ellen might be able to smell shit when she started sucking him off. Fortunately he stiffened up with such a nice mouth round his willy, and Ellen slobbered away minding her own business. She enjoyed giving head – having a boy shiver and spasm in time with her waggly tongue – and it was possible she was getting more pleasure off it than Johnnie. His brain was a cracked egg, half scrambled with poo-poo and half fried with sexstasy. He didn't attempt to bring Ellen off with his shitty fingers, and when she eventually boinged on top of him all Johnnie could think about was brown goo. His arsehole still felt sticky and awful and he imagined the hot aroma of faeces filling the small bedroom, and it terrified him. Ellen was horny and couldn't smell a thing, but just as she was reaching the sexy sunrise of an orgasm she started to feel Johnnie's stiffy subside and his cock slipped out from inside her. She was devastated, and overall it did get the sex off to the shittiest possible start. And if anything it's only gotten worse – now all Johnnie can do is give Ellen sore bits, no *petit mort* in sight unless you count Ellen wanting to kill her boyfriend. Nowadays she dreads going to bed, what with Johnnie always trying to put his leg over or trying to get her flaps going when she's dry as newspaper. Most porn gives boys the impression girls like to suffer during sex, and when Johnnie first bashed Ellen's delicate cervix he showed off to all the guys at the Linthorpe he'd 'reached the top'. Wowee! Fifty-four bad shags later, Ellen's seriously considering splashing out on a Rampant Rabbit or employing some sort of male escort, and she tries to think back to all these wonderful one-night stands she's had with handsome, very competent strangers. Not only has she forgotten how to orgasm, she's forgotten how to fake one. It's now eight-and-a-bit months since her last cock-in-fanny climax (a boy named Smithy who could draw circles and figure-8s with the end of his penis), summer's here, and Ellen wonders how much longer she can last without another fruity encounter. One particular balmy evening, she sits alone in Johnnie's bed, bored out of her skull. She peers out the window at little kids playing ball games on the grassy verges five storeys below. She thinks bad thoughts. Johnnie's out terrorising the neighbourhood (or so he said – he's actually having a pint in the Central with his mates and they're talking about Bello's new Lacoste shellsuit, shiny red it is), and there's nothing much to do but watch the world slowly turn. The kids outside are adorable – Ellen watches the girls steal the boys' football, the boys chase the girls, they all fall over in the clover, and they all laugh their heads off with funny terrapin expressions. The kids don't care that the playing field's all dusty and grubby and pooey, or that they're not getting orgasms. Seven-year-olds don't even know what an orgasm is, and they seem to be having a pretty fun time without one. Ellen wishes she was that age again, rolling around getting muddy in a flowery dress and hating boys and making fun out of dollies and twigs and old tyres, not drugs or booze or boys' limbs. Ellen sighs, all cosy in her jammies but her head hurts from all the weird thinking, or is it just a hangover? Last night was another shitty shag with Johnnie (really drunk, Johnnie spurted his load while Ellen was trying to insert him up her mousetrap twat), and she smothers her head in the sweaty pillows to the sound of cackling little lasses. Her brain's a puddle of piss, slightly wishing she hated Johnnie so they could go their separate ways but she doesn't. It's the fact that she otherwise gets on so well with Johnnie she doesn't have the heart to keep telling him he's a failure in bed. She doesn't want to split up with him just because he's a bad lay, but then again she doesn't want a split up her cunt every time she goes to bed with him. It's quite sad because obviously Johnnie knows he gives her very little pleasure, but his only frame of reference is pornography and over time he's learnt to shag exactly like the clueless misogynistic bastards in those films. And yet somehow they always make the girls squirt! Johnnie's confused, and more often than not he can be seen with a very sad head. He's a lot less talkative nowadays, so Ellen's glad she's got Pamela and Mandy and the rest of the gang upstairs to knock around with and have a laugh with. There's a party tonight in 6D, and Johnnie gave her a tenner in consolation for the bad sex. Bless him. She starts getting ready, co-ordinating her outfit with the pink sunset outside and feeling a bit less negative. She sniffs and slides on a rosy Umbro T-shirt with tights and denim miniskirt, and she goes overboard with the make-up because she thinks some boys might be there tonight. She gets a weird kick out of boys drooling over her, like it confirms her good-looking-ness or something. She doesn't think she's insecure; she just loves to be loved. She imagines herself as a free spirit, always swanning around the halls and walls of Peach House like it's the Chelsea Hotel in the sixties and she's Nico and she knows where all the parties are. Sometimes she goes to Mandy's, the stick-thin speed-freak who's always got something crap to tell you. Sometimes she goes to Angelo's, the hunky Sardinian who welcomes anyone as long as they've got booze or big boobs. Sometimes she goes to Pamela's if her mam and dad's away, the nursery worker with a permanently glazed expression on her face. Sometimes she goes to Bobby the Artist's, if he's not too fucked to open the door or talking to the wallpaper. It feels like a great place to be, and Ellen draws herself a smile out of pink lip-gloss. She runs the straighteners through her creamy waterfall hair, then whacks on a bit of CK Be and gazes at herself in the mirror plastered with grubby photos of friends and exes. Ellen's been living at Johnnie's for about three months, and nowadays the footy posters have been replaced with girly items such as stretch mirror, cuddly bunnies, photographs of people she used to snog and shag. She stays there rent free and she loves getting waited on hand and foot – Johnnie gives her anything she wants, from Americano pizzas to MDMA tablets, plus she's guaranteed £88.10 in her Halifax every fortnight. It's so class being on the dole, Ellen just loves drifting through her life like a princess on a throne carried about by court jesters or whoever. She laughs at that image in her head, then puts on her shoes and clomps out of the flat. She wibbles her bottom as she goes up the stairs, even though no one's watching, and she feels a million dollars or maybe a million pound depending on the exchange rate. When she lets herself into 6D everyone's sat around doing laughing gas, jibbering about like mental patients at a kids' birthday party. Whoosh laugh whoosh laugh whoosh laugh. Ellen says her hellos then sits on a pile of floppy deflated balloons, all multicoloured and pretty amongst the Super Skols and the ashtrays getting passed around with reefers on top of them. She takes a toot or two, and a can of lager magically walks into her hand from across the carpet. Angelo's there on the sofa arm (the boy who rents the flat), happily handing out drinks and whizzing the whip-cream cartridges into life in his dirty paws. Everyone's faces turn alabaster as they take up lungfuls of the stuff, some of them giggling like wet nellies and others tripping off a cliff into hippy heaven as the gas roly-polys round their system. Mandy perches cross-legged next to Dave Morton (the professional foot-baller brought up on Premier Road), completely chewing his ear off with her tales of owning a race-horse and riding it to victory in the Grand National. She seems to have lost her marbles over the years – perhaps it's down to nailing speed every day, although she always was a random cunt when she was at second-ary school with Pamela and Ellen. Pamela looks on at Mandy with glazed disgust because she wants to get into Dave herself, but apart from that she's enjoying blowing balloon after balloon into her air-pipes. Angelo likes to impress the girls and he sets them up with doublers, passing Ellen a big juicy watermelon-size one. After a count of one-two-three, they start sucking blowing sucking blowing sucking blowing with their cheeks going big and red like trumpet play-ers, and for twenty seconds the happy happy hardcore core's all repetitititive like a stuck stuck rec rec ord ord the squeaks squeaks of the ballooooooooons are all birds all birds flying ing over over head head with Ellellellellellellellellen riding a fire fire engine ing a fire engine through pink pink pine forest pink fire engine and then then there's monkeys monkeys top top hats top hats top hats evil cackling cackle-cackle and and then then the cackle hisssssing of sssssnakes no the hissing of balloons deflating and then she's back in the flat again. 'Fuck,' she says. Funny how laughing gas doesn't really make you laugh – it sends you to an altogether much weirder place. Ellen feels all shaken up and sober, and she curls up on the sofa cradling her knees. She makes a full-blown attempt next to get drunk, pilfering more lagers and big shots of vodka from people too busy dreaming to notice. Soon everyone's monged – some of them start acting horny, retreating back to their quarters to shag their knobs and fannies off with each other; others are just dead bodies. Mandy slurps Dave's lips off like a cream bun. Dave hasn't played a professional match for about a month (he got tackled from behind by a butch cunt from Carlisle), and he's quite enjoying all the time off getting wrecked on the sly. He's the sort of boy who thinks one sniff of NO_2 would send him insane for the rest of his life, but he's known Angelo since they played for Marton as youngsters and he still likes coming round for a can or two. Dave actually looks quite fucked, nodding off to the smurf-voice hardcore stuff, but Mandy's full of beans and drags him down the hall to fuck the hell out of him in her bare crusty bedroom. Pamela watches them leave over her sparkly blue bottle of Spectra, and she starts getting depressed and falls in a heap on Angelo's burgundy settee, with a full balloon of NO_2 clamped between her fingers. Suddenly the balloon flies from her hand, farting a trail of laughing gas that makes all the dust particles giggle, and it lands with a plip on Ellen's lap. Ellen grins. By about two or three most people have wandered off or passed out in strange places round the flat (Kev in a cupboard in the kitchen, Stacey soaking in the shower), but Ellen's feeling lovely and merry and she's got Pamela's Spectra to get through now. When the whip-cream things run out, Angelo slides up to Ellen and sits with her for a bit in front of the fuzzy television. 'How's it going?' he asks through the static. Angelo's been in Peach House about four months, and although he's shagged his way through many of the residents (an over-forty-year-old included), he's yet to snake-charm Ellen. Sex is his kick, and to be honest he's not bad looking – yummy hot-chocolate head, Pacific Ocean eyeballs, and black and white vests with massive muscles underneath. Girls have a hard time resisting him, what with his silkworm touch and his persistence – he claims to have bedded over five hundred lovers, and he's only twenty-four. Angelo preys on anything with a nice face or figure or just a fanny-hole and, even though he knows about Johnnie the big bad boyfriend, he can't stop himself placing a hand on Ellen's lap. He submerges the little girl in his whirlypool pupils and says to her, 'Ellen, you look a bit down.' Ellen says she's alright – in fact she's pretty mortalled now she's started on the cider, and she sees two or maybe even three Angelos towering over her. But she likes the look of them, and she lies back having a wee drunken smile to herself. She can be a flirt as well, and mainly just to amuse herself she does an awful pout and slaps Angelo on the left biceps. 'In fact, I'm *quite* alright,' she grins, thinking she's hilarious. Angelo feels his knob and balls starting to expand. He touches her on the thigh, totally in awe of Ellen the same way he was totally in awe of the other five hundred. 'I've got a pill if you want it,' Angelo ventures, 'it's up to you, like; just thought you needed cheering up or something.' Ellen's eyes flap open, suddenly all alert for about one and a half-ish seconds. 'Well I don't need cheering up like but I wouldn't say no though, would I,' Ellen grins. So they take the ecstasy together (Angelo having ninety-eight of them locked away in his Buddha pot in the bedroom, recently acquired from this boy on Kesteven Road, you know, down near the Total garage), and after about fifty minutes and a bit more leg-rubbing they can both feel it kicking in. Ellen probably less so than Angelo, what with her being so smashed and still drinking, but it adds nicely to the madness already sitting in her brain-box. They crouch together in the flicky sizzle of the television set, the only other people around lying comatose beneath the navy blue window blowing clouds from one edge of wallpaper to the other. It's a delightful feeling, and for a while Ellen and Angelo talk manically about how good the party was and how good the laughing gas was and how good the random shags were and how good the patches of vomit were, and Johnnie. The flat's a mess and so are their heads – Angelo's in rapture and he so desperately wants to slide his cock in the lady, and weirdly he seems to be getting better looking the more Ellen glances at him. Skimming a finger over her anklebone, Angelo raises an eyebrow and asks softly, in his dulcet Rudolph Valentino accent, 'So everything's perfect with Johnnie, then?' Angelo's quite cunning (after all, no relationship's perfect, is it?), and it's like a clarion call when Ellen replies, 'Ah, I dunno, well see I dunno if I should say like . . . it's just the sex . . . at the minute . . . isn't that great . . . oh I dunno, I think I just need a good shag ha ha ha ha.' And Ellen sits there sheepish for a second, then Angelo moves a bit closer and her lips accidentally fall on his and they keep falling for about a minute and falling and falling. For a second she regrets it, but then Angelo's hands are all over her neck and hips and tits and arse, and suddenly she's enjoying it. Perhaps Ellen's a selfish bitch, but surely if you're desperate for an orgasm you're entitled to have one even if it's not from your boyfriend. Even the feel of Angelo's big fat tongue in her mouth gets her all flustered – Johnnie's got a bit of a pointy one. 'Let's go in the bedroom,' Angelo whispers, all his hot breath giving Ellen a heatwave. She feels jittery and pissed and lurved-up, and she nods and practically drags the boy herself to the double bed. They strip each other off, Ellen stroking his knob through the straight trousers while she gets her Umbro shirt ripped off. She kneels topless on the covers then gives Angelo a blow-job, biting him through his Y-fronts then slipping them off and slurping up his big red-ender. Angelo's got a much larger cock than Johnnie, and she tugs it with two hands, tasting all the clear stuff coming out. It's brilliant just to treat each other like animals for one night, but when Ellen's knickers get whipped off and Angelo frigs her beautifully with two fingers she turns to glass and melts. On top of the pill she's also on the Pill, and she kisses Angelo's buffalo skin and mouth as she crawls into the girl-on-top position. Usually it's uncomfortable starting sex with Johnnie in this formation, but as Ellen squeezes Angelo's dick and slowly lowers herself round it she's absolutely dripping wet. Speaking of drips, two floors down Bobby the Artist still can't sleep. He sits upright in bed next to silent Georgie, thinking much too deeply about a strange dripping in the kitchen. Drip! All the money's run out now for drugs and food and booze, but that still hasn't stopped his mind acting strange. As he sits with his back up against the bronze headrest, Bobby glares at the opposite wall, hearing an excruciating weeny plop about every four or five seconds. Each drip feels like a depth charge going off in his skull. Drip! Is he imagining it? Outside the weather's humid, and even though he's boiling Bobby the Artist slips on his yellow and blue argyle to go and sort out the kitchen. He leaves Georgie dozing with no covers on and just her cerulean-with-pink-trim knickers, softly banging his sweaty painty feet onto carpet then Drip! onto linoleum. Bobby looks a mess (raggy hair, skinny legs under the argyle and his knob out), and perhaps the insomnia's down to drug withdrawal rather than innocent drips, but when it's 4.14am no one likes to get Chinese water tortured. Drip! Dawn's breaking, and for a bit Bobby gets distracted by the beautiful purple steamy sunrise stretching its rays under the drawn net curtains. He gets mesmerised by a lovely little laser beam, striking through a wee gap in the window, but then Drip! the drips are back, and louder. Louder! Bobby the Artist rubs his sore bonce. Drip!! Where to start? The taps: Bobby and Georgie made a huge spag bol this evening with cheesy bread and Parmesan on top and all that gourmet shite, and the

Artist knocks down all the dirty dishes to check the hot and cold taps but the sink's silent except for the big annoying crash he just made. The freezer: They defrosted the freezer the other week, and on the off-chance they messed it up Bobby checks whether it's leaking, but there's just rock-hard pizzas and mince and ice cubes and icicles hanging down like they've been growing a mini North Pole in the kitchen. For a bit he crouches and stares at the gritty frost and smoke in case it does something, but it doesn't. The kettle: Georgie likes cups of tea (with four sugars in them). She boils the kettle at least three times a day, and Bobby examines the adjacent wall and ceiling in case there's been a build-up of condensation and now it's decided to start dripping. But no. Antagonised, Bobby stands all huffy-and-puffy with his hands on his hips (a classic pissed-off pose). Holding his breath, Bobby listens really closely to the next four or five Drip!! Drip!! Drip!! Drip!!s, but it's not that obvious which direction they're coming from. His ears are ringing after listening to *Metal Machine Music* all night, and the drips seem to gain a more arrogant Splish! the more he can't find them. The boiler: Getting desperate, Bobby starts to dismantle the Baxi, uncovering all the fancy copper pipes and investigating each one and each one's little fittings for leakage, but unfortunately the plumbing's faultless. Splish! The tinned goods: Losing it, Bobby scrabbles through the various tins of tomatoes and tats and Heinzes in the lone cupboard, as if they could seep enough drippy liquid to keep a grown man out of bed. They're fine, of course. The floor: Bobby the Artist breaks down on the lino floor in a heap of argyle sweater and ball sac. His brain absolutely kills, and the wee droplets are now giant's feet stomping all round the kitchen. Boom!! Bobby's insane. He curls up in a ball, leaving snail-trails of sweat-marks along the plastic ground, totally exhausted but unable to drop off. It's as if he's forgotten how to fall asleep, and Bobby just sprawls there in a frustrating sleepy no-man's-land. Boom!! He tries to count sheep but the drips come at such strange intervals his mind becomes a knot of numbers and splishes and he wonders if it'll Boom!! ever unravel. The only consolation is that lovely colourful shard of daybreak squeezing under the curtain, and Bobby the Artist flicks his fingers through it smiling moronically. It's such a beautiful spectacle that Bobby pulls himself from the ground and tugs open the curtain completely, and that's when he sees the gorgeous bright rainbow arcing all the way from Berwick Hills to South Bank, and that's when he sees the slight rainfall dripping every three or four seconds on the metal window ledge. Drip! The following night Bobby the Artist can't sleep thanks to an obscure banging upstairs. Bang! It's actually Johnnie beating the shit out of Angelo, throwing him against the four walls and battering his kneecaps and almost breaking his own wrist thumping him round the face. He bishes him and bashes him and boshes him. He doesn't know for sure Ellen's cheated on him, but the walls of this tower block are incredibly thin, which blesses (or curses) the inhabitants with a strange sort of psychic sixth sense – or rather a sort of uncontrollable nosy awareness of what everybody's up to. Johnnie knows Ellen slept round Angelo's last night – he heard her voice coming out of his ceiling. And he knows what red-blooded bloodhounds like Angelo try to do to girls when they're in their pyjamas. Ellen came back this afternoon with her miniskirt on the wrong way and teethmarks on her Umbro top and pupils like coat buttons. Without even thinking, she told Johnnie Angelo was knocking out brilliant ecstasy, and maybe he should get hold of some of these 'sharks' himself. Just when she thought it was safe to go back in the water, splashing herself down on the sofa and putting an arm round Johnnie, her boyfriend leapt up, kicked an Americano box the length of the flat, then bounded upstairs to sort the cunt out for good. It's bad enough Ellen being round the Sardinian's all the time, but even worse is some prick like him stealing his pill business. Johnnie has a hard time as it is trying to pay the rent, but he credits himself with a good few volleys to Angelo's forehead and a scream of, 'You bastard!!' He wants to kill him, or at least kill his good looks, throwing precision toe-punts into his great cheekbones and thick greasy locks. Angelo begins spewing up blood, nervously spasming to and fro in his apartment, convinced Johnnie knows about him and Ellen (a great shag; one hour and thirty-three minutes of missionary, doggy, legs in the sky, blow-job, cunnilingus, three orgasms for Ellen and two for Angelo, the only disappointment being the 500 million hyperactive sperms he deposited in Ellen's womb, surfing wildly through her hot pipes desperately searching and barging into each other and racing round the fallopians, only to find she's on the Pill and there's no Mrs Egg and two hours later they all got knackered and they frizzled and fried in her belly and died, all the little sperms screaming, 'Nooo! And it was such a promising shag and all . . .'), and he keeps whining, 'I'm sorry . . . sorry . . . sorry sorry sorry.' He sort of resigns himself to the fact he's going to get murdered. Johnnie's not that barbaric though – he just enjoys roughing up/disciplining people he doesn't like. He sees it as a form of education. It killed him the other evening to hear Ellen describe Angelo as 'sweet', 'really funny' and 'a bit hunky' to Pamela outside his own front door, and sometimes he thinks Ellen doesn't appreciate him at all. Last night Johnnie gave her a tenner to get drunk and hopefully come back for a cuddle in bed or a roll in the hay (Ellen pretty much has to be drunk for him to see any action at all), but she had to go and spoil it all by getting pilled-up, not even phoning Johnnie, and ending up possibly sleeping in the bed of a man renowned for being seedy and fucking the shit out of anything with tits. Johnnie can't even handle the thought of one finger being placed on her, let alone in her. He has a habit of weaving sick tapestries in his head, and as he batters Angelo senseless all he can see is a Mediterranean man's penis sliding in and out of Ellen's vagina. Johnnie grits his teeth into tiny white treestumps. An odd tear clouds his vision as he kicks through Angelo's skull, splatters of crimson Jackson Pollocking round the room. Angelo's eyes are bruised and so podgy he can't really see anything, and he just lies there as Johnnie continues laying into him. It's not one of his better comedowns. Angelo curls up into a snail shape, but that only spurs Johnnie on to boot him up the arse, catching a stray bollock squashed between his elephanty thighs. Angelo screams.

Johnnie's expertise in the field of fighting dates back to him shattering Jamie Morris's shin after getting snowballed in the face when he was eight. Johnnie quickly realised he could get anything he wanted with a few threats and well-executed punches to the sides of the head: for instance money for the 65A, Astrobangers, cigarettes off lads in Day-Glo trackies, and once he even got a tramp to give up his can of Special Brew when he was in year seven. Back then Johnnie had total confidence in himself and total respect from everyone else, back when there were no adult troubles such as mediocre sex, spongers, piss-takers, no income, drug deals, monogamy. The worst thing that ever happened to Johnnie was growing up, although he does still feel slightly childish walloping Angelo's head once, twice, thrice, four times against the TV cabinet. Initially during a beating the body releases some sort of natural anaesthetic or force-field, and you don't get all that hurt, but by now it's completely worn off and Angelo writhes round the carpet, trailing blood like a red cape. His eye-slits are full of raspberry tears, making him blind and dazed and worried. At first he thought Johnnie would run out of steam after a handful of punches and bright kicks to Angelo's forehead, but it's quickly become clear he's in for twelve rounds of torture. Even Johnnie's arms are muddied with throbs and hot aches, his mind absolutely barmy with hatred. It's like there's a black voodoo monkey crawling round his brainwaves, tormenting him with a constant string of pictures: sperm spurting up his girlfriend's cervix, her lips slurping up slippy stiff dicks. Johnnie explodes with new-found fury, stamping rock-hard on Angelo's vested chest then flinging fists here and there at the jumble of fishy features that now make up the boy's face. 'Stop stop stop!' Angelo yelps in a desperate five-year-old's plea for help. Today he knows what it feels like to be dying, though in situations like this it's possible to conjure up some weird sort of superhuman strength, and Angelo spins over and manages to rattle one elbow into Johnnie's side. Johnnie doesn't like this. He gets his claws out, scrabbling and ripping at Angelo's swollen lumps and bumps, and in the process his black vest tears open revealing big defined pecs and shaved chest, Hulk Hogan style. You'd think Angelo had enough power to put up a decent fight, or at least a half-decent barrier, but in actual fact the muscles come from a diet of weight-gain milkshakes and steroids and they're more pleasing to the eye than really powerful. That fucking chest disgusts Johnnie (all hunky, rigid and brown like a leather sofa), but maybe there's a bit of envy too – Johnnie once considered taking steroids, but he's scared of needles, and needle-sized willies. As a result, he's a bit like Skeletor to Angelo's He-Man, and he doesn't see any reason why Ellen wouldn't go off gallivanting with this sexy cunt. He'd like to cut his throat. It's almost not enough for Angelo just to lie there with a few swellings and purple skin; Johnnie really wants to degrade him. He leaves Angelo soaking through the living room carpet, waltzing into the bathroom to find some sort of razor or cutting device. He scrambles through endless moisturisers, hair products, deodorants, creams, face-washes, dental hygiene stuff and handcare on the mouldy windowsill, until he finds Angelo's shaving bits. There's no old-school cutthroat flick-knife thing like gentlemen used in days of yore, but Johnnie uncovers some of those Wilkinson Sword double-edge numbers and staggers back into the lounge with one pressed in his palm. Alright, he might not be able to dissect the hairy animal with it, but he's sure he'll think of something. Johnnie catches his face in the mirror on the way out, all haggard and scary, and he does feel a bit of a sick cunt. He could probably do with a shave and all. Johnnie coughs, then laughs at Angelo – he looks like a wrestling figure with his arms and legs on the wrong way. Johnnie kneels down. 'Swallow one, you cunt,' he spits, unwrapping a dull silver blade from the paper, 'or I'll fucking kill you . . .' Angelo's totally shitting himself and delusional, pain spreading down every limb from the tips of his fingers to his toes and nose, and he genuinely believes Johnnie's insane enough to take his lovely life. After all, he's feeding him fucking razor blades, isn't he. It's a weird situation – Angelo feels strangely deserving of these horrors (to be honest, having shagged about sixty women already in relationships, Angelo always thought himself lucky not to have yet received a hiding, but always knew one was round the corner), but surely no one should have to stand for this. Johnnie just doesn't know when to stop – he loves Ellen so much but can't cope with all the pain she causes, and all he can do is take it out on other people and not her. A boy brought up on beating people up, Johnnie just doesn't know how to react any differently to such shitty affairs. Oh yeah, and those pills! Those fucking 'sharks', or whatever they're called. What a bastard. Johnnie pins Angelo's head down on the itchy carpet, clamps his nose shut, then pushes a razor blade between his lips and urges the cunt to swallow. Angelo screams but Johnnie wants to scream as well, getting convinced Angelo knows all about his inadequacy in bed, and his small knob, and his oddly minuscule balls, and that time he shit himself in Aruba. So, he sees no reason not to make Angelo eat a razor, and he prods the steel blade right down the Sardinian's tongue, being careful not to nick himself on it. Angelo squirms, panicking a sweaty diluted trail of blood around the apartment – he tries one more time to punch Johnnie's kneecap, but it's pretty futile and Johnnie just mutters, 'Fucking prick.' Then he gets a bit firmer and informs him, 'You swallow that fucking razor now or you're going out the window.' He points to the sky outside, all square and blue and delightful, but dropping six storeys isn't really the way Angelo would like to enjoy it. Angelo used to love taking girls out for dates at beer gardens and restaurants in the yummy summertime before bringing them home and banging them expertly in his bed or giving head up on the rooftop, and all these sorts of merry memories lightning-strike through his head as he lies there with a razor blade in his gob. So, your life does flash before your eyes before you die, after all! Johnnie restrains him, kneeling hard on his bulky shoulders, and Angelo supposes he's had an alright time on earth (if all it means is working five days a week so you can enjoy yourself at the weekends and sleep with lots of people). He shuts his eyes, sort of accepting it might be the end for him thanks to this horrible psycho/psychic cunt crouched on top of him. He's crying a bit because he doesn't want to swallow a Wilko

Sword, but something inside him thinks he should do it because he's been such a naughty boy – and after all it'd be better to eat a razor than plummet to a mushy death (and he's been beaten to such a pulp already he doubts it'll feel much worse than a sore throat) – so Angelo crunches his face and lets the blade slide down his gullet, lashing his legs out in mid-air as it starts gashing up the roof of his mouth. He screeches a banshee wail as the thing gets stuck halfway, latching onto the back of his throat, and he coughs out water-pistolly blood, gurgling and yelling obscenities that shake the tower block out of the concrete. It's more the choking sensation that gets to him – to be honest it hardly feels like his mouth's getting sliced up; it's all in his head. He gasps and retches for air, coughs battling peristalsis and the blade stammering up and down his food-pipe, and Angelo keeps screaming for a bit of sympathy. Johnnie's bored now anyway, and slowly rises from the floor, deciding to leave Angelo alone and get back down to his girlfriend – who he loves – and he takes probably one or two steps across the carpet when suddenly the door whams open and Alan Blunt the Cunt's standing there brandishing a candlestick holder. 'What the fuck's going on here?' Alan growls in his gravelly baritone, almost swinging at Johnnie without any sort of explanation. Alan Blunt's one of the stranger characters in the building, and his flat's the equivalent of the spooky mansion at the end of your street with the black cats roaming outside and the bats in the attic and dead bodies in the closet. There's rumours that Alan might have killed his wife (though it's more likely she just left him, Alan being a bit of a twisted fucker), or that he's a

43

paedo (Alan's favourite hangout of an afternoon is peering over the fence at Corpus Christi primary school), but Johnnie's not the sort of person to hold a grudge really and often he goes round to Alan's to help with DIY or have a nice cup of tea. Johnnie stops where he is on Angelo's stained floor, the dizzy light spreading his lanky shadow across the wall, and he holds his hands up to Alan and says, 'Don't worry, it's all sound, mate.' Alan Blunt the Cunt squints through his thick brown kiddy-fiddling glasses, his curly hair all matted with lack of sleep, and he smiles when he recognises Johnnie there in his lime shellsuit. 'What's going on? Youse are fucking keeping me up! I've got to drive the container tonight, you know,' Alan says, relaxing slightly. Although he's a nutty bastard, Alan does enjoy living in Peach House – it makes him feel less lonely, living in a big pink Tower of Babel, and in particular Johnnie's someone he gets on well with, often bumping into him and chatting about the football and the betting shop and the 4.45 at Doncaster. Johnnie wafts his hand at Angelo, writhing about like a worm stuck on tarmac, and he says to Alan, 'See this cunt there, he's been dealing drugs to little kids. Just thought he needed a ticking-off like.' Alan Blunt the Cunt hates drugs, hates the idea of youngsters becoming vegetables shooting shite up their veins and noses and, being a racist twat, he's also pleased to see a foreign person lying there in a jumble. Tears flooding his eyelids, Angelo coughs a couple of times and regurgitates the razor blade into his mouth again, keeping it clenched between his teeth though so as not to draw attention to himself. He hopes to God Alan doesn't pounce on him as well. Being a foreigner living next-door to a racist was always going to cause frictions, and rumour has it in his youth (the 1970s) Alan used to go around in a gang terrorising Paki shops and Paki houses and pizzerias and Turkish kebab inns. Today, though, Alan just stands in the threshold, his fluffy hand flexing on the candlestick, and he goes, 'Well, good lad, Johnnie. Just keep it down, alright?' Johnnie nods, feeling a bit softer in the head now it's all off his chest and Alan's here. He knows Alan's alright even though he's a bit of a cunt, and they walk out of Angelo's together laughing at the state of that silly Sardine. They actually high-five each other on the way down the corridor. Alan Blunt the Cunt offers Johnnie a cup of tea or Pot Noodle back at his but, even though he's pretty starving, Johnnie wants to get back downstairs with Ellen and he shakes Alan's hand and they say their cheerios on the grubby carpet outside 6E. Johnnie hopes Ellen hasn't run away during all this violence, and he hopes she hasn't really made the beast with two backsides with Angelo. What a mental evening. In the flat underneath Alan the Cunt's (5E), while Johnnie and Al say their goodbyes Ellen stands shaking in the silvery bathroom holding their Gary Rhodes frying pan aloft. Although she does love Johnnie sometimes he scares the hell out of her, and she stands around all guilty and paranoid about that amazing amazing fuck with Angelo. All she said to Johnnie was Angelo's got some incredible pills on the go, and suddenly Johnnie cracked and stormed upstairs, and you could hear him cracking Angelo's head off the walls and the furniture and especially the paper-thin floor. She's past herself

45

with worry that Angelo might spurt something out about them shagging, and she fucking hates herself even though the fuck was great. She can hear the fighting subsiding upstairs, but now every little creak and voice and slamming door around Peach House gives Ellen the willies as she waits for Johnnie to return. Paranoia! If Johnnie knows she's been a slag, is he going to give her the same treatment? To Ellen it sounded like Johnnie was gouging Angelo's eyeballs out or slicing his Jap's eye open or something like that. She dithers round the bathroom like a nervous little lamb, dressed in a white Ellesse tracksuit Johnnie bought her last month from the FirstSport catalogue she gets through the door. She can't understand how she could be such a bitch to Johnnie because he's so caring and sweet and protective, but then again she can understand because she got the ride of her life last night. Sex with Johnnie is devastating – often she's too dry to even bother attempting to put his penis inside her, or Ellen's too tired but Johnnie pushes her and pushes her until they have awful depressing zombie sex, or Ellen's on her period and – although she doesn't mind having sex on the blob – when they change positions Johnnie sees big globs of gooey cummy blood on his dick and it goes instantly limp, or occasionally Johnnie's so drunk he comes after two or three thrusts and Ellen feels shitty cleaning all his gunk out of herself for nothing. Alright, so Johnnie knows he's a bad shag, but surely that's no reason to go around cheating on the boy. But she did, and maybe in her head she expects to get murdered. That's why her and Gary Rhodes are hiding in the bathroom together. She hears Johnnie come through the front door, and she shudders, clutching the pan a bit higher. She can imagine the mad temper on his face – upside-down V eyebrows, eyes with the skinny red veins popping out, grit teeth, and those unusual twitches he gets when in the presence of bouncers, police, and other people he hates. Ellen's arms are too tiny for the great weight of the frying pan, and really she doesn't want to hurt Johnnie, but if these are her last few moments on earth she does want to go out with a bang. She glances at herself in the runny water-splashed bathroom mirror, and she thinks if she does happen to die this afternoon at least she's looking good for the paramedics – perhaps the sex yesterday has given her that bit of extra radiance. She strokes her hair. Ellen's not sure where to position herself in the tiny cube to surprise-attack Johnnie the best, but after a bit of scuttling around and climbing on things she decides to stop knocking things over and stands silently behind the door again. She practises a few swings of the pan, Ellen imagining in great detail the door handle getting depressed and the door slowly slowly squeaking open and Johnnie's bleedy trainer coming in then his evil scowling face and him saying, 'Here's Johnnie!' then Ellen swinging the pan 180 degrees and the metal connecting with Johnnie's head and clunking against his skull and Johnnie tumbling to the ground with a 'bump aargh' and the non-stick surface of the pan ending up very sticky and red. In the end, though, Johnnie just steps into the bathroom and disarms her very easily. He takes Gary Rhodes by the handle and yogs him casually onto the lino floor. Ellen bursts into tears (plan B) then hugs/suppresses Johnnie and whimpers, 'Did you kill him did you kill him?' Suddenly Ellen's a sopping tracksuit wrapped around Johnnie's, and she does an incredible puppy-dog-saved-from-drowning expression and almost tells Johnnie she's sorry and she loves him but she doesn't want to go overboard. Johnnie's natural instinct is to feel anxious (is she worried Angelo's dead because it means she can't shag him again?), but there's a teensy pink lever in his heart which gets triggered whenever Ellen's looking sad and vulnerable, and he smiles and strokes her platinum hair and says, 'Don't be daft. I just taught him a lesson, didn't I. He's a prick.' Ellen lands on her knees, shaking the bathtub and the sink and the stinky shower curtain, and she asks, 'Are you cross at me?' Johnnie goes, 'Naw, of course I'm not.' He's still got suspicions about her and Angelo, but he knows deep down taking them out on Ellen will only result in him or her getting dumped and more sadness for Johnnie and cold beds and the shitty rat-race of chasing girls again and the possibility of not getting shagged himself again for maybe three or four-plus months. That's not the life for him. He'd rather keep all the wonderful incredible things about Ellen and all the sickening dreadful things about her than not have anything of her at all. So, slightly grudgingly (but knowing in the back of his mind it's the right thing to do), Johnnie takes a breath, takes up Ellen in both of his arms and says, 'Don't worry, Ellen, I love you. That cunt Angelo, ah he should know better not to go around punting pills. I'm struggling enough, aren't I. He's a cunt, he's a cunt.' Ellen can't really believe Johnnie could beat Angelo to a pulp just because of ecstasy, but she's happy with the result and cuddles him back and swears in her head she'll never do anything to hurt him ever again, if she can. For Johnnie it feels instantly heavenly to have her back in his arms – just the feel of Ellen and her little heart-beat makes him feel happy again. The two of them are pretty knackered now and they retreat back into the lounge, holding hands, and they flop onto the settee like grandma and granddad. Johnnie's right arm stings from the wrist to the tip of his shoulder, but for the time being he doesn't mind Ellen lying on top of it. He feels a bit bad for making such a mess of Angelo's carpet and for disturbing the neighbours, but soon tiredness takes over with his head on Ellen's breast and he forgets all his worries, and slowly he begins to wink wink wink wink wink wink wink wink wink wink wink wink wink wink wink wink wink wink wink wink wink wink wink wink wink wink wink wink wink wink wink wink wink wink wink wink wink wink wink wink wink wink wink wink wink. Johnnie dreams about the tower block, imagining himself as the Don (all black slick-back hair and crisp suits and fishes in newspapers and tommy guns in violin cases), calling all the shots in the creaky crappy corridors of the building. Peach House isn't perfect, but it's not hell on earth either – the council tarted up the outside with double-glazing and pinky/yellowy/creamy-square pattern about five years back. It stands like a candy castle over the busy Cargo Fleet crossroad, lined with skinny brown chip-shops and newsagents and Lidl and the two other blocks Plum and Pear. Inside, Peach House is all beigey colour schemes turned fluorescent by striplights, the corridors all claustrophobic garden paths leading you round the lodgings. The landings are either too hot or too cold depending on the season or where the sun sits in the sky, and you have to watch for dead furniture and kiddies knock-a-door-running when traversing the gangways. Floor seven is a mirage of exotic smells and spices, floor two has a poster up encouraging you to KNOW YOUR LIMIT when it comes to drinking booze, and floor ten leads up to the roof where all the satellite dishes hang out and where Alan Blunt the Cunt may or may not have tried to commit suicide the year before. Tower blocks tend to house a really strange collection of people, ranging from skint young families to slightly frightening hermits, rowdy little drug-taking bastards who keep everyone up all night, depressed single middle-aged people and immigrants, and last week the lift broke and now from outside you can see them all charging up and down and up and down the stairways like ants. It's a pain in the arse one morning when Mrs Fletcher (a secretary at a solicitor's in town, who lives way up on floor eight) is late for work and has to battle about a million steps just to get to the bus stop outside. It's partly her own fault – there was an interesting article this morning in her *Observer* about Van Gogh being a nutcase and chopping his ear off and not being appreciated in his own time, and she sat in bed reading with her husband while the clock ticked way past 9am. It's so difficult getting out of bed since Mr Fletcher got laid off at the post office – nowadays he just sits in the floral armchair, checking Teletext for jobs, sipping cups of coffee getting colder and colder, spring-cleans the apartment, stays in bed till afternoon. It was incredibly tempting to stay under the covers with him this morning, enjoying the paper and pasties he purchased that morning from Premier, but now Mrs Fletcher's cursing herself because she'll never make it to the office for 9.30 and it's not fair Jennifer covering for her when the poor girl's got loads of filing and phone calls to answer herself. Mrs Fletcher grimaces, bobbing and weaving past carriers of rubbish as she charges down down down round round round. Her Elizabeth Duke watch tells her she's missed the 9.23 bus already, and she mutters something shitty under her breath and wonders if it's worth running down the stairs at all. Those new heels from Priceless still aren't worn in, and it'd probably be Mrs Fletcher's luck to snag one on a binbag and collapse all the way down to ground floor. If only the lift was working, there'd be none of this hassle. Apparently the men from the council have been informed about the faulty cable mechanism, but Mrs Fletcher's experience with authorities and councillors and workmen in general leads her to thinking it'll be weeks before it's even looked at/diagnosed. The world of work is very disappointing. She can't help but think Mr Fletcher was so hard done by losing his job at the post depot – he was a solid worker, never had a day off in eleven years, and he found pleasure inventing magical stories about the people on all the envelopes he sorted. When Mr Fletcher was at the PO he was as happy and radiant as the stallion she met twenty years ago in the George public house in Normanby, but as the mail became more automated, more and more workers lost their jobs and Mr Fletcher was one of the first to go in September. The Fletchers had to downsize from their cosy semi into Peach

House, and her husband blames himself and spites all technology and machinery, and he doesn't even like boiling the kettle any more. He has nightmares about a sort of *Terminator*ish world where all the robots and machines and tin cans wage war against the humans, and all the Luddites would have to go hide in some kind of underground Butlins holiday camp, awaiting death or batteries running out. He mopes around the house with nothing much to do. The Fletchers don't even have a garden he can potter about in, and living on floor eight makes him feel particularly housebound and lonely, cut off from the trees and the flowers and the streets and the human faces. Mrs Fletcher herself doesn't mind living in the sky – they've made the flat quite homely, kitted out with chintzy furniture, and the view's incredible – but this morning it's a nuisance and all she can do is just grumble, tumbling down the spirals and landings. She's reduced to a walking pace by the time she reaches floor four (and desperate for one of the ten Sterlings she limits herself to each day), and she's in an awful mood. She can't be bothered explaining why she's late to Mr Gosling when she's got no proper excuse, and he'll probably be on her back all day, and it's nowhere near the weekend. Mrs Fletcher's almost tempted to scuttle back upstairs and phone in sick, when suddenly she trips and stops and gazes at that 'Blob with Eyes' (58x81cm) Bobby the Artist discarded on the landing. Except to her it's not a blob with eyes; it's a dazzling masterpiece, a wacky celebration of colour and seaside, and the most beautiful sleeping beauty since *Sleeping Beauty*. Mrs Fletcher blinks, picks up the picture, and suddenly she doesn't give a shit about being late for work any more. She loves art, you know. She touches the surface, tracing the lumpy bumpy brushstrokes over the top of Georgie's over-the-top mascara. Mrs Fletcher wonders how such a gorgeous artwork could be chucked so brutally down the corridors of her block, and she's about to slip it in her briefcase when suddenly the door of 4E creaks open and the real Georgie staggers out of her Hansel and Gretel flat made of sweets, bleary-eyed. Georgie's got work at ten at Bhs, and she steps down the steps all grumpy and knackered. She's still a bit dazed after a great dream about a gigantic piñata, candy raining down on her as she bats the hell out of her boss Mr Hawkson strung way up high from a tree. She can't be fucked going to work either. Georgie scratches under her unflattering nylon uniform, hardly noticing Mrs Fletcher standing there with the painting halfway in her briefcase. Fletcher smiles sheepishly, suddenly recognising Georgie as the girl from the picture, and she asks her, 'Excuse me, is this your painting?' Georgie snaps out of her sickly trance, glances at Mrs Fletcher and the bit of paper in the quarter-light of the corridor, then croaks, 'Erm, naw, it's Bobby's, my boyfriend.' Georgie's pretty desperate to avoid all contact with human beings and just get to work, so shattered she is, and she tries to creep down the stairway but Mrs Fletcher pulls her up and carries on, 'I love it. It's so . . . raw. Yet, like, delicate.' Georgie says, 'Cheers,' wishing she hadn't stepped out the door at that very moment. She can't even stand eye contact with anyone when she's in this mood, although it's worse when someone you hate sits next to you on the bus and you're forced

53

to make small talk with them for twenty minutes. She picks out a bit of sleepy mascara, yawning a big O to herself while Mrs Fletcher persists, 'Can I speak to the artist?' Georgie shuts her mouth, then opens it again and says, 'I wouldn't if I was you. He's in bed, and like he hasn't been sleeping very well the last few days and he'll be really off with you. Nothing against you, by the way ...' Mrs Fletcher nods, glances again at 'Blob with Eyes' (58x81cm), then asks, 'Well, can I take his number? Sorry to be a nuisance, it's just my cousin Lewis is actually a dealer in art in London, and I'm sure he'd love to see some of Robert's work. It's really interesting stuff; I'd like to see more!' Georgie stares. 'It's Bobby, not Robert,' she says, 'but erm yeah, here you go then.' Giving Mrs Fletcher his number, Georgie urges her to phone 'at least after tea. He'll be in a bad mood with you otherwise.' Mrs Fletcher nods and grins, returning the painting to the grubby vinyl so as not to seem like a dodgy thieving cow. For a bit Georgie and Mrs Fletcher carry on down the stairs together, but on reaching floor two Georgie stops and pretends to tie her shoelace so she doesn't have to talk to that weirdo any more. Mrs Fletcher takes the hint and walks by herself to the hot magnifying-glass bus shelter, satisfied in her head that she might've discovered the New Van Gogh. If only she could get him to cut his ear off! Mrs Fletcher gets on the 65 pulling a smug grin, and while the bus starts and stops and stops and starts down Cargo Fleet Lane she pulls out her Mitsubishi 'brick' and dials her cousin's office. Bent Lewis sits on his grey spinning-chair in his gallery in Clerkenwell (that's in London), half flicking through slides of nude males and half daydreaming out the brushed aluminium windows. It's a lovely day in London as well, and Bent Lewis rolls up his salmon sleeves, answering the phone placed with brilliant feng shui between art books (*Francis Bacon: Portraits and Heads*, *Hockney's Pictures*, and *Robert Mapplethorpe*, the one with all the men's willies in it) and press releases with the names of artists and the names of artworks and the names of prices on them. 'Hello?' he ding-dongs, sweat collecting in the fat grooves of his neck. 'Hi, Lewis, it's Mary,' Mrs Fletcher says, the 65 turning up King's Road (that's not in London), where the Buccaneer is and the Majestic Bingo. She scrunches her eyes at the sunshine like a seashell shutting and says, 'You'll never guess what I've seen today. The New Van Gogh! There's this incredible young artist living in my block – God, I don't know how to describe it . . . sort of, imagine the love-child of Keith Haring and Basquiat, if they ever had sex that is . . . haw haw haw . . .' Back in Clerkenwell, Bent Lewis wakes up slightly in the groggy Cadmium Yellow heat – recently London's been getting him down, what with the trains beginning to smell and the gallery opening looming faster and faster and the lack of cheap young talent to hang in his white cube. Back in June he sent a few feelers out to the college degree shows, but found all the work to be trash. Fucking trash! Lewis's list is fairly uninspiring – he represents a couple of photographers (mostly nude portraits/commercial plop), an abstract painter he fucked at the Frieze art fair last year, a multimedia artist whose videos bore you to tears (his work 'Watching Paint Dry, 2001–2' is a particular no-no) but he's got a pretty face, and Lewis's ex-boyfriend Michael – a painter of still-lifes he's still on good terms with, and always tries to get back with when he's pissed on free champers. Bent Lewis watches a pigeon or two lingering on the warehouse roof across the road, chewing his nails, feeling an odd tear of hay fever or loneliness in his left eye. He swaps the telephone to his other ear, then tells Mrs Fletcher, 'Tell me more.' Fletcher shuffles on the bus seat, explaining, 'Well, I was coming down the stairs this morning, and there it was – this amazing little painting amongst the binbags and all that . . . even the paintings Bobby throws out are amazing!' Bent Lewis begins bouncing on his spinny chair, and he takes the Artist's number and takes a walk round the office beaming to himself. He loves Northerners. He spends the rest of the day obsessing over the New Van Gogh, imagining all the luscious paintings but also imagining the rusty stink of pennies and boys' bottoms on his fingers. On his way home (he gets the overland from Farringdon to Tulse Hill; it's always fucking busy) he squashes on a three-seater with two office workers doing crossword puzzles, and phones Bobby the Artist staring out the glass at the sun going down. The sun's going down up North as well, and Bobby throws down his paintbrushes in disgust at the shitty falling light. He's still on a mighty old comedown, slurping china tea feeling all Buddhist in his kangaroo PJs. He feels quite sad today for no particular reason. Bobby gazes at the large canvas perched against the pink couch, all these beautiful girls staring out of the slop like les Demoiselles d'Avignon but not as triangular and whorish. The new piece is called 'The Angels' (244x233cm)

– sort of a celebration of all the lovely ladies living in the tower block. The thing with Bobby is – although he's attached to Georgie – he'll always feel some sort of attraction or affection towards other girls. He enjoys following a strange sixties idealism, which involves taking many psychedelics, listening to far-out music and spreading lots of love. He wants to be Jack Kerouac – or the more hardcore one, Neal Cassady. He doesn't think he'll ever cheat on Georgie, but often he gets that sensation walking down a busy street that all the girls are better looking than his own, or that they'd do more drugs, or that they'd do much dirtier things in bed. He thinks it's natural to want sex every single day, but it seems an eight-hour shift at Bhs kills a girl's libido. He loves so many things about Georgie (her kitten face, her dressing-up box, her passion for sweets), but those are things he's gotten used to over the months and the napalm-ish excitement he felt for her when they first started going out has gradually dampened. Why is it that, as soon as you start living with a girl, you hardly seem to have sex with her any more? Breathing out a hot puff, Bobby the Artist leans into the canvas and applies a thick splurge of cream across Georgie's breasts. Georgie stands with a big flashing halo in the centre of all the others: Pamela from upstairs with a glazed expression in raunchy nurse gear (a perverted vision of her doing her shift at the kid's playschool), Ellen in miniskirt with fluorescent thighs, Mandy all skinny brushstrokes on speed babbling nonsense. Oh, drugs. All the money's gone now, hasn't it, and Bobby feels generally very depressed like he's carting a ton weight around with him. He owes £200 ticky to Johnnie and about £100 rent to Georgie, but fuck money – Bobby doesn't think you've been put on this world to worry about paper and coins, you've been put here to enjoy every one of your breaths like a drowned sailor finally pulled back up to the surface. He sighs. Bobby's destructive drug-taking stems from a terrible incident in his childhood: he discovered rock and roll. Ever since he saw the video for 'I Am the Walrus' on *Top of the Pops 2* aged eight and a half, Little Bobby knew he wanted to dedicate his life to drugs. But it didn't take long to spiral out of control, sending him into a horrible, vicious world of technicolour, sunshine, and fun. Now he reads Baudelaire's 'Intoxication' every morning when he gets out of bed. He wants it tattooed across his forehead. Sighing again, Bobby's incredibly tempted to go upstairs for more ticky off Johnnie but stops himself, suddenly put off by his screaming siren mobile phone. His ringtone is a garbled spaghetti of sounds he inputted high on mushrooms one evening, thinking he could hear exotic birds and rainforest animals every playback. He ceases the horridness, answering the phone to Bent Lewis with a paintbrush in his mouth and the word, 'Eh?' Bent Lewis: 'Hello, is that Bobby? This is Lewis from the +!Gallery' (pronounced with a big camp yelp – 'PPLLUUSS!' – which makes Bobby shit himself) 'in London. How do you do? I think my cousin has been in touch with you, no? She saw a wonderful painting of yours this morning, and I was wondering if you've ever thought about representation, or if you'd be interested in showing me some work perhaps? Your stuff sounds ideal for my opening exhibition . . .' Bobby the

Artist blinks once or twice, not sure if they've got the right number. Cousin? Paintings? Wiping his schnozzle, Bobby stares blankly at the wall and says again, 'Eh?' Bent Lewis: 'Oh yes, sorry, well obviously I need to see some paintings! Let's not jump the gun . . . Are you busy next week? I'd love to come up and see your studio – your work sounds *so* fantastic. I could make you a lot of money!' Bobby the Artist sniffs. 'Well, the flat's a bit of a state, like,' he mumbles, glancing at all the candy wrappers and all the druggy wrappers and splodges of acrylic and paintings and the ballerina/sailor/brownie outfits and the sleepy shoes and wormy fag butts. Bent Lewis: 'Oh, don't worry, you should've seen Francis Bacon's studio!' Suddenly becoming more animated, Bobby leap-frogs off the carpet and asks, 'You knew Francis Bacon?' Bent Lewis says, 'Yes,' although he actually means no. Back in Clerkenwell, Lewis nudges that book *7 Reece Mews* along his desk, the one with all the grimy oil-painty photos of Bacon's hideout. Through the telephone he hears lots of muffled bumping, which is Bobby jumping about the flat with glee. The Artist thinks he's speaking to some sort of hero or guardian angel. They arrange a date to meet up, Bobby scribing NEXT SATURDAY on the skirting-board with Georgie's Love That Pink lipstick, just as the girl herself trundles through the door in her Bhs stuff. She squirts her stinky work shoes onto the carpet, finding a space on a sofa arm until Bobby's off the phone, then she gives him a big hello hug. Bobby the Artist gives her a welcome-back snog on the lips, then bounces on the balls of his feet telling Georgie about the weird man on the phone and the exhibition and the Bacon. He's got the football-size eyes of a five-year-old, and Georgie starts bouncing too with the excitement of it all and the fact the creaky floorboards are quite fun. She'd forgotten all about Mrs Fletcher harassing her this morning, and she grins two pink crescents all proud of her boyfriend. In a way Bobby feels weird getting so over-the-top about 'fame' and 'money', but the way the world works you do need pennies in your back pocket, and there's no way he wants to die with this stupid world not knowing his name. In a torrent of inspiration, Bobby claws for his sable brush and whips jiggedy-jaggedy lemon yellow bits into each of the Angels' hair, getting put off for a split-second when his tummy has a wee rumble. Bobby the Artist hasn't eaten for days, his appetite suppressed so much by drugs a bite of sausage roll yesterday afternoon had to be spitten out, but now every little squeeze from Georgie reminds him just how empty he is. His cheeks look like black triangles as he kisses Georgie so up close – usually the mop-top hides all signs of malnutrition, and bad skin. Georgie, mirrorballs hidden by eyelids, spins Bobby onto the floor and gives him a big fat smackeroony anyway. She loves her boyfriend and she loves him getting back on his arty farty feet again, and the two of them roll around in the sweeties and the paint and they knock over Bobby's water pot, and the two of them are a mess and all. On an ordinary comedown this sort of behaviour would annoy Bobby, but today he's got London drooling at his feet, and he gives Georgie another huge huggle. She laughs, spinning him into the new painting, and suddenly he does get a bit tetchy and says,

'Actually, that's enough. I'm fucking starving. Howay.' Georgie doesn't really notice her boyfriend's topsy-turvy emotions, she just keeps beaming and does a little squeal and says, 'Ooh, I know what you can have! It's a special occasion, after all!' She scampers through to the kitchen and empties her work-bag onto the breakfast bar, cascading cut-price pick-'n'-mix and stolen bags of crisps like a crunchy waterfall. She tears open bags of Haribo and paper barber-shop bags of candy, chomping and smiling all the time like Minnie Mouse or Miss Piggy on Methylenedioxymethamphetamine. Her face is the sun breaking through her two cloudy cheeks. To celebrate Bobby's success, she 'cooks up' a sweety full-English breakfast for them both, which consists of: Starmix fried eggs, cola jelly-beans for sausages, pink shrimps for bacon, red Skittle tomatoes, two tiny toffee hash-browns, a fingerful of pink Nerds for baked beans, yucky Blackjack black pudding, two ready-salted KP Squares for toast, served with a Starmix milk bottle on a paper plate. Georgie's forehead twitches with hilarity as she brings Bobby the Artist his meal, with a dishcloth folded over her forearm like a proper waitress. Bobby gets the hystericals and loves her all over again, clearing a space on the shitty carpet for the plates. You have to eat the sweety full-English with your fingers, and it gets scoffed in an instant, Georgie being really adventurous and combining tastes, for example Nerds on Squares (beans on toast), shrimp squashed on jelly-bean (pigs in blankets), or a Skittle either side of the Blackjack (just gets rid of the taste of a Blackjack). Bobby picks at his food piece by piece, hands all shaky and white. Afterwards he gives

61

Georgie another smooch, and for ten seconds his life is perfect and if he were to die right now (for example his heart bursting, so full it is with glittering red bloooood) he'd be in too much rapture to notice. But then ten seconds later he's hungry again – the sweety full-English isn't known for being very filling – but there's fuck-all in the cupboards, unless you like eating bread sandwiches. Bobby's not the sort of house-husband to go pushing a trolley round Lidl very often; in fact, at times he can be quite a bad boyfriend, since living the bohemian dream involves not cleaning the apartment or washing the dishes or buying more milk when they run out of milk. He just wants to paint and be merry! Bobby the Artist sits there in the middle of a Stonehenge of canvases, feeling his belly grumble, and he wonders if Georgie would mind him eating her instead. Randy bastard. Eyes beaming, Georgie giggles as he creeps his hands up her legs like pervy spiders, and in all his light-headed derangement Bobby starts cackling too. He tugs down her Sooty and Sweep knickers. Georgie's a bit shy to open her legs dead wide because she's got a few in-grown hairs and all that, but she smiles serenely as Bobby's fingers slither up her cellulite. He slips his tongue into her sweaty cinnamon fanny, and all those feelings of starvation disappear down her minge-hole. Georgie aahs. It's a bit annoying getting shagged straight after a gruelling shift at work, and it's a shame the sex organs have to be so close to the poo organs – they can really stink sometimes. And the same goes for Bobby – he hasn't showered his mouldy sausage for a while, and she decides not to suck him off. She kisses his whiffy-fanny lips instead. And now for a cameo appearance from Mr Condom! He comes leaping out of his packaging, then Bobby and Georgie jump around gleefully on top of each other for about half an hour. It's intense! Bobby finds Mr Condom annoying though – he's a bit like an over-attentive waiter on your first date, but Georgie's scared of STDs and small children and she insists on him being there. Georgie's incredibly cautious about every-thing – she just wants a lovely comfortable life with no big shocks or scares, whereas Bobby favours a mad look-Mam-no-hands! sort of life. But whatever, the sex is still great. Bobby gets his own back on Mr Condom by suffocating him with white custard, then he screws him up in the bin with all the other gritty Mr Condoms. He goes for a wee in the bathroom – a foamy spunky one – then frog-jumps next to Georgie and swings his arms round her four or five times like Stretch Armstrong or just someone really really in love with their girlfriend. Over in the bin, Mr Condom sighs. Georgie's feeling a bit cold now all in the nude, and she gets changed into an old fairy costume and guzzles down a few jelly-beans. Her favourites from the Jelly Belly range are Peach, Plum and Juicy Pear – it makes her feel like she's eating up the tower blocks. 'Dessert?' she enquires, throwing Bobby one. Bobby nods, then he nuzzles her neck and says he loves her and Georgie grins and says it too. 'I'm so proud of you, hun!' she squeals. Bobby the Artist scours the carpet for a post-fuck fag, but all the packs are empty, and he has-n't got the guts to ask Georgie for a borrow. Money, you're such a pain! On top of selling canvases, occa-sionally Bobby gets commissions to paint murals for libraries or hospitals or kids' homes, but it's such a chore having to do it sober – the one time he dropped acid painting the Accident & Emergency, Bobby's brush spewed a load of porno doctors and nurses with syringes in their heads and patients racing naked on medicine cabinets. A day later it was covered sick Infirmary Green again. Bobby blinks, bingeing up a rollie out the stinky ashtray. He hopes to God this Lewis magics him some money soon. The last 'real job' Bobby ever had was working the fork-lift trucks at the B&Q Warehouse on the Portrack Lane Ind. Est., stacking bits of wood and garden furniture, drinking cups of tea and listening to the Fall's 'Industrial Estate' on his dinner-break. Surely to fuck he can get by without fags and drugs for just a little bit. He's got paintings to paint! Wheezing on the old rollie, Bobby the Artist pulls on his boxers again then washes his one-inch DIY brush and mixes up peach-pink on the pocked palette. To get peachy pink, you need three parts Cadmium Red to two parts Titanium White to one part Yellow Ochre. Then comes the tricky bit: applying it to the Angels' lips and cheeks without making them look like absolute harlots. Watching him work, Georgie straightens the white tutu, wondering who the hell all the girls are but she's not jealous. She has a few more Jelly Bellies, then plops through to the bathroom to give her minge a good old clean-out and sort her hair. She likes Mr Condom, but she hates his latex aftershave. In the front room she hears Bob put on My Bloody Valentine – lots of fuzzy-wuzzy songs perfect after a shag or during a painting. 'Loveless' actually reminds Bobby of his ex-girlfriend Gabrielle – the sex between them was great too but without much emotional content (to be honest, he found her pretentious and boring), and he used to enjoy putting on records after they'd shagged more than doing the deed itself. The song 'Loomer' oozes out the square speakers like pink lava, and Georgie comes back in the lounge all sleepy with just fake candy energy bubbling in her tummy. Surprisingly she's not absolutely obese, although she's always moaning to Bobby about her love-handles and big bum and shimmery cellulite – perhaps it's all the running around at work and all the running around after Bobby that keeps her somewhere in shape. However, Bobby glares at her gobbling more and more jelly-beans, and in his gobbledygook imagination he thinks Georgie looks a bit like a piglet. The fact she goes on about her weight so much only fuels the image in his head even brighter. He adds a bit extra paint to Georgie's cheeks then wipes it out with a paper towel, knowing she'll only kick off if she's immortalised chubby in one of his paintings. Bobby the Artist chews his brush. Two weeks ago he read Dear Deidre in the *Sun* (Alan Blunt the Cunt donates his newspapers sometimes for Bobby to paint on) and she said boys often expect their girlfriends to look slim and perfect, but in fact curves are the natural shape for rearing children and whatnot. But then again on Page 3 you've got skinny ninnies with their knockers out. Bobby the Artist has a bit of a cough, and he's just about to thin Georgie down with some white spirit when the front door goes rat-a-tat-tat and he staggers over to it, mop-top flopping this way and that. It's Ellen from upstairs, and she stands there in the hallway

65

wearing a clingfilm shellsuit and a sad expression. 'What's up?' Bobby the Artist asks, rolling up his sleeves. 'Oh nowt,' Ellen goes, but you can tell she's holding back and she dips her eyelashes and says, 'Well, actually it's Johnnie. He's been weird. You know he put Angelo Bashini in hospital the other night? Well he just seems dead uptight, like, I was wondering – if it's not too much trouble – could I stay here tonight? He's not at home and I'm worried he's gone mad, and I think Mandy's out with Dave, and Pamela's mam and dad are back, and I don't want to be alone . . .' Despite the comedown, Bobby reacts a bit too ecstatically and bangs the door wide open and smiles just as wide and says, 'Sound, Ellen, howay in! Make yourself at home.' Bobby leads Ellen through to the lounge and, although Ellen's been round loads of times for happenings and drugs and borrowing sugar, he says to her, 'Keep your shoes on if you want, this is the living room, soz it's messy, I'm painting and that, bathroom's over there, kitchen's through there, have what you want, you can sleep on the sofa if you like, I'll move this.' Bobby the Artist drags 'The Angels' (244x233cm) off the pink couch and into the bedroom, then he plumps the fuch- sia cushions and points where Ellen should park her bum. Ellen sits down, rustling skinny clingfilm fabric, grinning at Bobby being so weird and welcoming. On the floor, Georgie stares up with tired gobstopper eyes. A big orgasm on top of an eight-hour shift always knocks the poor girl for six, and she can hardly stay awake while Ellen retells the story of Johnnie going round Angelo's, knocking him round the flat, feeding him a razor blade, the shenanigans with Gary Rhodes, but missing out the bit about her shagging Angelo of course. Bobby the Artist gazes, listening intently, thinking a razor blade through the eyeball might've been a more lasting punishment but perhaps he's been watching too much *Chien Andalou* again. Ellen tells them Johnnie's been alright to her but he's clearly in a fiery mood and today he's gone missing from Peach House and he won't answer his phone and she doesn't know what to do, but thanks a lot for letting her stay. Bobby the Artist looks at her from his standing-up position in the doorframe, nodding in random places, thinking about her Golden Ratio face and the prospect of her possibly posing naked for 'The Angels' (244x233cm). Ellen oozes more sex than a sloppy de Kooning, and at times Bobby wishes he was single again and free to feel the completely different caresses and crevices of a completely different girl. It worries him that he'll never kiss another pair of lips ever again. Ellen feels a bit uncomfortable what with him staring at her so much and Georgie dying on the carpet, and after a bit of creaky silence she shuffles on the sofa and asks, 'Oi, what time do youse usually get up, cos I've got to sign on at half ten tomorrow.' Bobby the Artist clicks out of his trance, slightly paranoid in case Ellen's telepathic, but then he smiles and says, 'Oh, I dunno, I'll probably still be awake by then, I dunno . . . my sleeping's a bit fucked.' Ellen blows out a little laugh, then looks at Georgie at the bottom of the carpet and the worker bee says, 'Well, I've got the dentist at ten tomorrow, so I'll leave with you, if you want.' Georgie's rabid sweety-eating has resulted in her having a mouth full of silver and white fillings, big lumpy fissure seals and the odd rotten hole or brown crack in her molars, and tomorrow she's in for another two drillings. She hates the dentist – in total, since she was ten years old, she's had twenty-seven fillings, five teeth pulled out, plus a horrid old brace when she was fourteen. Nowadays her smile's pretty straight and you wouldn't know all her teeth are riddled with mercury and whatnot, but it's her mouth that causes her most grief in life. Bobby does all that bloody gurning and he's never even had a filling, lucky old so-and-so! Georgie's dentist tells her she's got soft gnashers and the deepness of the molars make for more crap getting stuck in than normal, but she'll never give up eating sweets for a man whose breath always smells of onion. Laid all crumply in her fairy outfit, Georgie pops another peach jelly-bean down her neck, enjoying the flavour, but the thought of getting her teeth buzzed tomorrow makes her all shaky and sad and her tummy feels fizzy with nerves. 'I didn't know you had the dentist, pet,' Bobby the Artist says, although it's typical of him to forget everything, and Georgie guesses it's the drugs killing off all his brain cells and generally turning him into a stupid person. She's too shattered to argue, though, and eventually she heads off to bed feeling depressed about the dentist and depressed that Bobby forgot and depressed that Bobby'll be up all night talking to Ellen, and she depresses the mattress and the bronzey pillow when she finally flops naked into bed. Bobby doesn't mean to be a dozy cunt. He's just excited to have a guest in the house, and he tries to run around the flat offering Ellen cups of tea or mouldy toast or Georgie's sweets or half a binge, but Ellen's just happy to be safe four storeys high in the sky.

When she woke up this morning in Johnnie's bed, there was just a ditch laid next to her instead of a boyfriend. She hopes Johnnie hasn't flipped again, storming around the town, mutilating young men in his path. She unzips her clingy top, lying back on the sofa while Bobby pervs, memorising her curves for 'The Angels' (244x233cm). He thinks Ellen's quite sound because she takes a lot of heavy-duty drugs and doesn't seem to give a shit about anything – she's like a sixties child in an eighties tracksuit, always enjoying herself, getting laid, doing pills, not going to work. She reminds him a bit of himself, except he doesn't have blonde hair and he's never shagged two men at once in San Antonio on holiday. He's not going to make a pass at her – he really couldn't do that to Georgie, and he doesn't fancy dining on razor blades either. He asks Ellen if she's got a spare ciggy, but no smoker ever has a spare cigarette, and she ends up going on her own to the bathroom to spark up the Richmonds Johnnie bought her so Bobby won't cadge off her. At around 5am Ellen starts getting tired and she figures she'd better get some sleep since she's at the dole tomorrow, despite Bobby the Artist rambling to her about primary colours and Josef Albers and optical illusions and other shite. He slaps some bright red next to some bright blue on this new painting he's doing called 'Bobby's Favourite Trip' (120x150cm), based on an afternoon in Spar when Bobby tried to climb into the confectionery counter, thinking all the gaudy chocolate bars were gaudy chocolate cars. He says, 'See how your eye flickers between the red and blue, like it can't tell which is nearer? It's called an illusion I think.' Ellen yawns and curls into a mollusc shape on the settee, opening one eye then saying, 'Ah right, well anyway that's nice but I think I'd best be off to sleep. You gonna stay up much longer?' Ellen nuzzles her head right into one of the cushions, completely shattered, while Bobby potters about in the living room, scrabbling for change for a two-litre bottle of cider from the shop across the road. When times are hard, he can often rustle £1.99 for White Strike and get pissed for a few hours – anything to avoid the boring lifeless ordeal of being sober. He uncovers a few 10 and 20ps from under the settee and round 'The Angels' (244x233cm) and 'Bobby's Favourite Trip' (120x150cm) and behind the telly and in Georgie's tweed purse, then he propels himself shopward. The boys at the Coca-Cola newsagent always sort him out for booze way before they're licensed, and there's that faint rock-and-roll scruffy charm buying gutrot cider at daft o'clock in the morning surrounded by paper boys and the dawn yawning. Bobby trundles back into Peach House with bare feet and his arm round the cider, and an hour or so later he's completely legless and Georgie and Ellen are just waking up with grumpy pale faces. He tries to make them a cup of tea in the kitchen but he just jibbers about like an octopus on downers, flapping his arms and knocking things over but really enjoying it. Georgie's less impressed, sorting her and Ellen a fried-egg sarnie each and still really pooing herself about the dentist. She's got on the geisha dressing-gown, and she tells Bobby to go to bed but he just laughs and says to her lighten up and he's a bit of a nuisance. She gives him a karate chop and makes herself the perfect white-

four-sugars cup of tea, then she sits in a huff in front of
GMTV. It's funny how you take normal days for grant-
ed, normal days where you don't have to have your
teeth drilled out, or you don't have to look after
Bobby, or you don't have your hay fever. Georgie sniffs
and sulks into her teacup, feeling all snotty and red-
eyed and nervous. It's one of those mornings the air
stinks and the sun's a big yellow circle, all the pretty
flowers opening their petals to it like slutty vaginas and
pissing out ping-pong pollen. Georgie gets hay fever
really awful every summer, and just when she thought
she'd get through June without a sneeze or a sniffle, she
wakes up on the morning of her dentist appointment
with sloppy marshmallow eyeballs and a throat full of
flames. Poor little blossom. Summer's a funny time for
Georgie in that she loves sunny weather and rolling
around in daisy patches, but she gets punished for it so
severely. She finishes off her tea and says cheerio to the
wobbly wino in the kitchen, then her and Ellen set off
into the thick slimy sunlight. There's a heatwave floating over Cargo Fleet Lane, and her and Ellen sit
together on the grassy slope instead of hanging out
with the silent cunts at the bus shelter. Georgie and
Ellen actually get on quite well – a relationship built
on drunken nights round each other's flats, often talking totally openly about boyfriends' cum faces, farting,
and so-and-so's (Mandy's) stinky fanny. The only thing
is Georgie really disagrees with people sponging off
the dole and being lazy, and she worries people like
Ellen will go nowhere in their beautiful massive lives.
Having said that, while the two of them sit there constructing a daisy-chain, Georgie wishes she was going

to the Jobcentre and getting £44 a week for nowt
rather than going to the dentist then a six-hour shift at
Bhs on minimum wage. The bad thing about work
today is she won't be in the mood for scoffing sweets
after getting her mouth carved out, and sitting amongst
the posters of rotten teeth and cartoon kids saying NO!
to sugary treats puts you on such a fucking guilt trip.
Slapping dark hair and bright sun out of her eyes,
Georgie positions herself in some lamp-post shadow
and asks Ellen, 'You and Johnnie aren't on the rocks, are
you?' Ellen sits in the buttercups with her top rolled up
to her turtle-green bra and shellsuit bottoms turned
up, and she squints at Georgie and goes, 'Naw, I don't
think so. I just want to give him space, know what I
mean? Give him some space and that. I think he's just
pissed off about Angelo, something to do with drugs or
something.' Georgie nods, thinking she's lucky in a way
that Bobby's not that violent or temperamental; he's
just plain mental. She stabs another daisy with her pink
nail and attaches it to their metre-long chain, and as the
65 bus comes wibbling into view from over the hill she
says, 'Here's the bus.' They jump on, Ellen hanging the
dainty chain round her neck and borrowing the fare
off Georgie, which she says she'll 'definitely get back'.
Georgie says it's okay with a blank face, sitting down
and worrying more about her left eye than a wee bit of
money. She's leaking all this yellow gooey stuff, probably because Georgie's rubbing her eyes with the same
hand she's been rubbing her nose with, but she can't
help it. She stares sadly at the backs of people's heads.
Keeping themselves occupied on the white-hot bus,
her and Ellen chatter a bit longer about boys and trou-

bles, Ellen asking things like, 'So is Bobby a good shag and that?' and Georgie replying things like, 'Aw yeah, it's the best. I mean, I haven't shagged loads of lads, but Bobby's incredible. Only sometimes he can get carried away, you know, like wanting to get tied up or wanting me to put a finger up his bum . . .' Ellen laughs and nods, but really she thinks Georgie's probably pretty frigid – or at least not very outgoing in bed – when really sex is like a blank page and you can either leave it pretty blank or you can squirt a thousand colours over it. Sometimes Ellen thinks of herself as being artistic like Bobby, but only when it comes to being a good shag – she's no good with a paintbrush, but incredibly creative with a man's hard penis. She smiles wistfully, remembering all the many willies squirting semen left right and centre like squeezy mayonnaise bottles, and she also thinks slightly about Angelo in hospital, unable to shag him because he's all bandaged up but she might've wanted to again. As the bus grumbles and drops everyone outside the Crown, Ellen guesses it's probably for the best Angelo's gone. She doesn't want her head caved in either. Ellen scuttles off towards the Jobcentre, feeling the sun melting drab brown Legoland, and she waves Georgie off lighting her last Richmond Superking. Georgie gives her a lonely little nod, pacing with her head down to the dental practice. The word 'practice' always makes her nervous – she hopes they've practised well enough by now not to make any mistakes. Georgie walks into the crinkly white surgery, the smell of mouthwash and plastic gloves sending a shiver down her spine, and she feels dismal telling the receptionist her name and that she's in for two fillings. The receptionist smiles but not with any sympathy, and tells Georgie to sit in the waiting room for ten minutes in between kids' toys and out-of-date women's magazines and the stereo chirping out CDs full of whale noises or the rainforest or a marmoset dying. Georgie knocks her knees together, waiting with her heart in her mouth on the ripped school-staff-roomy chairs. She'd much rather be at work, but it's funny how she always whinges about going to Bhs too, and she wonders to herself if she's got a fairly shitty life. Ellen and Bobby the Artist have it soooooo easy, being able to do what they want – they don't know what it's like working nine-to-five; what a way to make a living. It's fucking shite. It's just that Georgie has no choice – she figures you've got to make money to stay alive, and there's people out there doing much worse jobs and they might not even have a partner and they might eat ready-meals-for-one every night crying into the pasta or the shepherd's pie and then just go to bed. At least Georgie's life is exciting – what with living with complete nutcases – and she tries to hold her head high when the nurse in blue calls her name, leading her up the tight grubby staircase. But in the operating room it's torture – for starters Mr West aggravates her with lots of small-talk (nice weather today eh, see the footy, going anywhere nice this summer?), then he leans her right back in the grey leather seat and blinds poor Georgie with the rectangle light. Georgie's pulse is battering as the dentist cleans her molars with that cold sucky machine, the sound of it going through her like nails down a blackboard but much much worse. It's the fact Mr West never informs her what he's doing that gets to Georgie; he concentrates closed-mouthed as he starts drilling into Georgie's soft tooth, as if it's worse to actually say the word 'drill' to her than to just dive in with it completely unexpectedly. Georgie flinches, a weeny tear plopping out of her eye – at first the pain's not so bad, but then Mr West pushes down a bit harder and the drill goes whizz and bits of mouldy white gravel start flying out of her mouth. All the while the blue nurse still has that sicky sucky thing shoved in her gob like Georgie's giving a blow-job to all these metal instruments, and she starts crying like a little girl, wishing her mammy was here or at least Bobby the Artist to tell the surgeons to push off. Soon the pain's unbearable, and Mr West even has the nerve to poke into the cavity with this skinny spike, sending an electric shock round Georgie's skull and out through her eyeballs. She cries sloppy tears and makes the odd moan, trying to be a big girl but she's positive Mr West's hurting her on purpose, the sadistic little rotter. She clutches the arms of the leathery seat, wishing all the dentists of the world dead but at least she's forgotten about her hay fever. Her molars feel like big lightning-struck rocks, and even when Mr West fills the nerves in with white glob her mouth still kills and all she can think of is Ellen at the dole office, doing two minutes' work a fortnight then going out and getting pissed and not giving a shit for the next two weeks. Even Ellen's healthcare's free because she's signing on; Georgie has to pay the surgery forty-odd pound for the pleasure of having her teethies hurt. She pays up with a sour face and a fat lip, then trundles out of the surgery with a little bit of relief but mostly antagonism and numbness. It's eleven o'clock and she picks up the pace on her way to Bhs, not bearing to look at the Jobcentre as she scuttles past. Ellen's probably down the pub by now, with a cocktail in one hand. Lucky bitch. However, in actual fact Ellen's still sitting on the plaggy seats with her white giro booklet in hand, waiting very impatiently to get her name called by one of the grotesque blouse-mad JC assistants. It's shit weather in the Jobcentre – mostly grey and humid, some scattered fans about doing nowt. Ellen watches the plastic clock not moving in the corner of her eye, desperately wanting to get back outside and out of this fucking depressing zoo. They're funny old creatures, dole scum: man and wife with zebra tattoos probably been signing on for years, girl with peacock hair and little baby joey, bloke in grey seal suit probably got made redundant, little teenage cheetahs cheating the dole like Ellen. She feels a weird bond with all these people – the ones who sign on every first and third Thursday of the month around the half-ten mark. Johnnie used to be one. Ellen's got no intention of finding a job what with her leeching off her boyfriend and enjoying herself so much – she thinks people who work are absolute mugs. The dole people are mugs and all – when Ellen finally gets called to Desk Number One, the lady behind it asks her what she's been doing this week to find a job and Ellen says with a serious face, 'Aw loads . . . Been looking in the *Evening Gazette* but there was nowt suitable, came in the Jobcentre a few times to look for . . . vacancies, is it? . . . yeah, and my uncle Gary reckons he can get me a job at Morrison's, so I'm just waiting to hear from him really . . . oh yeah, and I checked the *Herald and Post* and all.' The lady nods, quite skeletal from years of hearing bullshit – Ellen doesn't really have an uncle Gary; she's got an aunty Diana, but she's a lesbian and works at the dog-track in Sunderland and Ellen doesn't think she could be fucked with that. She taps her feet up and down on the grey carpet tiles, signing her name under all her other signatures on the slip the lady hands her, seeing jackpot signs whizz round her eyeballs like her head's a one-armed bandit. 'Have you checked the vacancies today?' the lady asks, every bit of her creased like a hairless old ball sac. 'Yeah,' Ellen lies, but the ball sac still has a check through the database for her just in case. Ellen cringes, wishing very bad things on the dole lady and the dole lady's family. Blowing into a tissue, the lady glances at Ellen's details and spouts, 'So I see you're looking for jobs in either animal care, engineering, or computer management? Well what about this = Veterinarian Nurse, five days a week in Redcar, two years' experience minimum, ten pounds fifty an hour?' Ellen's belly smiles. She goes, 'Ah, I don't have the experience, sorry.' To be a professional dole merchant, you've got to have good qualifications in Excuse Making – the only subject Ellen really excelled at in school. The ball-sac lady gazes at her with a bit of contempt, but there's nothing she can say really and she stares at her computer again feeling shitty and annoyed – it's not like she loves working at the Jobcentre; all she wants herself is an easy life. The lady's had a million awful jobs (on the till at Netto, parking attendant, human filing cabinet at the Inland Revenue, school bog cleaner), and she doesn't see why some people (her) have to go through murder while others (Ellen) wake up to *Diagnosis Murder* at three in the afternoon and have no worries in the world. The lady purses her lips, clicks the cream keyboard, then snaps at Ellen, 'Well, you said you're looking at a job in Morrison's so I take it you're not against working in retail . . . well, what have we here: Sales Assistant, Asda South Bank, meets national minimum wage, full training given. Sounds ideal.' Ellen grins sour milk, stomach churning. 'Just give them a ring on this number,' the crinkly lady continues, printing out a wee slip of details, then, 'You can use the phone free of charge, over there.' In her head Ellen sees herself rimming the dole lady while getting whipped by the dole lady's devilish minions. The lady hands her the slip, then ushers Ellen away to the black tacky phone in a booth sat all on its lonesome. In full view of Mrs Ball Sac, Ellen picks up the receiver. She has a sulk to the sound of the dial tone, even the thought of getting up early for an interview let alone fucking working there bringing a tear to her eye. Why in this world can you not just do what you want? Cavemen got on alright without money and dole ladies and Asda. Ellen sits all tired and grumpy in the MDF booth, stalling for a bit then, in a flash of inspiration, she says to the dead phone, 'Hi, is that Asda? . . . Yeah, can I speak to Gloria please? . . . Oh, hi! Yeah, I hope so . . . I'd like to apply for the post of sales assistant, please . . . Oh, really? . . . Well great, yes, that'd be lovely. Monday. Nine fifty-five. Nice one . . . Okay, yep, will do . . . Alright, ta ra.' Ellen turns and smiles at the dole lady, giving her a dead corny thumbs-up and the lady nods, slightly suspicious but not really giving much of a shit now. She's got another person to see (girl with the peacock hair), and Ellen swivels in her swively chair grinning to herself. There's a sign above the phone saying NO PERSONAL CALLS, but Ellen decides she might as well give Johnnie a personal call seeing as it's free and she's free from the horrible lady too. Her breath crackles on the creaky black plastic. 'Where are you?' she asks when Johnnie picks up, and it's a relief to hear his voice, 'I've been dead worried. What are you up to?' Johnnie sniffs. 'I'm just in Lidl,' he replies, pushing the cagey trolley round the aisles while his Nanna picks up packs of potatoes and orange juices and chopped tomatoes and slings them in. 'Eh?' Ellen ehs, twizzling the wire round her little finger. 'Ah, I'm just helping Nanna out with the shopping, aren't I,' Johnnie says, his grandmother suddenly perking up with Choco Rice in one hand and wittering, 'Ooh is it Eleanor? Tell her hello from me, John, tell her hello from me.' Nanna stands there for a good minute with the box in her claw like a stone sculpture, staring at her grandson until he finally says, 'Yeah, Ellen, our Nanna says alright by the way.' Nanna grins and carries on loading the trolley (it's brilliant in Lidl, you can get noodles for 13p and eight Excelsiors for £4.49), Johnnie breaking his back trying to scoot it round with one hand. It's been a terrible couple of days for him – he doesn't mean to get paranoid all the time, but he had to run away after getting all upset about a couple of tissues in his dustbin. Of all the things! Early Tuesday morning, just before he disappeared, Johnnie woke up very proud to have Ellen back and to be feeling like a sort of hardcase Don figure around the block, and he decided to treat himself to his first wank in fif-teen days. Ellen was snoring. He got out the uncut video of *Arse Mania VI* (the one where five men prac-tically gang-rape a young girl), but when he reached for the box of mansize Kleenex he was dismayed to find the box empty. Scratching his head in very over-the-top confusion, Johnnie saw the bin next to Ellen's side of the bed was full of screwed-up tissues, glooped together in what looked like PVA. Shuddering, Johnnie quickly came to the conclusion that either Ellen's got a cold and a very very runny nose, or she's been seeping somebody else's semen. True to form, Johnnie Jealousy decided to believe the latter. After all, Johnnie hadn't wanked or shot spunk into Ellen for weeks (their last excruciating shag was cut short by the Express pizza boy), and he hadn't heard her sniffing recently. Johnnie fell to the floor in agony, imagining Angelo's thick jizz oozing out of Ellen's fanny bum and mouth. He cried a couple of tears. Getting wound up, Johnnie scrabbled round the carpet like a bull terrier, trying to gather up more clues and evidence. He felt certain Ellen's lacy blue knickers (the ones she wore not last night but the night before) smelt of another man's aftershave, and he started to see claw marks in her skinny exposed back, and he even dished the tis-sues out of the dustbin and took a lungful of their scent, and he felt fairly certain they ponged of semen. Johnnie dropped back down to the ground, feeling insane. He listened silently to Ellen's breath for twenty-five minutes, dreading her mumbling the word 'Angeloooo' in her sleep. But she just kept saying, 'Snore breath snore breath snore breath.' Twitching, he crept quietly out of the flat, not wanting to wake Ellen and argue with her, instead driving all the way to his Nanna's house in Eston with the heavy weight of Ellen and Angelo's naked bodies on top of his head. He's not sure if he's overreacting, or if he's being made a fool of, but either way it's been a painful couple of days. And just because of tissues! Occasionally Johnnie wishes he had the guts to just dump Ellen and be done with it, but he's paranoid too that he'll never go out with any-one more beautiful than Ellen, especially since he's no Brad Pitt himself, even though he's got strange psy-chotic Fight Club tendencies. Anyhow, after a couple of slap-up meals round Nanna's and a lonely lonely bed to sleep in last night, Johnnie quickly realised what he was missing. And strangely, he feels quite smug that it's Ellen phoning him and not the other way round, and he asks her, 'So, what you been up to, darling?' Ellen scrapes her foot along the crunchy grey carpet, then replies, 'Er, I've just finished at the doley. I was just wondering if I could come over? When are you done with your Nanna? You having dinner at hers?' Johnnie dodges a pot of mayonnaise, skidding off one wheel, then says, 'Naw naw, I'll come and meet you. That'd be mint. I'll just drop Nanna off in a bit . . . what say we meet at the flat in about half an hourish?' Ellen smiles a big cheesy grin and nods, then remembers to speak, 'Yeah alright.' The two of them say all their see you lat-ers, and Johnnie considers saying I love you but he doesn't want to sound too desperate – in his head he wants to be cool and nonchalant and play hard to get and make Ellen work a little bit, but really in this world if you love someone you should definitely tell them.

Oh well. He puts the phone down then carries on wheeling the groceries round Lidl with his nutty old granny, and he really doesn't feel that cool at all. His Nanna looks a bit like a white-haired Ronald McDonald, corned-beef legs dribbling out of her sensible shoes and her red cardigan slowly turning pale burgundy as the years go by. She smells of hospital beds, but she's got a great sense of humour and a terrible memory which only adds to the hilarity. 'Who was that?' she asks once Johnnie's off the phone. 'Ellen. You know, Eleanor or whatever you just . . .' he says. He can feel weeny sweat patches sprouting under his armpits – there's no air-conditioning in Lidl, but it makes up for it with the hazy rays of light beaming through the glass, the sort of sight that makes you realise you were right drawing the sun with blocky yellow stripes coming out when you were young. Johnnie was always a shit drawer at school – his suns were just orange spirals, or he wouldn't draw suns at all, just black clouds instead. Nanna's got a picture of his at home; this big dark stormcloud in the middle with an evil frowny face. Some teachers thought Johnnie was a disturbed little child, but then again he did go round at breaktime breaking other kids' toys. Johnnie gets pissed off and says 'fuck' when the trolley-wheel gets caught on a jelly–fishy Lidl bag on the ground and gets all mangled, but his Nanna's always in a good mood and she releases the jellyfish then says to him, 'Ho ho, someone got out the wrong side of bed today.' Johnnie didn't exactly get out the wrong side of bed, it's just that he didn't get out of it with Ellen this morning. In the last aisle Johnnie helps Nanna lift three bottles of cut-price

Hock into the trolley then pushes it to the cashiers at top speed, desperate now to get home – it's only been two days, but he's forgotten what Ellen kisses like, what she feels like, how she tastes. He's practically forgotten all about the tissues, and all. Shuddering, Johnnie almost starts getting a slight stiffy as him and Nanna load the shopping on the conveyor belt, but to avoid embarrassment he imagines Nanna all spread-eagled in one of those 50+ magazines you get in Premier, and it soon subsides. It's strange to think how many newsagents stock that kind of senile smut, but who actually has the nerve to step up to the counter and buy it? Johnnie wonders if, when his granddad was alive, did he prefer to see naked sixty-year-olds, or still get a kick out of shaven, supple Just Eighteens? Sweating, him and Nanna cram all the chunky bags into his Nissan Sunny out in the car park, then the two of them whittle off down the sunny street-stripe to Nanna's pad, Johnnie driving carefully because he doesn't want to worry his Nanna and he doesn't want to kill her either. On the way down Normanby Road, passing those loopy houses with the curvy brown roofies like futuristic farm stables, Nanna puts her hand on Johnnie's knee and asks softly, 'Now, love, have you seen your mother recently? You know she's going through a bit of a bad patch, and I'm sure she'd love to see you.' Johnnie sighs silently, feeling a bit unnerved by the granny-grip on his leg and the fact she's brought up his mam while he's manoeuvring that tricky cross-road down by the post office. Johnnie's mam's been suffering a bit of depression since she fell headfirst into the menopause, fluttering violently from hibernating in her dark bedroom for weeks on end to lashing out at family members like a prickly porcupine. She's never liked the idea of her sons (Barrie, Johnnie and Robbie) growing up to be failures, and with Robbie being the only one at home now (Barrie flew the nest to set up an unsuccessful twenty-four-hour booze delivery service with his ex-missus, and Tony the Dad goes off-shore for periods of three months on, one month off at the oil rigs), he gets most of the spines. Johnnie bites his lip as he swerves down curvy Windsor Road, nodding in certain places while his Nanna says, 'You see, you don't want your Robbie getting an earful every time he comes home late, gets his PE kit mucky, that sort of thing. She didn't even let him see his new girlfriend the other night! She's just lonely mind – I try my best to see her, but it's tricky with me not being so mobile now . . .' Once they reach Nanna's, Johnnie lugs all the shopping into her kitchen, saying to her, 'I dunno, it's just she just kicks off at me. You know how hard it is finding a job round here, Nanna; it's rock hard. And I'm really trying; I really am, but last time I went round she just started crying and chucked the plates at me.' Johnnie does want to see her, but it's the heartbreak of telling your mam you're pathetic and penniless and can't find a job (when in fact you're pathetic and penniless and punt pills and pilfer people) that puts him off. Johnnie coming round with a big Smiley Face when all he does in life is sell SmileyFaces to idiots is only going to depress her even more. But Johnnie promises his Nanna he'll give it a go, and she smiles and delves into her purse and hands him a crisp new fiver, to help tide him over. Johnnie kisses her goodbye and walks through her lovely lilac garden, chuffed about the money. He beeps the horn while Nanna waves cheery at the window, gently pulling off the drive then whacking his foot down once he's completely out of view. If only his mam and Nanna knew how talented he is in the field of criminal behaviour! It's not easy being a failure, you know. Over the years Johnnie's really honed his craft; sometimes he makes more money drug-dealing when he doesn't even have any drugs on him. Genius! Some of his favourite tricks of the trade range from 'hit-and-run' (where you literally hit and run away from someone who's just given you money/unveiled their wallet), 'lucky cellophane' (insert any piece of cellophane or other worthless plastic into a cigarette box, then sell to unsuspecting customers as 'drugs'), the 'unlucky cell phone' (advertise yourself as a trendy drug dealer to kids, then snatch their mobile when they go to take your number), and sometimes you've just got to be fearless and put your hand in people's pockets, or your elbow in people's car windows. Vroom-vroom-vrooming down Cargo Fleet, Johnnie spots a couple of youths in flammable tops who got ganj off him once at a party, and he considers for a second trying the old 'unlucky cell phone' on them, but today he's just not in the mood. It's 12.30pm and the sun's at pretty much full force, zapping the town with life – it's one of those days when all the playing fields are jolly and green and the sky's a neon sign and all the houses are pink pomegranates; everything looking completely beautiful. Sliding the Nissan Sunny into the Peach/Pear House car park, Johnnie smiles and spots Ellen impersonating a bright lamp-post by the edge of the road. He waves then parks up, being careful not to stall or crash into the five five-year-olds having a kickabout on the concrete. He gets out the car, then stepping-stones on his own shadow to where Ellen's parked herself. 'Hiya,' he says, all baby deer eyes and jailbird haircut. Ellen smiles, then for twenty-two seconds there's a sort of awkward silence, friction in the air like the streets and the trees are made of sandpaper. Johnnie looks at Ellen. She's so gorgeous, he hopes up to the cloudless sky she didn't sleep with Angelo etc. etc. 'I missed you!' she yelps, and she hugs him and Johnnie finally manages to relax. He can be a bit of a pushover and he trips over a big bucket of love and says, 'I missed you too.' They have a bit of a kiss and a bit of a grope, then Johnnie scrambles through his pocket for the fiver Nanna gave him, and he says, 'Here, Ellen, this is for you. I just wanna say sorry for being a dickhead. Soz for scaring you, you know, when I went mad at Angelo. It wasn't your fault. I'm alright now.' Ellen's eyes ping on when she sees the money, and it's annoying because deep down she's a right greedy cunt but it's hard to kick off at a girl when she's wrapped herself around you. To Johnnie a cuddle from Ellen's worth at least a fiver anyhow. The two of them squeeze and squeeze until it's too hot and sweaty, then Ellen pockets the money and says, 'Aww, Johnnie, I love you.' Johnnie says ahh he loves her as well and everything else then he says, 'So what you up to? Wanna nip down the park or something?' Ellen squints at the sun then covers her eyes with a hand full of rings and goes, 'Yeah! It's too nice to stay in the flat, isn't it . . .' After a bit more cuddling the two of them skip off to the adventure playground in Pally Park, linking pinkies rather than holding hands because it's far too sticky. The world's revolving like a microwave. Like Dorothy and her daft dog Toto, Ellen and Johnnie meander together down the yellow streets of heatwave; through the enchanted forest of council houses; past scary lads with footballs, tinheads on motorbikes and giant lions on deckchairs in threadbare gardens; down to the Emerald City. Pallister Park is beautiful in sunshine, dismal in winter, and the two of them zip across the crispy green grass with smiles the size of bananas. Firstly, Johnnie and Ellen climb the climbing frame, sitting at the summit with their legs dangling off, the fizz and flutter of birds, barks, cars, screams and ice-cream vans sounding around them. Then they jump off and spin on the roundabout for eighteen rotations, then they see-saw, then Johnnie has a go on the bouncy sheep thing on a spring but there's threat of him bashing his head on the ground so he gets off. Five minutes are spent having a fag on the park bench, Johnnie and Ellen chatting about the crinkly ball sac at the dole office, his mother's depression, and the lads over there having a wee against the railings. All the while Johnnie thinks how he'd love to put all thoughts of Angelo behind him and give shagging Ellen another go. He pecks her lemon meringue left cheek, then they stub out their fags and jump on the swings. There's nowhere he'd rather be than swinging with his girlfriend into the neverending sky. At first they start off gentle, the shiny flats and houses coming and going beneath them then, as the momentum builds, one minute you're in Pallister Park and the next minute you're in the Milky

Way. Johnnie dangles his feet in a cirrus cloud while Ellen kicks at fluffy aeroplane trails, both of them whizzing at high speed like happy demolition balls. Ellen thinks to herself, 'I can see my house from here,' but then again she does live in a big fuck-off tower block. Johnnie begins to show off, kicking harder and harder with every swing, and soon he's nearly going full-circle with the earth coming back in view over the back of his head. He's like a ghostly galleon, all pale and skeletal. While her boyfriend zooms back and forth on his back, Ellen starts getting tired and swings a bit less passionately, feeling her tight top stick to her flesh. She checks in the back of her miniskirt the fiver's still there and it is, then she gradually comes to a halt with a gleeful little face on her head. She glances at Johnnie being a blur next to her, and she thinks to herself everything's going to be fine and dandy between them. Then she thinks how easy it is to cheat on your boyfriend! After a bit, Johnnie starts getting sweaty too and he stops kicking his legs, gliding back down to earth like a feather. The sky and the land slowly become flat again – not big arcs of rainbow whoosh – and Johnnie eases himself into a more sedate swinging style. Squinting through burnt blue retinas, Johnnie sees the playground has emptied slightly, possibly due to his menacing presence or it could be the ice-cream van round the corner. Sparking up another Richmond, Johnnie yawns, eyeballing two big pigeons waddling about the coloured tarmac. One's a man bird and the other's a woman bird, and they look so downtrodden and scratty it seems out of place on such a happy day. The bloke pigeon has his neck feathers all puffed out, chasing the lady like Benny Hill on birdseed. The lady clearly wants nothing to do with him, scrabbling away on the hot ground or flying onto the climbing frame only to get followed a second later, the gadge pigeon pushing his neck out fatter and fatter and it's pure comedy watching the two of them. Johnnie laughs in his head but then he feels sad, thinking of all the human ladies in the same position in all the clubs and pubs in Britain or the whole universe. But then it's just Mother Nature's fault boys are always randy – after all it's a scientific fact the human race would disappear if no one wanted to have sex any more. Just as long as they don't want to have sex with your bird, that's all. Johnnie sighs then dismounts the swing, and him and Ellen walk off hand in hand through the smell of the playground. Ellen likes to take funny little penguin steps, while Johnnie prefers walking at ten-to-two, which means – if you happened to be standing on a clock-face – left foot would point at ten, right foot at two. It's a walk generally favoured by frogs and ruffians. Trundling towards Corpus Christi primary with their bodies pushed together, Johnnie tries his best to smile but he feels funny. He can't wait for the little things again, like nibbling Americano pizzas and stroking Ellen in bed and getting stroked back. He has to learn how to calm down. Fucking tissues! He clings her a bit closer, then the both of them laugh when they spot Alan Blunt the Cunt lurking by the primary school fence in his deer-hide jacket, perving over the pre-teens on their afternoon break. Alan's a weirdo but he's also rather friendly, and Johnnie blurts out 'Hello' as they amble past. Alan waves back, looking a bit grim in such heavy clothes and bags under his eyes, one hand still attached to the metal rungs. 'Now then, Johnnie,' he says stiffly. Alan gets on with most (white) people in Peach House, despite Johnnie piping monotonous earth-quaky trance through his pillow every night. It drives Alan to very murderous thoughts, but on the flipside Johnnie does help him put shelves up and he did bring a Sardinian to an inch of his life the other day. As well as hating foreigners, Alan also hates to see people in love, and he gazes at Johnnie and Ellen with a bit of disgust as they pace off into the shadows. Alan's wife disappeared four years back, and since then no one's succumbed to Racist Cunt Alan's racy racist charms. He adjusts his thick-rim gegs then turns back to the school playground, suddenly disappointed when the bell goes and all the kids scamper back indoors for their music lesson (yes, it's 1.30pm on a Thursday). Some weeks he likes to stay and listen to the recorders getting sucked and blown, but this afternoon he's promised Bobby the Artist he'll sit for a portrait and a piss-up, so he slowly detaches himself from the green gates and follows the lovebirds' footsteps up wide won-derful Cargo Fleet Lane. Alan Blunt the Cunt's not a big fan of the sun – on scorching days like this he tends to stay indoors watching the Toshiba telly, stepping out only to drive the containers at ICI and sit in dismal ferry terminals, or stare at the kids in the playground. He likes the children at Corpus Christi, since it's a Catholic school and they're mostly pale faces. Alan's always been a Cunt and he's always been Racist – he was a copper in the seventies and eighties, renowned for using his truncheon on anything with off-white skin at any opportunity. His wife came back from holiday having shagged an Italian stallion, and rumour has it he used his truncheon on her as well. Alan Blunt is a member of the Socialist Workers' Union in town, but he's also under the Hitlerish impression that Niggers, Nips, Pakis and Chinks are all out to get white people's jobs, out to terrorise white people's neighbourhoods, and out to shag white people's wives. He's the sort of person who says 'Fuck off back to Arabia, you fucking Paki' to people from India when he's had a bit too much to drink. He thinks the Chinese have suspicious eyes. He believes all Mediterranean men are big greasy STD carriers. Alan's father Larry used to show him books about lynchings in the Southern states of the US and Vietnam and race riots, making up joke captions and spazzy accents for all the poor victims. It's a wonder he didn't read Alan *Mein Kampf* at bedtime. Alan's father died years back after refusing a flu jab from a Bangladeshi nurse and, as Alan plods past the Thorntree cemetery where the daft bastard's buried, he feels glad that Larry Blunt the Cunt can't see what a lonely situation his son's in now. Alan steps across the hot-plate car park then bashes the code into the side of the tower block, yawning as he steps into the cool dark of the foyer. He hangs silently in the lift for about a minute, pressing buttons with chipolata fingers, but it's still fucking broke. The letting agency keep telling him it'll be fixed within a fortnight; every day you can see Alan lingering in there with the same tense expression. Hissing, he gives the lift panel a bit of a slap then proceeds up the six staircases like a grumpy tortoise. Alan's face is a crumpled crisp packet from too many years frowning. At his door (6E, but the E's fallen off) he finds Bobby the Artist sitting cross-legged supping a bubbly bottle of White Ace. Bobby's feeling half-cut already after just a litre of the stuff, but he's been huffing Lynx again all morning and his brain feels like mushy peas. Alan Blunt the Cunt stops for a sec on the mottled vinyl, then pushes his specs up and goes, 'What you drinking that shite for? Howay in and I'll get us a can of Special.' Bobby smiles and claps his hands, following Alan into the flat with his biggest argyle all sweaty and floppy round his skinny frame. In all those argyle sweaters, Bobby looks a bit like a sixties Mark E Smith, except Mark's a little city hobgoblin and Bobby's a six-foot elastic man. Yawning again, Alan Blunt the Cunt gets some Carlsberg Special out the fridge, then puts on Sinatra's 'On the Sunny Side of the Street' and tells Bobby to sit down and start drinking. Bobby the Artist dives into the brown knackered sofa. From that viewpoint, Alan's flat looks like the mad headquarters of a stalker or serial killer or other strange person, and yet it's also sort of homely. The walls are Blu Tacked with sun-dried pages of the *Sun* and *Mirror* singing out BOY KILLED BY RACIST THUGS and ASIAN GIRL, 18, RAPED and RAPPER KILLED IN GANGLAND SHOOTOUT, like black white and nicotine retro wallpaper. Frank Sinatra sits with other Franks on the mantelpiece instead of family photos, and the gramophone skips all his records. Mosquitoes lounge around the walls in piles of human blood. The Toshiba telly sits in the corner with its arms crossed, switched off. The floors are all bare, with only cans of Special Brew and shoes and dusty binoculars and cutted-out newspapers scattered about the underlay. It's one of those homes with so much character it practically talks to you. 'Hello,' says the wallpaper. Bobby the Artist pushes the frothy White Ace back in his Premier carrier and takes out a rolled sheet of cartridge paper, along with his crayons and watercolours. He sets everything out on the crusty floor, pinning the A1 paper flat with four more Carlsbergs they're going to drink. 'So you're doing a portrait then?' Alan Blunt asks, quickly taking Bobby's place on the sofa and going 'aahh' with his can in his mouth. 'Yeah, just a sketch like,' Bobby replies, 'I dunno, I might make it into a big canvas later like, but you never know.' Bobby the Artist starts out by crayoning Alan's head and glasses quite large and cartoony, with the suggestion of wavy b+w tabloids behind him and the grumpy Toshiba telly. Blur your eyes and the walls go into a kind of Bridget Riley, or is that just the Special Brew? Bobby the Artist burps then does a squiggle for Alan's sickly hair, the sun bursting in through the window like a magic yellow filter. 'So what you been up to today, Al?' Bobby asks, lifting one of the Carlsbergs to scribble a fag packet with centipede legs in the bottom left corner. 'Ah, not much; this and that, you know how it is,' Alan replies, too ashamed to talk about the Corpus Christi kiddies, even though everyone on the estate must've seen him gawping through the railings at one time or another. Alan doesn't think of himself as a pervert or a paedo, but he knows what people say about him behind shut doors. It's becoming a bit of an obsession for him. One of the kids in particular, Tiny Tina, plagues his beery dreams every night, so perfect she is in her dining-cloth dress

93

with her piggytails and rosy legs. 'Aaahh,' Alan says again, thinking about the girl but pretending it's the grog. 'How's the picture going?' he asks next, reddening, shuffling on the settee. The problem with drawing Alan Blunt the Cunt is he can't keep still at all, but Bobby uses it to his advantage and throws rapid marks across the paper, telling him, 'Er, it's going to be sort of abstract.' Alan Blunt nods, but he doesn't know a great deal about art except for the Constable print his father used to have above the Toshiba telly when it lived with his folks in Thorntree. However, Alan did once see some of Bobby's work at his degree show in college – these groovy, childish pictures of sunshines and flowers and body parts. They could've been done by a five-year-old, but that's not a bad thing in Alan's book. Slurping, Bobby mixes up some luminous pinky-red for all the *Sun* logos behind the Cunt, like the poppies in that very famous painting someone painted about poppies in the olden days. Without drugs, it's been a tricky week for the Artist – the boredom's the worst and the ever-so-slight downcast can't-be-bothered-to-talk-to-you feeling but, saying that, there's no drug in the world better than painting. Oh and the Special Brew's starting to kick in, and Bobby's brushstrokes start to flow much looser and stranger, and he ends up drawing an elephant trunk coming out of Alan's face. 'So, you up to owt later on?' Bobby asks, much happier to make small-talk now he's getting sloshed. 'Ah, well I've gotta drive the fucking truck tonight like, but God knows if I'm gonna be sober in time,' Alan replies, then takes a big guzzle and asks, 'Are you working nowadays, Bob?' Bobby the Artist glances up from the paper, then sort of stammers, 'No, er, it's shite like cos I haven't had any commissions for ages. But, er, well this weekend this dealer's coming up here to look at some paintings and maybe do something together, or something.' Perhaps the only bad thing about drinking is Bobby can feel himself getting slower and stupider the more drunk he gets, and he shifts uneasily on the floorboards. He sees photos scattered on the floor of Alan and his ex-wife with all her heads cut out, and he wonders if Alan pasted them on voodoo dolls or set them on fire or just threw them out the window. On the cartridge paper, Bobby draws lots of women's heads floating around in the background. 'Well good luck with it all,' Alan suddenly spouts, his chin on the Special Brew. He takes another sip, then changes his position again – hunched forward with goggly eyes. 'Cheers, Al,' Bobby replies. 'Hopefully I'll get some money for it; I'll have to take you out for a bevvy or summat.' With Alan Blunt the Cunt moving about so much, Bobby the Artist tries to bring the drawing to a close with one last curl on Alan's head and a few extra broken blood vessels, then he takes it out from under the Carlsbergs and hands it over. Bobby's satisfied with it – he always tries to show the good in people, but he does feel a little nervous while Alan glares at it. Eventually he burps and laughs and goes, 'Cheers, mate, that's lovely . . . Look, there's Sinatra in the background! Ho ho ho. Not sure about the elephant trunk, like . . .' Bobby the Artist pukes up a smile, then sups more Brew and goes, 'Soz yeah, it's a bit avant garde eh. You can have it though, if you want?' Alan Blunt claps his hands, then gets up off the sofa and replaces Frank's *The Man with the*

Golden Arm with Bobby's 'The Man with the Golden Can' (59.4x84.1cm) on the mantelpiece. He ruffles the Artist's shabby hair then goes, 'That means a lot to me, Bob,' and for the first time in a while he feels a connection and real joy and admiration for another human person. Bobby grins more gooey teeth and feels like his work here is done. What a beautiful day on floor six. Bobby swallows a load more Carlsberg then lazily packs his paints and crayons back in the Premier bag, not really wanting to leave Alan on his own but also not wanting Georgie to come home to an empty flat after she's been at work and had her teeth filled and all that. It's five o'clock already – doesn't time fly when you're getting pissed! Bobby watches Alan crush a can with his eyes all sad and soggy, and he can tell Alan wants him to stay and he can't help but kneel back down when Alan murmurs, 'Actually, Bobby, if you're not in a rush or owt, I've got something to show you. Something I've drawn – my own bit of art, I suppose. I'd be keen to know what you think.' Then Alan Blunt the Cunt goes rushing out to his bedroom and comes back brandishing an A3 tabloid mock-up he's devised with a headline reading HORRIBLE DRUG DEALER TAUGHT A LESSON BY THE BOY DOWN-STAIRS and a smaller sub-heading ANGELO BASHINI WAS MADE TO EAT RAZOR BLADES AFTER BEING CAUGHT SELLING FIVE-YEAR-OLDS SMACK – JOHNNIE HYDE SAYS 'NEXT TIME YOU'RE DEAD'. Even though it's a mental spin on the razor episode, the paper's been beautifully illustrated in ink with made-up images of Johnnie hitting Angelo and Angelo's head in bandages in hospital, as well as delicate hand-drawn courier text and red tempera logo. 'I had to make me own headline up cos the prick never pressed charges. There wasn't even a peep from the *Gazette*,' Alan explains, 'but what do you think? It's quite funny, isn't it . . .' Bobby the Artist scans a bit of the racist text (for example the 'reporter' ends the article with 'but at the end of the day, the daft cunt had it coming') and cringes, but as for craftsmanship it's a wonderful piece of bonkers Pop Art and he replies, 'It's lovely, mate.' Bobby the Artist feels uneasy when Racist Cunt Alan starts being a total Racist Cunt rather than just a Cunt or just plain Alan, but he holds the A3 drawing in both hands and keeps smiling. To be honest Bobby's going to miss Angelo. It's a real shame he's not in Peach House any more (rumour has it he's going to move back to his mam's in Sardinia once he's out of hospital), since Bobby used to have some right wild times up at Angelo's, for instance that time they threw Roman candles off the top of Peach House off their heads, thinking they could spell NOW THEN in fire-work – and it wasn't even Guy Fawkes night! Crazy days. Wistfully looking up at the Artexed ceiling, Bobby the Artist grins then hands the bit of A3 care-fully back to Alan, who swallows down a burp. 'Cheers, Bob, I mean I don't think it's in your league or owt, but I do love having a little scribble now and then . . . it keeps me occupied. It gets quite lonely up here, you know, being so high up off the ground.' Totally charmed by the old bastard, Bobby pats Alan Blunt on the shoulder. He reminds Bobby a bit of that artist Henry Darger, the one who did all his work on his lonesome in some Chicago apartment and it only got discovered once he'd popped his clogs. Henry left behind these great big fairytale panoramas, tracing little girls (and giving them little willies) and Disney animals and beautiful flowers. He could've been seen as some kind of paedo (like Alan), but some people reckon Henry was such an outsider he might've been unaware females don't have cocks. But anyhow, the paintings are absolutely delightful – each one of them depicts a scene from the epic million-page fairy story Henry made up, and the colours are all luminous and the Vivian Girls are all cute and morbid, and the composition's so natural and vibrant it almost makes Bobby cry just to see them in shitty reproductions. Bobby often wonders what it'd be like for Henry to have done all this wonderful art but never have found any recognition in his lifetime, and in a way it makes him sad because he's on the cusp of fame himself and he doesn't even feel that excited about it. All he feels is bored bored bored because he hasn't got any drugs to eat any more. But looking at Alan Blunt the Cunt, lumbered in a stinky flat with just his Toshiba telly and *Sun* cutouts, Bobby does realise in his heart he can't end up forty years old with no one having appreciated him for his artwork. Alan Blunt hardly even has anyone to appreciate him as a person, let alone as an artist. But saying that, perhaps it's best if the world doesn't see Alan's disgusting drawings. Firing himself up again, Bobby gives Alan a hug goodbye, and for the rest of the week he paints furiously, snorting coffee powder and getting pissed and chasing fame like a maniac with a carving knife. He completes 'The Angels' (244x233cm) and 'Bobby's Favourite Trip' (120x150cm) as well as something called 'Georgie on the Toilet' (60x80cm) and a large canvas with Alan peering lonely out of a TV set called 'Channel Alan' (200x151$\frac{3}{4}$cm) and, by the time Bent Lewis turns up at Peach House in his platinum BMW and paisley cravat, Bobby's got masterpiece after masterpiece lined up in the front room and the bedroom and one on the cistern in the bog. Bobby imagines the flat to be some sort of underground makeshift gallery like what you'd find in the East Village in the eighties or Shoreditch in the nineties. There's nothing Bent Lewis enjoys more than viewing art in a trendy squat or disused butcher's shop or North East tower block, and he's beside himself with glee walking up the patchy stairs to floor four with Bobby the Artist dressed like a trampy golfer. 'This is it,' Bobby says, pulling the sleeves of his smartest (blue) argyle sweater shyly as he shows Lewis into the flat. 'Gosh, it's like the Fun Gallery in New York . . . this one's very Keith Haring,' Bent Lewis yelps, pointing at 'Bobby's Favourite Trip' (120x150cm). He looks like your typical London art dealer: pink shirt, plush suit, posh shoes, cravat, creases in his face from thinking about conceptual art too much. Bobby shuffles on the clean carpet (him and Georgie hoovered it especially) while Bent Lewis lifts paintings and looks at them with his head on its side, Georgie peeking out from the kitchenette. Bobby mumbles a few embarrassed comments like, 'I was off my head when I did that one,' and, 'That's our lass in the nud,' but it goes down well with Bent Lewis – it's the first time he's heard an artist speak so candidly about his work, like how a commoner would explain their holiday snaps of Faliraki to you. He thinks

Bobby's very good looking – as well as a fairly good painter – and he loves watching Bobby trying to sell his work in an obviously hangovery state. To calm his nerves, the last few nights Bobby's been on a binge of Special Brew, Bombay Sapphire and Three Hammers, and to be honest it hasn't helped much. He only just rose in time this morning to fix up the flat. Georgie, still peering from the crusty breakfast bar, has been finding him unbearable now he's on solely the fighting juice – last night he accused her of not giving a shit about him or his artwork, and he refused to say good-night to her before bedtime, which upset her. Bobby hates himself this morning for acting like that, and he hates how booze can turn you into a dithering, manic-depressive aggressive cunt, with very bad breath. He adores Georgie and would never want to hurt her feelings, but sometimes on booze he feels so much weird antagonism towards her (for example when she moves his paints to sit down, when she leaves the light on in the bathroom, or when she says she's too tired to have sex with a jibbery drunk fool) and last night it worried him because he was THAT close to hitting her for no reason. You just get in such a foul mood sometimes! In the past Bobby and Georgie haven't really been ones to argue about anything, but mostly the fights stem from him wanting a rock-and-roll bohemian lifestyle, not a life where you worry about food and rent and clean carpets, except you have to. Today he feels all crappy, and now and then he catches Georgie's eye in the kitchen and gives her a little sorry blink. 'I love all of them,' Bent Lewis yips, his posh-tosser voice grating on Bobby slightly though he seems like a nice enough person. 'This one in particular,' Lewis continues, pointing out 'Boozy Bastard Bashes Bird' (81x58cm) – a wacky cathartic painting Bobby whipped up last night, 'has a real don't-give-a-fuck quality, like a cross between – say – Willem de Kooning and Liam Gallagher. It's great.' Bobby the Artist nods but smirks a little inside, clocking straight away Bent Lewis trying to butter him up with hip pop references and shite like that, and slowly he realises he's got Lewis wrapped around his finger. It's weird – no one's really spoken about his work since art college two years ago, and back then it was all 'maybe put some blue over there' or 'this area's a little unresolved'. Today it's all gasps of pleasure and slapping on the back. Bent Lewis doesn't usually drink before six but he desperately does want to appear credible to Bobby and he asks, 'Shall we have a drop of champagne?' and the answer's yes and he takes a fancy bottle of Laurent-Perrier from his bag of tricks and Bobby and Georgie's eyes both pop out. Georgie scrabbles like a budgerigar, washing three pint glasses in the sink, then comes through and says, 'Are these alright? Soz, the wine glasses got smashed a bit ago ...' Georgie feels a bit uncivilised, but she tries to strike a divine pose in her charity shop Jessica Rabbit dress while Lewis fills the glasses. 'No no no, it's fine,' he laughs. Imagine the stories he can tell the guys at the Tate, or the guys he vaguely knows at *Frieze* magazine! Giggling, Lewis sips the champers, glancing over the rim at Bobby with huge blackpool eyes, feeling absolutely giddy. Georgie follows Lewis's movements and sips hers delicately too. Bobby the Artist wallops his down, then gets a refill and asks, 'So you might want some of these for an exhibition and that?' Bent Lewis's face expands into a big gay balloon then he bellows, 'Oh definitely! I'll show you which of these would be perfect.' He stands up, then fingers all the canvases again and singles out 'Bobby's Favourite Trip', 'Georgie on the Toilet', 'Boozy Bastard Bashes Bird', 'Channel Alan', 'Stripy Socks', and 'The Angels'. 'I mean, basically, my gallery opens next month and I think these one two three four five six paintings would be ideal for the opening,' Lewis rambles, feeling the champoo going to his head already, 'it's sort of a group show – you'll like the other artists. I think your work will stand out particularly well. I can see them all fetching high prices. What I propose is – if you accept – you bring all the work down mid-August, we'll set up the show together ready for the 18th, and hopefully we'll both make lots of money! I'm going to suggest a sixty per cent commission. How that works is, say, if a painting is sold for a thousand pounds, you'd get four hundred and I'd get six. It's simple. Trust me, Bobby, I expect us to make lots of filthy lucre! Haw haw haw. Anyhow, would you like another refill?' Bobby nods, but it's weird how fancy Laurent-Perrier tastes about the same as the £1.49 Friscino Perry from over the road, and it's about the same percentage and all. And Bobby hates all the talk of money, as if that's all he's even bothered about. What he really wants is just a bit of fame before he dies of a drug overdose or perhaps natural causes. Bobby the Artist says, 'Well, don't worry too much about coin, mate, but yeah, nice one,' then carries on swallowing the champagne trying to get hammered. 'Oh yes, of course,' Bent Lewis interjects, 'but it's nice to have financial support, isn't it? I think you're going to make lots of dollars, Bobby, whether you like it or not!' Soon Bobby starts to feel fidgety with boozyness, and the aggressive pangs come back what with Lewis kissing his arse so much – it just seems rather fake and plastic like they're both Barbie dolls and someone else is playing with them. Bobby would much rather just get mortalled with the gadge and talk about artists they like or the parties or the women, not all this fucking oohing and aahing. However, Bobby does sort of agree it'd be nice to have some money and enjoy himself and get the rent in on time this month, and the exhibition malarkey sounds exciting too. The afternoon really picks up when Bent Lewis, art dealer extraordinaire, pulls out a wee baggy of cocaine he bought out of the gallery finances. 'Shall we adjourn to the bathroom?' Lewis asks with a slopey eyebrow, and at first Bobby thinks he means Bobby has to bum him in order to seal the deal and his stomach turns over, but then he sees the Charles and he laughs. Georgie politely declines the offer, swishing the Perrier, feeling like royalty despite her sixty-seventh period sandpapering her insides. Slightly grimacing, she listens to the boys cram in the bog, and they move 'Gurnica' (100x350cm) from the cistern to rack up a couple of white worms. Bobby hoovers his through his craggy white nostril, then blurts, 'Cheers, mate, for the sniff; you're sound, you.' Bent Lewis pats Bobby on the back like they're best mates, then snorts his own – more modest – line, and in his head he squeals the word, 'Yes!' He's a bit of a tosspot but Bobby supposes you have to be in a business where all deals are made by licking someone else's arse. 'I'm really excited about your future, Bobby,' Lewis says, gobshiteing in a look-at-me-I'm-on-drugs way, rolling his eyes round. 'Aye, top notch,' Bobby grins, feeling all fat-lipped and frozen from the dusty Charlie. 'So where'd you get it from?' he asks. 'Oh, down in London you can get cocaine delivered by cab nowadays – it's hot stuff, isn't it? – woo, haw haw haw,' Lewis explains, and Bobby wonders what sort of insane place his capital city is. The furthest south he's ever travelled is to his aunty's for hols in Leeds, and in his head Bobby always imagines London to be some cartoony citadel of smoking chimneys and Big Bens and Krays and people in suits drinking coffee and breathing cocaine and going hmmmm. It gives Bobby the Artist sparkly chills in his belly just to think he'll be there in a month! 'Cheers for sorting all this out for us, like, Lewis,' Bobby speaks, the aggression finally drifting off like a red helicopter. 'Oh, not at all, Bobby. Thank *you* for creating such lovely art,' Lewis jabbers. 'So I expect you'll be celebrating tonight then, eh?' Bent Lewis nudges Bobby in the ribs, which is quite irritating, and Bobby sort of ducks his shoulders a bit and says, 'Ah, well, I would do, but I haven't got a penny to my name at the minute, so probably just get a White Ace and sit in with the lass.' Bent Lewis gives him a glare of oh-my-God-no and says, 'That's not on – here, Bobby, have a drink on me,' then hands the Artist the twenty they snorted the coke through. Bobby licks the residue off, then remembers to say thanks and shakes Bent Lewis's shaky hand. What a dream come true – a real-life art dealer drooling over his work and handing him free money. But then he does feel slightly guilty and greedy (after all, he's never taken twenty quid off a stranger before in his life, and now he's got his new-found fame he doesn't want to always be expecting everything handed to him on a shiny plate), so Bobby the Artist lands his hand on Bent Lewis's forearm and asks, 'Lewis, would you like to stick around for another drink? I might have some Brew left in the fridge ...' Bent Lewis's eyes prise open all bewildered like the ugly duckling at a disco getting picked to dance by the school heartthrob. He grabs the Artist's hand again, shakes it again, then sort of holds on to it for a minute and says, 'I'd love to, Bobby, but I've promised I'd see Mary before I head off back to the Smoke. Do you know the Fletchers very well? No?' Bobby just shrugs, even though it was Mrs Fletcher who discovered 'Blob with Eyes' (58x81cm) all those days ago. 'She's my cousin,' Lewis continues, 'don't see her very often. Nice to kill two birds with one stone eh, coming here. I just hope I'm not too coked up to see her!' Bobby cringes. By now he just finds Lewis sort of comedy; a bit embarrassing like when your mam says she likes your taste in music when you're thirteen. The two of them shake hands another handful of times before Bent Lewis takes the trek to floor eight, Bobby shouting behind him, 'Thanks for the money!' and 'See you later, mate!' and all that pleasant stuff. When Bobby finally taps the door shut, he flops onto the clear carpet with a face like a fried egg. Georgie wanders over and gives her boyfriend a great massive hug, spilling a bit of her champagne on the floor but it doesn't matter now. They kiss for a long time. Bobby the Artist grins, feeling like he's been given the key to a secret silver castle. He's now part of the Art World, which he imagines is a sort of fantasy world with Kandinsky hills, Cubist crazy paving, money growing on trees, still-life foliage and lots of silly wankers. Georgie plants a slobbery rosy-red kiss on Bobby's neck and she sighs heavily, like saying, 'Ooh, well done,' in breath, then they start throwing each other round the room with glee, then twenty seconds later Bobby's in Johnnie's flat telling him and Ellen about the exhibition and telling them they have to come out tonight for a shindig. The last few days Johnnie and Ellen have been bored, crunching Americanos and watching American sitcoms on the box, and Bobby says he'll pay them both out in exchange for a couple pills for everyone, if that's alright. 'I should be able to pay my ticky off in a month and all, Johnnie,' Bobby promises with big round thank-you eyes. Johnnie's not bothered – he's in higher spirits now Ellen's back in the flat and the dustbin's been emptied of tissues, and even more chuffed now Bobby's got a break down in London. It saddens him slightly that Bobby has to go down South where apparently all the dickheads are, but he supposes that's just where you go to become famous. Johnnie ruffles the Artist's neverending hair and hugs him round the neck, getting all elated and saying, 'God, Bobby, you've made it, mate, you've made it,' then he goes scrabbling about in the vitamin tin and pulls out a goody-bag of a hundredish ecstasy, and gives Bobby a handful of fifteen or so. Bobby's face goes all happy and spastic and elastic. 'Cheers, Johnnie, I'll defo pay youse out tonight – fancy coming to the Indie Night, though?' The Indie

Night takes place at a place called the Arena and, although Bobby would never admit to listening to indie music, it is the sort of scene where lots of people take lots of old-fashioned drugs like speed and pills and occasionally mushrooms if they're in season (last October Bobby found himself clinging to the dark walls of the Arena like he was in some hellish cave, accidentally stumbling into the heavy-metal room). So Bobby pockets the pills, then there's two or three hours of getting ready and phoning people (Pamela, Mandy, Dave Morton and all those madheads from upstairs are over the Linny, and they agree to come over Arena later, on the promise of free E) and putting away paintings and putting on fresh jumpers, and Johnnie wheels the Sunny out of the car park and Bobby, Georgie and Ellen jump in. It's five minutes past seven and, as they drive, this half of the world gradually starts going dark blue and the wind starts smelling dusky and the birds start saying night-night to each other, and Bobby the Artist sticks his head out the window with puppy eyes of wonder. He feels like he's on ecstasy already – sometimes the world can do that to you. Sometimes it can be such a heart-choking beautiful place, like you've accidentally walked into a Turner painting. Bobby feels so humble and grateful and wobbly with joy crammed in a car full of his favourite people, and he thinks even if every dickhead and idiot in the world are out tonight as well he'll still have a wonderful time. Johnnie pulls into the Linthorpe car park, reversing at top speed into one of the white spaces. Being in such close proximity to two art colleges, the Linny is sort of the Beat Hotel of the North East, where all manner of beatniks and meatheads and thinkers and drinkers smash it into themselves. Three years back, Georgie and Bobby were studying their Art Foundations two minutes down the Roman Road, and they had their first drink together in the Linthorpe and their first kiss and their first toasted cheese sandwich. They failed their second term coursework after submitting their video collaboration 'Un Hommage de Monsieur Condom, 2005', which was basically forty mins of the pair making love in Georgie's parents' boudoir. The video still lives under the couple's bed in Peach House, and Bobby occasionally digs it out – not for sexual gratification, mind you – to remember what it's like to first go out with a girl and be excited about everything about her. He can't believe the teachers shunned it. Stepping into the Linny, Bobby squeezes Georgie's paw and can't help grinning in her face as they worm their way to the bar. The pub's quite hot and packed, and you can tell who's been on their hols recently because they've got roast chicken skin and rainbow braids in their hair, and all their mates have gone overboard with the fake tan to compensate. Georgie feels horribly pale in comparison – you'd think she'd see a lot of sun living so high in the blue sky, but in fact their flat faces north and she spends most of her time in Bhs watching sweeties getting old and sweaty instead. Saying that, she's kitted herself out in a white Victorian slip and wee winkle-pickers and she's stolen that daisy-chain off Ellen, and she does look the embodiment of summer. Bobby the Artist smirks. The hippy outfit is one of his favourites. 'I'll go look for the others,' Johnnie states, kicking about in his brown Kickers. It turns out Pamela, Dave and Mandy

have popped off to Isaac's instead – the Wetherspoon's
– so the Peach Housemates perch themselves round
one of the pint-size tables, working their way through
lots of pint-size drinks. It's nice to be back in the Linny
– Bobby doesn't recognise half as many faces as he used
to back in his heyday of sex, lectures and Ayingerbräu,
but at least the lager's still strong and cheap. He gets
about four rounds in with the twenty pound, and
everyone toasts him and he feels like a king and very
pleased to be alive. It's the first time in a while they've
all been out together, and how nice it is just to sit
around a table with your best mates laughing and talking and getting full of liquid! Bobby the Artist strokes
Georgie's knee under the flowery embroidered slip,
gazing out at the beer garden though it's not made of
beer it's made of trees and grass. Over the slopey table,
Johnnie and Ellen are having a bit of a snog, and it's
nice to see them so happy together. Bobby the Artist
knows they've been going through a tricky patch even
if he doesn't know all the details, but relationships are
meant to be all ups and downs, aren't they? Weird how
you get maybe a three-month honeymoon period,
then suddenly you're in a boring pantomime of breaking up and making up over and over and over and over.
'I love you,' Bobby says to Georgie in her fossil-shaped
ear, and she says it back. Soon there's lots of empty
glasses in the middle of the table (the glass-collector's
sick tonight, with some sort of summer cold or maybe
hay fever or lazyitis), and everyone's pissed and jabbering to each other and laughing loudly like fire alarms.
Just for the fun of it, Bobby and Johnnie and Ellen drop
a pill for the walk to the Arena, and Georgie drops an

antihistamine. The pollen count's astronomical today, and she can feel her eyes turning to mush the more she touches them. She sniffs and sniffs and sniffs en route to the Arena, the four of them striding up the Roman Road like marionettes on very wobbly wires. It's a lovely evening with all the brown stars out and a cool breeze dipping into the streets occasionally, although it's spoiled slightly when a boy in shellsuit bottoms shouts from across the road, 'Fucking pansies!' He's probably referring to Bobby the Artist, what with his long girly hair and strange fashion sense, or perhaps he's referring to Georgie's daisy-chain. Seething, Johnnie shouts back the word 'Eh?' and manages to give the boy in the shellsuit some dirty eyeballs. 'Get a fucking haircut,' the boy screams, but then he backs off and scuttles down the alley with his shoulders hunched round his earlobes. What a bastard. Bobby the Artist feels all upset now, clinging on to Georgie like a security blanket, although to be honest it's pretty common for someone in a town where everyone's got army haircuts to get abuse if they let it all hang out. Bobby's dream is to live in some sort of happy Shangri-La, where everyone's nice to each other and it's hot and you can have any haircut you want. Round here, everyone loves taking the piss out of each other – groups of lads will go out at night, call each other names, embarrass one another in front of the opposite sex, try to start fights with other groups of lads, and never in their life tell each other they love them. What a stupid world we live in where it's easier to say you hate someone than to say you love them. Bobby bobs his head, but once they get in the Arena he starts feeling comfortable again. They walk through the dark misty entrance. Then they drop another pill with a bottle of Holsten Pils, the sound of three rooms pounding different drumbeats and guitars in different keys, spinning their heads. The Indie Night is a bit of a safe haven, full of kids in their mam and dad's outfits and tight jeans dancing and hugging each other. Most of the kids think they're wild and dangerous, but in fact they're fairly harmless – they spend too much time in their bedrooms listening to music to be that fearsome. Bobby the Artist starts smiling again as the four of them weave their way up the slippy steps, to that dinky room where you're allowed to sit down. He can feel the pills ever so slightly casting spells on him, and he has his first gurn as he drops down on the sofa. Georgie kneels next to him, pinching her hippy skirt in two hands so it doesn't touch the scummy ground. She wishes she had the guts to try a pill, because Bobby looks so happy, but sometimes even the buzz off a vodka-Red Bull is too much for her. Johnnie and Ellen come over to sit with them, wibbling like flowerpot men with their jowls going all over the place. It's one of those nights you want to thank the heavens and angels that the world got made up and you got invited to play on it. Bobby has his first big rush of ecstasy just as Mandy, Pamela and Dave Morton come downstairs from the main bit, and he beams at them with a smile the size of a white brick. They're with a girl from the green tower block (Pear House) called Katey, and straight away he thinks she's good looking and very paintable and nice, but then he looks back at Georgie and his pupils go dilated and she climbs into them. She makes space for Mandy and Pamela on the crushy sofa, and Mandy quite surreptitiously keys up a bit of white powder. As usual her head's full of bizarre thoughts and her mouth's full of shit, and she tells Pamela, 'I want to be on the ceiling. Like Bowie in *Labyrinth*. But I wouldn't sing! I want to dance, how good would it be to dance up there! God, it's getting busy in here . . .' Pamela pulls a face, and says in the nicest possible way, 'Shut up.' Pamela's a bit grumpy tonight – she's knack-ered after a long shift at the nursery (the kids are hell sometimes, and every time she wants a cigarette she has to play hide-and-seek with them and run off to the furthest reaches of the playing field), her pill hasn't worked yet, and she's still gutted Mandy's shagging Dave Morton. Dave stands a bit awkwardly with a plas-tic pint in his fist, feeling a bit out of place in his Hackett jumper and Clarks loafers. He's back in train-ing now for the professional football team, and unfor-tunately he's got a drugs test tomorrow – so no pills for Dave tonight, as usual – and he gazes at Mandy through sleepy peepers. She's skinny as a climbing frame, and sometimes when Dave climbs into bed with her they knock hip-bones and kneecaps and their sex makes the most beautiful African clave music. Those two go off to the bathroom for a bit of a breather and an incoherent chit-chat, and Pamela slides up to Bobby and asks, 'How's it going?' Bobby grins and gurns and tells her about London and the bent art dealer, and they hug and Bobby gives her another pill since hers isn't working too well. Half an hour later Bobby and Georgie wander upstairs for a little boogie, and they find Pamela dancing manically on the stage with two boys round her waist and her arms in the air. Bobby laughs, feeling great, and him and his girlfriend swing each other like a couple in the fifties hearing rock and roll for the first time. Georgie's very floppy and gurgly and staggers to most of the songs, whereas Bobby's all focused and ecstatic and in his moon boots. They don't like the Libertines, so when those lot come on they retreat back to one of the park-bench affairs dotted around the walls and plonk down next to Johnnie and Ellen. The seat bounces in time with people's feet dancing in time to the music. It's quite difficult to talk, but Bobby shouts 'Alright' to Johnnie and Ellen and they both nod with big round cheery faces. Johnnie's got his arm round Ellen and she's hugging his right knee, and they look so happy and in love. Most of the night they've just been sat there watching kids dance, kissing each other, cuddling, telling each other really nice things. 'It's mint how we're back on track now,' Johnnie yells in Ellen's ear, touching her hip. How weird it was for them to be apart just because of Kleenex! Johnnie thinks it's his fault, and Ellen thinks it's hers. 'I proper missed you,' he says, all doe-eyed and creamy-mouthed, 'I proper did.' Ellen nods with her lids shut, lashes moving gently in time with the snare drum. 'I love yooou,' she gushes. Johnnie gives her another squeeze as the Libertines burst into the Kinks' 'Victoria', watching Bobby and Georgie totter off to the dancefloor again. Johnnie dribbles, 'I love you toooo,' then they have a luxurious snog and they laugh because it's all so wonderful and romantic and Hollywoodish. The disco lights for this particular song are red and blue, which equals purple. 'I still wanna say sorry for being weird last week,' Johnnie says, speaking very direct and dramatic like you do on pills sometimes. He goes, 'I shouldn't have done that to Angelo. I was just frustrated, I don't know why. I mean, I just get jealous when you're over his, but I'm not saying you shagged him or owt like that. I mean, you didn't, did you?' For a long long time Johnnie's wanted to know the truth about Ellen and Angelo (as long as the answer's no). It's been tearing him up – admittedly, he'd rather not know if the answer's yes (it'd kill him – he'd be inclined to dump Ellen, and the prospect of not being with her scares him), but when you're on pills you're probably in the best mindset to find out once and for all. At first Ellen looks at him and her heart goes squelch, still cuddling and holding hands with her boyfriend. She blinks an invisible tear back in her eye, then strokes his paw and says, 'Naw, of course I never.' Before Johnnie clocks her guilty doll's face, he swamps her with arms and hands and kisses, and he feels like his life's worthwhile again and all the crime's worthwhile and the drugs are worthwhile and the whole big struggle's worthwhile, all for Ellen. He shouts to her, 'I love you I love you,' then he needs to go to the toilet desperately and runs off quickly through groups of people bashing into each other. He pretends he's bursting for a piss, but in actual fact he locks himself in one of the cubicles and sits down and cries buckets of joy into his hands. He feels like he's the luckiest person on earth. It's been such a crazy rollercoaster with Ellen, and he's been so worried and worked-up about her (having stress-dreams at night where his teeth all crumble and fall out in big painful chunks), and now finally he feels thankful to be alive again. How fantastic it is, to be crying and crying and crying in that pissy-floored toilet! Johnnie gurgles saltwater, then wipes his streaming eyes with the bottom of his Lacoste T-shirt and rushes back out of that cubicle to go and hug Ellen again and maybe tell her he's been weeping with happiness or maybe not. In the end he doesn't need to; Ellen can see all the red and wet round his eyelids and, although she feels despicable for lying, she knows she's done the right thing. The two of them carry on kissing and singing each other's praises, and soon it's the end of the night and the lights gently pop on around them. Nights always go so fast when you're on ecstasy, since there's no time to be bored whatsoever. As Johnnie and Ellen sit there like teddy bears on a shop counter, gradually Bobby and Georgie and Mandy and all them congregate around with rusty limbs from dancing too much. Everyone looks lovely, all the couples wrapped up in each other like a perfect vision of the world, everyone smiling, everyone feeling wonderful inside. Pamela comes over in a bit, having lost her two new boyfriends and her left shoe, munching her lip gloss and dithering about. Katey, the one from the pear-coloured tower block, takes her under her wing and then they all stumble back down the steps and into the swirly night air. All the pillheads start wobbling about, chattering to strangers getting kicked out, not like Dave Morton and Georgie who stand all grumpy and knackered by the car park edges. Even though there's eight of them, Johnnie's still feeling dandy and he says, ''Ere, we can all squeeze in the Sunny like, if youse don't mind walking back to the Linny?' Johnnie starts marching off down Parliament Road with Ellen under his arm, and even though she goes 'Naw, Johnnie, I dunno if it's a good idea,' everyone else seems to think so, and the group of them follow the crinkled pavement back into town. It's a nice night for a stroll, but unfortunately they end up rousing all the families in the houses as the gobby e-heads pass by. 'Swear down, I'll be sound driving,' Mr and Mrs Evans from number 64 hear quite clearly out their open window. 'I'm still fucking buzzing, me,' little baby Shane hears from his cot in 55, waking up and bawling his eyes out. 'God, I never did get on that ceiling,' the dog from 49 catches, rushing out of his shitty kennel and barking as Mandy stampedes past. She craps herself, grabs onto Dave's bulky arm, then the two of them laugh and carry on pacing down the dead street. It takes about twenty-five minutes for the gang to reach the Linthorpe car park, rubbing shoulders with all the other people from other chucking-out times round town: the sad lonely people looking for girls and taxis, the rock-hard ruffians looking for a fight because they haven't pulled, the greedy pigs nibbling pizzas, and the happy drug fiends riding the streets like a conveyor belt. Johnnie and Ellen are first to reach the Nissan, sat on its tod in the cold lumpy car park. Johnnie's still gurning, and still happy to pile everyone into the Sunny, as long as they hurry up! Bobby the Artist and Georgie arrive after a bit, followed by Mandy and Dave Morton, who keep lagging behind for snogs and gropes in the veins of the town. Last come Pamela and Katey, keeping a safe distance behind Mandy so they can bitch about her as well as get fags from the twenty-four-hour shop and not share any with her. 'Howay, then, it's gonna be a fucking squeeze,' Johnnie gargles, waving his limbs about. He motions for Ellen to join him in the front, then Bobby and Georgie and Mandy and Dave get in the back with Katey laid across their laps, and Pamela grudgingly clambers in the boot although she's still buzzing her tits off. It's a bit like that trick where they try to squeeze loads of Chinks into a Mini, except on ecstasy. In particular, Bobby the Artist enjoys having Katey's left booby pressed into his groin and the other one pressed into his crushed hand. 'God, I bet youse fuck the suspension,' Johnnie slurps, setting off at about two miles an hour. Ahh, but it's nice to have all his friends squashed in one place like a Christmas stocking, and there's promise of a party back at Peach House once they reach dry land. Johnnie loves speeding, but he can only reach 41mph on Roman Road, and it's very obvious to all the people passing by it's a car chock-full of gurning gorillas. Johnnie tells them to keep their heads down in case there's any police, but in the back everyone's chatting and giggling and feeling each other up, not arsed. The town tumbles past the windows. Johnnie tries to floor it after the lights keep going green, but he's still getting overtaken by taxis and lads on pushbikes. The tank starts groaning as they reach Keith Road, which must have been named after a person called Keith. Johnnie slows to about 20mph going up and down the dips, the car feeling like a rock superglued to the earth. He gazes at the wonderful skinny trees straddling the avenue. Are they oak, beech, pine, or fir? He wonders how all the estates got their names – like Beechwood, Thorntree, Netherfields, Brambles

Farm – and he imagines the town a thousand years ago, all rolling plains and forests and men with straw in their mouths. He wonders if Keith used to be a famous farmer. Dreaming away, Johnnie finds himself in one of those lovely, thoughtful still-on-pills moods, jaw swinging from one side of his face to the other. Then suddenly, against all the odds, the Ford Focus in front slams on its brakes and, had Johnnie not been travelling at a girly 20mph, he might've ploughed into the back of it. 'Screeeech!' say all the tyres. The Sunny comes to a halt six centimetres from the Focus's bumper, and Johnnie just sits there in shocked silence with feet all shaky on the emergency stop pedals. 'Fucking hell!' Ellen shrieks. Johnnie stares into space. 'What a fucking dickhead,' Dave Morton says from the back. 'What's he fucking doing?!' Soon everyone in the back of the Sunny starts moaning and cursing the Focus, especially Katey since she's got an elbow in her spine. They all could've died. Johnnie bursts a cough out of his head. The last time he got blocked in by another car, he was down a back-alley and it was an angry taxi driver he'd just done a runner from. 'Here, mebbies just give him a beep,' Bobby suggests, quite contented really being squadged between all the girls. In the boot, Pamela's thinking, 'God, I wish I got those boys' numbers.' She's been occupying herself in there, quite enjoying the fairground aspect of getting thrown around. Why has it stopped? Back in the front, Johnnie squints, trying to see who's driving the Focus and whether they're eligible for a slap. Just as he's about to whack his paw on the lion-roar horn, the Focus driver leaps out of the car, looking quite moody. He seems about thirtyish, crew cut, navy blue jumper but not that muscly, and Johnnie reckons he could batter him given half a chance. Perhaps everyone's beginning to feel a bit paranoid coming down off the pills (Mandy whines: 'Is it an illusion?'), but Johnnie's convinced the fellow's after a fight. It's not unheard of round these parts for lads to throw bricks through people's windows just for kicks, but forcing someone to smash into the back of your own car? What a wanker. Johnnie's almost tempted to slide the Sunny into the cunt's path and wipe him out, but perhaps that's going a bit far. Instead, he clenches and unclenches his fists, firing himself up for a good old fashioned punch-up with the Black Rebel Ford Focus Club, when suddenly the man turns to face Johnnie and he sees the badge on his jumper CLEVELAND POLICE. Johnnie shits it. With eight of them crushed in the Sunny – most of them on pills, most of all the driver – Johnnie suddenly backs down, taps all the locks down, and puts his foot down. He pushes the Nissan into first then rams it over the left kerb, squeezing round the Focus and the wonderful spindly trees, then quickly down Keith's road. 'Fuck!' Dave Morton swears, dreading his expulsion from the famous football team. Everyone's a jittery mess. 'Can't believe the fucking scum tried to block us in!' Johnnie yells, all pissed off now that he didn't knack Mr Focus anyhow. He keeps glancing in the misty mirror as he tears down the remainder of the street, conjuring up 59mph this time, and fortunately there doesn't seem to be any following blue lights or woo-woo-woops! Just to be on the safe side, Johnnie ignores the red lights at Belle Vue roundabout as well as the reds further down Marton Road, and thankfully God decides not to send any innocent vehicles in his flight-path. The Ford Focus man fades into a teeny bug in the rear-view mirror. Mr Mark Regan, a dog lover, scratches underneath his CLEVELAND GAS LTD sweater, feeling a bit shaky too. He feels terrible. He watches the Nissan Sunny jet off towards Belle Vue in such a hurry, then glances down at the beautiful grey greyhound laid under his front wheels, splattered to death. He doesn't know what to do. Maybe he's a little tired from such a long shift at the power plant, but the hound just came out of nowhere and he couldn't stop the car in time. The sickly memory of the dog going thump on the left side of the bonnet then crunch underneath the tyres will haunt him for months. All he wanted was to get home as quickly as poss and get back into Barbara's arms, and now look what he's done. The greyhound lies twisted in a puddle of black blood. Sniffing back tears, Mark Regan stands shivering in the crisp silence of Keith Road, uncertain what to do. The image of the greyhound charging out of number 14's gate flashes in his memory bank, and he wonders if he really could've done anything to save its life. All around the murder scene, the houses are dark and silent and sinister. Getting his breath back, Mark Regan supposes the best thing to do is knock on door number 14 and explain what's happened, only it's half-past three in the morning and he can't see the news being taken very sportingly. 'Excuse me, sorry for waking you up, but I've murdered your dog,' he mumbles to himself, grimacing. Glancing up and down the street, Mark Regan rolls his sleeves above the elbow, dreading the repercussions. But, just as he's about to step into number 14's garden, Mark has a far better (less incriminating) idea. He swallows back a bit of sick, then crouches next to the beautiful grey greyhound and pulls it out from the wheels of his shiny Focus. The dog's absolutely saturated with blood, and it trails a dark red stripe as Mr Regan drags it into 14's front yard. At first one of the hind legs gets caught on the rusty metal gate but, after a bit of yanking, the leg snaps and comes free. Mark feels ill. He tugs the greyhound softly onto the patch of scrubby lawn, arranging its sticky limbs in a fairly decent order, then he gathers a couple of twigs from the hedging and sticks a makeshift cross in the soil. His red hands make him feel green. Sniffing and snortling, Mr Mark Regan tiptoes gently back to his car, hops in, then cringes when the engine makes a loud noise starting up. He tries to regulate his breathing, huff puff huff puff, then he drives off towards Belle Vue very very carefully, keeping a lookout for more stray animals. He can't wait to get back home to Barbara. He thinks he's done the noble thing, getting the beautiful dead grey greyhound off the road but, as he turns cautiously onto Marton Road, suddenly a horrible thought hits him: what if he hasn't put the hound in the right garden? Trembling, one mile ahead of Mr Regan, Johnnie and his cronies ease themselves to a 30mph dawdle the rest of the way home, hearts still stammering and mouths still squealing. The ones in the back try to keep their heads in each other's laps, out of sight. 'Was that aliens, trying to beam us up?!' Mandy thinks out loud, scratching her neck uncontrollably. 'I saw the green in his eyes . . .' she carries on, but to be fair it's not actually that spooky for a person to have green eyes. Johnnie shudders on the steering wheel, desperate to get home but feeling inclined to stop at every light now and stick to the speed limit. Ellen rubs his leg, trying to calm him down. He takes a breath of the hot sweaty air, skirting the estates rather than steaming through, and his forehead finally stops pouring out water as the juicy giant Peach looms into view. He says a little prayer up to God (his mam and dad are devout Catholics and, although Johnnie never goes to church with them, he does say hello to God now and then), then parks the Sunny out of sight between a Volvo estate and the Biffa bins. 'Thank fuck for that,' he mumbles, though he's still on the para. What did the bobbies want? Did they get his registration? Why did he run two red lights? He's vibrating like a five-foot dildo, huffing and puffing the tangy night air. Ellen gives him a hug, watching everyone tumble out of the Nissan like toys tumbling out of a toy-box, and Pamela emerges from the boot looking white and ghostly. Her dress has twizzled itself 180 degrees round her abdomen, and she stumbles into Peach House repeating, 'That was mint, that was mint.' Even when someone explains to her about the police she's still smiling and her eyes are dropping out everywhere. Falling around, the lot of them proceed into the building, Johnnie and Ellen tagging on the end of the line after locking up the stupid car. From up one floor Bobby the Artist yells, 'Howay round mine, there's more pills to be had. Johnnie! Johnnie! Party round ours . . .' Johnnie hears the words, but he's too exasperated and stressed to carry on with the others, and for some reason Ellen keeps feeling his arse and snogging his ear-lobes and the two of them scuttle off to 5E instead. Ellen puts the chain on the door and drags him through to the red/white bedroom. Johnnie tries to ignore all thoughts of Ford Focuses when Ellen starts to undress, almost frenzied as she unbuttons her top and slides out of the patent miniskirt. Johnnie's heart starts beating in a 4/5 tempo, tugging off garments and letting them fly around like jazzy poltergeists. In his checked boxers, Johnnie clambers onto the bed and envelops Ellen in a great big swampy hug. He pushes her down on the mattress, trying to be quite macho and sexy with his firm kissing and ultra hands-on approach. Ellen mmmms with pleasure, egging him on, and she leans back on her hands as Johnnie tears off her knicks. For some reason Ellen's shaven all her fanny hair off (bored in the shower, plus paranoid she found a crab-egg after shagging Angelo but it was actually a bit of fluff), and Johnnie smiles as he slides his finger down her rashed gash. She's quite drippy. 'Do you want me to lick you out?' he asks, giving her a Sean Connery eyebrow. 'Mmm, yes police, Johnnie,' Ellen replies, opening her grand canyon legs. Johnnie's not quite sure what he just heard (the party's just started beneath them, to the sound of Bardo Pond's 'Dilate' at volume 88), but in any case he jumps into Ellen's fanny face-first. He gargles her name in her wee hole. He has a bit of trouble opening her flaps with his mouth, and at one point he accidentally bites down on her clit and a bit of lip, and Ellen reels back in pain. Johnnie says sorry and, realising he's spoiled the moment, sits up all sheepish with a floppy knob. Ellen tells him not to

123

worry though and, despite the sore bits, carries on kissing him on the lips and elsewhere. 'Here, I'll sort you out,' she says. Ellen gets down on all-fours, looking into his eyes like a sex-crazed slut, and she takes his dangly cock in one hand and starts kneading it, stretching it, stroking it, embarrassing it. What a waste of time. 'Why carn't you get it up?' she asks, slightly ashamed of herself. 'Is it me?' Johnnie just shrugs then shakes his head, thundery pangs of frustration clanging him about the head. He's desperate for a shag, but his brain's all in tatters and the more he tells his dick to liven up, the more it defies him. It's just one of those nights – a fucking shit one. And the more Johnnie tugs and curses his flaccid wobbly bits, the more Ellen thinks it's her fault. 'Aw, Johnnie, I was looking Ford to this all night,' she continues, biting her lip in a provocative manner, but it's still no use. Johnnie feels a little heave-ho in his stomach, bordering on sickness, and he wishes there was a pair of scissors nearby to just put his cock out of its misery. Grrr! And it doesn't really help when Ellen starts wanking herself off in front of him. She does look quite lovely, sliding one finger round her cunt with her tits out and a filthy look on her face, but Johnnie's knob's still just a sad old grave-marker that's fallen down. 'Police, Johnnie,' Ellen pleads, trying to be sexy, 'just Focus on me, Johnnie . . . Copper look at *that* . . .' Ellen opens her flaps so Johnnie can see her inserting a couple slender fingers, but Johnnie's sure his mind's all twisted and he's hearing things, and he just lies back on the bed with a growl. He wants to kill himself. What follows is the sad procedure of Johnnie and Ellen ashamedly putting back on clothes, all furtive and awkward like children in a swimming-pool changing room. They can hardly look at each other, and Johnnie hates how such a promising night can suddenly turn sour, like a delicate vase of flowers falling off a mantel-piece. Falling off a mantelpiece, smashing into a million pieces, and inside that vase there's not only flowers but a Polaroid of Johnnie's small floppy penis, and all his friends and family are there to see it and laugh. Gritting his teeth, Johnnie tries to console himself and convince himself the floppy-on was due to the pills or the police mishap earlier on, but anyhow he still feels like a cock. All aggravated, he sits on the edge of the bed with his head in the palms of his hands. He wonders if all that pain and hard work keeping Ellen was just a waste, and he's absolutely certain in his head they'll never have sex again. He rolls into the foetal position like a snail going to sleep, his mind completely ravaged, and Ellen paus-es there looking at him, not sure whether to hug him or go away. She's slightly tempted to nip downstairs and see what the party's like; after all, it's not the first time Johnnie's fucked up in bed and there's no point hang-ing round with him if he's going to be in a bad mood. The only confusing thing for her is Johnnie didn't seem receptive to all her best moves (the wanking worked wonders for Angelo the other week, but let's not mention that), and Ellen feels a bit deflated and unattractive. Johnnie sinks slowly slowly into the bed-covers. After a large amount of silence, Ellen decides to forget the party and crawls under the duvet with him, next to the ton-weight clamping down one half. She says 'good night' and that depresses Johnnie even more – they've only been going out about half a year, and they're lucky if they have sex once a month. Johnnie worries they'll turn into one of those couples that never have sex; instead they'll go for nice walks and do the garden instead of each other, and it'll be all Johnnie's fault. For another half-hour he stares blankly at the red and white wallpaper, too wired and anxious to sleep, and he wonders what it is that makes him so pathetic in bed. Is his technique really that much shitter than all the other boys Ellen's nailed? He loves her so much and he really wants to please her, but what can he do? He considers putting on *Slutty Cheerleaders From Hell Vol. IV*, to double-check how to have sex, but the idea of it makes his tummy gurgle. He rolls over on the bed, but seeing Ellen's back turned towards him makes him feel even worse. He wonders whether it's better to be happy and lonely, or sad and married? His brain's like a melon getting scooped out. It keeps him awake the rest of the night, especially with that song 'Ganges' rumbling like a forest fire under the floorboards at a million decibels, and Johnnie prays up to the sky that him and Ellen will have sex again, and that they'll get to sleep too. Even Alan Blunt the Cunt can hear the dreaded music, one storey higher, and he paces round and round his apartment, making a sort of raincloud sound on Johnnie and Ellen's ceiling. Alan's been drinking, and even though it's a relaxant he too can't sleep what with all that fucking racket. What he hates most about teenagers is their ability to listen to blitzkriegy-loud music without their ears bursting off the sides of their heads. Whenever he puts on Sinatra it has to be at a pleasant volume, otherwise you lose all the subtlety of the strings, the swooping arrangements, and Frank's voice farts at you instead of showering you with perfume. Alan Blunt the Cunt spent the evening at the Brambles Farm Hotel, opposite Peach House on the whoosh-whoosh nee-naw crossroad, where they happened to have a bit of karaoke on. Alan only intended to go for one glass of McEwan's 80 – since he feels awkward and depressed drinking there on his own – but he happened upon a fellow ex-copper and sat there sharing stories and dropping more and more pints into his belly, and after a bit he blocked out the embarrassedness with a feeling of being completely smashed. When his partner in crime eventually headed home to his wife and four delinquent children, Alan was seeing stars and he even had the courage to warble 'Under My Skin' on the karaoke. Despite lots of slur-ring, it was a fine performance. When they were younger, Alan and his brother Ronny used to duet on all sorts of Sinatra or Dean Martin standards, getting up at family barbecues or wedding receptions or funerals to croon 'I Get a Kick Out of You' or 'Mambo Italiano' to wet-eyed nannas and granddads. Thirty years and three hundred thousand Regals later, Alan's voice has become nothing short of heavenly, and he felt like Frank himself this evening in the Brambles. Pissed as a fanny, he thought he was serenading a caberet concert hall, and all the workmen were cool cats in zoot suits and all the wrinkly wives were Ingrid Bergmans or Kim Novaks. After the karaoke, Alan Blunt scoffed a burger from the shop and waltzed back to the flat in high spirits. It's only now, coma setting in and his brain rotting like an amp speaker leaking battery fluid, Alan feels sad again and he wishes himself dead. Funny how booze squirts you full of confidence, diluting all your worries and troubles, only to be pissed out of you again, revealing your nightmares like a murky tide going out. It's called a hangover. Trembling, Alan Blunt wonders what it'd be like to hang over the edge of a ten-storey tower block. He wonders if he can fit through the slightly open window. Shaking his head, he's not sure why he feels so shitty all of a sudden. He got scolded this morning for turning up to work late, he owes a bottomless amount of money to the Loan Company, he's forty years old and it's doubtful he'll kiss any women again, and he feels all embarrassed now for singing in the local. Fucking hell, why did he have to jump up on that tabletop?? Sniffing, Alan staggers into the rumbling kitchen – the noise is just as loud there too – and he bonks his head off the double-glazing a few times. He's losing it. Sub-woofers are the worst – you can try drowning out the sound with 'My Way' on full-blast but it's like bouncing two bassy footballs round your flat, the two tempos colliding and making your inner ear all seasick. Sometimes Alan gets so radgy he'll storm downstairs with a baseball bat or candle-stick holder, but then again he hates to get on bad terms with his neighbours, and it's so much easier (and disappointing) to just hide your head under a pillow until the onslaught stops. At least Bobby the Artist lis-tens to music with real-life vocals and instruments – that boy Johnnie from downstairs puts his robot music on so loud you can only imagine him dancing round his flat with ears bleeding, and when Angelo lived next-door the most awful booom-booom-booom ragga music came on at six like clockwork, heralding his return from working at the tyre factory. God, and those lyrics! Anyone would think black people hated everyone, always referring to ladies as bitches and prozzies (despite wanting to shag them all) and swinging guns around and things. Alan puts on the kettle and scratches his knob. It's been years since he last had sex, and it was a nauseating affair with a fat bird he used to talk to in the Cargo Fleet Club. She was there tonight at the Brambles, but he didn't look over and in his heart he's glad she didn't come over to talk to him. Sex, to Alan, is a dirty old raindrop now evaporated into the gloomy grey sky. There's not too much in his life now that makes him happy, except perhaps visiting Tiny Tina at Corpus Christi. Last week a lady came to school to make kites with the kids, and Tiny Tina was a picture of perfection in her little gingham dress, sprinting down the length of the field clutching the lovely smiley-face kite she'd made. Alan thinks he could make her smile. Face pressed between the rungs of the anti-paedophile fence, he gazed at her longingly, wishing he could take her home. Oh, the things he could do with her! Misting over, Alan Blunt the Cunt imagines Tina sat on his lap giving him a big squeeze. On kite day he saw her trip over and graze her knee, and Alan wanted to jump the fence and put a plaster on or kiss her leg better, but he didn't have the guts. Or the plaster. Pouring a cup of coffee (he thinks it'll sober him up), Alan plots Tina's Big Kidnap. He's so desperate for company, he'd gladly go to jail for twenty-five years just to spend twenty-four glorious hours with the girl. Scratching under his teary glasses, Alan wonders when his life went so tits up. He pounds his feet into the living room in slippers, then sits down to the sound of 'Despite the Roar' kicking in with all them distorted guitars. Bloody rock music; it's a wonder Bobby the Artist doesn't get a fucking rock in his face sometimes. Alan has a big dramatic groan to himself. He's still drunk, and with every blink the room shifts leftwards in a sickly, uncontrollable manner. Left. Left. Left. Left. Alan Blunt rarely vomits, but his stomach's full of lashing waves and rotting old sailboats. He mumbles a swearword, clutching his gut, trying his best to sink into a coma on the sofa. He spills coffee on his trousers. Then one minute later he's off to sleep, just him and his belly ache and a thousand bad dreams, then in the morning he feels alright again. He gets up and finishes off the cold coffee, totally oblivious to all his evil thoughts the night before. The flat's silent again (silence is the subtle sound of feet and doors and birds), and he opens the curtains to a bright summery eleven and a half o'clock. Sitting back on the musty couch, Alan vaguely remembers Bobby's awful cannonball music, and he vaguely remembers being upset about something. Never mind. Hangovers bring a certain cloudy depression, but nothing compared to your lowest shitty pissed maudlin moment. He feels like a dried-up old plant that needs watering, and he runs the cold tap into his mouth for two minutes. Alan hopes to God he didn't offend anyone last night, or show himself up too much. Although he hates excessive noise and obnoxious bastards, he can't imagine ever living anywhere else. He loves knowing everyone's secret business, and he loves sharing his worldly wit and wisdom with everybody. For example, he once had a lovely, heated discussion with Mrs Fletcher in the foyer about government immigration legislation, and just before Bobby the Artist sets sail to London he gives him the advice to 'steer clear of Brixton – it's full of blacks and drug dealers'. Racist Cunt Alan feels he's a sort of father figure to the residents of Peach House (although he's by no means the oldest), and he's always there to celebrate people's birthdays or greet new tenants, whether invited or not. For instance, when Bobby the Artist steps onto the 65A on the first leg of his journey to the capital, Alan's face is there amongst all the young ones waving him off. Georgie feels uncontrollably upset, getting hugged by Ellen and Pamela, standing there on the gritty pavement as the bus wobbles off down Cargo Fleet. Bobby the Artist waves and waves and waves until Georgie, his friends, and then the tower block itself disintegrate into dots on the blobby horizon. He feels weird and nervous, all his travel and hotel and itinerary prearranged by Bent Lewis, getting pushed into a strange southern city without any brakes or stabilisers on. He stares as the town where he grew up dribbles away, all the beautiful grey maisons and green muddy playing fields and famous bridges and pepperpot cooling towers and the underpass where he first fell off his bike disappearing slowly into specks as well. Goodbye lovely factory town. On the back of his crumpled itinerary (labelled MONDAY to FRIDAY), Bobby scribbles three quick pencil drawings of the town and its funny frowny residents – one last memory of the place to keep in his pocket once he gets munched up by the scary monster called London. He doesn't want to leave but he does want to be a famous artist, and his stomach puts itself in a knot and then a double-knot as he turns the itinerary over again and re-reads the list. MONDAY: Bobby the Artist loads the six canvases into the boot of the National Express, each one of them carefully bubble-wrapped and tagged by him and Georgie the night before. They got all gluey and stuck to each other, and they couldn't help popping loads of the bubbles for fun. On the coach, Bobby sits near the back surrounded by Geordies and children scoffing sweets, and he wishes he had some head-phones and Merzbow to drown out those silly fuckers. He's in a bad mood because he doesn't want to leave home. And he feels like he's on a fucking school trip, the driver stressing that no food or drink and especial-ly no drugs are allowed on the bus. Well the chance would be a fine thing. At services somewhere just west of Shitsville, Bobby feels like a right nerd tramping into Burger King with the rest of the National Express goons, and he orders a bacon-double-cheeseburger and munches it all self-consciously on his own on a red squashy seat. He's on expenses (which means Bent Lewis pays for everything Bobby buys on his arty excursion), and it's strange getting into the routine of putting receipts in your pocket instead of screwing them up and booting them far as you can down the street. In a way he's very tempted to exploit getting everything paid for, and he considers getting another burger and chips and Coke and maybe even an ice cream, but he doesn't want to spew up, does he. Back on the bus, Bobby the Artist tries to sleep for the remaining three hours, but the Geordies are too loud and annoying. He looks out the window, but after a while you get bored of the same old patchwork fields and the odd white pillows floating about in the sky. The view finally starts getting exciting when the coach sneaks through the outskirts of London, Bobby the Artist observing the boulevards of Barnet, then the posh pillared mansions of St John's Wood, then Victoria Station where the buses go to sleep. Bobby gets off and, although the itinerary says 'get a cab immediately to the +!Gallery', he's far too parched and sits in the Shakespeare instead with all his paintings, and he buys each of them a pint. It's not a myth – drinks in London are extremely expensive, so thank God he's on expenses. Bobby the Artist perches at a table in the corner, gurgling lager, staring in awe at all the people running around outside in such a rush! It's like everyone turned up for the London marathon in suits and casual clothes, and decided to run wherever they wanted, like a caucus-race. Madness. Bobby's also shocked how many different sorts of people there are – people with faces all the colours of the rainbow, all shapes and sizes, all sorts of straights and gays and inbetweenies. After just one sip of Kronenbourg, he spots a man with a Mohican sporting leopard hotpants and a pink furry coat, strolling the highway. Bobby laughs into his glass. He feels sort of underdressed, but also safe and happy to be just a face in the crowd for once – back home you can get beaten up just for having slightly colour-ful shoes. After swallowing the rest of the pints, Bobby the Artist bundles the canvases together again and struggles with them out onto the whizzing street. Accidentally he annoys everyone, causing an obstruc-tion on their precious little pavement. Frowning,

Bobby hails a taxi then whooshes to the gallery on Clerkenwell Road, under a tepee of bubble-wrap and slight drunkenness. Bent Lewis is stood there waiting, and he welcomes Bobby with a great big cheery hug and then a more civilised shake of the hand. 'Welcome to London,' Lewis sings, the sun smashing into his fluorescent teeth. Bent Lewis leads Bobby the Artist into the gallery, which is a huge white box with the aroma of cement and oil paint stuck to the air. Lewis shows him the other works featured in the upcoming exhibition, but Bobby's not all that interested. There's a few monochrome prints of flower petals and sex organs (quite commercial, but nice if you like things that are black and white), abstract paintings with 300-word explanations next to them, and a set of lively photographs taken in some crap nightclub or other. Bobby's not totally impressed, but it warms his heart when Bent Lewis leads him into the vast empty Gallery 2 and says, 'We reserved the largest space for you.' Bobby the Artist has a little spin in the big white sugarcube, the yellow argyle sticking to his chest because it's been sweaty dragging all those paintings across town. Him and Bent Lewis pull the canvases into the chilly space and unwrap them, Lewis yelping at the sight of each one as they get unveiled. 'Wonderful stuff,' he says. 'Gosh, I'd forgotten that one!' Bent Lewis explains next that time is of the essence since the gallery opens on Thursday, and he wants Bobby to come in early each morning to sort the hanging. Bobby was actually hoping to enjoy a few casual days in London exploring the Big Bens and the drinking dens, but it's exciting too imagining the paintings nailed up all professional and jazzy. Him and Lewis arrange to meet at the gallery at 9.30 tomorrow morning, then they shake hands and all that rigmarole, and Lewis escorts him back out onto the road going vroombroomvroombroomvroom. 'So what do I do now?' Bobby the Artist asks, since there's nothing on his itinerary to tell him how to spend his leisure time. 'I'm not sure!' Bent Lewis giggles, awed and also slightly jealous of Bobby the wee fawn in the big bad city for the first time. 'I'd invite you out for a drink – and maybe a snort, haw haw – but I'm meeting a very important client for supper . . . there's Farringdon tube down there' (Lewis points down there). 'Have an explore! The city's your oyster, my friend.' Bobby the Artist smiles skew-whiff, and it's only when he finds himself in Farringdon station he realises an Oyster's that daft card that lets you travel on the trains and buses and that. You have to bash it on the little pad to get through the gates, and at rush-hour it's a bit like being at the dog-track with all the funny greyhounds bursting out the traps. No one in London likes to talk to each other – on the tube, everyone avoids eye contact at all costs. At one point Bobby asks a fellow passenger what time it is, but he gets completely blanked and it makes him sad. He doesn't feel very comfortable, and he has the first pang in his heart of: Aaargh, where's Georgie? On Alan Blunt the Cunt's advice, Bobby's first port of call is Brixton, and although it does seem to be a largely black community it's pretty cosmopolitan and not a 'fucking hellhole', as Alan put it. Bobby the Artist pushes down Atlantic Road then Coldharbour Lane, dodging ticket touts for the Academy and ginger cunts trying to scrounge money off people who look pretty skint themselves. The hum of people and traffic sounds like one big ghetto-blaster, and within a moment or two there's a stocky black fellow offering him a menu of, 'Skunk, hash, pills?' Bobby goes round the corner with him to score a twenty-bag of weed, and the fellow tells him, 'This shit's the bomb, bruv, I smoke it myself, gets you right off your bonce and that,' or words to that effect. Bobby waits to see the goods before handing over any coin (he knows what Johnnie's like to unsuspecting customers, giving them a jab in the eye then running off), but the black guy seems trustworthy and quite amicable. He loves how he talks in such a rhythmical, Bob Marley manner. 'Can I get a receipt off you?' Bobby asks, pocketing the skunk, but a split-second later his friend has tootled off down Coldharbour, and Bobby shrugs and decides to head back to the tube. He does his Oyster again on the yellow pad, it says beep yes, then he gets the sky blue line to Oxford Circus. The trains are less busy now, but when he gets off all the shops are still open and people are milling around with armfuls of designer clothes and shoes and records and other silly bits and bobs. There's a man on the corner talking about Jesus. His head in the clouds, Bobby gets some small green Rizla and a twenty-four pack of crisps from a newsagent, asking the hairy man at the counter if he knows where the Saint Georges Hotel is. Bobby gets told to head up Regent Street, past tables with people on them sipping coffees and shops beginning to shut their metal eyelids, and when he finally reaches the Saint Georges it reminds him of Peach House except much fatter and not pink. There's a bar and restaurant on the top floor, and he grins, imagining sipping cocktails on top of the world. He checks in, then takes the lift up to floor seven, staring with spiral pupils at how smart and spotless the place is. The dodgy lift at Peach House smells of disinfected wee and crap sex. When Bobby the Artist keycards his door open, ker-clink, the first thing he does is bellyflop onto the double-bed and gaze out the window at the BT tower and Centrepoint and the big Duchamp bike wheel. It feels weird being at the edge of fame and fortune in the most famous city of them all, and it also feels weird being at the edge of the double-bed and he falls off by accident. Bomping his head off the floor, Bobby the Artist lies there in a daze, tweety birds ballroom dancing round his temples. What an unusual day. Bobby the Artist unpacks his things – he was so overloaded with canvases, all he's brought is a toothbrush, two socks, one boxers, cigs, HB pencil, and the itinerary – then adopts a lounging pose on the mattress and mechanically sparks up joints and gets stoned for a bit. He considers taking a shower, but after a few Happy Fags he can't be fussed and instead just slouches there, turning into part of the furniture. The wallpaper goes slightly Indian and arabesque for half an hour and he eats a lot of crisps. But it's boring not being able to tell Georgie all his wacky spacky thoughts, and sooner or later he starts drifting off to sleep on the sinking-sand covers. It's been a busy day, after all, and completely insane to think he was drinking tea with Georgie in the flat this morning and now he's here. He wants to give her a ring but the hotel phone doesn't seem to spit out receipts, and he wants to raid the mini-bar but he feels too much like a giant and it worries him. After one more smelly joint he resigns himself to a deep dingy sleep, weird dreams of big cities unfolding in his head like the pages of comic books. Snore snore snore. TUESDAY: The sun wakes him up, grinning through the window. Bobby the Artist can't be arsed sharing croissants and all that continental shite with the tourist types he observed yesterday in reception, so he smokes the rest of the ganj for breakfast and sets off to Clerkenwell at 10.02 by the hotel clock. Maybe it's the smokes, but everything seems to be staring at him on the tube this morning. He wishes he packed more than just the yellow argyle; he feels a bit of a scruffbag when he turns up to the gallery late, and Bent Lewis is standing there all immaculate in an Outrageous Orange shirt, like a work of art himself. The other pieces in the exhibition look a lot more innovative and appealing on skunk this morn. 'How are you today?' Bent Lewis asks, clinging to Bobby's arm as they step through to Gallery 2. 'A bit stoned like,' Bobby replies. Bent Lewis's face ruptures like a sunflower, laughing hysterically in that squeaky gay tone he has, and it sets Bobby off too because it's fucking giggly reefy. The whiteness of the gallery almost blinds the poor boy to death. Squinting, Bobby the Artist sees Lewis has leant the paintings against the walls in a certain arrangement, with all these tools and spirit levels and stepladders and tape measures and fancy things relaxing in the middle of the space. 'I think this arrangement gives the works a fabulous tension, a sort of ambiguous narrative flowing from one painting to the next . . .' Lewis begins, smugly waving his paws about but, for the sake of being different, Bobby pushes him aside and starts wildly bashing in nails and throwing up the canvases in the wrong order, at wonky heights and angles. Bent Lewis looks fabulously tense as the paintings go up. '*Voilá*,' Bobby the Artist puffs, putting down the hammer. Lewis frowns at first, then his eyebrows lift and all his hairs stand on end and he starts raving, 'I see, I see . . . yes yes . . . you're completely right – a very raw hang. It's like, well, I suppose it's like two fingers up to the stuck-up art world, isn't it?' Bobby the Artist nods, but to be honest he just wanted to get the paintings up as quick as poss so he can enjoy all the sights of London while the ganjy feeling lasts. All the characters in the paintings have a little smirk. Bent Lewis stands still, slack-jawed. Having said that, when Bobby the Artist dashes off merely forty-five minutes after turning up, Lewis can't help straightening the paintings slightly and he air-freshens the space of Bobby's BO. Stinking out the Circle Line, Bobby the Artist stands all the way to the Westminster stop, feeling cheery about the exhibition and all the beautiful ladies hopping on and off in slinky summer outfits. He's starting to like London. Bobby wafts a bit of air under his sweater, racing up the escalator then diving into the sunny breeze rubbing shoulders with Japs and Yankees oohing and aahing at Big Ben standing there all erect on the Thames. It's like a giant gold grandfather clock, and Bobby stares at it for thirteen puffs of a Regal. On the last puff, he turns his back and starts ambling up Whitehall, following the signs to TRAFALGAR SQUARE. He tries to see the Prime Minister's house at Downing Street but there's a big black fence keeping your eyes out, and when he gets to the square he's annoyed to see Nelson's Column hidden in scaffolding, getting spring cleaned. Sighing and sweating, Bobby sits for a bit on a lion's paw, then goes wandering over to Leicester Square but there's no celebs or premieres, and he goes to Carnaby Street but there's no sixties people just Reebok and Diesel, and he tries Buckingham Palace but the Queen's not in. There's loads of queens on Old Compton Street, but it freaks him out slightly getting eyed-up by a muscly bald T-shirted person. Bobby gets lost in Selfridges, and he even gets lost in McDonald's. Plopping himself down on a red bench, he puts his chin in an eggcuppy fist and sulks at London. All that great British history like beefeaters and Chelsea girls and mods and men in big white ruffles seems to have swirled down a plughole in the Thames. Now it's just a town full of shops and clowns and adverts – London probably cries itself to sleep every night, missing the good old days. Bobby misses the North East, and he really misses Georgie. It's funny how, after living with her for months and getting so used to her little intricacies and getting used to arguing with her, just two days apart gives him insane withdrawal symptoms, and he'd do anything to have just one little cuddle with her or a single lingering kiss. He never wants to be apart from her again. Sprinting into a BT phone box, Bobby the Artist dials her number but he only has 20p and he only gets to talk to her for a minute. Georgie sounds well – she tells him quickly she loves him and she's dead proud of him, and she also tells him Alan Blunt the Cunt caused a scene in the chippy last night after the two Korean boys tried to charge him for the HP sauce. Bobby cringes, smiling, but his skin feels slightly frosted with sadness because he wishes he was there with her. When the phone dies, Bobby dies a bit inside, and he's left holding the limp telephone with all the call-card girls leering at him. He bashes it down on its holder, then screams silently with his hands like tense eagle claws, then slips out onto Oxford Street again and composes himself as he goes to find the nearest watering hole. Weaving through rampant shoppers, Bobby can't possibly face the city sober. He ducks into the Ship on Wardour Street, makes himself comfy at the table over in the corner, and all he wants to see of London now sits in a bottle on top of the counter. He's green and his name is Gordon. WEDNESDAY: Bobby the Artist turns up to the gallery at 2.36pm wearing a terrifying hangover like a crown of thorns. He ended up with his head down the bog last night, sicking up, and his hair's still soaked with toilet water when he trails into the gallery space on such a fairytale summer afternoon. His stomach still feels turbulent, and he remembers nothing past the seventh supersonic in the Ship, but he smiles earnestly at Bent Lewis when he arrives. Bobby bought all the drinks on expenses, but let's not mention that to Lewis, shall we. Instead, Bobby shakes the fairy's hand as usual and asks, 'What's the crack then?' Bent Lewis grimaces, sniffing the Artist's eau de toilette of sweat, sicky dribble and hotel lino, then replies, 'Ah, well, we're just waiting for the card stock to arrive with the printed labels, then we'll discuss how we might want to present the titles, prices, etc. If you're feeling up to it, that is . . .' To be fair, Bent Lewis is starting to get a bit aggravated about Bobby's awful punctuality and increasing body odour, although in his heart he knows these incredible paintings could never be painted by a clean-cut, always-on-time sensible human being. If only he could get Bobby the Artist to die young, Bent Lewis would make an absolute killing. But as it stands, he just wants his first exhibition to run smoothly. 'I've marked up a basic price list,' he explains, handing Bobby this laminated bit of paper, 'but prices can fluctuate – hopefully for the best, if I do my job right!' The figures make Bobby's eyes roll back (ranging from £750 for 'Georgie on the Toilet' to £4,000 for 'The Angels'). He only got £100 to paint the Fireman Sam mural at Corpus Christi, where Alan Blunt the Cunt nowadays pervs over young girls. Squinting, Bobby's too hungover to speak. Taking that as bewilderment and joy, Bent Lewis bashes the Artist on the back and yippety-yaps, 'I think we'll have no problem off-loading all these works – you're going to be a star, mate! I could see this one, in particular, making an excellent commercial poster. Or an album cover even . . .' Bent Lewis motions limp-wristy at 'Bobby's Favourite Trip' (the one with the Artist climbing into the bright shopping shelves, six inches tall) and, although Bobby wants the world to see his work, he cringes at the thought of some wanky student having his image on their dusty cum-crusted wall. 'I mean, I think you'll go down very well with *the kids*,' Bent Lewis continues, sunny sky slapping him on the face. 'You've got a great future ahead. Trust me, Bobby, I'll take care of everything. We're mates, me and you.' Bobby just stands there perfectly still, like the Statue of

David got put in the exhibition too except it got pissed up on gin the night before. He doesn't really think of Bent Lewis as a mate per se, after all they've never been out on the town together and they've never snorted coke off a Page 3 model's tits yet, like he thought they might. London's slowly becoming a disappointment to Bobby – everyone's so obsessed with money, and less interested in getting to know each other. Down the Linthorpe back home, you can get mortalled with total strangers on just a tenner; down here you need twice the money for half the pleasure. For someone like Bent Lewis it's a great place to be, always in contact with clients and wankers and always invited to the latest trendy private view, but for someone normal like Bobby it's a nightmare. He always did imagine London to be a wonderful crazy castle of hedonism and history and people living in cardboard boxes, but as well as that it's full of brainwashed people in suits chasing pound notes round the city. Down the tube, you can bash into someone and say sorry sorry sorry and you won't get any reaction. Getting exasperated, Bobby the Artist's brain starts to t t h h r r o o b b, and he sits down with a gasp on the gallery floor. 'So the painting titles are going to be dead professional and that?' he asks, looking up at Lewis all distorted from his mouse-eye view. 'Yes yes, they're made by a lovely little printer off Old Street. They're couriering them over as soon as they're ready.' Bent Lewis smiles at the sweet efficiency of it all, but of course Bobby has to go and throw a spanner in the works and mumbles, 'Righty ho, but, but I thought maybe it might look better if I just scribble all the titles in felt-tip. Have you got a felt-tip?' Unfortunately for Lewis, he's got a felt-tip. He screws his nose up as Bobby jumps to attention, snatches the permanent marker, and hurriedly scrawls the titles and dates and dimensions straight onto the whitewashed walls. Bobby's handwriting is like that of a ten-year-old girl – his teachers tried to get him to join everything up and put dots instead of circles and punctuate everything perfectly, but it's quite typical of Bobby to ignore anyone like that. 'What do you reckon?' he asks Lewis. Sweating, the two of them twirl once in the finished space like cassette-rollers, and at first Bent Lewis is devastated, but then he tries to convince himself it looks primitive, or seductive, or not bad. In any case, by now he just can't be bothered arguing. 'It might just work!' Lewis guffaws, feeling like a loon. 'So we're done and dusted now then, eh?' Bobby asks, proud as punch to have his very own art exhibition. Look at it! 'Yes, we'll just have to wait and see what happens tomorrow!' Bent Lewis replies, knowing it'll cause a storm but the art world can be awfully harsh sometimes. It's one of those industries you either get your arse licked and roses thrown at you, or you get criticised to death by people who never made it as artists but know lots of long fancy words. 'So I'm free to go, then?' Bobby the Artist asks, tongue lolling at the prospect of drinking the Saint Georges dry the rest of the day. So much twirling round Gallery 2 has made his head go funny. 'Of course yes, cheers Bobby,' Bent Lewis says, then, 'What are your plans?' Bobby the Artist picks a bit of black bogey out of his nose (smoggy London gives you that), then sniffs and says, 'Oh I'm just gonna get wrecked again.' Bent Lewis lets out a belly-laugh like a flock of cawing birds, then his face becomes serious again and he says, 'Oh yes, that reminds me. A friend of mine, Francis Fuller, gave me a present to give you. He's very interested in seeing your work tomorrow – he could prove to be a very important buyer.' Bent Lewis smiles, then takes great pride in looking over his shoulder once or twice (to add tension), then palms a chunky wrap of coke into Bobby's hand. Bobby the Artist grins appreciatively, sliding it into his Magic Pocket (the tiny compartment situated above your right pocket, perfect for hiding drugs and johnnies and other embarrassing things). 'Admittedly I've already had a little dab myself,' Bent Lewis continues, trying to be cooooool, 'but there's about two or three grams there for yourself. This stuff is top notch, mate. One word of advice though: don't get too *wrecked* tonight, as you put it, and don't forget the private view starts at six o'clock tomorrow!' Who does Bent Lewis think he is: giving Bobby three g of Charlie then telling him not to get wrecked! He nods though, leaving the +!Gallery to the sound of Bent Lewis's hysterical, camp laughter. Bobby sticks out his pink bottom lip as he stumbles down Farringdon Road and into the tube, humming softly to himself while the train rattles back to Oxford Circus. Bobby races his shadow back to the hotel, and it's about evening-time when he finally gets sat in the Heights; the restaurant/bar thing located at the very top of the Saint Georges. There's a tear-jerking, dramatic view over the city with all its spires and blocks and squares and towers and colours and lots of lovely sky as well, and Bobby gets a Guinness then a Carlsberg then another Carlsberg then a bit of sniff to perk him up then another Guinness then a whisky then a bit more sniff then a gin and tonic for hair of the dog then another sniff then another Carlsberg, sitting by the window. But it's not much fun being famous and being on your own. By about ten o'clock Bobby's mortalled again and bored of the same old pitch-black view, and he plucks up the courage to go and sit with these three pretty girls who've been catching his eye all night, although it could just be the double-vision. Full of cokey confidence, Bobby asks, 'Can I sit here?' The girls giggle and nod, then he plonks himself down sharply between the lasses. They coo, 'How are you?' Bobby replies, 'Ah, I'm a bit spaced out. Been a mad old day, like . . .' The girls (one blonde, one brunette, one ginger) snigger and swoon over Bobby's exotic accent, and they look at each other and smile like squirrels as Bobby recounts his day, how he's an artist, and how he's got an exhibition tomorrow night and they can come if they want. The girls flutter their eyeballs and say they'd love to, only they're flying to Milan tomorrow afternoon. Bobby clocks them instantly as spoilt little brats – not only do they have the posh accent, they're all decked out in delicate designer dresses and they're only about seventeen. The ginge one wears shabby hippy slippers though, to appear bohemian and anti-capitalist or shite like that. The brunette one's got a CND badge dangling off her Louis Vuitton satchel. The blonde one's got quite nice tits. Glazing over, Bobby coughs then chats to them for a bit, finding out where they're from and what subjects they do and what jobs Mummy and Daddy do. It turns out they go to an all-girl school somewhere boring outside London, which sounds a bit *Carry On*-ish but probably a bit shit getting segregated like that. He submerges himself in another gin and tonic, the girls entertaining him with their soft plummy voices. 'I like your hair,' the blonde bird says, since she's into guitar music. All the girls are giddy and heavy-lidded, and after a bit more conversing Bobby invites them down to his room for a go of the Charlie. In the lift his brainwaves mosaic together an image of him snorting it off the girls' thighs, spanking their smooth pink hides, chucking the telly out the window, but under such lonely circumstances he'll settle for a nice conversation instead. He's just a bit drunk and flustered. In his room, Bobby gets the girls to sit on the bed then he racks up four lines, each one the length of this sentence. 'I love coke, I could really do with a line right now!' the brunette titters, trying her best to impress the mysterious mop-topped artist. Bobby just laughs, sucking up the first line. The brunette goes next since she's apparently so desperate, then the blonde, then the ginger. All three of them are mouth-wateringly gorgeous, the way posh girls often are – after all, their beautiful pristine genes come from a long line of wealthy men bedding gold-digging big-titted stunners. The blonde bird's mother was actually a Miss Sussex, and her dad's a rich banker in the City. The girls intrigue/annoy Bobby, since they were obviously born with silver spoons in their gobs and yet they talk as if they've had it really tough. 'My sister used to squat with ten people above a *kebab shop*,' the ginger one brags, having trouble snorting the shit though her ever so weeny nostril. 'And I ran away from home two years ago and had to sleep on the beach,' the brunette explains, with a very feel-sorry-for-me expression. Bobby the Artist nods, but he thinks girls like them only do things like that for attention, or they've got no identity at all in dull, stuffy Suburbialand so they try to adopt the maddest personality they can muster. That's why most Goths come from nice houses in the posh parts of town, not haunted castles. 'So do youse do many drugs?' Bobby asks, licking up the girls' crumbs. 'Oh, I love drugs!' they chorus, then the brunette takes over: 'I've done absolutely everything, you know; pills, poppers, skunk. I did ketamine at Glastonbury, and you'll never guess what happened: I went really small! It was like I was on fucking acid or something . . . but I'd never do acid though, or crack . . . I just know if I got into crack I'd do it too much and just overdose and die, I'm that sort of person. This one time my friend thought he was in hell after, I don't know, *loads* of ketamine, and this other time there was a boy who threw himself off a building after doing acid . . . it's true.' Bobby the Artist cringes then lights up one of the girls' Marlboro Lights, getting steamy-eyed as he tells them, 'Ah, acid's class though. I've never had a bad buzz, like . . .' The girls' jaws drop but then they try to adopt a cool expression, and the brunette goes, 'Oh, yeah, well I'd totally do acid . . . it'd be so fun . . .' Bobby shudders, getting the Charles out again. He makes four little white snakes on the melamine chest of drawers, then the snakes climb one by one through a rolled-up fiver into everyone's nose and slither round and round the brain. He offers the girls a packet of crisps, but the coke has eaten up their appetites for them and they

decline. Soon they're off their faces, lips numb with
snowflakes, and talking more and more shite as the
night turns dusky blue to wavy navy. 'I'd love to be an
artist too. I want to help the world through art, like,
start a revolution versus war and poverty, through art,
you know what I mean?' the ginge one babbles, but
Bobby the Artist doesn't know what she means. 'The
upper classes should be shot! It's up to us working class
to open the world's eyes to injustice and mistreatment
of people. If I ever get stinking rich, I'd give most of it
to charity. Or spend it all on ketamine!' the brunette
guffaws, in the most pompous accent known to man. 'I
mean, yeah, my daddy's not even rich by any means, for
instance he used to live in a terraced house . . .' the
blondie explains, and Bobby feels exhausted to hear
such a pretty thing speak such silly words. By their
third snort of dandruff the girls are just babbling high-
pitched white noise, which is sometimes used as a torture device in far-away countries. 'Everyone should be
vegetarian coke's so fun it makes me more intelligent
you know I wish we had some smack that'd be so fun
Milan tomorrow Daddy's given me five hundred euros
allowance I could spend it in one day he might want
to buy some of your paintings he's in property it's like
the same thing lahdeedahdeedah . . .' Bobby the Artist
feels sick and bored, wishing he'd never invited down
such irritating cunts, and he wants to be alone again.
He sits on the corner of the bed with his knees up,
covering his mouth, trying to give off bad body language. The girls start to calm down and shut up as the
cocaine fades from thick white cloud to clear sky in
their skulls. Bobby hates them. Even if they were to

149

suddenly rip off their clothes and pounce on Bobby he wouldn't like them any better, and it's definitely for the best when the girls start collecting their things together and start edging towards the door. Some boys (in particular, those who are off their head) would cheat on their girlfriends if they thought they could get away with it but, as the pretentious princesses waddle off back to their rooms, Bobby's pleased that God made them annoying little shits and didn't force him to have sex with them and be unfaithful to Georgie. He's never cheated on her, and if he carries on successfully dodging beautiful ladies, he thinks he'll stay with her for ever. Oh, Georgie! He fills his brain up with pictures of his girlfriend, then he puts his brain on the pillow and all the pictures turn into beautiful dreams as he falls into slumber. Kerplunk. THURSDAY: The build-up to the exhibition starts with a build-up of diarrhoea in Bobby the Artist's panties. Sat on the tube to Farringdon at 6.45pm, he hasn't actually soiled himself (not like Johnnie that first night he bonked Ellen), but he feels deathly nervous zipping through the black tunnels and white stations black tunnels and white stations. He finally managed a shower this afternoon at the hotel, spent the rest of the day combing his hair a different way, all the while fretting about the private view. As he leaves the tube and wobbles towards Clerkenwell Road like a lonely clown with a down-turned mouth, Bobby wonders if he'll have to explain his art to everybody, if he'll have to make pleasant conversation to complete dickheads with lots of money/power, if he'll be forced to sign his soul away to the Devil. The thought of free champagne and getting lashed is the only thing keeping his feet plodding in the right direction. To be fair, there's also a weeny bit of excitement at seeing his artworks in a real living, breathing exhibition, with real people there, but that feeling's just a tiny ladybird fluttering in his heart – not like the humongous slathering, gnashing dragon tunnelling through his guts. Nevertheless, Bobby the Artist keeps his head held high as he paces through the glass doors of the +!Gallery, and his eyelashes stutter at the sight of the space completely chock-a-block with people holding wine glasses and curious expressions on their faces. Bobby grabs a couple of red wines from the table with the tablecloth, then barges through to Gallery 2 but all you can see are people's faces, not paintings. Bent Lewis is there, entertaining a circle of floppy-haired gayboys, and as soon as he claps eyes on our humble artist he claps his hands and says, 'Bobby! You're here! You simply must meet some friends of mine . . .' So Bobby has to shake hands with lots of weird strangers – most of whom are fancy-dressed art dealers, wacky art critics or elderly gay abstract painters – and he stands stock-still when Bent Lewis explains to them, 'So this is the artist. He grew up on a council estate up North, and he only paints under the influence of psychedelic drugs. Pretty fucked up, don't you think? Pretty raw.' That's not strictly true, Bobby thinks to himself. Quite a few of these paintings were created under the influence of boredom, or when he's been Three Hammered. But Bent Lewis is in his element, and Bobby the Artist doesn't think it'd be appropriate to interrupt him, so he just keeps shhhhtum as Lewis continues, 'The works are anti-establishment, anti-art.

If Liam Gallagher were a Surrealist, you'd get Bobby. Just look at him, he's a fucking genius.' Bobby the Artist nods, but he's just nodding at the waiter person offering to top up his glass. It's quite depressing how bullshitty the world seems down here, how everyone's probably telling lies throughout the building just to punt a few canvases with pigment on them. Bobby hears Bent Lewis spurt out, 'I discovered Bobby in a grimy North East tower block,' and he cringes. How dare he describe Peach House as grimy! Bobby chews his lip, then decides to have a wander about. He's got no motivation to talk to anyone – everyone seems so pompous and boring, and they're twice his age, and they all laugh like pretentious pumping bumholes. Round the corner near the b+w flower prints, a pissed-up knobhead rambles to Bobby, 'Hello, I love "Bobby's Favourite Shop", and the one with the girl pissing! But you'll never make any money in the art world. You're naïve. Lewis, I don't know, he's just a fucking novice, he doesn't know what he's doing. Neither do you. I do love the paintings though . . . fabulous . . .' But Bobby doesn't care – he does at least have respect for Bent Lewis taking a chance on him, after all it's not every day a lad from his town gets an exhibition in the magical city of London. He swallows a few more cupfuls of wine then tries to escape from the pissed-up knobhead, the problem with these events being you can end up getting lumbered with soul-destroying dreary people. Bobby tells the knobhead, 'Actually mate, I'm dying for a lag. Cheerio,' then heads sharpish to the tablecloth again for another top-up then down to the bog in the basement. Down there, it's a white room as well and he wonders if the three mirrors screwed to the wall are art too. He splashes his face, then stares at himself and tries to tell himself it's okay and he's famous and he's happy. But he just feels drunk, not particularly happy, and when he gets back upstairs in the gallery he tries to avoid everyone's glances. At one point, he finds himself mumbling sweet nothings to the joyful Georgie of 'Stripy Socks' (45x35cm), when suddenly Bent Lewis bowls over and mutters in his stuttery ears, 'Bobby, mate, I'm about to introduce you to Francis Fuller, a *very* important art dealer. He's just offered me three point six K for "The Angels". He's really worth getting to know . . .' Suddenly face-to-face with Francis the important art dealer, Bobby the Artist has to fishing-line himself out of all that sprawling drunken water for a moment, shaking the guy's hand and giving him a reasonable smile. Francis Fuller, dressed head-to-toe in indigo with a turquoise shirt underneath like the Joker out of *Batman*, grins under his stuck-up nose and babbles, 'Very pleased to meet you, Bobby. I'm so very impressed with the exhibition. Very interesting hang. In particular, I absolutely adore "The Angles", there's something so tneconni dna lufecaep about it and I'm desaelp ylbidercni os to put in an offer dnif uoy epoh I hcihw substantial.' Bobby's so pissed he can't make head nor tail what Francis is saying, but he tries to appear interested and jovial, and he keeps repeating, 'That's mint, sound, cheers, that's mint, yeah it's dead exciting exciting exciting . . .' He bobs his head this way and that, then he slurs, 'You haven't got more coke, have you? This party's a bit fucking shite if you ask me, er . . .' Bent Lewis snorts and raises an eyebrow, then decides to usher Bobby the Artist outside the gallery before he makes any more ludicrous comments. But Bobby knows he's right – what kind of party is it if he's not with his friends and he's not got Georgie and he's not got anything to talk to anyone about. Inside there, it's like a silly sort of gladiators where all these pricks compete against each other to see who's the most powerful or most wealthy or most talented, except no one ever wins. Out on the humming humid street, Bent Lewis ruffles Bobby's hair and giggles, 'You're quite *wrecked*, aren't you, Bobby?' The Artist looks at him through fishy porthole eyes, then a sudden sort of clarity comes over him and he says, 'Too right. Look, Lewis, maybe me and you should get ourselves to a boozer or summat. Get out of here and that . . .' Bent Lewis glances down the road, then back into the fluorescent gallery. It's his opening night and part of him wants to stay and entertain all the wonderful people, but he's also weirdly magnetised to Bobby, and he swings a lanky arm round the Artist. Bent Lewis suggests they take a cab to the Colony Room, which is this members-only club where lots of famous artists like to get drunk. Lewis thinks he can get in, so he sticks his arm out into the road then sticks Bobby the Piss Artist in the back, and they both ride off bumpy bumpy into Soho. The lights all turn to stripes. When the boys get to Dean Street, Bent Lewis pays the driver (who can't wait to get home and tell the wife about the two strange benders he drove to the Colony, singing 'Live Forever' at the tops of their voices) then he leads Bobby up the rickety staircase and into the club. It's like being in an emerald, all of it painted green with a mish-mash of modern art stuck to the walls and a few mirrors and all your favourite records blasting out the hi-fi. Bent Lewis nods his head at a few of the other heads in there, then gives Bobby a twenty to get a bottle of cider named after André Breton. Bobby's eyes are still all over the place but he manages to say the right words to the barman. He wonders if Francis Bacon ever wobbled in the same spot as him. It's a bit like your living room, only full of artworks and famous people and a fully stocked booze cabinet. Bobby the Artist doesn't recognise any celebs or anyone, but then again he hardly recognises his own face when he clocks himself in one of the mirrors. He hasn't shaven for donkeys, and the yellow argyle has started sagging round his frame like a wet towel, and his eyes are just sacks with eyeballs sticking out the tops. He leans on the bar while Bent Lewis chats to a few people, foot tapping to Britpop and tongue lapping at André Breton. Soon he's absolutely wasted, every sip sending him a bit loopy like his brain's on a turntable and someone keeps switching it on and off. He's enjoying himself! The crack with the Colony is it's a teeny place so everyone's sort of encouraged to make conversation with each other, and now and then someone comes over and asks what Bobby does (Art? Writing? Rock star?) and he manages to mumble 'Artist' and ramble a bit of shite or other before slinking off back to his drink. He supposes the downside of the place is it's also very difficult to get away from anyone, although when Bent Lewis returns from all his little conversations he happens to have a bit of speed in his pocket and he offers Bobby in the bog with him. There's only one loo so they squeeze in tight together, and they hoover two healthy lines up their hooters. Bobby slurps a bit of sloppy white bogey down his throat, then blinks at Lewis and goes, 'Nice one, Lewis. I was starting to get a bit spazzy like on the drink; I'm sound now. Cheers, matey, for everything and . . . and, you know, the exhibition's mint and that . . .' Bobby's baggy eyes are shiny with tears but it's just the drinkie-winkies making him all daft and sentimental, and Bent Lewis sort of reads it wrong and starts stroking Bobby's face and looking deep into those beautiful globular eyes of his. The two of them stand silently on the chessboard toilet floor, and Bent Lewis that stupid old queen tries to make a move on Bobby, putting an arm round his waist and slanting his face sideways for a bit of a kiss. Bobby the Artist's heart bursts at first, then he sort of shoves Bent Lewis and slobbers, 'Ah soz, naw . . . naw . . .' Then he fumbles with the lock and staggers quickly out of the lavatory, feeling sickened at first then slightly distraught for Lewis, and he turns back and says to him, 'Soz, you know, you're sound and that, I like you . . . we're mates, aren't we . . .' Bent Lewis, slightly subdued, nods his face then pats Bobby gingerly on the back and he's pissed as well and all he can say is, 'I'm sorry, I'm sorry, haw haw haw . . . good speed, though. Here, you have the rest . . .' Bobby smiles, feeling strangely sober now, and he goes back to the bar to enjoy the speedy buzz on his own and spend more of Lewis's twenty on drinks while the gayboy flounces round the green walls trying to 'get contacts' as well as get a blow-job. And all of a sudden it's really entertaining to watch him; the stuffy art world doesn't seem so serious any more, although when Bent Lewis finally persuades another poor victim (this time, a first-time author from the South West who writes about conceptual Cornish pasties) into the bathroom with another chat-up line, Bobby the Artist decides it's time to go and he says bye-bye to the barman then nips invisibly down the stairs, like a ghost without his white sheet on. Back out on the bustling Soho streets, Chinks chinking glasses in Chinky restaurants and promoters promoting and tourists getting attracted by all the tourist attractions, Bobby decides the night's still fairly young and he searches for a while for somewhere else to drink, but after eleven in the West End it seems the only places open are trendy annoying clubs with banging choons on and beautiful people outside with clipboards picking beautiful/rich people off the street to come and play in their shite tacky discotheques. So Bobby thinks fuck it and walks back to his hotel in ever-so-slight despair. Everyone gets in his way. He's just about to have a big real-life cry, pissed and missing Georgie-weorgie again, when suddenly he remembers the mini-bar sitting untouched in his stark-white room. Hopefully the gallery won't mind paying for one more night of debauchery. After Bent Lewis's gay escapades in the Colon Room, Bobby thinks to himself, 'Fuck it; I could always bribe the cunt, couldn't I . . .' FRIDAY: Bobby the Artist's London adventure ends with him on the tube back to Victoria at four in the afternoon, head full of little builders bashing him with big hammers. He stayed in bed this morning with another foul hangover, answering calls to various snobby art dealers and agents and scouts and magazines and pests. So far 'The Angels' (244x233cm), 'Bobby's Favourite Trip' (120x150cm), 'Channel Alan' (200x151$\frac{3}{4}$cm) and 'Boozy Bastard Bashes Bird' (21x58cm) have been sold to collectors for lots of pounds, and yet still Bobby was laid under the covers without a penny to his name. It's all very well being on expenses, but you've got to have money in the first place to exchange for lovely things and receipts. So Bobby mustered up the courage to tube across the city, to borrow £350 off Bent Lewis. In actual fact he only intended to ask for three pound fifty for a few more cans, but when he said the words 'three fifty' he couldn't exactly decline the gadge posting hundreds of pounds into his hand. Bent Lewis seemed quite sheepish after last night's fun and games, and Bobby used it to his advantage, walking out of there with a couple of left-over bottles of Moët and some +!Gallery stationery. He staggered away from the gallery feeling like a prince. He could get used to all this free money. As a treat for Georgie, he stopped off at the Trocadero to get her a luxury pick-'n'-mix, but now he's sat down down down in the deep dark tube all the sweets are starting to sweat and turn to mush. He scratches a spot under his mop-top, trying to avoid looking at everyone not looking at him on the busy train. As the tunnels and platforms zip by and the doors open close open close, Bobby grips the £350 in his pocket, thinking up ways to spend it like all the paint materials in the world, all the fancy dinners him and Georgie could eat, all the nights out dancing and cavorting, all the pills, thrills, and paying off all the bills. At Warren Street, the carriage is still packed and a tramp gets on and starts this dramatic speech about being homeless and needing only £1.84 to get into a hostel tonight for a roof over his head and a good square meal. The squarest meal Bobby can think of would be Bird's Eye potato waffles. The tramp looks like quite a sad character in this oversized denim jacket and grey stubble like Pinhead out of *Hellraiser*, and in a way he wants to help him but when he delves into his pocket for change there's nothing but the roll of twenties, and he doesn't really have the will to hand any of that over. But then he feels like such a cunt – the tramp steps empty-handed off the silent, menacing train at Green Park, and suddenly Bobby realises he's just as shitty and ignorant as everyone else. London people are so cold and miserable and weird, and so is he. All stunned and trembly, Bobby the Artist gets up to chase after the tramp but then suddenly the doors start beeping and shutting and he doesn't know what to do and half as a hesitation and half as a punishment he lets the doors shut on his head and he yelps and feels his brain crush like a big strawberry in a vice. Everybody stares as Bobby flops back into his seat, hair all flat and eyes waterfalling. He feels so guilty for having so much money so unexpectedly. He feels like a twat and he wants to go home. He winces as a violet bump rises on the top of his bonce, but he doesn't want to give it a rub in front of these people because it'll only give them the satisfaction of having seen him hurt himself and they'll laugh. He waits till he's safely in busy Victoria coach station, and he hides in a café toilet and sadly checks his head for blood but he's okay. He's alright. Bobby clutches the candy-stripe candy bag as he walks to the right gate, past all those grey depressive faces of people not wanting to go home (or they're just knackered and grumpy), and he says one last goodbye to London but to be honest he's not bothered if he never sees it again. The long journey home's actually quite enjoyable, packed on the bus with those beautiful sane people of the North East, chatting away about the football and getting out on the lash as soon as they get back. It's a Friday, after all. Bobby the Artist drifts off into a bit of a sleep round about the Midlands, all their voices permeating his dreams like lines from a script typewritten by his brain, and they're happy dreams. Oh the accents! He wakes up well before he has to get off, but it takes about an hour to adjust to wakey wakeyness and he's still a bit groggy as he stumbles about the bus station of his home town, looking for Georgie. The bus station's very brown – like all the walls are covered in Dairy Milks – and Georgie stands out in her pastel blue power-suit, standing over there by the butcher's. She looks like Basquiat's muse Suzanne Mallouk with her Love That Red lipstick, and Bobby runs over and grabs her and kisses it off her. She's been to the hairdressers today and had a brutal bob done, and she looks so delightfully different, as if they've been apart for months and months and months. 'I love you I love you,' is all Bobby can really tell Georgie about London. He's not in the mood to go into the exhibition, the wankers, the Colony, the coke ladies and the tramp, and they get the 65 back home talking about the tower block instead. He's missed it so much, or rather he's missed the people who live in it and the town it sits on. Scuttling through the streets all grey and boring and wonderful, Bobby the Artist squeezes Georgie in absolute rapture – it's funny how important it is to have someone there to kiss and cuddle when your life starts getting all intense and weird. He gives Georgie the sweets, and her mirrorball eyes reel back at all the pretty gummies and fizzies and chewies and chockies. 'As if they do sour cherries in London!' she squeals, kissing him non-stop with candy coming out of her gob. Georgie's in heaven – it's been lonely and also slightly frightening not having Bobby in the flat with her, Georgie having to fill the double- bed with her petite frame, cooking for one, and the silence silence silence. Plus the horrible, sad experience of not being touched for one week. So, once they make it back home and get the door locked and jump crash-bang-wallop onto the comfy bed, Bobby the Artist and Georgie the eighties throwback throw back the covers and roll around creasing them up, hugging each other to death and giving each other very passionate exaggerated kisses, making up for lost time. Bobby nuzzles his face into Georgie's perfume-counter neck, then he comes back up for air and says, 'Ah, I've got this for you too!' He whips out the money in his trousers and gives Georgie the £100 he owes her for rent, then he kisses her a bit more, and a little bit more after that. Georgie's ecstatic – she stares at the money in wonder for a moment, then gets back to stuffing her face in the sweet bag. Grinning, Bobby the Artist decides to leave her to it, sneaking off to the bathroom 'for a wee' then fumbling with that wrap of speed Lewis gave him and snorting a good healthy line up his left nostril. Since London Bobby's been favouring the left nostril after the right one became a bit bloody and scabby round the edges, and it's much too tempting to pick your scabs and now he's made quite a mess of it. Being right-handed it seems most natural to snort your drugs up the right nostril, but Bobby's worried he'll lose his septum although it might mean he could do a head-stand and tip powder right down his conk and never have to chop up lines again. Bobby used to love the rit-ual of lining up white powder like a giant snow-plough, but compared to just guzzling up a pill it is a bit of a rigmarole. But so what – Bobby's got drugs in his system and he's got his girlfriend back and he's happy! He wraps up the wrap again and taps it into his Magic Pocket, and he strolls back into the lounge with a deadpan sort of expression. Georgie's too busy pol-ishing off the pick-'n'-mix to notice a speedy glint in her boy's eye, and she smiles and tosses him a white chocolate mouse and says, 'Squeak!' Bobby the Artist munches down the rodent before his appetite com-pletely disappears, then hops next to Georgie and throws his arms round her like a scarf. He nuzzles her neck a little bit, then tells her he loves her and Georgie goes 'aah', all drunk on sweets, and says back, 'I love you too! I'm dead proud of you, darling . . .' In a bit Georgie goes through to the bedroom and slips on her comfy netball uniform (her position was always GD), and Bobby slips into the bathroom again and sniffs another white slug off the toilet cover. A sparky silver thread spins up his nervous system, and for a bit Bobby just dithers in the bathroom gurning slightly and feel-ing excited about every toiletry and every fitting and every surface in the little white room. For a millisec-

162

ond he wants to give the bathroom a good spring-clean and he almost gets the detergents out, but then he gets his bearings back and remembers Georgie and he bounces out the door knocking over the Toilet Duck. 'Quack,' says the duck, meaning ouch. Bobby tries to harness feeling so supercharged as he steps into the living room again, but when he sees Georgie in the pleated navy skirt and she hugs him all tight and lovely and kisses him first on the cheek then the lips then the neck, Bobby the Artist feels his heart speed up and his lungs turn to butterfly wings pumping glorious silver sequins round his airways. *Let's have sex*, they think simultaneously, couples having strange mind-reading powers after months and months of trying to figure each other out. Panting, Georgie starts rubbing her hands round Bobby's biological erogenous zones, turning his trousers into a tent with lots of rude organs camping underneath. Bobby sucks all the freckles and moles off her chest, pulling the GD bib wheeeeeeeeeee over her head and flicking Georgie's turquoise bra off her shoulders then kissing her tits, and he's got so much energy – plus he's very impatient – Bobby tugs off his sweaty sweater himself and gives Georgie a helping hand with his zip. Then comes the enormous anticipation of someone putting their mitts on your cock and balls. Georgie smiles to herself and keeps him hanging on for a bit, which in a way is even better though it makes the Artist want to explode and after one or two tugs he moans 'whoah' then screams '*whoah!*' and Georgie lets go giggling, then suddenly her face is all serious and Bobby pulls her polished pine legs apart and slithers a hand up her skirt where her fanny's got a bit of five o'clock shadow like a pin cushion but her lips are nice and slippy, and he slides some lubricunt round and round, mixing clockwise with anticlockwise with figure 8 until Georgie's shagging the air with pleasure bashing her feet about. Then, Bobby starts scrabbling frantically across the carpet for Mr Condom, sending five or six multicolour Durexes flying through the air, and he struggles getting the packet open and Georgie has to roll Mr Condom down Mr Penis for him and she has to help insert him into Mrs Vagina. They shag at double-speed: Inthekitchentheydospoonsonthebreakfastbaramongstallthecutlerythenin thebathroomtheyshowereachotherwithhotkissesandGe orgiekneelsonthepisserwhileBobbydoesheruptheshitter thenintheloungetheybounceupanddownonthesofa theninthebedroomtheysqueakthespringsofthemattress. Meanwhile, down in Vaginaland, Mr Condom's beginning to feel a bit iffy. He's overheating. For some reason, the shagging seems to be twice as fast this evening, and he grimaces as he gets flung willy-nilly in and out of the pink tunnel. He starts getting friction burns, hanging onto Bobby's stiff penis for dear life, headbutting Georgie's cervix at 180 beats per minute. 'Help me!' he yells in the darkness, feeling himself melting. The sex only seems to be getting faster though, and Mr Condom squeezes his eyes shut as Bobby groans and the friction starts getting unbearable and Mr Condom thinks he's going to be sick and the searing pain the searing pain and Bobby groans again and suddenly squirts a gallon of white molten lava from his Jap's eye, exploding through Mr Condom's heavy reservoir end and Mr Condom screams and screams and vomits ice cream into Georgie's vagina. Shivering and spasming, Bobby suddenly feels the endorphins kick in and he falls onto the carpet with a happy bump. Georgie's all smiley too, and for a minute the flat's silent except for the delicate surround-sound of creaking footsteps, doors going open-shut, mumbling kids, and TV crackle. All pooped, Georgie shuts her peepers, looking forward to a post-coital cuddle and perhaps more sweets, but when she reopens them Bobby's back in the bathroom doing another line of speed then he's all hyper again and he jumps back into his clothes and jumps out the door in a sudden flash of yellow argyle. Fickle bastard. Panting heavily, Bobby charges up one flight of stairs with money falling out of his pockets. Before he forgets, he zips round Johnnie's to pay back the £200 ticky, and rid himself of more stinky lucre. It's one of the only wondrous feelings money can really give you – giving it to someone else. Bobby the Artist feels like some sort of Father Christmas figure as he stands outside 5E, oblivious now to how tight-arsed he felt this morning in London. Johnnie answers the door in his Boro dressing-gown, at first looking all unkempt and glum but then he clocks the Artist and a smile rises on his face like an upside-down rainbow, and he gives him a hug. 'How do, Bobby! How was the what-do-you-call-it-again? The Smoke?' Johnnie asks, teeth chattering. 'Sound, sound,' Bobby replies instinctively, but then he really thinks about it and adds, 'Ah, it was crap. I'm glad to be back like.' Johnnie nods, scratching his knackers under the flannely fabric. 'Aye right, the South's full of dickhead wankers, isn't it,' Johnnie states, not that he really knows or anything. Johnnie leans his shoulder against the doorframe, feeling a little bit exhausted with life but he's happy to talk. Since Bobby left for London, Ellen's been sleeping round Johnnie's every night, but instead of sex they've just been having excruciating, boring cuddles and dry kisses. Despite Johnnie's best efforts to suggest new things such as tying each other up, role-playing, sado-masochism, or giving each other foreplay, Ellen just doesn't seem interested in shagging him any more. He's frustrated. On Wednesday afternoon he bought a handful of men's magazines, hoping to amass a ton of new sex techniques and try them out on Ellen, but all the lurid lusty girls in the photos just disheartened him because they all seem so up for sex and being right sordid little minxes, whereas Ellen (and all other real-life girls, for that matter) don't want your willy twenty-four hours a day, and they don't always want to suck it on demand. But it's not like Johnnie really wants all that, he just wants to know she's still into him. He feels like he's losing her again, after that terrible, terrible performance on Indie Night. What a flop. When Bobby called by, him and Ellen were napping in the messy boudoir, or at least Her Majesty was – Johnnie can't sleep nowadays, for the fear she's dreaming of sleeping with someone else, or dreaming up ways to get rid of him. He's frightened they're just going to end up as 'friends'. He's been getting pissed on his own at the Brambles Farm Hotel and getting into fights with strangers and locals – on Tuesday evening he battered Joe Lucy because he might've accidentally looked at Ellen's legs. Johnnie's started stealing from his grandmother and stealing from the newsagent down the road (they've got a 'no-run' policy, so if you get out the door you're home and dry), desperately trying to please Ellen with gifts such as fags and pizzas and pasties out of Greggs, and he feels like a bit of an arsehole. 'You feeling alright?' Bobby the Artist asks, snapping Johnnie out of the gloomy daze. Johnnie nods – he's not the sort of person to whinge whinge whinge, like a fanny – he doesn't want any attention, he just wants to 'Go for a pint in a bit?' Naturally Bob's eyes sparkle over with bright Dulux varnish, and he grins and says, 'Yeah, yeah, defo. But first, Johnnie, I've got something to give you. Here's that ticky I owe you.' His fingers are twitching with joy as he hands over the £200, and it's worth every penny to see all Johnnie's frown lines and crow's feet melt away like he's just put on Oil of Olay. Johnnie hugs Bobby again, and the first thing he does is hide it away in the empty *Anal Adventures* video where Ellen won't find it, then he goes back in the bedroom to get changed and say goodbye to the mannequin. He feels brighter stepping down the steps with Bobby. The Artist feels lighter to have all that money out of his hands – he thinks the best days of your life are definitely those days with no pennies in your pocket where you still manage to get by and have a good time, you and your mates sacrificing food for booze and occasionally finding the money to buy each other a drink or two, all of you in the same bittersweet boat and all of you paddling the oars together. But now it feels weird to be rich and famous, money having that strange curse that makes you seem like a tight twat if you don't automatically throw it at all your friends and neighbours. For now Bobby can smile and enjoy the peasant life again down the pub with Johnnie, but merely days later his phone's overloaded with the squeals and whines of art collectors and magazines, and cheques for £2,000 and £3,000 and millions and trillions of pounds start dropping through the letterbox (or, rather, appearing in the post-racks, since they don't have a letterbox). Bobby feels like a scared little girl under an acid rainfall of gold coins. His initial reaction is to run and hide behind the sofa (especially when getting hounded by pretentious journalists asking 'the meaning' of this and that, or the 'context' or the 'blah blah blah'), but you can always turn your phone off or flush it down the toilet, and when Bobby does get a quiet moment in the flat to really think about his new stardom, it does actually seem pretty incredible. Okay, so it's all a wild whirlwind Bobby's got no control over, but at least he doesn't have to work in an office and he doesn't have a shitty boss to answer to and he'll never have to make shitty conversation with anyone over a shitty water-cooler. So, instead of chucking the money out the window, Bobby decides to get on with it and enjoy the high life – he spends his pennies on one hundred ecstasy pills, fifty tabs of acid, twenty-five grams of coke and twenty-five grams of ket (to be mixed into the powerful concoction known as CK). He comes home from Lidl with a trolley full of exotic wines, spirits and beers (he doesn't mind losing the quid he pushed in the trolley slot), and him and Georgie spend the whole of an evening arranging a bar in the kitchen then drinking it. One morning, high on the CK stuff and wandering around town like a circus clown scaring children, Bobby pops into Bhs and orders Georgie to make herself a £100 pick-'n'-mix, much to the amusement of the mams and nans passing through but much to the disgust of her boss Mr Hawkson, who hates to see Georgie going out with such a dreadful tramp, although he doesn't realise it's acceptable to look this way nowadays. Georgie doesn't give a shite – she loves Bobby's big heart and big old argyle sweaters, although the £100 pick-'n'-mix does subsequently fill her out quite a bit and it causes them both some dismay. However, by this time Bobby's on a strict diet of pills-on-toast for breakfast, acid for dinner and CK for tea, and his attention begins wandering elsewhere. Oh, and his trousers start dropping off his hipbones. As soon as his picture's printed on the front of the *Gazette* with the headline LOCAL ARTIST MAKES IT BIG! (with Bobby standing all gay and moody next to 'The Angels'), lots of people from the tower block start drooling over him and sucking up to him and telling all their friends about him and then yelling at them to get their hands off him, he's theirs. The girls Ellen, Mandy and Pamela start paying a lot more attention to him, popping down to his flat when Georgie's at work, for a line of CK or a free ten-pound note, and soon they start adopting the role of groupies, or stalkers. Bobby begins to enjoy the power money gives him, and – on top of the heroic drug intake – the rickety fence between dream and reality starts to float away in the wind. In days of yore, artists used to pay prostitutes to lie about naked in front of canvases, pretending to be religious figures, and one afternoon Pamela comes down for a smoke and Bobby offers her £50 to pose topless for 'Lady From Upstairs'

(41x123cm), which she accepts. And before you know it, word gets around and soon all the girls are sitting for Bobby, competing against each other to get their hands in the Artist's pants, and pockets. They think he might be able to make them famous too. And it's hard not to get swept up in all the commotion – Bobby starts acting strange, living up to his famous artist status, buying expensive argyles from the Scottish Highlands to paint in (not like those Pringle knock-offs Johnnie found round the back of Binns a year back), throwing money at girls, painting them in various shades and sizes, buying Johnnie and Ellen lots of Americanos. He even starts huffing Chanel instead of Lynx, and one psychedelic afternoon in September he accidentally swallows ten tabs of acid while sitting on the toilet. Bobby starts mumbling to himself, gurgling, the shapes of sinks becoming white elephants with beady winking eyes, and the clownfishes on the bath curtain darting about chattering to each other. For a minute he thinks he's Salvador Dalí, growing a curly moustache in the mirror. *Hola!* Salvador laughs – he can't even tell if his eyes are open or shut or not. Freaking out, Salvador puts his head in his hands, serving another gust of Chanel into his sleeve. Watch out Sal, here comes the automatic writing! Holistic chicken made tea don't you hedgerow all oil trousers ink sprayed salmon on its chest possibly a frog leopard print snout man looking grumpy boulevard legs eleven prostitute hamsters won fifty pounds at a masquerade after leaving four cups of juicy lemon spiked a nut on the dame of Duke York post-natal dream dismay and a forehead keeps singing on the phone to conker forest of evil and wormy stretch ouch bastard gondolier tra la la Cornetto Tonga hand grenade hooray hippo snarling under grasp only showing remorse for the budgie that sung sweetly so sweetly but died after having injection to the neck holy water tomato onion banana ketchup see-saw then Ellen Ellen Ellen. 'Bobby, what are you doing?' Ellen asks, stepping into the bathroom and it's really her, not a mirage. 'I let myself in, door was open,' she continues, fluffing her gold hair. She looks at Bobby the Artist laid upside-down in the bath, arms and legs flailing. He rubs his eyes. He mumbles something quite bonkers like, 'I'm fishing,' then he sits up really straight and says, 'Fuck. What are you doing here?' Ellen smiles, strokes her hair again, then replies, 'Well, you said you were going to paint me, remember?' Ellen, like the other girls in the block, has started taking a real shine to Bobby – in fact, she's always thought he's very attractive and different and lovely, and the past few days she's enjoyed coming round and watching him draw and smoking draw with him. Bobby doesn't remember saying he'd paint her, but then again he doesn't even remember the clownfish now, and he starts to stand up and get his head together like a thousand puzzle pieces chucked across the floor. The acid's still going strong and real-life objects keep turning to dreams and dreams keep turning to objects, and to be honest the idea of painting in such a psychotic state excites him very much. Bobby the Artist slides into the living room with his back against the wall, avoiding the white water rapids in the closet, then finds any old bit of canvas and pins it to his brand-new multipurpose easel. He squirts fresh acrylic onto a fresh palette, watching in awe the multicoloured dog turds squirting out of the tubes. 'So, how do you want me?' Ellen asks, biting her tongue. She can tell Bobby's off his rocker, but she's had a litre of vodka and all, and she tries to stand there all provocative in her Lycra top and blue miniskirt. Bobby, distracted for a second by the VCR smiling at him, blinks once or twice then says to Ellen, 'Aw, however you want . . . do what you want.' Ellen turns her lips into a sort of red heart-shape, still twizzling that lemon hair of hers. 'Shall we take this into the bedroom?' she asks with eyebrows like archways, and Bobby's a bit too fucked to really understand the proposition. 'Sound, well er, well the easel's a bit bulky like but . . . alright then,' he mumbles. He drags the easel leg by leg into the boudoir, Ellen licking her lips and getting all randy and excited. 'Horny little cunts,' says the VCR, behind their backs. In the bronze bedroom, Ellen stands perfectly still by the window, adopting a languid pose while Bobby takes ages setting up the canvas again. He thinks he sees a winking hippo in his pile of argyle sweaters, the whole room pulsing with joy. He starts laughing hysterically. Sniffing, Ellen does a dramatic yawn then suggests, 'I can take all my clothes off, if you want?' She knows there's a couple of hours before Georgie gets home, and she's sure Georgie wouldn't feed her raw razor blades even if they did get up to something naughty. Suddenly waking up, Bobby the Artist gulps then grins and says, 'Oh aye, sound. I'll give you some coin, like . . .' Ellen's eyes fl-flicker like light-bulbs as Bobby delves into one of his argyle socks, removing a few twenty pound notes and handing them to Ellen in super slow-motion. She finds it quite arousing being treated like a sort of harlot and, as she posts the money into her fake Prada handbag, she wonders just how she'll get Bobby's clothes off as well. 'You're dead sweet,' she breathes. Blinking casually, Ellen pulls off her tight Lycra top like a peeled banana, but instead of yellow flesh she's got tanning underneath and her best bra from H&M. Her heart's pumping. She thinks she prefers shagging random lads rather than despairing all the time over regular, monotonous sex. *Ah, if only Johnnie was a stallion in bed*, she thinks to herself, unsnapping her bra and flinging it all choreographed over Bobby's easel. Her and the lasses from upstairs once went to lap-dancing classes at a workshop in Newcastle – to impress their fellas as well as getting a bit in shape – and Ellen swivels her hips like a sultry cobra while Bobby the Artist gets his brushes together. He's intrigued at how soft and malleable the wood feels in his fingers. They almost seem to droop in his hands like Dalí's floppy clocks, and he sings a few bars of laughter in his head. It's only when Ellen shimmies her blue skirt down her legs and pulls down her pants that Bobby snaps out of it. Sometimes seeing beautiful girls naked can be a slight disappointment (after all, clothes were invented to hide all your shameful bits), but Ellen standing there all perfect and naked and with shaved doo-dah and pyramid tits makes Bobby's hands tremble, and all the brushes plop out of his fingers like a pile of slimy snakes. Ellen lets out a little embarrassed giggle for him, and she thinks Bobby looks even cuter as he bends over like Mr Stretchy to pick them up again, and she says to him, 'Don't worry about them. *Leave them.*' She does a little cough, waiting for Bobby to pounce on her, but he just stands up again all flustered and says, 'Aw right, yeah, good idea; I'll get the palette knives out.' Ellen chortles. She's a bit confused about Bobby's playing-hard-to-get behaviour, but he's definitely worth the effort. A little birdy (Georgie) once told her he's a brilliant shag and, although it does feel weird being stark naked in Georgie's bedroom, Ellen manages to keep focused. She strikes the ultimate slutty pose, hands on hips with tits aiming skyward and a face like a dribbling orgasmic puppy. 'Get on the bed then,' Bobby says, and she shudders with pleasure. She crawls pussycatty onto the bronze covers, all the springs underneath squeaking and giggling. Bobby's eyes are turning windmills. 'Fucking hell,' he drools, Ellen knelt in the doggy position with her holes exposed, opening and closing. She does wonder for a second if Bobby's going to take her there and then without any foreplay or even touching or kissing, but in the braincell next door to that one she thinks that might be rather spectacular too. But Bobby's got other things on his mind and, as he starts furiously slapping paint onto the raggy old bit of canvas, it quickly dawns on Ellen she's going to be crouched in that uncomfy position for at least half an hour, with not one whiff of sex. There's only that faint whiff of fresh acrylic paint, which is sort of chemicals mixed with fish piss. Bobby smiles to himself, blissfully unaware that he could've slotted his penis in her and she wouldn't care, instead feverishly painting with lots of pinks and creams and bubblegums. On the canvas, Ellen's skinny legs start to grow really stick-thin and exaggerated like a lanky Modigliani – it's a nice change not to be painting Georgie's chubby thighs for once. Oh, how many sweets that woman eats! He finds it strange how Georgie keeps complaining about getting fat but she still keeps nailing the Haribo, and it seems the more she talks about it, the bigger she gets. If only she could keep her mouth shut . . . Sighing a sizeable siren, Bobby the Artist carries on painting, adding spunky white where the light catches Ellen's thigh, creamy pink wiggly bits round her tits, and a squirt of blood-orange up her fanny hole. To be honest it's a bit of a shambles, all the colours flowing into each other and getting muddy, but it was Ellen's idea to paint it with a fucking palette knife, wasn't it. He's not sure what to do – everything looks so different on LSD (and so disappointing in the morning), and it's hard to tell what changes to make when the shapes keep changing themselves. After a bit, Ellen (still spread-eagled on the duvet cover) starts getting deep-vein thrombosis in her arms and legs – and she starts feeling silly being so exposed like that on Georgie's bed – and she asks Bobby, 'Are you nearly done yet?' Bobby steps back, blinking at the blob with fanny and bum on the canvas. '*Voilá*,' he says, adding one last splurge of pinky green yellow. Bobby's got a humdinger of a headache now the acid's beginning to wear off, like a beautiful tide going out leaving behind lots of rusty ships and rotting fish, and he flops onto the bed with a groan and a wail. Ellen blows out a scream of relief, then she quickly pulls on her fluorescent clothes again. She has a little shiver, then steps round the easel to inspect the 'Blob with Fanny and Bum' (?x?cm). Ellen smiles, feeling strangely aroused at Bobby having given her precious bits such close scrutiny. 'Nice arse, eh?' Ellen says to Bobby, trying one last time to get him turned on, but Bobby's just a broken toy on the bedcovers. He's so exhausted – it really takes it out of you, painting naked lasses. Ellen scrunches her face up, a bit drained herself and annoyed for not having gotten a shag, but to be fair Bobby looks completely dead – it's not worth raping him. Ellen has one last glance at herself on the canvas, then at Bobby facedown on the bed, then tugs another twenty or forty quid out of his argyle sock and leaves the flat. Bobby the Artist snores a little 'See you later' when the door slams, emotionally knackered but unable to sleep, like he's plugged into the a/c mains and he can't reach the switch to turn himself off. He lies there for five minutes with his eyes open but pushed pitch-black into the pillow, then he grumbles and gets up and puts on his kangaroo pyjamas, and tries again. But it's still no use – the tower block's too noisy, and his brain's too much of an open encyclopaedia with all the pages torn out and thrown about. When Georgie gets home from Bhs he can't really be bothered to talk to her, instead playing dead on the bedcovers while his head fizzes and pops and splutters. Georgie sniffs. She looks at him, then looks at the porny portrait of Ellen with sad glittery eyes, and retires to the living room to make soup and eat Cherry Drops on her own in silence. She doesn't see or speak to her boyfriend for the rest of the night, and in the morning when he wakes up and she's back in the Bhs, Bobby's skull still wrecks but with a little more clarity or reality in there, like someone's opened a few windows in his brain and let the day in. He wakes up to very aggressive knocking on the front door.

Sitting bolt upright in bed, Bobby rubs his matted sweaty hair, mouth full of shaving foam. 'Bobby?! Bobby?!' the front door yells, with a real tenseness in its voice. 'It's Johnnie – open up!' Bobby the Artist sniffs, wondering what Johnnie wants and why he sounds so irate. He thuds out of bed in his undercrackers, pulling on a pink argyle then sipping some old Soave and searching about for relevant trousers. Suddenly it dawns on Bobby he's got a naked picture of Johnnie's girlfriend standing there for all the world to see. Panicking, he quickly tugs on some corduroy drain-pipes, then scrabbles through the overturned rubbish for more paints and a paintbrush not completely caked in acrylic. 'Bobby!! Open the fucking door,' Johnnie stresses, sounding quite impatient. Bobby trembles. The portrait of Ellen towers over him all randy and deli-cious, bearing all the horrible sins of Bobby's pervy mind, like Dorian Gray doing a centrefold for *Men Only*. He's got no idea how he got Ellen in such an uncompromising position last night, and it's certainly not something he wants her boyfriend – the notorious jealous headcase – to lay his peepers on. So Bobby scoops big blobs of fluorescent green onto the horse-hair brush, and rapidly covers over Ellen's naked toosh with one thick stroke, then her left tit, then the whole of 'Blob with Fanny and Bum' (?x?cm). Breathing sharply, Bobby the Artist feels like such a cunt and falls cross-legged to the ground with a thud. All censored like that, the painting makes him think of this famous Gustav Klimt piece, which he learnt about at art col-lege down the Roman Road. 'Portrait of Adele Bloch-Bauer' is this wonderful gold thing, with Adele peep-ing out all serene from these huge pretty patterns covering the canvas. Well it turned out Gustav Klimt was shagging this bird Adele (who was the wife of a sugar baron, who'd paid him to do the portrait), and the crazy ornate patterns were just there to cover up the saucy naked sketches underneath. Gustav told the sugar baron the gold represented his wealth, and the poor unfortunate fellow was over the moon with it. 'Bobby!! Bobby!!' the front door screams again. 'Two seconds!' Bobby replies, trying to sound chirpy. He sways cautiously towards the shrieking door, then undoes the catch and gently swings it open. In storms Johnnie, face all red and sweaty, and armed with a hammer. It's an Estwing curved claw hammer, weighing in at 0.57kg, with a 2.5cm diameter polished steel head at one end, razor-sharp claw at the other, a 9cm long solid-forged neck, black rubber shock reduction grip with the Estwing logo printed on both sides, and Johnnie's right hand wrapped around it. It could easily pummel an artist's head in. 'Er, how's it going, friend?' Bobby asks softly, telling himself in his head he's a friend he's a friend he's a friend. Johnnie raises the hammer. 'What's going on with you and Ellen?!' he squeals, purple veins popping out of his forehead like strangled worms. 'Er,' Bobby mumbles, feeling a bit dumb. 'I know all them lasses from upstairs are coming down and getting their tits out for you,' Johnnie snaps, throwing his left hand at all the softcore canvases perched behind the fluorescent green abstract expressionist one, 'Katey's obsessed with you now, lucky cunt. I know Ellen's been down here, and all. And she came back with loads of money last night . . . Have you fucking shagged her or something? Are you shagging all of them?' Johnnie starts to speak really panicky, and it's typical of him to wind himself up all the time to the point of frenzy, and he ends up clutching the walls and frothing at the mouth. His heart feels like a wrecking-ball, and it pounds his insides. Bobby the Artist puts his hands up in mercy, then tries to pat Johnnie on the side and say, 'I couldn't cheat on Georgie, don't worry, mate.' Johnnie's hand slackens on the hammer grip, and his eyes dip like flying saucers as he speaks. 'You've got it so fucking good though, Bobby. I mean, as if all the birds are all over you now . . . bastard . . . God, if you've fucking laid a finger on Ellen . . .' Johnnie's fist tightens again. He's so desperate to put that hammerhead through somebody's skull, and out the other side. Sniffling, Bobby explains, 'Johnnie, I know I'm getting popular and that, but there's no need to go mad . . . Erm, I'm going to be in demand, know what I mean? It's natural,' though he definitely feels like a wanker standing amongst all the porny pictures of ladies in their underduds. 'All these lasses mean nowt to me,' he continues, 'they're just models. You know, like, mannequins. I've just been getting wrecked, you know, painting them in a daze and that. Half the time I don't even know they're naked. You're not missing much.' As if to prove his point, Bobby the Artist starts scrabbling through the litter round the TV, searching for something. He chucks video cases and acrylic tubes and old sweets out from underneath him, like an ostrich burying its head in the carpet. Johnnie raises an eyebrow. Half a minute later Bobby comes up trumps, handing Johnnie a scuffed VCR tape with 'Un Hommage de Monsieur

Condom, 2005' emblazoned on the sleeve. 'Look, Johnnie, here, have this video. I don't know if it's any consolation like, but it's got me and Georgie shagging on it. I might've seen the girls upstairs with their tits out and that, but this is proper off it . . . Georgie's fanny and that . . . go on, take it, I don't mind.' At first Johnnie feels sickened by such a weird gesture, but then again he is an avid fan of pornography, and he clutches the video in a sweaty claw. Now he's not sure if he wants to punch a wall down or pull his pants down. 'You dirty bastard,' Johnnie scoffs. Bobby the Artist puts his hands in the surrender position again. He knows that – when faced with madheads of Johnnie's nature – it's best just to smile and nod and agree with them. Bobby sniffs up a few wet bogies, then strokes his own hair nervously and says, 'Howay, Johnnie, we're mates, me and you. Look, here, have this as well . . .' And Bobby rifles through his pockets for another fifty or sixty quid, and handshakes it into Johnnie's palm. Johnnie's eyes brighten, then he slowly starts to grin again and hugs Bobby round the neck. The hammer goes plonk to the ground. 'Cheers, man,' he says, feeling daft now for going so schizo. Bobby the Artist feels like a bit of a knob and all. The two of them stand silently in the faint glow of white clouds, not sure what else to say, and Bobby puts on one of the jangly Stone Roses best ofs to try and lighten the mood. 'Fools Gold' twangs out of the rusty speakers – that song about how people who come into a bit of money can turn into complete dicks. Shuddering, Bobby the Artist looks to the ground. He's starting to hate himself. It's all very well bribing Johnnie to avoid a hammer through the face, but somehow Bobby feels his personality's getting taken over completely by money. The other day Georgie caught him constructing a house out of money, the pound coins all elegant pillars and stairways, and the notes all lovely balconies and mezzanine floors. Soon all his paintings will be about arrogance and greed and backstabbing. Sighing, Bobby the Artist watches a bird flop past the window. Johnnie clutches the money in his Henri Lloyd jacket, feeling a lot calmer, and with Bambi-ish eyes he tells Bobby, 'Soz, you know, for having a go at you. I, I know you wouldn't fuck about with Ellen . . .' Bobby the Artist tries to interject and say all those typical things like no-no-it's-alright and don't-be-daft, but Johnnie stops him midbreath and continues, 'You're a good mate of mine . . . it's just I've been fucking frustrated recently like . . .' Bobby picks a bit of fluorescent green out of his fingernail, looking at the carpet, then he glances at Johnnie and asks, 'How come?' Johnnie flaps his eyelids like big Chinese fans, then he sighs the word 'Urrgh!' and explains, 'I feel daft for saying it like, but I'm going through a shit patch with Ellen. I mean, don't get me wrong, I'm a mint shag and that, it's just I'm having a bit of trouble pleasing her, you know, in the sack and that. It's driving me mad. I dunno what's wrong with me.' Bobby the Artist continues staring at the carpet while Johnnie speaks, feeling a bit guilty and embarrassed listening to a hardcase speaking so candidly about his shit sex-life. Bobby rubs his neck nervously, then offers, 'Erm, I'm sure you'll be alright. She loves you.' Johnnie's eyebrows do a Mexican wave, then his face drops again and he says, 'But it's not alright, mate.

I'm serious. It's like, I keep blowing my load dead early, or I can't get it up, or she's dry as owt . . .' Bobby suppresses a snigger in his belly. Johnnie almost starts gyrating in the doorway, all the stress and panic getting to him again, but Bobby pats his tense shoulder and looks him in the eye and suggests, 'Look, Johnnie, maybe you've just got to relax a bit. I mean, take her out for a romantic meal or something – girls go mad for that. Take things slow, treat her nice and all that . . . just *relax*. And watch that video – maybe me and Georgie can teach you a thing or two!' Johnnie smirks. As Bobby speaks, he starts to take on the appearance of some sort of oracle or agony uncle, and there's something about Bobby's soothing smoky voice that seeps into Johnnie's psyche and turns all his raging lava into pink cotton wool. Johnnie realises he's been a bit of a cunt recently, a bit of a fucking drama queen. Blinking and breathing softer softer, Johnnie stumbles round the flat, picking up a mucky ashtray, putting it back down. He feels embarrassed. 'Look, I'd better go,' he murmurs, edging towards the door again. 'My mam's off work today,' he carries on, 'and I promised I'd pop round. She's not very well.' Bobby nods, shut-lipped. Bobby's met Jean a few times before and, although she suffers from hideous bouts of depression, she can be quite a hoot when she's on the Teacher's or the diazepam. Karaoke, Christmas 2006 was a riot! 'Well, say hello from me, eh,' Bobby states, touching Johnnie on the back again, 'and, you know, keep your chin up. Oh, and don't forget your hammer . . .' Bobby giggles, handing over the Estwing, but it's a sickly sort of laughter tinged with absolute terror. Johnnie nods and gives his friend a very modest hug, then clip-clops out of the flat with feet at ten-to-two. Once the door shuts safely behind the psycho, Bobby the Artist throws himself headfirst at the settee. He lands with a soft crunch. What a fucking day. Six weeks ago everything was alright, but since coming back from London he can feel all the cogs and gears in his head slowly rusting and malfunctioning and falling to bits. He's not sure if it's him who's changed, or everyone else. Rolling off the sofa, Bobby the Artist feels stupid for painting all the girls and feeling like a king and being an absolute dickhead. It's not 1901, and he's not Gustav Klimt. He lights a cigarette. He's smoking Marlboro Lights nowadays, instead of Regals. Blowing out smoke, Bobby the Artist wants to put his fucking head in the oven. In total disgust, he piles all the girly paintings one on top of the other, binds them with string, then wraps them in two layers of brown parcel paper. Bent Lewis loves shit artwork – maybe he might want them. Scribbling the +!Gallery address across the brown paper, Bobby feels a bit better getting those paintings out of his sight, and he has a little sniff of the Magic Marker to celebrate. Wheee, for five seconds he feels light-headed and cheery, then all of a sudden he feels incredibly alone and downcast again. This room used to be full of artwork. Now it's more like an insane asylum, where boys with skinhead haircuts come round to batter you with hammers, and where girls with tantalising titties come over to pester you, and where your girlfriend can't stop eating the house down. Bobby's beginning to find people rather scary. He bangs his chin against the heavy parcel. He's even begun getting bad press. Or, rather, he's been getting a mix of good press (*Time Out* described 'The Angels' as 'a joyous flurry of brushstrokes and breasts') and bad press (*Modern Painters* described Bobby as a 'juvenile, contrived Basquiat rip-off'), but for some reason human beings can't help but believe the bad stuff. Bobby doesn't even want to be in the spotlight; he'd much rather be behind the sofa. Trembling, Bobby the Artist sniffs then plods through to the bedroom, slides open his Fourth Drawer Down, and removes a big swag-bag of Loveheart pills. He downs a couple with another swig of manky Soave, then trundles back through to the lounge and starts to squeeze himself firmly behind the pink settee. Squashed between the backboard and bumpy wallpaper, Bobby thinks he can hear rats scampering through the wall cavity behind him, or perhaps that's just rats scampering around his brain-pipes. He shudders. In times of crisis, all you can really do is try and block out whatever's making you feel sad. And with that in mind, Bobby downs another eleven ecstasy pills, then flops down underneath the sofa, making a sad chalky outline of sweat on the bright blue carpet. Bon voyage! Meanwhile, Johnnie sets sail down Cargo Fleet Lane on the good ship Nissan Sunny, sticking it into fifth, which is a bit naughty actually because it's a 30mph speed limit you know. He's still in quite a psychotic mood, swerving over Coke cans and bird corpses on the wide, silky tarmac. He glances at 'Un Hommage de Monsieur Condom, 2005' and the hammer stuffed in the glove box, trying his best to relax, like he's been told. He feels like a cock now for kicking off at Bobby over nothing – it's becoming quite a habit of his lately. Breathing carefully in then carefully out and so on and so on, Johnnie screeches the car to 29mph in time for the speed camera, then back to 45ish once he's gone round the bend. He wants to get to his mam's as quick as possible, and just get it over with. She's going to be a nightmare. Johnnie's mam got diagnosed with depression back in June, and the hardest thing about it is no one really knows what triggered it off. Alright, so she's going through the menopause and all her sons are frustrating and Tony the Dad spends more time off-shore or down the Brunnies than with poor Jean, but it's not like she's got cancer or she's got no money or her dog just died. Perhaps it's genetic – after all, Johnnie can have mood swings now and then, you know. Dissolving on the racing seat, Johnnie smashes his foot further into the accelerator, not really fussed if he kills himself. He's in such a strange, unexplainable mood. He stares straight ahead as all the gloomy houses whizz past, and it's quite a shock when he pulls up outside Jean's house in Ormesby to find his mother in extremely high spirits. She's been on a new mix of tablets for a week or so, and she gives her son a great big cuddle when he arrives, squeezing the sweat out of him like a bright J-cloth. 'Come in, come in,' she says, scarpering through to the living room in her odd Snoopy and Bugs Bunny slippers. Jean's looking well – she had her hair cut-and-coloured rosy black at Classy Cutz last Tuesday, plus she's been going to aromatherapy in her best mate's garage four weeks running. She feels like a new woman. 'I'm just in the middle of something, John Boy,' she explains, 'but howay in, sit down, sit down.' Johnnie plods gently into the sitting room, to see the

PlayStation 2 hooked up to the telly and Dance Dance Revolution paused on the screen; that game you see in arcades where gayboys and pre-pubescent girls bop around on the metal pads with the arrows going in synch with the cartoon person on TV. Jean bought the DVD thing and the metal floorpad off the internet, and since it arrived last weekend she's been on it non-stop. Her GP at James Cook told her exercise can help combat depression, but instead of self-consciously jogging round Albert Park on rainy afternoons she decided to plump for the dancing. Johnnie glances at his trainers as Jean kicks off her slippers and hops back on the pads, standing poised in front of the butch bloke with the Afro on the screen. She unpauses the action, then suddenly jumps back to life as the awful cheesy Eurotrance starts up, leap-frogging about and jiggling her arse. She's actually pretty good. Johnnie giggles into his chest, pretending to stare at the carpet but seeing his mother make a tit out of herself is much more captivating. She seems so different from the miserable woman of stone he saw at his aunty's birthday barbecue back in May, though it still makes him cringe a bit. Jean grunts and pants as she criss-crosses, kicks, and stamps her feet to the thumping soundtrack, and she does really well to keep in time with the funky fella on TV. She looks a right picture in pink leggings and white crusty cardigan, sweat patches spiralling out of her armpits. It's been so important for her having the DVD, after all it's kept her mind off feeling down and wanting to die and other sad things like that. On Prozac she feels a bit like a cheery zombie, but at least it gives her a kick up the arse now and then. She bops about like a little girl at her first school disco. At the end of this particular dance, Jean's totted up lots of points but it's not a TOP SCORE, and she says to Johnnie, 'Ah, bloody hell, I could've done better if the door hadn't gone.' Johnnie feels compelled to say sorry, but before his lips hinge open Jean's through in the kitchen brewing teas and chattering to him all out of breath. 'I'm getting good at it now . . . but it's tricky – I could do with the handrail, cos when the steps speed up I get all off-balance. But it's more expensive . . . and it looks like a fucking Zimmer frame – I'm not that old *yet*!' Jean comes back into the lounge with hands made of cups of tea, then collapses onto the settee next to her son, totally pooped. She pats his bony knee, then flops her head backwards into the cushions, smiling constantly. The side-effects of the tablets haven't been too nasty or horrific, unless you count the weird dreams she had three nights in a row where she was a nun stapled to a cross in the town centre, with all these horrible peasants chucking huge carrots at her. Terrible stuff. 'So, how are you, then?' she asks, much more willing and able to talk now she's on the new medication. 'You're a bit quiet,' she adds, then she slurps a gobful of tea. 'Ah, I'm alright,' Johnnie mumbles. 'Well I hope so,' Jean says. 'You're looking a bit gaunt. Are you eating? Do you want owt to eat, son?' Johnnie hugs his mug of tea, shaking his head, and he replies, 'Nah, I'm fine. Just a bit knackered. Anyway, you must be too . . . you're a bit of a whizz on the old dance game, eh?' Jean snorts up a laugh, then offers Johnnie a go on it but he politely says no fucking way mate. He glances round the room at the old familiar wallpaper and Sylvanian

Family ornaments and butter-wouldn't-melt school photos of himself, as well as the ones they got done in Whitby where you have to dress as Victorian dandies or military men or old waistcoated wallies. Johnnie hides a snigger in the tubes of his belly. He's starting to lighten up. He shuffles his trainers on the flower pattern, leaving behind vaguely muddy footprints, then asks his mam, 'So you've been alright, then?' Jean turns her head 180 degrees like an owl spotting a delicious mouse, but instead of devouring her own son she replies, 'Oh yeah, I've been great. Back to my old self. These pills are a breath of fresh air. Never felt better. It's like, ooh, it's like I'm all in love with life again!' Jean's voice rings in his ears and tingles his fingers and toes, like someone playing a wonderful miniature piano on his mother's tongue. How amazing it is to hear your mother's back to normal, after months and months of wobbling on the railings of Suicide Mountain. Johnnie remembers the onset of her menopause well, Jean spending every evening in floods of tears, scolding Johnnie for not having a job, Robbie for getting under her feet and banging his new girlfriend too loudly in the bedroom next door, and even Barrie got the brunt of it despite being the blessed first son, making it to business college in Stockton but happening to phone her for a £500 loan at a very very wrong wrong time. Jean used to smash plates in disgust at having to wash up after 'useless pricks'. Tony the Dad got slapped once for calling her a bossy boots, and she threw his favourite ELO record out the back door. Time after time, she'd come home from her job at Sainsbury's with bags of fish and tartar sauce and potatoes and frozen peas (or beans for Robbie), only to chuck them all in the flip-top bin in a huff and run upstairs crying hysterically after someone says 'hello' to her the wrong way or if someone looks at her a certain way. It seems so unbelievable and far-fetched to think a couple of teeny weeny tablets could suck out all Jean's negativeness, but here she is slapping her son's thigh in joy and smiling like a loony escapee from the Heartbreak Hotel. 'So, what've you been up to, John Boy?' Jean asks as she rises and totters back to Dance Dance Revolution. She loads up a new game, then stands poised on the metal pads with her bum all exposed in tight trousers. She looks idiotic, but the fact she's been so depressed and now she's standing there all carefree and exuberant makes Johnnie hold her in his heart as an absolute heroine. He looks up to her with wet, wobbly eyes as she bursts into dance – this time it's a Macarena-ish salsa with lots of daft lunges and sort of star-jumps and general bottom shaking. Johnnie doesn't know what to say. Yes he's been feeling depressed as well, but it's nothing compared to the sad murky swamp his mother's had to swim out of. What the hell's even wrong with him! It's only that he's getting a hard time off Ellen he's so tetchy, and he shouldn't have kicked off at Bobby or taken money off him. He spends a moment staring at his knees, feeling like a right dumb wanker. 'Ah, I haven't been up to much really . . .' he eventually replies, scratching himself. After a few more spectacular dances on the telly screen, Jean racking up TOP SCORE after TOP SCORE what with her son's encouragement, Johnnie decides to say his goodbyes and, instead of the usual awkward creeping out the door with Jean bawling blue murder, they have a huge sweaty cuddle and a kiss. Standing halfway in and out of the house, Johnnie wipes his eyes, and Jean takes his shaky hand and says, 'Thanks so much for coming, love. You sure you're feeling alright? Here, swear down, have a couple of these Prozac things. They'll sort you right out – I can get you some more from Angie next door, if you want.' And she presses two white circles into Johnnie's palm, and it's only when he gets out in the garden and sees the crisp Mitsubishi logo stamped into the sides he realises Jean's been taking ecstasy all this time, not Prozac. Johnnie laughs in his ribcage. He drives through the falling fog in the grumbling Sunny, Jean waving frantically at the door and giving him phone-me signals with her hand and beaming teethy grins at him. Johnnie watches her shrink in the rear-view mirror, tossing mist here and there as he slips down Allendale Road. Bobby the Artist went to primary school round here, where he began to develop himself as an artist, finger-painting foldy butterflies and stamping cut-off potatoes into food colouring. Experimental little bastard. Turning the corner onto Cargo Fleet Lane, waiting ages for the roundabout to stop spinning, Johnnie opens and shuts his mouth a number of times, gazing in the direction of the beautiful beautiful tower blocks. Jean's luxury madness has really put things in perspective for him; for ages and ages he's felt like the saddest boy on the planet and his life's a disaster and everything's crap, but in fact there's a lot of people in the world worse off than him and they get on with it a lot better than he does. So he promises he'll try and relax more, like Bobby told him to. And he promises to take more ecstasy. Good old Jean. Parking the Nissan again in the pigeon-grey car park, Johnnie sneezes, then removes the car keys and 'Un Hommage de Monsieur Condom, 2005,' and heads towards Peach House. Brr! It's chilly all of a sudden. He's only got on the thin Henri Lloyd jacket, and it's that time of year already where the earth starts to slant away from the sun and summertime gets shipped off to Australia and South America on frosty little speedboats. Shivering, Johnnie darts up the spiral staircase, desperate for a long, loving embrace from his girlfriend on a day of such violence. Johnnie whips open the door of 5E, kicking off his shoes and scampering into the bedroom, only to find Ellen's disappeared from beneath the Boro quilt. Panicking, he checks the £200's still there in the *Anal Adventures* vid (and it is), and he hopes for a second she hasn't gone off gallivanting with any men, but then he tells himself to shush. She's probably just gone out for a walk with the girls, to pick flowers and bake cakes and do cartwheels. Sniffing, Johnnie drops softly to the ground. As is habit whenever he finds himself alone in the flat, Johnnie considers poking the *Anal* video into the moist VCR slot and indulging himself in a fine, lengthy wank, when suddenly he remembers he's got Bobby and Georgie's live sex show in his mitts. His heart bounces. Adopting a cross-legged, trousers-round-the-ankles position one metre in front of the telly, Johnnie presses 'Un Hommage de Monsieur Condom, 2005' into the VCR and accidentally presses STOP, then he presses PLAY three times to compensate. The screen goes snowy, then it bursts into life. Picture the scene:

Interior. A double-bed with Spiderman covers in a bedroom at the back of a house in Linthorpe, March 2005. Bobby's the first to enter the stage, and Johnnie giggles at him with a lot shorter haircut and an Eclipse sweater on. He's not stiff yet, but things start to perk up when a much skinnier, Just Seventeen Georgie joins her boyfriend on screen. All's quiet as they start to strip each other off, clothes flying around like poltergeists, exposing white limbs and even whiter rude bits. *Is this art??* Johnnie wonders, scratching his chin. Three minutes and fifty-one seconds in, there's a good shot of Georgie's arse, and Johnnie feels his prick gradually standing to attention like a balloon getting blown up. He starts getting all hot in the face, anticipating the hardcore shagging and skullfucking and bum love and money shot and filthy stuff. Georgie sucks her boyfriend's willy for a bit, but then – just as it all starts getting interesting – something incredibly strange happens: Bobby gives his girlfriend some foreplay. Frowning, Johnnie watches Bobby lick her out; a boring scene which lasts about five or six minutes, culminating in a writhing orgasm for Georgie. Johnnie raises his eyebrow. She seems to be enjoying it. Once Georgie's got her bearings back, the two of them indulge in a long-winded bout of stroking one another, which seems a bit schmaltzy and ultimately leads to Johnnie's knob flopping. He pulls his trousers up, a bit disappointed. He's beginning to cotton on that real-life sex isn't as rampant or acrobatic as porno sex – when Bobby eventually slides his tail into Georgie, they shag at half the normal speed of pornstars. Johnnie even tries fast-forwarding the action to spice it up a bit, but then it just looks daft. 'Where's

all the crazy sexual positions?' Johnnie wonders, thinking back to the time he made Ellen do a headstand and
he stuck his knob in her bum and she went mad at him
and kicked him in the knackers. Resuming the tape to
normal speed, Johnnie retreats back to the sofa, not
turned at all, but very intrigued about his friends'
weird, romantic style of lovemaking. He scratches his
head. Georgie and Bobby stay in the spoons for a good
five minutes, then the girl-on-top position, then a bit
of casual doggy, all the time kissing each other and
smiling and looking like they're having a great time.
Shock horror, at one point they even start talking to
each other! Bobby: *You alright?* Georgie: *Yeah, it's mint.*
Bobby: *Woooooooooah. Groan groan groan.* The grand
finale of 'Un Hommage de Monsieur Condom, 2005'
involves Bobby ejaculating inside Mr Condom inside
Georgie, then they have a great big cuddle. Then they
dispose of Mr Condom very carefully in a wrapped-up
tissue. Switching off the VCR, all of a sudden Johnnie
realises how wrong he's been, always trying to shove his
cock in unwanted places, pouring semen over Ellen,
gagging her, roughing her up. Whoops! Rubbing his
nose, Johnnie takes out the video, then he sits for three
or four minutes gazing at the ceiling. He feels enlight-
ened. As if sex is all about love, not just getting your
end away! Johnnie supposes, in a way, sex is all about
relaxing as well. Blinking, he charges into the bedroom for his new Siemens mobile, then dials up Ellen
to see what she's up to, and whether or not she's up for
a wondrous, *ultra-relaxing* night out in Time this
evening. 'No hassle, love, no pressure, we'll just have a
quiet one,' he stresses, once she picks up. Ellen's sat on

someone's double-bed way up on floor nine, but don't worry; it's only Mandy's. They've been talking shit all afternoon, and Ellen's relieved to finally hear a normal person's voice again. In fact, she was just thinking how much she'd like to spend time with Johnnie again, after that weird calamity with Bobby the Artist shunning her. She's incredibly pissed off about posing starkers in front of him, and not getting any action – she likes to think she feels used or exploited, but in her heart she's just gutted and doesn't want anything to do with him any more. Complex bastard. Fame's obviously gone to his head; he thinks he's some totally serious artiste now. Bouncing on Mandy's mattress, she tells Johnnie she'll pop down in a minute, and she thinks he sounds strangely chirpy this afternoon. She hangs up, then Ellen grabs her fake Prada bag from Mandy's floor and kisses the nutcase goodbye. 'Cheerio,' she says, clomping out the door. 'Fishcakes,' replies Mandy. Ellen raises her eyebrows, marching down four storeys and shaking her head. Johnnie's there waiting with the front door open, and he twirls his girlfriend four or five rotations when she enters. They're both very pleased to see each other. 'You're in a good mood!' she laughs, but she's not complaining. Before they head out, Ellen pops through to the bedroom to get changed, and there's a spring in her step that hasn't been there for weeks. Jumping on top of Johnnie's bed, she chucks off some clothes then puts on new ones then chucks those off and puts on different ones. She picks pants without any brown period stains in them, and a bra that doesn't give her two pairs of tits. She makes sure to brush her teeth, pouting and striking various poses in the bathroom mirror, then the two of them dash out the house all jit-tery and merry. Johnnie tells Ellen about his mam and the Dance Dance Revolution and the ecstasy, and they swing hands all the way to the bus stop. He's so excit-ed about what he's going to do to her tonight! Despite selling most of his pills to Bobby the Artist this last half-week or so, he's still got five of the blighters in his back pocket (plus the Mitsubishis off Jean), and he can't wait to grin and gurn the night away with Ellen. They only have to wait five minutes before an Arriva comes, Johnnie trying his best to be cool and relaxed and stretching his legs and going 'aaah' all the time. He even goes as far as to say to Ellen, 'Mmm, I feel really good and relaxed, me.' Ellen nods and frowns. They get out at the chocolate bus station, wandering down its tiled, disinfected aisles then out again to the deathly quiet concrete streets. Turn a few corners and you get to the Princess Alice, which is this lovely green and white pub with people bantering and piling out into the street, and Johnnie casually furrows to the bar without bash-ing into any of them. 'Bark!' a dog says down the street. Ellen keeps a tight grip of Johnnie's hand as they stand at the cramped bar, wondering where his typical hard-man mannerisms have gone. Johnnie actually comes across as slightly camp as he rests there on the thick wood with floppy limbs. 'Pint of Carlsberg and a gin and tonic please, mate, thank you,' he says to the brick shithouse behind the bar. He gets a little raised eye-brow, then his drinks. Stood there in the rammed pub, Johnnie and Ellen aren't sure where to sit so they linger with their glasses at the bar, trying their best to talk to each other in the rumble-grumble-mumble of everybody's chatter. 'God, I'm looking forward to tonight!' Johnnie grins, holding Ellen close to him like a valuable suitcase. 'Aye,' Ellen agrees, 'I haven't done pills for a while like . . .' Ellen strokes Johnnie's arm under his shirt cuff, feeling strangely grateful for him staying with her all this time. She's glad she didn't hump Bobby the Artist now. If she really thinks about it, Johnnie would've only gone and put Bobby in hospital with severed oesophagus or disfigurement of the face, and if Bobby was willing to cheat on bonny Georgie he'd probably be inclined to cheat on Ellen too, if they ever got together. Johnnie, bless his heart, has never cheated on anyone ever (unless you count Nicola Purcell smacking her lips on him in the Linny when he was seeing this bird Sharon). Johnnie has a certain respectability about him (despite being seen as a lowlife by certain mams and dads who are against drugs and tracksuits and skinheads because the TV tells them so), and he really wants to make things work with Ellen and have a future with her and have kids not yet but some time, and all that marrying each other shite. And hopefully, soon he'll be shagging her correctly. Occasionally Johnnie does wonder if he'd be happier going out with a virgin, taking her under his wing and stretching her fanny out and adapting her to his rough, crappy shagging style and giving her orgasm after orgasm, but then again virgins are generally quite dreary and clueless as people, and it wouldn't be that worth it. Just standing here arm in arm with Ellen and pint in hand, the uphill treacherous struggle with her seems all the more worthwhile. He still feels very protective and anxious about her, but he tries his hardest not to get wound up by all the leering faces in the pub tonight. The trick is to keep a cool head! Marshy – the frog-eyed lad with a slice out of one ear – keeps looking over at Ellen from the bandit, but Johnnie just catches his frog eye and smiles. Dav – the boxer who used to fancy Ellen and tried to get off with her numerous times before he knew Johnnie was going out with her – sits over there under the telly, but Johnnie just ignores him. He ignores Darren as well, and Maresy and Gill, all of them fucking chauvinistic wankers getting pissed and slagging off women like they're rock stars on a tour bus full of groupies (but their band Whirlwind are absolutely gash). Usually even the longhairs annoy Johnnie, slumped there all gay and languid in their tight jeans and talking all deep about music and how hardcore they all are, but Johnnie avoids knitting his eyebrows or passing comment. 'Bark!' a doggy shouts, off down the street. Johnnie sniffs, keeping his eyes fixed on Ellen rather than all these dumb cretins. He gets another Carlsberg and sups it calmly, feeling all the knots in his brain untie and unribbon until his mind's just a blank cassette playing happily backwards and forwards. He smiles at his girlfriend, trying to remember Bobby and Georgie's slow, sumptuous moves from that video. He grins. It's a quarter to ten, and Johnnie and Ellen decide to leave the Alice, with big red hearts like gongs. Ellen's excited to be out with Johnnie again – she sees tonight as some sort of turning point. Johnnie seems different, and she likes that. He seems much more laid back, and as they walk down Corporation Road he's beaming and he's got a spring in his step, like an innocent man newly released from jail. The world seems much prettier to him, for example the yellow moon dangling in the dusky blackcurrant sky, or the various pubs and bars humming and sprinkling colour on the street like overgrown TVs, and all the people going by without pissing him off. In the queue at Time, Johnnie and Ellen stand behind a group of raucous curly-haired girls, trying not to listen to them. Ellen strokes her boyfriend's belly and she can't stop kissing him. She's in love again. They both can't wait to drop the Es and breeze around like a pair of Siamese twins, and one of them can't wait to get back to the flat afterwards and try out all the new moves from 'Un Hommage de Monsieur Condom, 2005'. However, what neither of them has realised is tonight Cleveland Police are undertaking Operation Nighthawk, which means zero tolerance on drugs and violence and drunk-and-disorderliness, and there's lots more bobbies and lots more undercover secret agents and lots more patrol cars and vans. And sniffer dogs. 'Bark!' a big dark Labrador screams at Johnnie, on the end of its lead. 'Bark bark barky bark!' it adds. All the colour falls out of Johnnie's face and down his large intestine. His heart turns to a hard red brick. The stocky police officer holding the leash puts a hand on Johnnie's wibbly shoulder and says quite politely, 'Can you step aside please?' but, as Johnnie stumbles off the pavement all devastated, everyone's looking over and gawping and a few lads from the queue surreptitiously tiptoe off down the street trying not to get sniffed themselves. Ellen starts screaming at the officers, telling them they're wrong they're wrong, but the sniffer dog keeps saying 'I'm right I'm right' in bark-language. Johnnie's absolutely horrified and sweaty, but he decides to remain calm, and he doesn't say a word or bat an eyelid when he gets chucked in the back of the van. The cage doors slam, then he's off brum-brum-brum to the police station without even a kiss goodbye or a glance from Ellen. She's left standing paralysed on the creaky concrete. The queue for Time means nothing to her now. She doesn't know what to do. She starts walking aimlessly back into town, suddenly all the cold stars projecting a feeling of sadness and loneliness and shit and gloom. In a weird selfish way she's glad it wasn't her holding the pills tonight and her in the back of the van, but she was having such a nice time with Johnnie, it's a shock to be suddenly on her own. The pavements have the silent, tense atmosphere of just suffering a tornado or earthquake or something. She goes past the rows and rows of pubs and clowny pissheads, feeling lost in her own home town. The image of Johnnie getting locked up in a horrid cell really grabs at her stomach, twisting and twirling her pipes and organs. She suddenly feels sober. Deflated, she sits underneath the big cardboard Corporation House like a homeless person. She's in no mood to go to a club alone – she just wants her boyfriend. She's not very keen either to go back to her mam's in Eston and tell her the reason she's home early, and then her mam slag off Johnnie and be a bitch to her the rest of the evening. Ellen and her mam get on alright, but they're the only ones in that boring old semi and they get on each other's nerves quite a bit. Ellen's mam's probably just jealous of her having a boyfriend and being more attractive and nubile and smoother. Resting her chin in cupped hands, Ellen wishes life could be easy, not full of disasters all the time and premature ejaculations and policemen. She gets up from the bench, adjusts her top so her boobs aren't falling out, then decides to wander towards the police station in case she can see Johnnie or maybe it's been a case of mistaken identity and he's been released. She tumbles in high heels between the house of cardboard and the town hall, taxis beeping at her and men drooling at her legs, but she keeps her head up and a blank expression on it. She's not interested in any other boys but Johnnie. They're all zombies. The police station lies there over the top of the gardens, all blocky and modernist like a white Rubik's cube. She imagines Johnnie in there in handcuffs, getting touched and searched and tortured, and she's surprised at herself for a tear dribbling out of one eye. He really does mean something to her, and all those memories of her cheating on him and nailing Angelo and trying it on with Bobby and ignoring Johnnie make her dizzy as she steps over the forecourt of the cop shop. There's always a certain paranoia and guilty feeling walking into a police station, but when she gets to the desk all the police people seem okay, sipping polystyrene coffees and sorting through paperwork. 'Hello,' she says to the slightly dykeish female one at the counter. 'Er,' she mumbles, 'my boyfriend Johnnie Hyde just got taken in, er, I'm not sure why. Is he getting released? We were gonna go to Time.' The female officer furrows her brow, rummages papers and taps a computer, then tells Ellen to use the old phone over there and ring the extension 1242 and ask them instead. Ellen nods and sighs, feeling like it's her who's done the bad deed. Ellen tick-tocks her heels over to the dingy phone booth; one of those with the pod affair that goes over you and your head. She types in the number, but the line's dead so she goes back over to the desk and goes, 'The line's dead.' The female officer stands up from her comfy office chair, then gets someone else to tap the computer keys for her, and this fellow seems much more amiable with his bushy white eyebrows and dimples, and he tells Ellen, 'Right, he's been put in a cell overnight, until he sobers up. He should be released sometime in the morning. But questioning won't start till at least nine thirty, and we've taken a lot of people in tonight, so I suggest you go home and get some sleep, and come back tomorrow.' PC Bushy Eyebrows scribbles a number down for Ellen, telling her to phone back at about nine o'clock when they should have a better idea when he might be out. Ellen lingers for a second at the counter in case they've got more information and because she's got nothing better to do until nine, but the female one says, 'Right, thanks a lot, then,' in a nasty tone, which means 'Right, get lost, then,' so Ellen swallows a gulp and makes a move back onto the streets again. She still doesn't want to go back to her mam's though. She sits for a bit in Central Gardens, watching the sky for forty-five minutes and it's strange and beautiful how much it changes in that time, clouds stretching like the stuff in a huge indigo lava lamp, and stars gently shifting pattern as the earth turns. But then after a bit it gets boring. Ellen smokes her last cigarette: a Richmond. She walks over to the Bottle of Notes, that Claes Oldenburg sculpture thing they wanted to paint red and white to match the colours of the football team. She sees ducks roosting in the pond. Getting chilly, Ellen strides out of the park and down past the side of the Empire, where the bouncers are headbutting someone. Ellen goes to McDonald's, but the restaurant part's shut so she has to walk through the drive-thru, pretending to be a motor car. She parks at one of the counters, then orders the Big Mac meal with Diet Coke from the gormless cunt serving. She sits on the pavement outside the American Golf shop to eat her burger, and wonders to herself how many people play golf in this humdrum industrial town. While she eats, she feels annoyed at herself for spending money on food, and disappointed not to have any vodka to mix with her Coke. She looks at the metal spikes and columns of the ICI factory, like a space-age silver Parthenon. The smoke mingles with clouds, and slowly slowly slowly the dark sky gets riddled with candy floss. Ellen walks to the furthest bin in the car park to dispose of the McDonald's wrappers, killing time. Her phone says 2.03am and she perches on the brick wall to input the cop shop number into her contacts. It's too freezing to stay in one place though. She wanders down Wilson Street and watches people leaving the clubs after their brilliant nights out. She scowls at a police car growling past. Ellen ducks under Albert Bridge, which marks the old part of town famously known as Over the Border. For some reason prostitutes and general unsavouries like to station themselves near train stations, and Ellen feels a little unsafe wandering about in her miniskirt in the witching hour, but tonight it's all pretty quiet and she paces quickly to

Ferry Road to look at the fluorescent blue Transporter Bridge in all its lanky glory. All the time she's thinking about Johnnie, hoping he's alright. She stares at the prickly lights across the other side of the river, but everyone except the power stations are in bed. She heads back after ten minutes standing there. She goes to a kebab shop on Linthorpe Road and orders a can of Lilt so she can sit inside until it shuts. At half three, she decides to trudge through fancy Captain Cook Square (though it's a graveyard at this time of night), past all the shops with their grilles down like medieval portcullises, with the intention of falling asleep on a bench in the empty bus station. Her eyes are starting to sag and clam up, and her feet are getting achy. But imagine her dismay to find the station all locked up and – as if that wasn't enough – an icy gust of wind comes suddenly shooting up her skirt and she has a big horrible shiver. Distress! There's still a good five hours before she's allowed to phone the police, and she's beginning to feel awful and fluey, but in her heart she holds a lot of pride in sticking around for her boyfriend. After all, he's in a worse position than her right now. But at least he's got a bed. Sniffling, Ellen considers going back to Eston and sneaking in through the back door to bed, but the taxi costs about six pound to get to suburbia and she's spent all her pennies on McDonald's instead. She curses herself. Giving in, she finds a spot to lie down and sleep in the five-storey car park, nestling herself in a manky corner out of the wind and out of the CCTV. She's so incredibly knackered she falls asleep instantly, but wakes up at half-hourly intervals desperately checking her bag's still there and what time it is, then Plonk! off to sleep again. She has twisted, meaningful dreams about Johnnie. One, he's shackled in war-torn Siberia and Ellen comes in dressed as a baddie, but she's really a goodie and kisses him on the mush and releases him from the clasps of evil with a handy blowtorch. In another, they're both barking dogs humping each other senseless. She dreams how horrible it'd be for Johnnie to leave the station and nobody being there to greet him, and it's that image that keeps waking her up clambering for her phone. Finally, it gets to 8.49am and Ellen thinks fuck it and rings the station anyway. A man answers. 'Hello, just like wondering if my boyfriend Johnnie Hyde's been released yet?' Ellen murmurs, the town awful silent around her but beginning to lighten up. She stands, staring off the edge of the Zetland car park, odd worker bees and men in fluorescent jackets stumbling past beneath her. She rubs her crusty eyes, feeling a bit of a sty in the left one, listening carefully as the gadge replies, 'Yes, he's in questioning right now. Should be out in about half an hour . . .' Ellen pops the phone back in her bag, then tries to do her hair and some lipstick in her free Glamour mirror before heading down the breezeblock steps and through the square again. Shops are starting to open, bread getting delivered, and gradually more and more people start appearing on the streets like blood cells flowing round your system as your body wakes up. Ellen looks like death as she staggers over to the police station, though her heart's beating quickly and she's excited to see her boy. When she reaches the cop shop, Johnnie's already there waiting for her, squatting by the rails outside with a tab hanging out his mouth. Ellen clatters up the pavement and grabs him and gives him a big squeeze, asking how he is and what went on and what's going to happen. 'It's alright, it's alright,' Johnnie replies, 'I only had seven on me, didn't I, so I got away with a caution like. "Personal use" and all that. Fucking lucky. Thank fuck Bobby's been buying loads off me, cos I might've took them all out with me.' Johnnie hugs Ellen again, so pleased and relieved she's here, but also extremely aggravated having spent ten hours in the stinky police station. All that calmness and serenity he'd been working on so hard has gone right out the fucking window. 'It was mad in there like,' Johnnie says. 'Couldn't really sleep; the bed was sick. And my cell was next-door to this fruitcake prozzy screaming her head off. But . . . it's mint being out. Howay, let's get ourselves a drink.' Ellen smiles, absolutely delighted she's not losing her man, and she asks him for a few tokes on that Regal because she's really gasping. They walk and smoke back into town, arm in arm. How amazing both those arms feel to be linked again! Johnnie feels emotionally shattered, but it's funny how wonderful and colourful and pleasing the world seems when you've had a stint behind bars. He never wants to go back there, despite enjoying a modest English brekkie this morning. The bacon was fucking plastic, mind you. It sounds like such a Hollywood cliché, but after such a great escape he feels like quitting crime altogether. For once in his life he's got a bit of respect for the zombies going round in their suits and uniforms, with their comfy lives. But before any rash decisions, he really needs a drink. Johnnie and Ellen aim their heels towards Linthorpe

Road and the old faithful 24/7 off-licence, and as they cut through the warm Cleveland Centre they spot Georgie and her brutal bob slinking into Bhs, but she's too far off and too sleepy, and in any case she's slightly late for work and she tries to duck unnoticed through the scary entrance. She's in a terrible mood this morning. Ever since she saw that nudie portrait of Ellen in her and Bobby's bedroom, she's been in such low spirits and she's been eating lots more junk food and sweets and crisps, and it depresses her that she's getting obese. This morning she's already consumed two Mars bars, one half bag of Haribo, jam on toast and two cups of tea. She feels all shit and bloated. Perhaps, she thinks, sweets are her drug, and every drug seems to come with a downside. Scoffing sugary treats makes her feel brilliant for five minutes then suddenly all downcast and irritable, a bit like crack. Flattening her Bhs shirt down her podgy belly, Georgie scampers behind the sweety counter, feeling Mr Hawkson's hawky eyes on her, but she doesn't turn around or say anything. 'Late again?' he enquires, trying to inject a bit of humour in his tone but he's just a cunt. 'Yeah, sorry. Buses,' is all Georgie can manage, trying to hide behind her eyelashes and get on with serving customers. Only there's no one to serve yet, and there's an awkward bit of silence as her and Mr Hawkson stand amongst the bright candies and glittery packets. Curving his curly eyebrows, Hawkson tries again with her. 'You know it's *really important* to get in on time, Georgina,' he says, 'I don't want to be like your headmaster or anything but, ehm, if you're not careful I might have to issue you with your first official warning.' Very very biting,

Georgie flashes him a look of sheer disgust and says, *'Nice one*, cheers.' And then, the next thing she knows Mr Hawkson's scuttling back to the office to type her out a lovely posh STATEMENT OF WARNING, and it ruins her day. She keeps her head down after that, seething while she dishes sweets into the boxes and scales, mumbling obscenities while she faces-up the selection boxes and Quality Streets. Serving the schoolkids seems like such a chore this afternoon, and isn't it just typical they act like such bastards when you're not having a very good day. They're not meant to use their fingers in the pick-'n'-mix! 'Use the tongs! Use the tongs!' she spits, feeling like an old lady. In the quiet moments, where she gets to enjoy a Crunchie or Boost with Guarana, all Georgie can do is stare lifeless-ly at Sport&Soccer across the mall thinking about Bobby. He seems like such an idiot now he's a 'famous artist' – so flirty with other girls (what did he get up to with Ellen when she posed starkers for that painting?), so stressed out (alright, so he's got more paintings to do and more phone calls to answer, but it's not exactly a nine-to-five slog), and he hardly seems to talk to Georgie any more (little bastard). It's the not talking part that's really getting to Georgie – she thinks it's something to do with him taking drugs and getting skinny, or her not taking any drugs and getting fat. But surely drugs aren't the be-all and end-all of everything? She thinks they're pretty boring as a matter of fact. His drug taking is getting incredibly tedious – after all, he seems to be doing it on every single fucking page. Georgie used to have miles more fun with Bobby the Artist on Vat 69 or Londinium Gin, putting records on and painting and going to bed at similar times, before every other little bastard got involved. Now it's as if Bobby thinks he's some sort of Old Master or New Romantic, employing prostitutes to sit around his flat all day and paint and sniff coke off them. Georgie nearly sicks up a bit of her Crunchie. She hopes to the Lord Bobby hasn't been cheating, but then again who wouldn't cheat on a fat slob like her? After work, Georgie's still in a bad mood – and she really can't face going back to the flat when she knows Bobby'll be there with all his new friends, smoking Es out of a bong or sniffing horse tranquilliser, and getting naked on all the clean work surfaces – so she gets the 63 instead of the 65 and rides through the industrial estates with all their burning frosty flares and *Blade Runner* pipes and lattices and cooling towers puffing out nimbostratuses with that tiny layer of black soot collecting in their crevices, and she takes her sadness all the way to the seaside. It's a funny little sea resort, Redcar, what with its close proximity to such overbearing rusty blast furnaces and black generators and, as Georgie stands on the promenade sucking a lemon top and looking out to sea, she wonders if there's any three-legged fishies or Siamese crabs in there like people say so. She watches the tankers lining up on the horizon like grey matchsticks, waiting to float down the Tees and dump their gear off. Shivering, Georgie's a bit annoyed she's wearing her Bhs outfit when she's got a perfectly good sailor suit at home. Having said that, she hardly wears the fancy dress any more, since Bobby's paying so little attention to her. She misses him. Gazing across such a grey, wavy ice rink, frothing at the mouth, she really really misses him. It's such sad weather, and she's such a sad sad girl you'd need a painter there anyway just to capture all the perfect melancholy. She dreads to think what Bobby's doing instead. Daubing pink acrylic across Katey's cream knockers? Snorting Special K round Pamela's bum-hole? Shagging Johnnie's girlfriend between her beautiful bronze bedsheets? Up on saucy, sordid floor four of Peach House, however, Bobby the Artist is actually having a mental breakdown. Look at him chewing up the carpet! Look at him punching down the walls! Poor Bobby's stressed out – it's not easy being a famous person, boo hoo hoo. Everyone keeps coming round demanding paintings (Mr and Mrs Fletcher, the ones who got Bobby the London gig, were over earlier asking if they could pose for a personal portrait, but Bobby was all twisted on the CK and frightened and had to slam the door in their faces), or asking him for free money, or threatening him with hammers and big knockers. On top of all that, there's a point where taking drugs becomes not very fun, for example when the thirteenth ecstasy of the day makes you feel all tired and irritable. He writhes around on the floor. Bobby made a heroic attempt this afternoon to get fucked, ingesting handful after handful of pills and, while he did manage to block out the stresses for a little bit, now he just feels like death. There's a poltergeisty chill wind coming in through the whistling window, and Bobby considers making some acid-on-cream-crackers in the kitchen, but even that's too much effort. He's not even hungry – it's just he's getting really ill not eating five or six days on the bounce, and it'd probably be a good idea to poke something down his neck. He chews a handful of salt and vinegar Discos, then spits them back out again. He feels like a little baby. Oh, if only Georgie was here to look after him! His heart feels really sore. He doesn't even feel like he's spoken to Georgie for days, despite probably sleeping in the same bed together every night, but he's not even sure. He wishes he didn't have to manage a girlfriend who always seems pissed off at him. Yes, she's getting fatter, but the only bad thing about it is her inability to smile any more because of it. He doesn't really care if she ends up looking like a Space Hopper – at least then he might be able to ride around on her more. The stresses! Bobby the Artist tumbles back through to the lounge, gritting his teeth anxiously or gurning or a bit of both. He flops onto the sofa, wishing he was a bit of fluff not a human being. The whole reason he got into drugs was to detach himself from horrible, boring Realityland, and for a while he got used to being all happy and bohemian and poor and he felt he'd discovered who he really was, until he accidentally sold some paintings and suddenly everyone else discovered who he was and paid him lots of attention and paid him lots of money, and dragged him out of that fairytale lifestyle. What a drag. Bobby the Artist glances out the window at the sky moving gently from one side to the other. He hopes he hasn't annoyed Georgie too much, him being quite the dickhead of late. Spluttering, Bobby the Artist stands up from the sunken ship sofa, puts his kangaroo pyjama top on as a coat, then marches out the flat feeling extremely sinister. At the doormat, there's a cheque from Francis Fuller for £3,600 for 'The Angels'

(244x233cm), but Bobby just kicks it aside and carries on charging out the tower block. He wishes he'd never sold his angels. Bobby goes down to Premier to buy Georgie a lovely Sarah Lee chocolate gateau, and on the way the streets feel really morbid and unfamiliar, like he's a young explorer lost in the Doldrums or Badlands or Teesside Park or somewhere. It's crazy to think he hasn't left Peach House for weeks – sometimes that tower block has the power to become a sort of dreamland for him; a little high-rise town of its own, like nothing else really matters outside the striplit corridors or chicken-coop lodgings. It's quite unnerving, actually, having to cross roads again and interact with strangers. In Premier, Bobby nervously peruses the skinny aisles for gateau, feeling the laser-beam eyes of the owner drilling into his back, feeling his legs start to spiral and melt like Cornettos. He shakily lifts the £2.49 cake out of the freezer compartment, then chooses a route through the aisles to the counter without coming into contact with other customers. As he walks, each step seems so fake and deliberate and clumsy, and he begins to panic, wondering whether to say, 'Just this, thanks,' or, 'Hi,' or, 'How are you?' or nothing at all to the guy serving. He wonders why he's being so anxious, but it's hard to switch it off. When he finally makes it to the desk, he squeaks, 'Hi, alright, how are you, just this ta,' but the assistant just stares right through him, bagging up the gateau then putting out his hand like a zombie. It makes his tummy churn. Bobby the Artist passes him a fiver and waits nervously for his change, then darts back to the flat as fast as he can without getting squashed by cars. Scrabbling up the staircase, Bobby tries to breathe steady and not faint all the way back down to ground floor. He clicks open the door softly, then takes off his kangaroo top and stuffs it behind the radiator. He feels so ravaged from one minor excursion to the shop, he has to scamper through to the bedroom and light up his Coca-Cola bong. Pamela foolishly left her ounce of tac round the other night, and Bobby shudders as he sparks up the manky chillum bit. Last Tuesday, him and Pamela felt like Sooty and Sweep in a Chinese opium den, all tingling and giggling and playing hide-and-seek in the green swampy smoke. Teeth chattering, Bobby the Artist does occasionally think he overdoes it a bit with drugs, but they've been nothing but friendly to him in the past. To compensate for such weird weird anxieties, he stuffs in a bit extra tac, then lights her up again and sucks the living daylights out of the gloopy Coke bottle. Aah, he feels a lot better after that, and he trundles back into the lounge with the chocolate gateau, smiling. It's becoming lovely and dusky outside. Scratching a lump under the greasy mop-top, Bobby switches on the Dr Seuss lamp-stand, then suddenly his heart pops inside him and the Sarah Lee cake drops from his hand. Splat! For some reason, there's skulls all over the carpet this evening. Surely it wasn't like that when they first bought it from DFS? Panicking, Bobby the Artist rubs his eyes to shreds, wondering if it's a mirage. He gets down on his hands and knees, digging his nails into the soft weave. He screams. Lo and behold, there's six thousand tiny skull-and-crossbones embedded in the carpet, and if you listen to them really closely they're all laughing at you. Or is that just the boiler filling up?

Bobby the Artist leaps backwards onto the sofa. His eyes are bulging out of their sockets, and he has a little cardiac arrest, choking for air. Is this his punishment for taking too many pills? He shivers. Other things around the room are different too: the fuchsia cushions are all bloody organs like hearts and lungs and livers and spleens, the radiators are all tombstones, and there are faces in the curtains that look a bit like Michael Jackson. Trembling, Bobby the Artist sees in perfect clarity him losing all his marbles plop-plop-plop down a porcelain bathtub. 'Fucking hell,' he mumbles. How charming, for his head to be doing things like this to him! Sitting against the pink glass settee, all the colour drains from poor Bobby's face. He coughs. Centipedes rush into his brain, guzzling holes through the tender pink flesh. Flapping his arms about, Bobby takes a few attempts to clamber onto the sofa, throwing bloody organs everywhere. He coughs again, sicking a bit of acidy bile into his mouth, then he chokes it back down. The settee feels about two centimetres long. He tries to sit on it lengthways, then he tries to sit on it widthways. Balling himself up, for a second he thinks he's getting comfy, when suddenly the skulls in the carpet let out a piercing, blood-curdling scream. No, pardon me, that's actually just his phone going off in his trousers. Scared shitless, Bobby launches himself off the sofa, scrabbling with his trousers for about half a minute, then finally retrieving his mobile and answering it. 'Hello?' Bobby mumbles, trying to stop mind-power turning his phone into a six-foot anaconda. 'Hello! Bobby! Good to speak to you – you're not busy are you?' the snake replies. It's actually Bent Lewis, phoning from his plush rosebush-smelling office in London, all squeaky and cheerful and you can tell by the tone of his voice he's wearing a bright pink shirt. 'No, er, don't worry,' Bobby speaks, feeling a bit confused and detached like he's walked into somebody else's dream. 'Lovely,' Lewis chirps. 'You see, I was just ringing about those paintings you sent me recently . . . now, don't get me wrong – they're *interesting* but, I don't know, it just seems you might've lost your touch somewhat. I mean, we all love looking at girls with their *legs open*, but where's the soul? What's happened to all the stories? You should be telling stories, Bobby, not all this wanking around, mate . . .' Bobby nods along passively with Bent Lewis's lah-dee-dah voice, then suddenly he starts feeling all sick again and he doesn't want to listen and he slams the phone off the skully carpet. The skulls disappear for a second, then return again with new recruits. 'Fuck off,' he snaps at the empty room. He thinks Bent Lewis is just trying to get back at him, for not shagging him in the Colon. He stares utterly depressed at the upholstery and the furniture. Sniffing, Bobby the Artist shuffles again in his trainers. For some reason his feet feel far too big and uncomfy for his shoes. Getting jittery, he tries wiggling and wriggling his toes, slamming them up and down on the ground, cursing them, untying and retying the laces. No good, though. Wincing, Bobby gets up again to make himself a glass of water (a queer, desperate attempt to flush out all the toxins), but as he walks he feels his feet gradually turn to skeletons then all the bones crack and crumble to dust in his size 10 Trim-Trabbs. He screams the first letter of the alphabet, kicking off the nasty trainers, tears forming in the sides of his mouth. He shakes his feet frantically, then jabbers off to the bedroom to sink his head into a pillow. He drops himself flat onto the bronze bedcovers, but he's far too wired and petrified to sleep. 'You're going insane,' the left-hand compartment of his brain teases him. 'You're never coming out of this trip, unfortunately,' the right-hand compartment goads, 'if it *is* a trip, that is!' Hiding in the bedroom, Bobby hears Georgie come in from work but he's too frightened to talk to anyone human so he ignores her and pretends she doesn't exist. Georgie sees the squashed Sarah Lee gateau on the living room floor, shouts 'Hello' to Bobby, but she doesn't get any reply and she's not sure whether to eat the cake or not. She knows Bobby's home (his shoes are over there in the kitchen), and she wonders why he's ignoring her. She feels like having a big cry on the sofa but she restrains herself, instead just sitting there in silence for a while in the grey miserable lounge. Back in the bedroom, all colourless and treacherous, Bobby the Artist watches with horror as coats hung on hooks begin to morph into bleeding animal carcasses, but before the visions get too intense his mind says *stop stop stop* and he slams on the brain-brakes and his heart starts panting, and the visions go away. It's a constant struggle to keep his brain from taking the piss out of him. He's not sure what's happening to him. Bobby gets up to check if his pupils are dilated, but it seems someone's replaced the mirror with a portrait of Dracula. Dracula screams, then leaps back onto the bed. Aaaargh! Bobby trembles on the stone mattress, papping himself, and yet there's also a strange admiration for his brain conjuring up such horrific scenes. By heck, the power of the mind! But the more Bobby keeps telling himself it's just mind over matter, the more the room keeps tormenting him. Stubs in the ashtray turn into filthy bugs and maggots. Every single object in the room seems sinister – even Georgie's flowery knickers, and the picture of the two bunnies above the chest of drawers. Trembling, Bobby the Artist sinks his head back into the pillows. He tries to lie still for a bit – and for a few seconds it's alright – until, all of a sudden, footsteps start approaching outside the bedroom door. The steps are quite heavy, like they're carrying the weight of some sort of ogre or troll or the big brown mammoth thing out of *Labyrinth*. Bobby the Artist pulls the bronze covers up to his eyelids. The footsteps are getting closer and closer, and you can hear the beastie grunting as it approaches Bobby's boudoir. It's like there's some bloodthirsty demon out there. Probably with awful decaying teeth to gnaw on him, and horns spurting out semen and AIDS-infected blood, and claws caked in poo to scrape into him, and horrid breath, and eyes seeping smelly pus, and a belly full of young artists. The bedroom door begins to open. Bobby yelps, scrabbling around on the mattress in total desperation, but it turns out the monster's only Georgie, and she looks at him with diagonal eyebrows as he lies squealing on the bed. She wonders what his problem is. She asks him if he wants pasta sauce for tea. 'Soz soz soz, I can't talk to you,' Bobby the Artist snaps, shuddering in his sweaty argyle gown. He knows in his head it's rude to snap, but he's feeling so twisted the last thing he's capable of is a pleasant conversation with someone. He buries his head in the duvet again. Georgie's face drops, then she turns and scuttles out of the bedroom, mortified. Bobby just stays quiet, glad to be alone again. He can't speak at all. Fucking monsters. He has a little sigh to himself, hoping to God it's all over. He tries to lie still for a bit – and for a few seconds it's alright – until, all of a sudden, footsteps start approaching outside the bedroom door. The steps are quite heavy, like they're carrying the weight of some sort of ogre or troll or the big brown mammoth thing out of *Labyrinth*. Bobby the Artist pulls the bronze covers up to his eyelids again. The footsteps are getting closer and closer, and you can hear the beastie grunting as it approaches Bobby's bedroom. It's like there's some bloodthirsty demon out there. Probably with slimy green tentacles to strangle him, and snakes for hair spitting out venom and vomit, and eyes falling out on dangly stalks, and horrid BO, and tongue dripping smelly period blood, and a belly full of young artists. The tower block begins to shake. Bobby yelps, scrabbling around on the mattress in total desperation, but it turns out the monster's only Alan Blunt the Cunt going down the corridor to work his shift at ICI. Alan's been on the piss all afternoon, and he'd definitely own up to feeling a bit beastly this evening. He staggers insect-like round the block, losing his way, gurgling, trying to find the right stairs to ground floor. It's funny how, after a crate of Newcastle Brown, you can forget the most basic, familiar things. He burps. Fifteen minutes later he's out on windswept Cargo Fleet Lane, getting later and later, and he slumps over to Premier like wobbly raspberry jelly. It's no fun driving the big tanker without a few nibbles or a copy of the *Sun* – he hopes there's some really disgusting stories in there today. Stumbling out of the newsagent, Alan has a shifty glance at Keeley on Page 3 then ambles back towards Peach House and unlocks his battered Ford Escort. He calls his car Bryan. Bryan's been really faithful to Alan Blunt over the years, despite grudgingly driving him places when he's had too much to drink. Bryan often has flashbacks about all those scratches and dents in his bodywork, and his eyesight still hasn't recovered from that time Alan smashed into the back of a Punto on Ormesby roundabout and Bryan's headlight got caved in. But the two of them are like brothers, and on the odd occasion when Alan's feeling particularly lonely he has been known to talk to Bryan on their trips out together. 'Hello, Bryan,' Alan slathers, splattering spit down his chin. He gets in the front seat, whacks the engine on, then sits for a bit while the car warms up, finally spinning it off the tarmac and onto busy Cargo Fleet. Alan's a fairly competent driver even when he's drunk – after all, driving the HGV as an occupation makes the Ford Escort seem really nifty; a bit like playing keepy-uppies with a ping-pong ball before moving on to a size 6 Mitre. But having said that, it's been a while since Alan's been this drunk for work and, as he hurtles unknowingly into the charging two-lane traffic of Longlands Road, Alan realises it's going to be a bit of a mission getting to work this eve. And God knows what it'll be like driving the container! Alan does an accidental wheel-spin coming onto the trunk road. He knows he's far too mortalled to be transporting gas, but he knows how lonely it gets at home and he'd be lost without anything to do on the nights. Usually, when he's been out on the lash, Alan just downs a couple ProPlus with a couple coffees and he's sound, and he makes a mental note to visit the ICI canteen as soon as he gets to the plant. In any case, the job today is just taking the empty cab and chassis back to Hull to get reloaded and reserviced, so it's not as if he's driving with loads of dangerous chemicals on his back. Alan concedes, burping and spluttering, that he'll be fine and dandy. Blinking heavily, Alan misses a few chances to join the roundabout at Grangetown, gazing lazily at the smoking towers and the kids playing football on the Wilf Mannion recky below. He wonders how Tiny Tina's getting on this evening in her little gingham dress; he can't wait to kidnap her. Perhaps she'd like to drive with him in the tankers. 'Beep beep beep!' the cars behind sing out, and Bryan shudders into life and jumps hastily into the revolving traffic on the round-about. There's a near-miss between Bryan and this yellow Seicento, then the two of them slip off down the A1085 into the metal-clunking, fire-spunking fortress called ICI. It's a strange old place. The trees they put up to hide the cubey eyesores and big flare-stack stiffies have all withered to grey twiglets from the pollution. Ravens swoop overhead, ready to peck your eyes out. And all the men are fluorescent. Aah, it's like a second home though. Foot jittering on the accelerator, Alan Blunt the Cunt pulls into the crowded car park, foaming slightly at the mouth. Still pissed up, Alan gets out of the Escort, forgets to lock up then remembers, then tries his best to stroll soberly into the building with the canteen in it. He wipes a bit of condensation off his thick brown gegs, slipping slightly on the lino and laughing. The room smells of polystyrene cups. Alan Blunt hobbles over to the counter, smiles a load of furry teeth at Gloria the ex-dinnerlady, then orders a strong coffee three sugars please. He tries not to keel over, keeping one hand on the tray rack. He considers scranning one of the sandwiches but he's not sure his stomach could take it; even the sight of the swirling whirlpool coffee makes him gag slightly. He feels himself staring at Gloria all mole-eyed. Lifting the coffee up round the rim, he pours in the sugars, stir stir stir, pays Gloria, then staggers over to the empty school tables and sits down. The canteen has that cold morbid feel of a hospital waiting room, and he can see his breath. Banging his bum down on a foam seat, Alan feels his head bob in drunken knackeredness towards the table, absolutely fucked, then he takes a sip of coffee all hot and spicy into his belly. He looks at his watch, which says 5.11pm – only nineteen minutes until drive-time. He really cannot be bothered. He glances up at the few others in the canteen – there's Henderson the lab technician going bald years before his time, there's Miss Adams the Enron receptionist still wearing eighties power suits (today's shade is violet), there's Barnes the plastic analyser with the daft lopsided face after his stroke last summer, and there's Alan Blunt the Cunt's boss David H. Stephenson. 'Are you alright there, Alan?' Stephenson asks, unfortunately clocking him over the spinning cake machine. Alan looks up at him from his steamy coffee, or rather he looks a bit past him then a bit before him then Bang! right into Stephenson's beady eyes. 'Er, ey up,' Alan

mumbles, trying to act natural and all that. The paranoia of being caught pissed on the job just makes it
worse though, makes Alan's head clogged with lots of
unnecessary thoughts and cover-ups, and he blows it
completely by spurting out, 'What's your problem?'
Stephenson glares at him. He's heard rumours of Alan
getting pissed before work and heard the words 'alcoholic' and 'nutcase' batted about the plant before, and
he can see Alan's eyeballs wobbling all over the place
and mouth all sloppy and slurring like he's got a slippery haddock for a tongue, and breath worse than an
old man's undercrackers. 'You're not driving the tanker
tonight, are you?' Stephenson asks, with that harsh tone
of a headteacher. David H. Stephenson is much higher
up the ladder than Alan, co-ordinating the fleet of gas
tankers on their various excursions up and down the
country and abroad, and he has a habit of feeling
incredibly superior to those underneath him, especially the no-hopers like Alan. Alan Blunt the Cunt swallows down more manky coffee, then squints his eyes
and protests, 'Aye, but there's no gas on it tonight. Just
the cab and that, mate. It's, er, it's alright mate.'
Stephenson rolls up his M&S sleeves, disgusted that
anyone as trolleyed as Alan could even consider putting
his life – and the lives of others, such as pregnant single mothers and children – at risk driving a fucking
huge Leyland cab and chassis down public streets in
that state. Stephenson has no points on his licence, and
he passed his driving test years and years ago with only
one minor. Flicking back his Brylcreemy barnet,
Stephenson snarls at Alan, 'You're drunk, aren't you?'
Alan shrugs, still trying to convince himself he's alright

but it's hard work, and he repeats, 'Naw naw, it's only the . . . there's no gas tonight. I'm not gonna blow anyone up . . .' Stephenson snorts, disgusted. He screws his face up, as if he's just seen a tramp shit on his freshly pruned, plumed garden. As if it makes any difference, Alan sits up a bit straighter and reels off in a drippy monotone, 'It's sound, mate. I know the roads like the, er, back of my hand. I could get to Hull with my fucking eyes shut. Not that I'm going to, like, but . . .' Since beginning the tanker job five years back, the veins and wires in Alan's brain have slowly formed a British road map but, even so, he's still miles and miles over the drink-drive limit and the insanity limit. 'You're not going anywhere, sonny,' Stephenson states, using that same tone of voice his two boys face when coming home late from badminton. 'You're a disgrace, Alan,' he continues, 'and don't think I won't bring this up with Roberts,' (his boss) 'or Charvelstone' (his boss's boss). Gurgling slightly, Alan coughs up a bit of waxy phlegm. In his spinning teacup head, Alan doesn't really give a fuck what Stephenson says, but when David H. orders him to down the coffee and 'get the hell off the premises' he does feel a pang of stupidity and regret. 'Well, should I come back tomorrow?' Alan Blunt yells back at Stephenson as he plods back out of the canteen. 'Don't count on it,' Stephenson spits, catching the eyes of his peers, feeling like God. Recently, at the annual chemicals conference in Coventry, he was proud to note his wife was the most beautiful of all the ICI wives. 'I'll speak to Roberts,' Stephenson adds, as Alan disappears out the door, 'and I'll let you know. But don't hold your breath.' Sort of downcast, Alan Blunt the Cunt waddles back to his Ford Escort, pleased he parked Bryan out of sight of the cafeteria so shitty Stephenson can't see him drive off. He jumps into the M-reg, then scuttles hastily out of the Ind. Est. After that coffee he feels a bit sick in the guts, but also a bit livelier and more perceptive on the roads, and he knows he could've driven the cab down to Hull no bother. Speeding down the trunk road, skidding whoosh whoosh over all the roundabouts, Alan figures Stephenson won't say anything – he's all mouth and no chinos, that sort of wanker. It's not as if Alan was caught drinking behind the wheel; he was only caught drinking coffee in the canteen. Shock! Horror! Alan sighs. He gets back to Peach House and puts another brew on and sticks *Emmerdale* on. He gets a phone call around 7.23pm from David H. Stephenson telling him he's getting the sack and that his HGV and dangerous substances licence could be under threat and never to come back to the power plant ever again, and Alan Blunt sits down on the knackered sofa and changes the channels a few times. He sees a cloud out of the window. The wind seems to be blowing quite fiercely. After a couple sips of tea, Alan leaves his cup on the side then goes downstairs for a litre bottle of Bell's, remembering first to wrap himself up. He tucks his red SACRE BLEU FRANCK QUEDRUE scarf into his deerhide jacket, then walks sadly across the road, not bothering really to look both ways but there's nothing coming anyway. He buys the whisky, staring dumbly at the two Pakistani boys serving. He tumbles back up the stairs of Peach House. He swallows the whole bottle of Bell's, blacks out on the sunken settee, then goes back down to the shop in the crystally misty morning for another one. In the same clothes as last night, Alan looks like the gruesome ghost of a football manager, and the boys at the shop make jokes to each other in a foreign language and Alan considers bashing them over the head with the bottle but the booze is too precious to lose. He doesn't bother saying thank you or goodbye to them. Back on the autumnal estate, Alan gazes up at the three towers shivering like fat icepops, then glances at his watch under the deerhide sleeve. It's 10.15am – the kids at Corpus Christi will be on morning break – and, huddling the bottle of Bell's in his mitts, Alan smiles and breathes circles of steam and marches sharply towards the school gates. Oh Tiny Tina, there you are skipping around in a great oversized parka! And bare legs! How naughty! Tiny Tina, pulling her own pigtails as she darts amongst the boys and girls, smiles jubilantly to be out in the fresh air. Her class have just been learning about the Egyptians, and she prances around dreaming of Pharaohs and pyramids. 'I'm Cleopatra I'm Cleopatra!' Little Tracy yelps, over by the hop-scotch. 'No I'm Cleopatra I'm Cleopatra!' her friend Little Nicole screams, going down the slide. Tomorrow they'll be Florence Nightingales or Joans of Arc. Skipping past, Tiny Tina giggles to herself, skidding on the slippy tarmac. She thinks the Egyptians are great. Her teacher Carol can be quite disgusting though, telling the kids how the mummies get their brains scooped out of their noses with a long hook. Tina hopes her own mummy won't get her brains scooped out. Sniffling, Tiny Tina keeps dashing round the playground, trying her best

not to think about the gory bits. She runs to the opposite side of the playground, following the painted yellow lines of the netball court. She plays trains for a bit,
but she's the only carriage. Over by the frosty gate, she
spots Mr Spooks staring at her, but she carries on
charging round the playground regardless. Mr Spooks
is her name for the scary old man who stands at the
fence every other day, staring at the kiddies. He's
frightening! Mr Spooks coughs, then takes a swig from
a bright gold bottle. Zipping up mummy's coat, Tiny
Tina jumps around on the spot getting chilly, wondering if the boys over by the compost heap will let her
join in their cops and robbers game. Just as she's about
to sprint off over there, Mr Spooks coughs again and,
for the first time ever, shouts something at her. 'Come
here, darling!' Alan Blunt the Cunt spurts, clutching the
Bell's and one bar of the sticky, frosty fence. His face is
full of remorse and booze and bogies. 'Aaargh!' Tiny
Tina yelps, almost bursting into tears to hear such a
horrible voice. She's worried he wants to hook her
brains out. 'Aaargh!' she screams again, rushing over to
her teacher Carol, who stands every breaktime by the
cloakroom door making sure none of the kids get in.
Tiny Tina throws her little plasticine arms round
Corpus Christi Carol's legs, not yet crying but it's
brewing inside her like a storm big enough to capsize
several boats. 'What is it what is it?' Carol asks, stroking
Tina's piggytails, then all of a sudden she sees Alan
standing over by the gates in his musty deerhide jacket and she storms over to confront him. Alan has been
a nuisance to Corpus Christi for a good seven months
– the amount of time Tina has been at the school,

incidentally. A day seldom goes by when he's not standing there at the gates ogling the schoolgirls, but whenever she tries to have eye contact with him Alan just wanders off sadly without causing a fuss. Today though, Alan's hammered, and he stares viciously at the lanky woman striding across the yard. Corpus Christi Carol spits through the bars, 'What do you want?' Alan, slightly taken aback, points at Tiny Tina (who instantly jumps behind Carol like she's been zapped by lightning) then slurs, 'Look, just let me talk to her. L-let me play with her.' Disgusted, Corpus Christi Carol screws all her wrinkles up then, spotting the Bell's bottle vibrating in Alan's fist, snarls, 'Look, I think you'd better leave.' Sobs welling up in Tina's and Mr Spooks's eyes, Alan brings his face closer to the bars of the primary school and calls to the little girl, 'Come here! Come here! Come here!' Bursting into full-blown tears, Tiny Tina bursts off across the playground and hides herself safely in the girls' toilets. She trembles on the shut seat, crying for her mummy. Back in the yard, absolutely distraught, Alan takes a long desperate slug of whisky. Then he has a splutter, still clutching the metal fence. 'Look, if you don't leave, I'm calling the police!' Corpus Christi Carol yells. Alan Blunt's head drops, and he mumbles to himself, 'I *am* the fucking police.' But his police days are long gone of course, and he nods gravely at Carol then turns and staggers off across the road. There's still not enough cars on Cargo Fleet Lane to run him over. The walk back to Peach House seems to take forever. Every four or five steps, Alan stops to drink from the Bell's. He hears the primary school bell go off in the distance. So much for

Tina's Big Kidnap. A tear drops out of his eye, then tears start dropping out of the sky as well, and Alan quickens his pace before the deerhide jacket gets absolutely drenched. What a terrible day. He ducks into Ladbrokes before heading up the tower, which is like a wee garden shed glued to the side of the Brambles Farm Hotel. Slumping on the desk, he puts a fiver E/W on all the horses with the saddest names at Cheltenham and Musselburgh, and none of them wins him any money. Sniffing, Alan slurps more drink then makes the gloomy ascent back up Peach House. In the safety of the tower block, Alan shakes off a few drips and drops, sparking up his last Regal. He takes alternate sucks on the fag and the glass bottle, feeling really fucked again and not totally sure what's going on. All the bad news of a shitty grey day seems like a dull unspecific kick to the head. Sniffing and snortling, Alan Blunt the Cunt unlocks the door to his flat. He's dismayed to find Johnnie and Ellen pounding the *Cream Anthems Vol. 6* at full volume through his bedroom wall. They've just come home from some twenty-four-hour bender round town, but that's no fucking excuse. Alan has a good long stare out of his bedroom window, the tiny toy-town houses spinning round down below and the primary school only just out of view. He slams the curtains shut. The clocks went back the other day; now even the afternoons feel really dark and miserable. He wonders if he's getting the SAD disorder. Finishing the fag, Alan sits down on his unmade beige bed, immersing himself in booze and moody spiralling thoughts, until suddenly he's disturbed by his fat mobile phone going off in the deerhide jacket. 'Who the fuck could that be?' he asks himself. Corpus Christi Carol phoning to apologise? David H. Stephenson offering him his job back? Tiny Tina? Alan lifts himself from the bed and lifts the heavy walkie-talkie to his ear. 'Yeah?' he says. Surprise surprise, it's more bad news. Alan Blunt crumples in a heap again on the sweaty bed. It's the Loan Company, demanding two months' missed payments, and reminding him politely that he may face legal action or bailiffs should he fail to pay up. The persuasive cunt on the other end gets Alan to promise he'll 'definitely have the cash by Thursday', then he wishes Alan good day and hangs up. All red-faced and panicky, Alan slams the phone down, then turns it off at the OFF button. He puts it down the toilet and has a shit on top of it. Two minutes later, two floors down, Bobby the Artist sees a phone-shaped turd fly past the window. It refused to flush. Blinking curly eyelashes, Bobby can't tell if he's hallucinating or not. He's defrosting a sheet of acid in the kitchen, trying to weigh up the pros and cons of swallowing it. The Scary Incident with the Cannabis put the fear of God in him, but without drugs it's been a miserable boring day, and the three cans of Kronenbourg he devoured earlier have only worsened his mood. Johnnie dropped off another load of Class As last night, and he hopes to God he doesn't see evil things again. He figures Pamela must've gotten a bad batch of resin and it's not really his mind falling apart, and his drug days aren't over and he won't die from psychological devastation. Plus, it's lovely and orange and autumny today and Bobby wants to go down the park to attempt some sketches and kick-start his career as an artist again, and he couldn't possibly do it sober. Packing up a few HB and 2B pencils and putty rubber and sharpener, Bobby reassures himself again and again he'll be okay, then he rips off five of the strawberry blotters and casually pokes them down the chute with the last two sips of warm Kronenbourg. He plods through to the living room. This morning Bobby was pleased to find the skulls had disappeared from the carpet; however, they now seem to have been replaced by loads of swastikas on the wallpaper. Bobby shakes his head, pulling on a second argyle sweater, then he scampers down the staircase two or three steps at a time. Maybe it's just the living room that's going mental, not him. Bobby the Artist steps out onto the leafy car park, drawing pad clutched firmly under his turquoise sleeve. The sun's in and out of clouds as he wanders through the estate; it's chilly willy. He coughs into the sky. It's funny how different you feel walking on your own than with a group of friends – you become so aware and paranoid about how you look, how many steps to take before mounting that kerb there, and Bobby finds himself getting in people's way a lot more. He's like a sleepwalker. Gazing straight ahead, Bobby successfully dodges a banana skin on the edge of Cargo Fleet Lane, and he hopes no one put it there on purpose to trip him up. He sighs into his chest, looking forward to getting to the safety of the park. Picking up the pace down Cranmore Road, Bobby whistles 'Strawberry Fields Forever', waiting for the acid to kick in. Every so often he thinks the trees might be getting a bit greener, or the sky might be getting a bit faster, but it's all just in his head. Wandering onwards, he wishes he'd brought some gloves – his fingers are like frozen chips. He shoves his mitts in his corduroy pockets then carries on down the street, his mind drifting slightly like a kite getting caught on the breeze. Down past the bungalows at Addington Drive, Bobby the Artist feels his pupils gently dilate and, lo and behold, the pavements start to get swirly and he smiles into the collar of his top. So far so good. The sun comes out at 3.33pm and suddenly the estate's all beautiful and Bobby starts to skip between the lovely letterboxes and wheelie bins and drain covers. He admires the black and white spots of that bright Dalmatian over there. It doesn't even seem that cold any more – weather just seems a figment of imagination; if Bobby wants to be warm, he's warm. Look! The beck's all full of diamonds and crystals! Grinning away, Bobby enjoys just *derive*-ing about the estate, everything seeming new and exciting – especially the red of that red pool of blood up Chertsey Avenue! He's in a brilliant mood. Bobby's so pleased he's not a paranoid wreck, and he continues pacing along Cranmore getting deeper and deeper into the trip. At 4.44pm it all goes horribly wrong. The sun creeps behind a cumulonimbus, and suddenly the street seems a bit more sinister and daunting, and Bobby's heart stammers at the darkness closing in. He feels cold again. He shivers in his two jumpers, and then he makes a fatal mistake – he wonders what it'd be like if he started getting paranoid again. The thought of it makes his ribcage clatter, and he catches a glimpse of his reflection in a car windscreen and he thinks he sees Dracula again. 'Shit,' Dracula mumbles, in the darkened glass. Trembling, Bobby nearly falls off the kerb, wishing he was back in the flat. He has a bit of an internal monologue with himself, repeating, 'It'll be alright, it'll be alright,' but he knows it's not going to be alright. Nevertheless, he reckons things might be better in the park, and he tries to walk very cool and nonchalant down the rest of Cranmore Road. He avoids eye contact with his own reflection in the passing cars. All wobbly, Bobby the Artist keeps a tight grip of his sketchpad and pencils, trying his best to think light, happy thoughts like stroking kittens and playing beach volleyball and picking dandelions and sawing young children's arms and legs off. Whoops! Spluttering, Bobby the Artist continues down the rock-hard pavement, keeping his eyes fixed on that patch of green field up ahead but it seems fucking miles away now. He cringes. There seem to be people in the bushes laughing at him. Is Halloween a bit earlier this year, or is it just the acid? The more Bobby tells himself to relax and remember it's just a drug it's just a drug it's just a drug, the worse the whole ordeal gets, as if his brain's got a huge revolting grin and it's sniggering at him. It's like throwing a pack of cards in the air and all of them landing face-up jokers. Carrying on down the street, Bobby watches wide-eyed as trees start to take on the appearance of witches' claws, erupting from people's front gardens. Birds on rooftops that started out as pigeons fly off as black bloodthirsty crows and ravens, circling overhead and chanting 'Bobby Bobby Bobby'. This is completely uncharted territory for him – previously, the worst trips Bobby ever had were when he thought people were talking about him behind his back, or those few occasions the liberty caps didn't work. Head down,

Bobby tries to jog the rest of the way to the park, but his feet keep turning to brittle skeletons again and the concrete keeps getting harder and harder. 'Why me? Why me?' he whines to himself. After one last surge of energy – and a hop-skip-and-a-jump over some mangled entrails – Bobby the Artist finally reaches the gate of Pallister Park. The sun's still sitting firmly behind closed cloudy curtains, but things feel a bit safer being in an open area with lots of people milling about. There's a few lads playing football over by the muddy goalposts, and Bobby sits for a bit watching the ball plop this way and that. The bench he's sitting on feels like a giant ice cube. Squinting, Bobby the Artist flips open the sketchbook on his lap, then sharpens his pencils one by one onto the blustery grass. He thinks the best tonic is to concentrate on drawing something pretty for a while, rather than thinking all the time about death and executions and mutilated babies and all that. Keeping one eye on the football and one eye on the 220gsm cartridge paper from Jarreds, Bobby the Artist sketches a flurry of legs and Lotto boots and skidmarks and two-footed challenges. It's a pretty raucous kickabout! Scribbling furiously, Bobby gets engrossed in the action, following the lads' movements round the page in a muddle, like Mark Tobey or Cy Twombly drawing out team tactics on a chalkboard. He starts to cheer up, the sun winking now and then through the little transparent bits in clouds. He keeps focused on the boys' charging boots, like a lovely eight-legged horse kicking the hell out of the moon. Bobby nearly dribbles, he's enjoying himself so much. It's only when he glances up at the boys' faces that the pencil freezes in his grip. The lead breaks, and Bobby throws a load of stomach mush into his mouth. As the lads continue kicking, lunging and yelling, Bobby realises with terror they're a team of hideous gangly gargoyles. The boys' noses grow massive and hooked with hairs sprouting out, and their teeth are piranhas', and their hair starts falling out in mouldy clumps, and their ears are all pointed, and their eyes are like the eyes that spy on you behind medieval portraits in haunted castles. Bobby the Artist retches, flinging his sketchbook twenty-four yards down the path. He tries to avert his eyes, but all the other kids and grown-ups in the park are the same disgusting, bug-eyed ghouls. Some lovers over there by the playground are actually feeding off each other, ripping off strips of flesh with maggots and flies pouring out. Petrified, Bobby the Artist swallows his own tongue, then darts out of the park with legs getting all tangled up together. The walk home is horribly unfamiliar. More piranha-toothed hook-noses are staggering about the opposite side of the street in Ellesse sportswear, all of them staring at Bobby and licking their lips. He strides the rest of the way with his head to the ground – at least the tarmac's not turning into anything spooky. He's so shaky! Up the stairs of the flat, he hopes to God he doesn't bump into anyone. There's only one thing for it now – his head's so fucked, all he can do is put himself to bed and hope no gremlins jump in with him. He's still quivering as he slots the key into the slit, and he tries to ignore the bug-eyed goblin on the sofa as he kicks off his shoes and runs to bed. 'Not even a hello?' Georgie asks, chewing Chewits sadly on the pink couch. Bobby the

Artist throws himself under the covers. Georgie sighs orange flavour. She rubs her glitterball eyes with her Bhs sleeve. She scratches her slightly less brutal bob. The weather's still quite overcast, and Georgie feels her chin begin to shake in all the sadness and shadows. She's not sure what to do – Bobby the Artist doesn't seem to like her any more. She's worried this might be the end for them. She's very paranoid herself, and incredibly grouchy after another poop day at Bhs. She thinks he might be cheating on her, but then again Ellen or Pamela or anyone don't seem to have been over recently. She can usually smell their over-the-top perfumes in the flat or, more obviously, see Bobby's filthy paintings of them in her bedroom. It's heart-breaking enough that Bobby's seen those girls in the nude, never mind whether he's done anything rude with them or not. It makes her sick to think those dole bitches might know what Bobby's knob looks, feels or tastes like, flaunting round her flat while she's out earning a living in sweety hell. She can feel herself getting fatter and fatter, and she doesn't even like sweets any more. She just comfort eats, gradually turning into a massive cushion. Georgie holds back the tears, holds back the urge to burst into Bobby's bedroom and scream at him. She feels neglected. It's never been like Bobby to not talk to her – one thing she loved most in the past was chatting to him for hours about the surrealists or space rock or paranoiac-critical method; ever since he got famous, he hasn't spoken about any of it at all. She used to love dressing up for him, lying round the living room in sailor suits and netball skirts and ballerina cozzies with Bobby feverishly swiping at a canvas – nowadays, she just comes home and sits in the tight Bhs uniform all night. And it's getting tighter. Bobby sleeps in his clothes now, so she does too. It's a sad old life. And horrible to think Bobby seemed so much happier before he went down to London! Georgie feels shitty about all his skinny groupies, but worse than all that is Bobby's love affair with drugs. She read on the internet this week that you can really lose your sense of reality on psychedelics (she read a great analogy about reality being like a beautiful flowerbed and how every time you do drugs it's like trampling on the flowers, and the more and more times you do it the less likely those beautiful flowers will ever grow back), and his general attitude is certainly starting to resemble that of a paranoid, detached zombie. She wants the old Bobby back. Sighing, Georgie glances at the scraps of empty canvas and ripped paper strewn around the lounge. He hardly seems to have painted anything decent for months – just boring busty birds, but at least they've flown off now. Fucking filth. Shoving one more fizzy Chewit down her throat, Georgie cringes, sitting in a pile of uncashed cheques and mountainous sweets. She used to be creative herself once, back when she first met Bobby at the art college, sculpting pirate ships and double-decker buses out of cardboard boxes from Tesco. She could even be a good painter herself – after all, she paints her own self-portrait every morning; in Max Factor. But she never wanted to become famous though – after all, her dad said artists just have their heads in the clouds and they won't ever amount to anything, and she wonders if that's true of Bobby. She sighs. She so dearly wants to help him get better.

Reminiscing raspberry-eyed about their daft days at school, Georgie tips out her bags of sweets onto the carpet and makes a little portrait of Bobby, using fried eggs for eyes, Parma Violets for teeth, and a big sour cherry for his nose. She kisses Bobby's lips, then she can't help gobbling him up. 'Mm-mm!' she yums. She understands a little how people could get addicted to drugs, since she can't even kick her own bloody candy habit. Bobby's left a few ecstasy pills knocking about on the carpet, and Georgie's almost tempted to sample one, just to see what all the fuss is about. She's aware she won't be able to cure him without understanding exactly what happens to you on pills, but then again she's seen how much damage drugs have caused him and she doesn't want all that pain for herself thank you very much. Instead, she just looks at the pretty patterns on the ecstasy (Mitsubishis, Shreks, Lovehearts), and copies them down with a nail scissor onto a few of her Parma Violets. Concentrating, she carefully engraves the sharp Mitsi logo into the first one, cracking the edge a bit, but you can still tell what it's meant to be. Blowing off the dust, Georgie admires her handiwork, then swallows the Mitsi Violet with a swig of fizzy pop. For five minutes Georgie pretends to be off her head – waving her arms in the air, faux-gurning, rolling her eyes like pool balls – but after a bit she just feels bloated. For the next couple of hours – instead of guzzling sweeties and feeling sorry for herself – Georgie carves fifty Mitsubishi and Loveheart logos into her Parma Violets, crushes two packets of Trebor XXX mints into six grams of brain-freeze 'cocaine', and sticks together twenty-five Looney Tunes sugar-papers (from a box of fairy-cake mix) to make a sheet of blotter acid. She feels good to be occupied in something creative again. Chewing her lips, Georgie gathers up her little array of medicines onto a sheet of plain A4, then tiptoes through to the bedroom, where Bobby's snoring under a cave of bronze bedcover. His face, peeking out of an air gap, looks so delicate and bewildering, like a fragile puppet-head. Georgie's desperate to wake him up and show him her Class A candy, but he doesn't half look peaceful for the first time in ages, and he'd probably get in a grump with her. Lingering there in the dusty light, Georgie wants to just drop the silly sweets and jump into bed with him, but then all of a sudden a really brilliant idea strikes her. Twitching her nose, Georgie creeps across the lumpy carpet, A4 paper aloft like a floppy old dinner tray. She knows exactly where Bobby the Artist keeps all his drugs and drug paraphernalia, and she holds her breath as she slides open his Fourth Drawer Down. Georgie pokes her hand into the sock where the drugs live, digging out a couple of baggys containing fifty-six ecstasy pills, half a gram of speed, and two grams-ish of cocaine. Fingers steady, Georgie replaces the pills with her Mitsi Parma Violets, then she pours the speed and coke into the wastepaper basket and fills up the baggys with crushed Trebor. Feeling quite dastardly but overall the Saint of Peach House, Georgie skips through to the kitchen and swaps Bobby's acid with cake papers in the freezer. She has an ecstatic shiver, then slams the freezer door shut and flexes her toes on the lino. Georgie chucks the real acid and the fifty-six ecstasy pills out the front-room window, and she imagines the pills each planting an ecstasy tree in the car park gardens. Big pink trees, probably! Before she gets too excited, though, Georgie decides to put something sedate on the stereo (she likes the Crimea) and puts on the kettle, and she refuses to have any sugars in her tea. In between bitter sips from the Power Rangers mug, Georgie smiles to the music and gives the flat a huge spring-clean, even if it's autumn. She washes and wipes and hoovers up everything related to bad memories (crusty bongs, pillbags, Rizla, etc.), and once she's finished the flat feels peculiarly empty. She arranges Bobby's painting materials in a neat pile next to the sofa, folds up his argyle sweaters, then hops into bed with him all shattered and giddy. Undressing, Georgie feels so much happier – she strips naked, stretching, rubbing the restrictive bra marks off her boobies. She yaaaaawwns. Slipping underneath the cover, she touches Bobby's side but he's absolutely paralysed, and they both just lie there silent like marble Roman statues. Up close, Georgie sniffs Bobby's dirty candlewax hair, and she snuggles into him like he's an unwashed comfort blanket. She doesn't want anyone – or any drugs – to take her Bobby away. Yawning again, she spoons him and starts dropping off, just as the Artist starts stirring and mumbling loudly, 'Don't hurt me.' Georgie's eyes ping open with horror. 'Don't hurt me, don't hurt me,' Bobby repeats, slightly writhing around in his sleep. Georgie lets go of him and turns over. She sighs. She wishes she could just click her fingers and everything be alright for him. Squelching her head deep into the pillow, half an hour later Georgie's fast asleep, dreaming of miniature elephants, and half an hour after that Bobby the Artist wakes up screaming air. He's been in and out of slumbers all evening. Sweaty and nervous, he glances at the back of Georgie's head, and worms start wiggling out of her dark bird's-nest hair. Sitting bolt upright, Bobby wonders what the hell's happening to him. He's got so much to give! Shivering, Bobby the Artist says a little prayer, staring up to the heavens, although sadly he doesn't actually believe in God. He glances nervously round the bedroom. Thankfully that bastard swastika wallpaper seems to have been taken down, and there's no more Michael Jacksons in the curtains. However, all the furniture seems to have been replaced by the apparatus of a horrible horrible torture chamber. Shuddering, Bobby clutches the covers up round his forehead, big sloppy heart choking him in his throat. He blinks nervously at the Homebase gallows, IKEA stretching-rack and matching stocks, shiny guillotine, GAK iron maiden and various ball-gags, whips, rusty chains and cats-o'-nine-tails. Georgie continues sleeping soundly beside him, her breaths becoming the deathly gasps and groans of torture victims, echoing off the horrid machinery. Bobby the Artist knows it's just his mind turning the bedroom into a Chamber of Horrors, not some evil Laurence Llewelyn-Bowen, but he wonders why he's got such a nasty bastard for a brain. Sniffing, Bobby concentrates on the various torture devices, trying with all his might to turn them back into furniture. He remembers an essay he studied at college, where André Breton says (like Leonardo da Vinci before him) if you stare into a crystal ball or cracks in the wall long enough, soon you'll start seeing obscure objects and images. On the other hand, Bobby figures if you focus long and hard enough on the illusory objects and images (for example, guillotines and gallows and cats-o'-nine-tails), soon enough they'll turn back into a crystal ball, or cracks in the wall, or your furniture. So, gritting his teeth, Bobby the Artist battles the torture chamber with mind power for fifteen minutes. By the end of it he's sweating profusely, but at least he gets his bedroom back to normal. He stares breathlessly at the Homebase clothes rack, IKEA desk and matching chest-of-drawers, Georgie's shiny dresser, Georgie's GAK suitcase, and various socks, tights, belts, and plugs and wires. Phew-ee! All exhausted, Bobby bumps his head back against the headboard. To celebrate, he decides to crack open a bottle of Bellabrusco, bought for £1.99 across the road. Holding the weight of one and a half litres in his trembly paws, Bobby coaxes paralysis out of the hefty glass container, getting completely hammered in just under half an hour. He chucks the empty bottle across the carpet, then chucks his head back on the pillow and burps and falls straight back to sleep. Next thing he knows, Bobby's woken at 8.30am by Georgie getting ready for work in a daze, then again at 11.05am by Johnnie battering on the door. Bobby tumbles out of bed. At first he thinks it's a *déjà vu*, and has he slept with Ellen and is Johnnie going to smash him up? Para para para. But Johnnie seems in incredibly high spirits, jiggling around in a new Le Coq Sportif tracksuit, and he says, 'Now then, Bobby, how's it going?' Bobby does a nervous grin. 'Er, not too bad,' he replies, still feeling quivery after The Scary Incident with the Acid and all the other scary incidents. He doesn't feel right at all, and he finds it a bit of an effort speaking to Johnnie when they go to sit in the kitchen. Johnnie helps himself to a handful of Skittles, fidgeting about on the stool, asking his pal, 'So how's the art coming on? Any good?' Bobby stares blankly at a crawling teaspoon on the crumby breakfast bar. 'Er, not too bad,' he repeats, then he says, 'Erm,' then he says nothing at all. He's had a few cheques through for various paintings ('Bobby's Favourite Trip' went for two grand, 'Boozy Bastard Bashes Bird' went for one and a half), but money just annoys him now and it's a drag having to log everything in his fucking tax book like Lewis told him to. And as for painting, Bobby hasn't done anything of value for ages, unless you count the lovely sketch he did the other day of a man with his head chopped off. Shifting his bum, Johnnie can see Bobby's a bit distant and moody but, instead of reading the signs and leaving him to it, he grins his teeth one by one and announces, 'I've got some good news, by the way.' Bobby raises a caterpillar. 'Yeah, well did you hear how I got banged up the other week?' Johnnie continues. 'Yeah? Well that's not the good news like, but it was alright anyway; I had pills and that on me but only five or so. Got off with a caution; daft cunts. But anyway, I've decided to pack it in. I'm giving up all this shite; you know, drugs, and stealing and all that. It's like what you said about being relaxed – I'm never fucking relaxed when I'm out and about causing trouble, you know, always watching my back and that. I'm just gonna get myself a job or something . . .' Johnnie's eyes are bright as golf balls as he speaks, genuinely excited about the prospect. He's twenty-one years old, after all

– stealing phones and dealing drugs and robbing people's purses just seems ever so babyish now. Crossing his legs, Johnnie breathes a really big sigh of relief – he's so proud for those words to be finally flying around like the spores of a dreamclock. He's going straight! Grinning, Johnnie glances at Bobby and carries on, 'Anyway, since I've given up dealing, I'm not gonna be taking drugs any more. But . . . I've been keeping this last gram of ket in my shoebox for a rainy day and well, it's not raining or owt, but I wondered if you'd be up for one last dabble? To celebrate and that . . .' Bobby watches corpse-like as Johnnie scrabbles through his pockets then plops a healthy bag of ketamine on the melamine, then for some reason they both start laughing haw haw haw. In his heart Bobby knows it's a foolish idea to go shoving more psychedelia up his nostrils, but then again it's Johnnie's last day of drugs and he'd be a fool to turn down such a generous offer. Perhaps the Special K won't send him doolally. The boys adjourn to the living room. The bare walls watch over them gobsmacked as they cut up lines of Kicking K with the credit card Bobby's been awarded by the Visa company. Four lines later, Bobby the Artist splits the card in two and hurls it in the bin overflowing with acrylic tubes and papers and sweet wrappers. He tries to forget about The Scary Incident with the Acid (even though that entails thinking about it a little bit), putting his feet up on the settee. The ketamine kicks in, numbing his limbs, sticking him to the sides of the sofa. Objects and patterns begin to flutter about the flat. Johnnie, glued to the floor, starts to giggle and run his hands through the carpet, imagining the most beautiful shiny flowers growing from where Bobby saw skulls buried a couple of days ago. He's catapulted back in time to his back garden in Ormesby, him and his brothers playing in the long unmown grass with toy cars and punctured footballs. Johnnie feels lovely, sitting there in the soppy flower bed, his head all free and happy for the first time in years. Bobby, on the other hand, suddenly begins to panic as the settee starts getting uncomfortable under his skinny frame. Not again! Absolutely paralysed from the sniffy stuff, Bobby can do nothing but lie still as needles begin to erupt from the sofa, ripping and severing the soft pink fabric. Next thing he knows, he's lying on a bed of nails, all twelve thousand pins stuck deep into his white flesh. With every wriggle, Bobby the Artist feels himself sinking deeper into the nails, until some needles start sticking their heads out of his chest and neck and scrotum and forehead. He screams the word '   '. This is Bobby's black period. Sweating, Bobby glances at Johnnie while shifting about on the pins, and lo and behold his friend's gleeful face starts to turn gnomish and hooky-nosed and horrible, with big grey flappy ears and sloppy fangs. He looks away. Drenched in perspiration, Bobby the Artist lubricates the bed of nails, sliding further and further in. During this ordeal, Alan Blunt the Cunt taps on the door three times (he's in dire straits, sad and desperate to talk to someone), but Bobby thinks it's the Hangman – or even worse, the Grim Reaper – and doesn't dare answer it. In any case, his limbs are completely numb; except for the searing needle pain, of course. Hyperventilating, Bobby just hopes he doesn't forget how to breathe, and he has to keep telling himself in out in out and shake it all about. Johnnie stares at him with blood dribbling out the corners of his gob. Squirming about, Bobby manages to swallow down a bit of bile, then finally musters up a few words: 'Johnnie . . . eh, maybe you'd better go . . .' Bits of stringy flesh peel off Johnnie's face. He sticks his big red tongue out. 'Oh, er, aye sound,' he mumbles, claws and penises and horns growing out of his eyeballs. Johnnie was quite enjoying himself just then, in the flower bed. He can tell when someone's having a bad trip, though – his mate Ronson once saw Hell in Sainsbury's car park, and he would've thrown himself onto the busy flyover had Johnnie not been there to look after him. The next day Ronson was fine, and they had a delicious Sunday dinner round his mam's with all the trimmings. Recalling that Bisto, Johnnie stands up from the daisy patch, licking his lips. He's in heaven. 'You alright, mate?' he asks, grinning his pearly off-whites/piranha gnashers. Bobby just grumbles though, fear and panic and all those other words tumbling about his system. He lets out a sustained, blood-boiling scream, and after a bit Johnnie gets the picture and starts readying himself on the sofa arm, checks his appearance three or four times in the TV set, says goodbye to every single one of the carpet flowers, then leans right over Bobby the Artist and growls, 'I hope, er, you're alright . . . take care, mate . . . er, take care.' Bobby just stares at him though, with weeping eyes. Shutting the door behind him softly, Johnnie feels a bit guilty leaving his friend in such a sorry state, but Bobby's a big boy and surely he knows how to combat a bad trip. It's just the drugs, it's just the drugs. Slinking down the staircase with heavy limbs, past 4B's fuzzy WELCOME mat, Johnnie's still firmly under the influence himself. With his new breezy state of mind, the world seems so simple and wondrous – hanging around with people having bad trips is pretty bad crack like. He slides down the slimy banister. Shivering, Johnnie catches the 65A into the town centre, and by the time he reaches Doggy the ketamine's beginning to fade off and he stares out the window at the scenery slowly becoming dull again. Off the bus, Johnnie strides peacefully between the mad chain stores and concrete blocks and gothic castles, head full of blank paper. For the first time in his life he wants to earn an honest crust; it's hard work as it is running around stealing wallets and selling drugs and avoiding policemen, it might actually be more of a doss having a nine-to-five occupation. There's always the dole – if they'd have him back – but it'd be depressing hanging out with the same bad characters on the New Deal; opportunist cunts like Bello who got him into twocking mobiles and suchlike. Keeping his head up, Johnnie goes into an off-licence on Borough Road for a pack of ten Royals, and he asks the assistant if they've got any jobs going. 'No, sorry mate,' the skinhead lad says, ding-a-linging the till. Nodding, Johnnie strolls a bit further down the road, popping into the Crown and then into Isaac's to see if they need bar staff. He's never poured a pint before in his life, but he likes the idea of working around pissheads, and he's also under the false impression that being behind a bar feels the same as being out on the lash. However, the lovely barmaid at the Crown and the fatty gadge at Wetherspoon's both turn him down, especially with no CV and no experience to speak of. The boy with spots at WHSmith turns him away as well. So does Superdrug. So do all the sports shops. Getting disheartened, and getting more and more cold and sober as the day goes silvery grey, Johnnie stops for a pint in the Central to calm his nerves. He looks at the people whizzing about Corporation Road, doing their daily jobs and errands and it looks like such a settled, easy life. And he can't wait to have that amazing safe-ty-net: a wage. Strangely, he's even looking forward to getting up at the crack of dawn and coming home knackered after excruciating days at the grind, throw-ing himself on the sofa between Ellen's Care-Bear arms. Maybe she'll even have dinner ready for him! Finishing his Kronenbourg, Johnnie gets up to leave and asks the glass-collector if they've got any 'vacan-cies' (a term he picked up from the boy at WHSmith), but no, they haven't. Back outside, he can't be bothered asking at the Hairy Lemon because it's got such a silly name. All sullen again, Johnnie's head drops to the ground and he follows it into the gaudy Cleveland Centre, kicking bits of receipts and fag butts in really clichéd upsetness. He wanders the aisles aimlessly for a bit. He sees a pair of trainers he likes in Sport&Soccer, but he can't afford them. Hands in pockets, Johnnie scampers into Bhs on the off-chance Georgie's on her shift. Bored, she stands there behind the sweety count-er, scoffing stick after stick of carrot dipped in humous. She's begun eating healthy since adopting her third pink spare tyre round her belly, although it's hard work what with all the kids coming in to buy their advent calendars ready for December the first. 'Oh, hiya,

Johnnie,' she says, with orange teeth. Johnnie smiles. He's surprised how much weight she's put on recently and how spotty she's becoming but, in the way that baby hippos are cute, she's still quite attractive. 'Alright, Georgie?' he asks. 'Not bad,' she replies, swallowing. 'Not very busy. What you been up to?' Johnnie shrugs. 'Not a lot,' he says. 'I was round yours today, mind; me and Bobby done a bit of Special K . . . it was mint . . .' Georgie gulps. Just when she thought she'd ridden the flat of drugs, Johnnie goes and forces more shite up her boyfriend's nose – that's the problem living so close to drug dealers. Bastards!! 'How is he??' she asks, calming down. 'Er, I dunno. I think his head's a bit fucked like . . .' Georgie looks at Johnnie with eyeballs starting to glisten. She's never really liked Johnnie, especially since he's sort of the devil sitting on Bobby's right shoulder, and she's the angel. 'Where is he now?' she asks, dipping another carrot stick. 'Dunno; at home I guess like,' is the reply. Georgie nods, wishing she could get Bobby to a doctor/psychiatrist/hippy spiritual healer. She looks around Bhs and the boring beige shopping arcade – she feels so locked and useless in her crap dead-end job. Johnnie, on the other hand, stares at her with a little bit of envy, then stares at the till and the brightly coloured shelves, trying to figure them out. 'Any chance you've got any jobs going here like?' he asks, and Georgie's a bit taken aback to hear that pop out of his mouth. She gargles some humous. 'Ah, I dunno,' she replies, just as Mr Hawkson her evil boss starts coming over to have a go at her. He strides across the dingy chewing-gummed carpet in his sticky polyester shirt, eyebrows like droopy knitted scarves, and he takes one look at Johnnie in his Le Coq Sportif tracky top and spouts, 'Who's this?' Johnnie feels a bit of an angry squirm in his belly, but he chokes it back trying to remain ca(argh)lm. 'This is Johnnie,' Georgie answers softly. 'He's looking for a job here.' Mr Hawkson splutters out this dreadful sarky laughter. 'Well tell him we're fully manned,' he snaps, then turns one hundred and seventy degrees and scuttles off back to his lair; the pokey office up by Menswear. 'Ignore him, he's an idiot,' Georgie says, although her body language is a bit stiffer and colder now Hawkson's been over. 'Ah, right,' Johnnie goes, gently walking backwards on his way out of the shop, 'I'll be off now, anyway. I'll see you later, eh, take care. Oh, and I hope Bobby's alright and all that.' Left with those words, Georgie feels a bit sad and subdued for the rest of her shift. Once Hawkson gives her the OK to grab her coat and leave the sweety labyrinth, Georgie stampedes sharply to the bus station through the chilly, slowly freezing town. She goes via Virgin Megastore, picking up a sale copy of Television's *Marquee Moon* for her and the boy to enjoy. Perhaps it'll be something to have a conversation about – they haven't spoken in a long long time. Clutching the yellow/red bag in her mitts as she sits on the 65 back to Peach House, she tries to replay memories of when the two of them were happy together, but it's a bit like staring up at stars on a dark night when you're drowning in a pond. So distant. She remembers her and Bobby taking their bikes up the Eston Hills and watching the chemically sunset when there was supposed to be a meteor shower, but there was too much brown fog to see any shooting stars. She remembers dancing with

248

Bobby to Bardo Pond the night she wore the sailor gear, spinning each other like ships' compasses. She hopes to God *Marquee Moon* has some songs to boogie to. Georgie feels a new sense of optimism as she charges up the tower block to her boyfriend, but when she gets in the door she realises with a bit of dismay and fear he's not there. Where is he? Naturally, Bobby's gone a bit mad after Johnnie left him on that horrible bed of nails. Although the very visual aspect of the trip died down after a short while (the needles turned back into pink thread), Bobby was left with a horrible sense his brain's been bent and stretched beyond repair. He couldn't stop thinking about Syd Barrett and Bri Wilson and everyone else who ever lost the plot on acid, and it feels like he's falling down the same stairs as them. At one point he picked up a bit of fluff from the carpet, examining it between his forefinger and thumb, and he burst out laughing for quarter of an hour, unable to work out what it was or where it had come from. 'What are you?!' he yelled at the bit of fluff. Later, Bobby the Artist started sorting frantically through the pile of post mounting on the side, finding on top a letter from Francis Fuller, that poncey art dealer he met all those moons ago in Londres. Frothing at the mouth, Bobby tore open the envelope and out fluttered a fancy perfumed note expressing Francis's gratitude for having 'The Angels' (244x233cm) to hang in his downstairs loo or somewhere like that. Tears in his eyes, Bobby slumped crash bang wallop onto the tough carpet, wishing all his favourite paintings weren't now in the claws of horrible money-gurgling entrepreneurs. That one, 'The Angels' (244x233cm), symbolised all

Bobby's love for the girls in the block – and for people in general – but now they're all devils. He used to be able to talk to people, without having to give them lots of money to be his friend. In a fit of rage, he grabbed Fuller's £3,600 cheque (still sitting there grinning at him next to the doormat) and stormed into the kitchen and set one of the knobs on full power and burned the cheque to death. The paper went all curly then frazzled into dust on the greasy cooker. Remembering to switch off the hob (after all, he's not *that* mad!), Bobby the Artist blew the dust into black snowflakes then returned to the lounge. Feeling itchy and claustrophobic in the tiny flat, Bobby wondered if he'd ever face the great outdoors again. All the staying inside has started giving him a yellow face and hands. Sniffing, Bobby glanced out the window, trying to figure out how sinister the town looked at that particular moment. He rated it about 6/10. Gathering up his medication (speedy coke from the Fourth Drawer Down, acid from the freezer), a clove of garlic, and a stake carved from one of his paintbrushes, Bobby decided to go out and face his fears. After all, he needed the fucking fresh air and all. Wrapped in three argyle sweaters (red then yellow then blue), Bobby went scuttling out of the haunted house. Now, unsure where he's heading, Bobby walks in circles round the estate in some sort of trippy malady. As he passes passers-by along lengthy Marshall Avenue, Bobby can't even look them in the face for fear they might turn into gargoyles or demons. His uncle's Transit van bleeps past with a piranha-toothed goblin in the front, and Bobby doesn't have a clue how to react. He takes a sharpish left down Ferndale Avenue, eyes fixed on the pavement. Safe things to look at are: pavements, houses, skies without clouds, beautiful girls. Dangerous things to look at are: all other people, spindly trees, clouds, shadows, animals, dark corners/blind corners. Bobby walks on, scared of everything. 'Oh-oh, I hope that witch's eyes don't fall out,' he thinks. 'Oh God, I hope there's not a medieval-style lynching round this corner,' he thinks. As he gets to Corpus Christi, with the sporadic traffic speeding past this way and that, Bobby feels a strange compulsion to throw himself in the middle of the road, just to see what it feels like. Ooh, searing metal slicing flesh! Spluttering, Bobby wishes he wasn't becoming such a morbid cunt. Head to the ground, he continues strolling the spooky highways and byways, and before long he finds himself lost in a vast maze of boring identical semi-detached housing – it's called suburbia. Trying to retrace his footsteps to Peach House, all the streets just look the same, and he starts walking round and round in circles getting panicky. Curse those fucking soulless seventies prefabs! Clutching the garlic and stake, Bobby finds himself inadvertently walking out of town, following the road-signs in all the wrong directions. Soon the landscape starts changing from beige cubes and driveways to green carpets and zoomy A-roads, and Bobby's not sure if it's all just an elaborate hallucination. He half wishes he was back indoors with the kettle on and Georgie round his neck, but the idea of getting lost for one evening appeals to him too. That fucking tower block's been making him very reclusive. Thinking back to books he gobbled up in art college like *The Dharma*

Bums or *Siddhartha* (where the protagonists go off to live in isolation and end up all transcendent and purified), Bobby wonders if the countryside might have a similar healing effect on him. Feeling a bit *Withnail&I*ish, clomping through heavy grass in his Adidas trainers, Bobby the Artist veers off the A-road, setting his sights on the big black hill in the distance. He figures the only way he'll be able to get over his torture is by going to the scariest place in the area (that woodland over there looks pretty sinister . . .) and swallowing the rest of his drugs in one last fight for his marbles back. He successfully overcame the IKEA torture chamber six hours ago, and he likes the idea of his Ego, Id and Superego going twelve rounds with each other in a spooky venue. He hopes Dracula comes back – he can't wait to give that daft cunt what-for! He feels ready. Touching the bag of narcotics tucked in his Magic Pocket, Bobby the Artist makes a beeline for the Big Hill, lunging ketamine-legged over tall bushes and down sickly swamps. The weather's reasonable but it's damp underfoot, and Bobby feels his feet turn to sticky toffee puddings as he manoeuvres over the whistling farmland. The fields are sleepy patchwork quilts, stitched together with annoying great fences and hedgerows Bobby has to clamber over. He wonders if he's feeling a bit transcendental already, but no, that's just the frostbite. Panting, Bobby the Artist holds the stake and garlic aloft whenever a fierce dog barks or a crow caws or a cow says moo. He's shivering. Plodding onwards, Bobby wishes he'd brought along some booze to warm his cockles, but then again he thinks a sober head might be the order of the day, to ensure a crystal-clear trip. There's a slight anxiety that his plan might go to pot and he'll wake up tomorrow in Acid Casualty at James Cook Hospital and he'll never be the same again, but he's only going to be battling his own imagination – how hard can that be? Bobby the Artist has always considered himself to be more of a lover than a fighter, but if any hook-noses or piranha-tooths come his way tonight there's going to be trouble! Psyching himself up, Bobby the Artist clenches his fists together, stamping his feet closer closer to the foot of the hill. He begins to throw ecstasy pills down his throat, in a valiant attempt to stay warm and happy. It's tricky having to dry-swallow them, Bobby conjuring mouthful after mouthful of gloopy spittle like a knackered old washing machine. Instantly, the placebo effect of whacking a few pills down the chute gives Bobby a spurt of energy over the last of the rickety fences. Breathing heavily, he feels sort of satisfied and stands hands-on-hips for a minute with the Big Hill leaning over him. The sky's cold and full of stars, like God made up a huge negative dot-to-dot puzzle but forgot to put the numbers on. Bobby scrapes a bit of mud from his trainers onto a spooky-looking bush, but he's not scared. He's not scared. He's just a bit chilly, that's all. Tucking his hands into his sleeves, Bobby sneezes then begins the ascent up the hill. The Big Hill looks a little like the Matterhorn from this angle, the cap all jagged after the mines in its belly collapsed a hundred years ago. Clouds slink around the peak like slimy puddles. Crackling a few twigs, Bobby the Artist tries to judge a safe route into the pitch black pine forest but it's far too blinding. He ends up tripping over filthy treestumps, losing his feet in bottomless bogs and crashing headfirst into branches. The owls and bats laugh at him. Sighing, Bobby the Artist wonders if he should've turned back ages ago. His trainer falls asleep in another puddle. Bogies waterfall out of his red clown nose. A big gust of icy air shoots up his jumpers. Bobby the Artist growls, panting, working his way up a tricky steep bit. He falls on his backside. If an artist falls in a forest and no one is around to hear, does he make a sound? 'Fucking *hell*!!' Bobby screams. Sniffing, he gets up and grabs the nearest conifer, shoes full of pine needles. For fifty yards it's easier scrabbling along the ground like a mop-haired Dulux dog, Bobby submitting himself to the soggy earth; a caveman in golfwear. Isn't it bracing!? In actual fact it's fucking frustrating, and Bobby's relieved to finally reach a levelled-out bit, and he flops down on a treetrunk with a gasp. Wet bummed, the Artist wipes his schnozzle and figures this is as good a place as any to take silly amounts of drugs and face his fears/death/runny nose. Birds flutter away, leaving him to it. A mole diverts his tunnel. Wood mice scamper off, giving Bobby a bit of privacy. And now, let the festivities begin! Slightly cagey and blue-fingered, Bobby removes his pouch of medicines from his trouser pocket, then divides up the Looney Tunes acid and starts poking it bit by bit down his neck. He gobbles up five more ecstasy tablets, hoping the MDMA will combat any untoward negative thinking. Lastly, he hoovers a huge wedge of speedy cokemix up his left nostril, sniffing the spicy white shite off a groove in his wrist. Then he twiddles his thumbs for a bit, waiting for something to happen. He's almost tempted to go all tribal, for example ripping all his clothes off and leaping round a campfire, but to be honest he's quite settled as he is on this treetrunk. He's got no idea what time it is except sometime round nighttime, and he wonders if Georgie's noticed he's gone. He hopes she's missing him, but he hopes she doesn't phone the police and send a search party into the woods – he'd fucking shit himself if loads of rozzers turned up with spotlights while he's tripping his bonce off. The clearing seems pretty secluded though – all he has for company is a bunch of dying Christmas trees and an internal monologue. Shuffling on the crispy trunk, Bobby the Artist gets himself comfortable for an evening in hell. He wonders what ghoulies are going to visit him tonight – strange to think they're all in his head already, but until recently they'd never really been acquainted with each other. He wonders if every human has these same horrible demons lurking about in the caverns of their brains, or if it's just those with insecurities or shyness or depression or anxiety. After all, as the saying goes, you're only ever using ten per cent of your noggin at any one time – perhaps the other ninety per cent is like a dingy waiting room full of monsters and horrid sea creatures and zombies. Or perhaps it's just useless squidgy pink blubber. Stupid old brain! Sighing, Bobby knocks his knees together, awaiting delirium. At one point a dog wails from the east of the forest, and Bobby thinks the spooky hallucinations are beginning, but don't worry it's actually just a dog wailing from the east of the forest. Anticipation! Having a little shiver, Bobby expects the frostiness to play a major part in tonight's trip – he imagines the trees all dropping fat icicles through his skull, or him becoming encased in ice David Blaine-style and dying. But, to be fair, it's actually a little warmer in the clearing, and rubbing your hands and legs together works quite well in generating heat. He wishes he had the tools to build a proper campfire, but a couple of hours down the line he'll probably be in a totally different mindset, and probably end up setting fire to himself or the animals of Farthing Wood. Best just to stick where he is, he concedes. Squirming his arms right into the torso of his jumpers, sleeves flopping dead by his sides, Bobby watches his steamy breath closely for ghosts or skeletons. He wonders what came first: the horror film or the bad trip? Where do these horrible images come from? Any minute now, he expects the whole woodland to turn into some sort of gruesome garden – crawling with lice and dead bodies and owls pecking his eyes out with rusty beaks – but, more than an hour after dropping the acid/E/speed concoction, the forest seems quite the same. Confused, Bobby strains his eyes, then shovels the rest of the drugs into his mouth. Feeling slightly suicidal, Bobby chucks eighteen more Mitsis and eight more blotters down his helter-skelter food pipe. He wants some action! After all, he hasn't come to the forest to sit on a freezing treetrunk all night. He wants to chase poltergeists, whip lanky Frankensteins red raw, and re-murder the living dead. He wants the demons to fear *him* this time! But, two hours and much thumb-twiddling later, the sun's beginning to come up and still no sign of any monsters. It's a miracle! It only took a few tabs to send him potty during The Scary Incident with the Acid, so why then have fifteen of the blighters not touched him in the slightest? He hasn't had a single gurn all night. Scratching his chin, Bobby shifts his weight on the trunk, all the trees becoming gold and tangerine as the sun yawns and wakes up. It's going to be a beautiful day. Bobby the Artist has a bit of a stretch himself, feeling quite knackered now and confused. There's a vague disappointment at having such an abnormally high tolerance for drugs all of a sudden, but ultimately happiness for not having another Cosmic Trip from Hell. He takes three attempts at chucking the empty drug wrappers up the nearest conifer, then has one last look round the clearing for demonic strangers and wanders off. He drops the smelly garlic and stake down a rabbit-hole. The descent from the Big Hill is a lot easier, Bobby gathering speed as he makes ski-trails in the pine needles. He kicks cones out of his path. Rubbing his eyes, Bobby the Artist traces a safe route back to the A-road from such a high vantage point, avoiding muddy fallow fields and hazardous spiky hedgerows. A farmer's out on his tractor in one of the green fields, chasing sheep, and Bobby gives him a big cheesy 'Hello' as he clambers over the last fence and onto the hard shoulder. The farmer ignores him though. There's not many cars zooming around at this time in the morning, and Bobby collapses on the skinny lay-by all pooped. He considers for a second hitchhiking back to Peach House, but he's got two pound fifty in his pocket and before long the 65A Arriva comes jetting past. Bobby gives a thumbs-up to the driver, handing over the money, then he sits at the back casually brushing leaves and dirt off his golf outfit. The driver glances occasionally at Bobby as he pulls back onto the dual carriageway, wondering if he's homeless. The driver's got saggy eyelids, squinting at the road, trundling at a snail's pace towards the round-about on this bitterest of glittery mornings. He's pretty shattered himself. He and his wife were up till two last night after a few drinkies down the Golden Lion in Loftus, and he's dreading facing the schoolkids in a couple of hours. Little shits. Although he was a fairly lippy youngster himself, back in the seventies you at least used to respect your elders, and the police, and the bus driver. Huffing out air, the driver glances again at Bobby the Artist dozing in his mirror. You don't half get some scruffy characters on the bus, he thinks to himself. He glares at Bobby's mud-crusted argyle sweater. It seems like such an undignified job sometimes, driving the bus, dealing with gobby youths and smack addicts not paying their fares, doils fighting at the back, tracksuits swerving in front of you on their bikes. He sighs. He wonders what Bobby's story is. It looks like he's been sleeping in a ditch, dirty bugger. Sliding gracefully down Ormesby Bank, the driver stares blue-eyed at the fuzzy panoramic view of the town stretching its arms out for a big hug. He wishes he was a skydiving instructor. There'd be none of this unglamorous chauffeuring old ladies and scabby adolescents; just vast blue sky and a parachute and some counting. He scratches his eyeballs. In his mirror, Bobby the Artist slowly starts turning green, crushed in a heap on the left-hand seat. Unwittingly he drops off to sleep halfway down Cargo Fleet, unaware of the bus steaming past Peach Plum and Pear Houses. Further into town, the driver picks up a few more passengers:

mostly young professionals starting work at 8am and the lovely Mrs Turner from North Ormesby who always says good morning and coughs like a metronome on the lonesome seat near the front. Gaining speed, the bus kerplunks heavily round Borough Road, all the windows and handrails and seat-fittings buzzing like rattlesnakes. Once in sight of the bus station, the driver has a nervous shiver, knowing the return journey entails picking up lots of grumpy lads and feisty young lasses in school uniforms. He grudgingly twizzles the fluorescent destination to read mirror-image LOFTUS, pulling into the parking bay. He whooshes open the front door, letting out Mrs Turner and the professional zombies. Yawning into his hand, the driver's just about to press the doors shut when suddenly he realises somebody's missing. Bobby's completely disappeared from his rear-view mirror. He leans his head out of the glass cabin, hoping the little shit hasn't been sick or OD'd or fallen into a coma. Such lowlifes! Such an annoyance! Perhaps Monsieur Driver just got out the wrong side of bed this morning, but he scowls and grumbles as he trudges down the aisle to sort out the golfer. 'Hang on hang on hang on,' he shouts at the rowdy kids waiting to get on, with candy fags and Astrobangers hanging out their mouths. Reaching the end of the bus, the driver plonks himself down on the back seat to find Bobby the Artist laid in a ball on the furry, grubby floor. He must've dropped off. 'Wakey wakey!' he yells, turning his nose up at the Artist's brown soggy trousers. Has the bastard shit himself? All Vaseline-eyed, Bobby returns from Dreamworld to find a big hefty man towering over him. Spluttering, Bobby scrabbles back onto his seat, feeling a bit embarrassed and awkward, and he asks, 'Where are we? Bus station? Shite . . . you can't drive me back to Cargo Fleet, can you?' The driver glares at him with dismal disgust. He shakes his head. 'Get off the bus,' he snaps, all moody eyebrows. 'What are you, on drugs or something?' Bobby the Artist wipes a bit of crispy sleep out of his eyes. 'Erm, I don't know . . . I think so . . .' he replies, confused, getting ushered back down the aisle with the driver's hand clamped round his elbow. Bobby tries to say sorry and see you later to the man but his mouth's full of gunge, and he nearly trips up when he hits the bus station tiles. He sucks in air. It's cold. He wishes he had money to get back home, and he wishes he didn't snap all his bank cards up. Hmming to himself, Bobby the Artist staggers out of the station in a daze. Outside, the morning's all frosty and bright like a big blue icepop, and all the streets seem incredibly sober as Bobby waltzes round the shops with their shutters shut. He coughs clouds into the sky. He's still vaguely waiting for his trip to begin, but being straight on such a beautiful morning feels quite uplifting too. The sunshine makes all the colours more vibrant than any sunshine acid ever could. Feeling happier but still incredibly knacked, Bobby the Artist begins a slow, meandering stroll back to Peach House. His flat lives about two miles away, past threatening flyovers and treacherous supermarket car parks, but it's pleasant being out at such an early hour, everything silent and cold and fairytale-ish. En route to Peach House Bobby's legs start turning to jelly, but that's tiredness, not drugs. He feels content getting his first bit of exercise in months, although by the time he reaches Longlands crossroads he's suffering from dizzy spells and weak knees. He slumps for two seconds on the edge of the pavement, getting his breath back, dreading the four-storey ascent to his bed. It's been such an ordeal getting home, it's already 11.15 when Bobby finally peels himself from the kerb, and he decides to pop in the Brambles Farm for a nice refreshing glass of tapwater. The hardcore locals snigger at Bobby – what with his long buoyant hair and drink of water – but the Artist guzzles it down proudly, sat just to the left of the bar between the bar-heater and Sky Sports News. He stays there for the duration of the tapwater and one of the landlord's Regals, then he returns to the great outdoors all rejuvenated and wet-lipped. He feels like he might've detoxed all those shitty useless drugs out of his system, and he makes a vow to have a poo and a wee when he gets in, just to make sure. He sits on the toilet singing along to the water pipes. Then he stumbles into the bedroom, strips off the three argyle sweaters, mucky trousers and stinking argyle socks, and falls into bed like a scuba diver. Splish!! Straight away he's asleep, churning the bedcovers and snoring and dreaming of empty spaces, and that's how Georgie finds him five hours later, face down in the pillows. She has a great big watermelon smile to herself. She's been worried sick about Bobby since he disappeared last night, although she imagined he was probably just round Johnnie's getting forced to do lots of drugs again. Slipping out of her skirt and sticky blouse, Georgie gently jumps on top of the lump in the bed. She plants a few kisses on his lips, reviving

the sleeping beauty. She frowns at the crispy mud pasted on one of his cheeks, like he's been using a very
wrong colour foundation. Blinking, Bobby the Artist
rolls over, rising from the Black Sea. 'Yawn,' he says,
smiling at Georgie. She looks particularly angelic this
evening, what with her head in the way of the lamp-
shade, causing a halo. 'How are you feeling?' she asks,
stroking Bob's chin. 'Alright,' he replies. Georgie
sprawls out on the remaining bit of mattress, staring at
the ceiling. She's feeling healthier now she's eating
more vegetables than sweets – today at work she gobbled a tuna salad from M&S, and she feels surprisingly
energised despite swallowing only leaves all day. She
realises sweets just give you that superficial sugar buzz
for half an hour, then they knacker you out. She feels
like an ex-addict herself – thank God she's discovered
slow-burning carbohydrates! Moving a hand over
Bobby's hip, all she wants now is her boyfriend to be
happy again. 'Bobbbbeeey?' she enquires, 'what do
drugs do for you again?' Bobby the Artist scrabbles in
the covers, trying to sit upright. He feels a bit groggy,
having just woken out of a coma, and he takes a minute
untangling his thoughts, sniffing loudly. 'Nothing,
apparently,' he murmurs, taking a big gulp of air then
submerging himself in pillows again. 'I did something
silly last night,' Bobby continues, 'I went into the
woods, like, to do all the drugs like and sort my head
out. It didn't work though. Well, I mean, the drugs did-
n't work anyway – it's like I've got a massive tolerance
all of a sudden. I don't know if it's really doing it for
me any more, you know, drugs and that . . .' Georgie
smiles. 'Ooh, that's weird,' she says, biting her lip. She

decides not to tell Bobby the Artist she replaced all his Class A drugs with sweets. Instead, she rolls on top of him and gives him a squeeze. And, for the first time in weeks, Bobby goes 'mmmm!' and strokes her back, and they have a lovely lingering kiss even though he hasn't brushed his teeth in a while. What a strange couple of months. Georgie's glad she's hung on, and she's glad Bobby's giving up drugs 'of his own accord'. She has a grin to herself, then the two of them turn to jigsaws, sticking to each other perfectly in the warm double-bed. It's only about six but it's delightful not to move from that spot, and soon their eyes start caving in and they drop into dreams. 'Night night, darling,' Georgie whispers, unaware she's about to have the happiest dreams of her life. She wakes up the next morning full of beans, and she has a really fun day at work, chatting to all the customers and nibbling rabbit food and thinking about Bobby. Her boyfriend, way up high in the tower block, wakes up at about noon with a crush-ing headache like his skull's been replaced with a rusty cannonball. He swings one leg after the other off the mattress, then puts on some clothes and coughs up some fluorescent bile into a glass. Georgie's made him a salt and vinegar crisp sarnie, and on top of it there's a note: HOPE YOU'RE OK. RING ME IF YOU NEED ANYTHING. LOVE XX. Smiling a pink banana, Bobby scratches his head and thanks the Lord he's got Georgie. He yawns. He's feeling fucking grog-gy this morning, suffering the greatest comedown in a long time, but it's good to be sober at least. He feels like he can look at lampshades and carrier bags and pencils again without overanalysing them or turning them into monsters. He can even look at himself in the mirror again without seeing Dracula, although he is still pretty dishevelled and his hair's all over the place. He's feeling a lot better though, mentally, and he downs the crisp sarnie with a glass of cool water. It's weird being on a detox diet all of a sudden, like some sort of fanny or supermodel, but to be honest towards the end all the rock-and-rollness has been getting a bit laboured and depressing. It's nice being on planet Earth again. Right on cue, the sun gets a teeny bit brighter and the one cloud Bobby can see out the bedroom window seems to be a smiling bunny-rabbit. Clouds, you're not even scary any more! Heart jumping with glee, Bobby darts into the lounge and he rings Georgie off the house phone and he has to say he loves her. 'I love you!' he says. After that, Bobby the Artist gets out his Crayola crayon set from Georgie's perfectly stacked pile by the TV, and he sketches his girlfriend with a great big heart and not one ounce of fat either. He's just about to add long wavy mascara when suddenly he's disturbed by his phone going off in a crumpled pair of old trousers. 'Now then!' he ping-pongs, expecting it to be Georgie again. But in fact it's just that daft cunt from London. Bent Lewis puts on his trendy-with-the-kids voice and says to Bobby, 'Hello, mate! Long time no speak . . . how's it going, mate?' Bobby the Artist flops back onto his bed like a grey ribbon getting dropped. 'Oh, I'm alright,' he answers. 'Good, good,' Lewis says, eyeing up the sexy headshot Bobby shot in the tower block car park. 'Have you managed to do any more painting?' he continues. 'See, I've had lots of offers for commissions and suchlike . . .' Bobby the Artist creases his face up.

It's been a while since he last thought about putting paint to paper/canvas/carpet. 'Not really,' he replies. 'Like, I dunno if I'm gonna be able to paint anything for a bit . . . I feel all under pressure, know what I mean? . . . My head's been a bit of a mess, and you did-n't like those nudie paintings I did recently, did you, so . . .' Over in Clerkenwell, Bent Lewis spins back and forth on his spinny chair like a record trying to start. Creak creak! 'Hmm,' he hmms, 'well, I don't know what to say. You had such potential, Bobby! But, I guess there's other things you could do. You've got a very saleable personality; in fact I've come up with a few ideas to get you back in the public eye, if you're inter-ested.' Bobby the Artist raises a lazy eyebrow. Miles away, stroking an abstract paperweight, Bent Lewis reels off 789 business proposals for Bobby's next career move. Here's a small excerpt: '#782: Greetings card illustrator. #783: Television presenter, possibly for a hip, edgy modern art programme. #784: Art workshops, preferably for deprived kids in tower blocks like Bobby's = great PR! #785: Create a range of funky, paint-splatter argyle sweaters, to bring Pringle into the twenty-first century. #786: Hospital murals again, but this time not on acid. #787: Painter/decorator. #788: The person who sits in the corners of galleries and museums, telling visitors not to breathe on the master-pieces. #789: Rent boy?' Bent Lewis licks his lips, com-ing to an end. 'Fuck off,' Bobby the Artist snaps. And with that he turns off his phone and lodges it under one of the heavy legs of the bed, then he jumps up and down fifteen times on the boingy bronze bedcovers. Cheerio telephone! Gasping for breath, Bobby finds himself in hysterics, wandering back through to the lounge for a fag and a sit down. Maybe being popular just isn't for him. He preferred his life so much more when him and Georgie made fun on the cheap, for example posing for portraits or flying paper aeroplanes out the window. He wished he could walk into a pub without everyone expecting a drink off him, or calling him a tight twat if he doesn't automatically buy everyone a round. Perhaps the worst bit of all though was feeling a bit lost, like all being famous is about is getting lots of initial success and then a slow decline into mediocrity and backlash and paranoia. It feels good to knock it on the head for a bit, and he hopes he won't have to become a total recluse to get his life back to normal again. After that fag, Bobby the Artist tears open all the scattered post left here and there on the side, arranging it into piles of cheques, bills, junk and 'miscellaneous'. He slips the cheques into his blue Halifax book, slings on an extra jumper, then scurries out of the tower block into the sunny white afternoon. Racing back into town, Bobby clutches the book in his pocket, making it sweaty, imagining with a grin all the cheques going up in flames like the 'Angels' one. What a lovely fuck-you it would be to Lewis and co., to throw their money back in their faces! What an incredible publicity stunt! No. No. No. Losing it again, Bobby the Artist wishes fame wasn't so fucking tantalising. He feels his head getting muddy again. Pacing through town, Bobby the Artist tries his best not to step on any cracks. He skips up Linthorpe Road to the Halifax, smiling at all the lovely passers-by not turning into zombies any more. Waiting in the queue, Bobby catches his breath staring at the ticking clock. It's 3.34pm. He has a little cough. By 3.39pm Bobby's cashed the £12,000 worth of cheques. He pays back in about £5,000 to live on happily the next year or so with Georgie, then he catches the bus back home to Peach House and strolls up to door 5E and calls for Johnnie and hands him an A5 brown envelope with the other £7,000 in. Johnnie's been having trouble recently trying to get a job, especially round these parts, and there's nothing Bobby the Artist would hate more than to see Johnnie relapse into a life of stinking crime and frustration again. At least £7,000 should get him a few Americano pizzas and that. All milky-eyed and shocked, Johnnie leaps out the door and gives his friend an enormous squeeze. Bobby giggles. He's glad they're back in each other's good books again, and weirdly he feels like some sort of born-again Christian, or Father Christmas. Sniffing, Johnnie offers him inside for a smoke and a can of budget lager with Ellen (who's there sat waving from the brown settee), but Bobby the Artist smiles humbly and shakes his head and says it's alright. He actually wants to go back downstairs and start painting again. For the first time in donkeys' he feels like he's got some stories to tell again – alright, so they're all probably going to involve skully carpets and goblins and torture chambers, but at least they'll only be there in paint on canvas, not there in his head and bedroom. Spinning grins this way and that, Johnnie watches the Artist toddle off back downstairs, hands shaking with the money in between them. He turns to Ellen and they both start gawping at each other. They've been getting on well again the last couple of weeks, but with a bit of a lack of money it's been hard to keep each other really entertained. They're still yet to have sex again, but Ellen likes the new Johnnie – the one who doesn't wake up in the middle of the night screaming 'Police! Police?' any more – and she's considering getting herself off the dole too, but only if the right job comes along. Professional babysitter would be great, or someone who tests the comfiness of couches in DFS. She saw a poster recently, Sellotaped on the door of Teesside University, advertising drug-testing and a payment of £800 to go with it, but she's not sure if they're the drugs she's thinking of. All they've had in the flat is a quickly shrinking block of tac and a twelve-pack of budget lager – it's been a difficult couple of weeks. 'Yey yey yey yey!' Ellen yelps at the sight of all that money. Johnnie considers throwing all the fifty-quid notes up in the air, like a daft Lottery winner in a soap opera, but the flat's a bit of a tip and it could be difficult collecting them up again. What if one of those fifty quids fell in Ellen's manky tomato soup!? Breathing in out in out really sharply, Johnnie just dithers about the flat in wibbly ecstasy, unsure what to do with himself. After a while he launches himself panting onto the sofa and gives Ellen a passionate bear hug. It's as if the Angel Gabriel has come down from Heaven and blessed them! The living room seems much brighter and happier, all the video recorders and thrown leaflets and pizza boxes smiling at one another. That old grey town out the window suddenly looks silver; no, make that gold. All wrapped up on the sofa, Johnnie and Ellen are sort of speechless except for a few 'Fuck fuck fucks' or 'Wheeeees'. To celebrate, they decide to go out on the piss or, better than that, go for a fancy meal somewhere in town. They feel like film-stars, charging round the flat getting spruced up and putting on perfumes, Johnnie checking the money on the mantelpiece every half minute to see if it's still real. 'Fucking hell, it's still reeeeal!' he yelps for the sixteenth time. Ellen laughs through her teeth through in the bedroom, getting a bit bored of that now. She wiggles her shiny legs through the hole in a miniskirt, puts on lots of slap and the glamorous cowl-necked thing, heart going bang bang bang all the time like an auction mal-let auctioning off lots of happiness. Johnnie juggles a Ben Sherman shirt out of his drawer and onto his top half, then swaps tracky bottoms for Burton trousers and pokes £150 into one of their pockets. Ellen suddenly has a little moment of 'Shit, do I look alright??' but they both look like gods, and their faces are colour-wheels. Passing Alan Blunt the Cunt on the way out, Johnnie and Ellen yelp in unison, 'Now then, Alan!' but he's looking a bit down and dismal in his soggy brown cardy, and he pretty much blanks them. But never mind! Johnnie and Ellen are in a bubble of absolute glee like two happy critters in a hamster-ball, and they race out of the flat giggling and showing their teeth. They decide to get the bus because Johnnie's not driv-ing drunk any more. He's gotten used to his new life already – he feels much more easy-going, and even when three cocky youngsters get on at the Buccaneer, chanting, 'Fat cunt, fat cunt, you fat bastard!' at perfect-ly normal people on the street outside, he manages to keep his head. Johnnie and Ellen step off the bus on Linthorpe Road feeling like millionaires, now and then catching their reflections in car mirrors and pizza-shop windows and smiling. The street's not too busy tonight, just odd people slowly parking their bums on seats in pubs, workers waiting around for buses home and shop assistants starting to put their shops to bed. It's a foul old drizzly evening, but who gives a shit when you've got money in your pocket and your best friend round your waist. 'I love you,' Ellen whispers in Johnnie's ear as they mount the ramp thing into Joe Rigatoni's, that swanky Italian restaurant opposite Kwik Save car park. The last time she came to Joe's was after her cousin's wedding three years back, which ended in tragedy – everyone got pissed and the groom started a fight with the page-boy and, worse than that, they got divorced a few months after, didn't they. Sitting down with Johnnie at a moody candle-lit table in the corner, Ellen holds his hand with two of hers and she feels absolutely elated to be with him. 'Look at us,' she says, 'two kids from a scruffy old flat in a place like this . . .' Johnnie laughs. He doesn't think it really makes a difference where they're from though; he just wants to have a laugh and get lashed and stuffed. They stare lovingly into each other's eyes like the lady and the tramp. The rest of the restaurant's fairly empty, just lots of waiters waiting around and the odd other couple sat far far away gobbling pasta and shrieking with laughter now and then. Johnnie and Ellen snigger at their *bellissimo* lives. They order the half pasta half pizza (Pasta: lasagne for him, spag bol for her. Pizza: Americano!), and Johnnie gets a pint of Kronenbourg and Ellen gets a bottle of Chardonnay. They're not foolish enough to guzzle down the Krug or Moët & Chandon; they're not fucking *that* loaded. Waiting for their food, Johnnie and Ellen start bouncing up and down on their seats, banging their cutlery like Oliver Twists at the China Buffet King. 'God, this is amazing!' Johnnie mutters, all dreamy and puff-cheeked, 'What a . . . Bobby's an absolute star!' He looks at Ellen, her face all radiant in the wee candles like she's been cast out of gold, and his teeth almost fall out he's smiling so much. But then suddenly it all turns a bit sour, and his jaw drops. The food gets served, which is marvellous, but who should be carrying the steamy plates but Angelo Bashini, Ellen's old flame. Angelo was supposed to move back to Sardinia, but instead he's living in Acklam now in a flat with his new girlfriend, and he's got a great job in a fancy restaurant (this one), and he stands there handing out the pizza/pasta with an arrogant grin and a much smarter shirt on than Johnnie's. 'Hello, Ellen,' Angelo drawls all Conneryish, one big hairy hand on her cream-cake shoulder. He knows Johnnie won't have the gall to lash out at him in such a high-profile location, and he takes sly glances at his arch adversary to see if he's riling him up. Angelo raises a curly eyebrow, staring down Ellen's top and pouting really exaggerated, wearing such tight tailored trousers you can tell he's got a big knob. Usually this sort of behaviour would rot Johnnie's insides, make him completely insane, and Angelo knows he's pushing his luck if he wants to go home in one piece. But today Johnnie just looks at him all nonchalant, scratches his chin and spouts, 'Waiter, be a darling and get us that bottle of Krug.' Angelo cackles, partly because Johnnie pronounces it wrong, and partly because Ben Sherman and champagne simply do not mix. 'I'm afraid I'll have to ask for the money in advance, *sir*,' Angelo says dead-pan, wanting to embarrass Johnnie and inside his tummy's all knotted with excitement. Johnnie whips two of the fifty-pound notes onto the tablecloth. 'Run along then,' he spits, and Angelo has no choice but to toddle off, desperately trying to check those notes in the dim light but they're genuine anyhow. 'Bravo,' Ellen smiles, and the two of them spend the rest of the night glugging champers out of the bottle and burping ha-ha-ha and hee-hee-hee and all the other sorts of laughs. Angelo spends the rest of the night lurking in the kitchen, mortified. He tries to console himself that his life's better than Johnnie's, that Ellen wasn't a good shag anyway, but if he's honest he's not happy at all working horrific hours at Joe's, and the flat at Acklam has no hot water, and that bird he's with snogged another man last weekend and although she says it means nothing he knows it probably does. Isn't life cruel sometimes! Back on table *undici*, Johnnie and Ellen are falling arse over tit in love all over again. Johnnie's so fun and laid-back and wealthy, he's falling in love with himself a little bit too. It's as if he scribbled all his fears and secrets and doubts onto tiny bits of paper and tied them to the legs of seagulls, and let them whizz off in every direction. Never before has he felt so free and cheery. It's taken this long to realise Angelo's just a fucking wanker, not a threat. The same goes for all other hot-blooded, sleazy macho men. Wankers; all of you, wankers! Absolutely beaming (and full up), Johnnie pays £27.90 for the meal, leaving no tip for the waiters just in case Angelo gets a slice. Then, striding out into the baby blue night, Johnnie and Ellen stroke fingers and make jokes about Angelo, and they think up ways to spend seven thousand pounds. Holidays! Food! Booze! Sky telly! New curtains! Oh, it's all too much for them as they wander back to the bus station, delirious. Not even a few specks and spots of rain can dampen their mood – they duck under cover into the Dairy Milk depot, traipsing round the tiled aisles without a care in the world. It's one of those many days in your life where you say this is the best day of your life. Smirking at each other, Johnnie and Ellen smoke a tab outside queue number eight, watching all the buses splishing and splashing around the courtyard. By the time they hop on the right one (Johnnie feels like a knob paying with a tenner, but luckily the driver doesn't have a go at him), the rain's wandered off elsewhere, and the two of them sit at the back kissing passionately, the raindrops all sliding sideways off the windows as the bus steams forward. They get to Peach House at about half six, swinging each other round and round the car park all giddy and merry. At the fortified front door they spot a soggy Chinese man standing there solemnly in a navy blue suit, though it could've been pale blue to start with. Johnnie and Ellen can't help sniggering at how desperate and minuscule he looks, bashing his fingers into the metal keypad and getting annoyed. 'Are you trying to get in, mate?' Johnnie asks, suppressing the laughter for a bit. The Chinese man nods, his straight black hair even straighter and blacker in the rain. 'Here, then,' Johnnie goes, whacking in the code then holding the door open for him. Still in fits of giggles, him and Ellen charge upstairs frantically, leaving the man to wait for-ever and ever for the cranky lift (it's finally fixed, but it's making quite curious sounds nowadays as it travels at tortoise-speed up and down the shaft). 'God, we haven't had a Chinese for fucking ages, have we,' Johnnie states, quarter way up the tower block, burst-ing into hysterics again. He burps bubbles. The rumble of the lift going down passes them as they reach fourth floor, then it quietly clunks to the ground and the alu-minium doors shunt open. Shaking drippy drops from his hair, the Chinese man sighs then steps into the dank lift. He's feeling shattered after being at work since 9.30am, and it hasn't really helped getting soaked in the process. He's dying to get home and see his new wife – him and Lily got hitched two months back, had a two-week honeymoon in Hong Kong which was ram-pant and beautiful, and he still gets dragonflies in his tummy whenever he thinks about her. At least this is his last job of the day – it would be a bloody block of flats though, wouldn't it. He finds people who live in flats much ruder and harder to cope with than ordinary people like him who live in ordinary houses. Sniffing, the Chinese man gets out on floor six, hoping to Buddha he isn't getting a cold. Holding his briefcase close to his chest, he takes a bit of a breath then knocks twice on the door marked 6E, except the E's fallen off. He waits, glancing up and down the corridor. After a couple more knocks; Alan Blunt the Cunt finally comes to the door, dressed in his brown cardigan and beige cords and slippers. He peers at the little man through thick tortoiseshell glasses. 'Yeah?' Alan says. 'Hello, Alan Blunt? I'm Mr Wong from the Loan

Company. I'm here to talk about your current payment plan. Can I come in, please?' Alan's stomach does a full loop-the-loop and his chin drops like a bowling ball down a mountain. At first he considers slamming the door in the man's face, but then he thinks it might not be completely bad news and he's only a little Chink and he's not exactly going to cause Alan much harm. Mr Wong strides into the bare living room, straight away clocking the racy tabloids glued to the walls, but he tries to remain calm. It does feel a bit like walking into Hell, though. And, as if the cuttings aren't bad enough, Alan's just been cooking scrambled eggs and that happens to be Mr Wong's least favourite food too. Standing erect rather than plonking himself on the battered couch, Mr Wong explains to Alan, 'We've noticed you haven't been keeping up to date with your payments, Mr Blunt, and that cheque you sent last week bounced, I'm afraid. Now, I know this time of year can be a little tough on the pockets – what with Christmas coming up – but I'm afraid we're going to need last month's payment in full before the tenth, or else you could face court action, or risk having your belongings repossessed . . .' Alan Blunt listens to the words fall like bird droppings out of Mr Wong's mouth. The Chinaman stands really cold and stiff while he talks, which only adds to Alan's antagonism. As the horror of the situation dawns on him, Alan's whole skeleton starts shuddering and his veins all turn to ropes. His forehead gets sweaty. 'Well, I dunno like, because see I got laid off by ICI so I might just have to like wait and see . . .' Alan blurts, wishing he'd figured out a better excuse in his head and not nailed those three Super

Tennents earlier. Mr Wong glares at him blankly, then speaks like a computer, 'You owe the Loan Company £289.63 including interest for last month's missed payment, plus a further £267.81 for this coming month, Mr Blunt.' Alan nods gravely, mouth starting to gather white slop in the corners, and he screws his eyes up and snaps, 'Well I can't get it.' Mr Wong keeps staring unsympathetically, desperate to get home to his lovely wife and away from this pathetic bastard. He spits back at Alan, 'Well then I'm afraid we have no choice but to contact the bailiffs . . .' Alan gulps, getting even angrier and shakier. He starts to hear an awful repetitive banging like an out-of-tune snare drum coming from downstairs, and it's a horrible soundtrack to his suffering. Bang! Bang! Bang!! Fucking hell. Alan feels his ankles and brain vibrate, and the red veins in his temples start bangbangbanging too. He curses Johnnie and Ellen. What the fuck are they doing down there? Uncontrollable twitches begin to sprout about Alan's face, and all the while Mr Wong just stands there like a passive Buddhist statuette. 'Get out of my fucking flat, you Chinky shit!' Alan Blunt the Cunt screams, unable to keep his composure any longer. Mr Wong finally shows a bit of emotion: dropped jaw. Wong tries to say, 'Well, if you don't keep up the payments you could easily *lose* this flat,' but before he knows it Alan's lunging across the room and gets both slippery hands round the little man's neck. Fingers stab in like knitting needles. Go for the jugular go for the jugular, the little devil on Alan's shoulder yelps in his ear. Heart racing, Alan just can't help himself from beating this person to a pulp. He's had a very hard couple of weeks. 'No no no!' Mr Wong screams, legs and arms kicking out like a woodlouse turned upside down. He tries to guard his precious little head, tucking it into his chest, but Alan's kicks are much too probing and soon his cheeks and eyeballs are all bruised and he starts weeping out salty blood. The banging keeps on going downstairs, and Alan Blunt the Cunt stops for a second to rub his temples, all wound up and dizzy. Mr Wong takes the opportunity to whip out his company mobile and phone 999, but all he manages to say is 'Help police' before Alan takes another swing at him and the phone spins out of his hand and splits open. 'You daft cunt!' Alan roars, launching a thousand more boots to the poor noodle-nibbler's noddle. Mr Wong makes a little gurgle, desperately scrabbling for the door, but then suddenly he's quiet and still and he goes to sleep face-down on Alan's filthy underlay. He seeps out a little strawberry sauce. Panting, Mr Blunt gives Mr Wong a nudge on the shoulder, but he doesn't seem to be moving. Alan bites his lip. Then all in one go he starts panicking and shitting himself, realising the Chinaman might be dead and the police might be on their way too – don't they have satellites in the sky to track every mobile on earth? Alan glances gingerly at Mr Wong's phone, all broken there on the carpet like a dead spaceship. He feels a strange sensation of being watched. Shaking manically, Alan Blunt grabs the mobile and takes it up to floor eight and kicks it down one of the corridors (where the Fletchers live), but he doubts if that'll put the satellites off the scent at all. After all, there's still a dead Chinese person in his flat. Breaths hovering in his gullet, Alan speedily stumbles back down to 6E, realising his time's probably up. He's got no clue how he's going to save himself. He feels sick looking at Mr Wong now oozing blood along the tatty skirting-board, and he slams the door sharply behind him and deadlocks it and does the chain. Oh God. Next, Alan Blunt the Cunt breaks into tears, staggering aimlessly round and round the messy flat. He stops once or twice at the blurry window, staring down at Cargo Fleet Lane and the tiny bit of Corpus Christi field not blotted out by houses, and he thinks for a second about Tiny Tina. He spites Corpus Christi Carol for not letting him talk to the girl. Such a lovely little girl. Carol doesn't know anything about him – he's not a bad man; he's just lonely, and he needs someone to play with. Sniffing up snot and sobs, Alan steps into his bedroom and sits for a minute on the unmade mattress. He cries hysterically for about fifteen minutes, then he gets over it and starts to breathe a bit more casually. He slides open the top drawer of his bedside cabinet, and for the first time in months he takes out The Photo. The Photo was taken in the living room of 57 Queens Road in 1998, and it was Christmas then too – you can see the prickly Chrimbo tree and the star decorations, and all the presents freshly unwrapped on the burgundy carpet. The Photo's starting to get dog-eared, but you can still make out Alan sat there with sideburns on the sofa and his ex-wife Barbara, and their one and only daughter Tiny Tina perched on his corduroy knee. Tina was only two years old there, back before Alan and Babs got the divorce, back before Barbara got custody over Tina and told Alan never to go near her or the kid ever again. It was only recently Alan realised

Tiny Tina was a pupil at Corpus Christi – by chance one September morning he was on his way to the barber's at Ormesby shops, and he recognised those gorgeous goldilocks a mile off. What joy it was finally to see her again, after all those years! But horrible as well to think she doesn't even know who he is, and that he scares her, and that Corpus Christi Carol won't let him come back to the school gates and see her any more. Sniffing again, Alan Blunt puts back The Photo and plods back through to the lounge. Hello, Mr Wong; still there are we? Shuddering, Alan feels absolutely shit and he wishes he hadn't fucked up his life so spectacularly. It's almost laughable, how horrific things have ended up. Standing stock-still on the itchy ground, Alan wonders if he could squeeze Mr Wong into the refrigerator. He shrugs, shaking his head. Better still, he wonders if he could squeeze himself out of the living-room window, and sadly he starts to clamber on top of the flaky white windowsill. He unlocks the window handles, slides them outward and open, then gently pushes his head and shoulders through the tight gap. For safety reasons the windows don't open out very far, but if you put your mind to it you can definitely throw yourself out of one. Alan Blunt puts his head to the breeze. It's chilly out there. He looks down at all the tree circles and ribbony pavements and matchbox houses, and it seems a hell of a long way down. Alan's stomach turns over, imagining the bloody crunch of his body smashing to bits on the street. For a second he thinks about that great Chrimbo film *It's a Wonderful Life*, and he wonders if he really does want to kill himself or not. But, unlike Jimmy Stewart, who had lots of lovely kids in that film and a stunning wife, Alan's just got a Toshiba telly and a battered old couch and a corpse for company. Squeezing himself a bit further through the window, Alan glances back into the flat. It's not a wonderful life. With no more Alan Blunt, Tiny Tina won't be so scared going to school any more, and Corpus Christi Carol's job will be much easier and perhaps she'll be able to teach Tina better, and Barbara won't have to go through the hell and rigmarole of launching a restraining order against her former husband, and Alan himself won't have to go through the horrible ordeal of losing his flat and his possessions, landing a life sentence in jail for a murder he committed when pissed, and never talk to anybody ever again anyway. So, weeping hailstones, Alan clambers unsteadily out of the tower, takes a glance at the town spread out before him, then drops himself from the ledge with one last push of courage and devastation. There's almost a weird rush of ecstasy as he flies through the air, and there might even be a glimpse of Alan's falling, flailing body as he whizzes past 5E's bedroom window, but Johnnie's too busy giving Ellen the ride of her life to notice. The two of them moan with crazed pleasure, Johnnie doing swirly deep strokes with his knob rather than horrible pornographic blam-blam-BLAMs. They writhe about on top of the bed covers, changing into different positions like taking it in turns to ride on top of a beautiful horse. Johnnie smiles to himself, Ellen sliding herself into the doggy position, and he strokes his fingers down her back and hips as he strokes his willy up and down inside her fanny. He feels like a character in *The Joy of Sex*. He tries to remember all the subtle tips and techniques from 'Un Hommage de Monsieur Condom, 2005', but when it comes down to it all he has to remember is to enjoy himself, and remain calm, and he breathes blissfully in time with the sexual intercoursing. For the first time since he's been shagging Ellen, he's not worried about spurting early, drying up, getting a floppy dangle-on, hurting his girlfriend, or hurting himself. He doesn't have to watch the door any more or watch his back; instead he just watches Ellen's back as the two of them squeak the springs of the mattress. 'Bang bang bang,' the bedhead says against the wall – it's enough to drive the neighbours insane. Changing into spoons (the most underrated of all the sex positions), Ellen shuts her eyes in heavenly flutters as she guides Johnnie up her hole again. She's amazed by Johnnie's sudden expertise in bed – rather than being skewered on a stick and shot to death, it's like she's sliding up and down a six-inch rainbow. Or maybe it's just that Johnnie's got money now that turns her on so much. She eeeeees with glee. Her fanny's absolutely soaking, and she groans as Johnnie reaches for it with his fingers. For five minutes he rips off Bobby and Georgie's sex vid, searching out Ellen's clit and rubbing it round-round-round like they do 22 mins 46 secs into the film. Johnnie carries on thrusting, and concentrating so hard on twirling Ellen's little joystick helps him from springing a leak too early. The rush is incredible, much better than ecstasy or stealing somebody's telephone. Kissing Ellen's neck, he continues getting her off with his fingers, and he feels the earth rumble as she starts writhing like an epilepsy victim, moaning very seriously. After half a minute of gyrating, Ellen starts to convulse and she has a great orchestral orgasm, kicking her legs and squawking like a cockatoo. At first Johnnie's not sure what she's doing, then slowly he begins to smile and two seconds later he's shutting his eyes and squirting hot white sperm into Ellen's belly. The two of them roll off each other giggling and wheezing. 'Wowee,' Ellen breathes, a wonderful pink grin felt-tipped across her face. She gives Johnnie a hug and kisses him on the lips, and she thanks the lord she's got the most bestest boyfriend in the world. Blinking sweaty blinks, Johnnie grins back at her. He feels proud of himself, and slightly surprised how easy it is to get a girl off and how incredibly wrong he's been trying to do it in the past. It's dusk and the room feels frosty now without all the shagging in it, so Johnnie and Ellen jump under the duvet and continue the kissing and smiling down there. They both say 'I love you,' then they laugh for saying it at the same time. Ellen snakes an arm out of the bed, pulling a few tissues out of the Kleenex tub to mop up Johnnie's slime from inside her. Johnnie manages not to lose his rag over them this time. Panting, Ellen tries to slam-dunk the tissues into the waste basket but misses, then she turns back round in the bed and swings her arms round Johnnie and double-knots them. It feels so perfect and gorgeous to be just lingering amongst the bed covers, not like the old days after an awkward fuck where one of them would have to leave the room or fall straight asleep to avoid an argument. Getting her breath back, Ellen can't believe how brilliant her relationship's just got. She does feel awful about shagging Angelo and lying about it to Johnnie, but that's all history now; back then Johnnie wasn't half the man he is now. She bites into the duvet cover, absolutely ecstatic. There's no reason to cheat on him ever again – that sex was womb-blowing! She hugs Johnnie round the neck, then the two of them just lie there kissing and staring and breathing on each other. 'Let's do it again!' Ellen suddenly yelps, and they both fall about the double mattress in fits of laughter. Meanwhile, Alan Blunt the Cunt carries on falling falling falling off the tower block. After that initial burst of excitement and panic, Alan enters a new phase: absolutely shitting his pants. He braces himself for the inevitable smash of bones and brains and guts splashing across the tarmac and his skull getting crushed. Screams and tears are all traffic-jammed in his throat. He starts to slip out of his wool-ly brown cardigan, and there might even be a glimpse of Alan's falling, flailing body as he whizzes past 4E's living-room window, but Bobby the Artist's too busy making a salad in the kitchen with Georgie to notice. Weirdly, Bobby and Georgie can't help giggling and enjoying themselves, chopping up lettuce leaves and grinding black pepper and pouring on Caesar dressing (but not too much, mind you). Georgie's been eating incredibly healthy, and somehow she's got Bobby hooked on it too. Salad seems to keep the monsters away. Bobby watches his girlfriend tossing the leaves in a Greek-goddess outfit, grinning to himself. She's final-ly dressing up for him again. Georgie sprinkles on a bit more dressing, then twirls round and gives him a great big smooch, asking him softly, 'So you're feeling better now then, honey?' Bobby the Artist nods silently, showing his dimples. He wishes he could tell Georgie all the terrible things that have been happening to him, but he doesn't want to depress her. Georgie's just relieved it all seems to be over for him, whatever it was. Grabbing his skinny biceps, she plants a big snog on the Artist's lips, then spins him a bit too fiercely in the miniature kitchen. Whizzing off in different directions, Georgie has to steady herself on the edge of the breakfast bar. She pulls a stretch of clingfilm over the Caesar salad, then glances at Bobby and speaks a bit slower, 'Er, I've got something to tell you, by the way, Bobby.' Georgie's breathing gets a bit staggered. She's been keeping a little secret from him for the past few months, and she's been desperate to get it off her chest but – until now – Bobby never seemed capable of listening. Today, the Artist looks at her with a deadly serious white face, ears open. 'Maybe we'd best go in the living room,' Georgie says, and the two of them trundle nervously into the lounge and park themselves on the two sofa arms. She hopes to God it doesn't split them up. She takes two lungfuls of air and flicks her dark bob behind one ear. Holding his clean hands, Georgie asks Bobby if he remembers the last time they had sex (about two and a half months ago), which was a bit rampant after Bobby got back from London and ate some speed and Georgie ate some sweets. It was great sex, but Georgie had a weird feeling that night that Mr Condom had been sick in her tummy, and when she woke the next morning she felt a little bit queasy herself. She rummaged through the rubbish bin, but she couldn't find Mr Condom anywhere. She decided to forget about it. But three or four weeks later she didn't get her period, and she went to Boots for a pregnancy test and lo and behold she's got a baby inside her. It turns out Mr Condom must've split while they were having sex, and Mr Sperm must've kissed Mrs Egg in Georgie's womb. It's weird because for a month or so Georgie's been getting heavier and heavier, and it never occurred to her it could be a baby. All hunched on the sofa, Bobby the Artist's jaw flops open and his eyes fall out. Georgie says she's not even sure if she wants to keep it or not (although secretly she definitely does), and she strokes Bobby's hand and adds, 'I mean, there's no need to worry. I can get an abortion and that . . .' Bobby the Artist mumbles two empty speech marks. At first his eyes are slightly glazed with terror, but then he shuts his lids and imagines a baby in a nappy gargling happily, and really a little person isn't that scary at all. He's seen worse things in his life. The beaming grin on his face lets Georgie know he's okay, then suddenly Bobby's off scuttling round the flat in absolute delight. Big hefty tears start jumping out of his diving-board eyes. He gives Georgie a gigantic squeeze, but then he eases off, not wanting to squash the little one. He's totally buzzing, and Georgie can't help chasing him round the carpet, showing off all her teeth. Eventually they dive on top of each other, giggling hysterically. 'That's mint news!' Bobby the Artist yells. 'I mean, it can't be that hard looking after a kid, can it?' Laughing, Georgie clutches her stomach, then replies, 'Well, it hasn't been that hard so far . . .' Rolling over, Bobby gives her a big cheesy grin and kisses her earhole. Then, he puts his head against her belly, listening for kicks and gurgles. 'Maybe we could move out of this place,' he suggests, coming up for air. 'I mean, we'll need extra room for the baby and that . . . We might have to get that fucking money back off Johnnie, though . . .' Bobby has a nervous twitch. Georgie shrugs, smiling at her boyfriend being all funny and over the top, although she likes the idea of getting a new place together and getting back on planet Earth again. Breathing deeply, she rubs Bobby's knee, absolutely over the moon that he wants to keep the baby. No more need to feel guilty having that little tadpole in there! Sniffing and snortling, Bobby matches his palms up with Georgie's, then gives the Greek goddess a big kiss and a cuddle. 'It's dead exciting!' he yelps, panting like a lunatic. Georgie sniggers, stroking Bobby's kneecaps and she whispers, 'I know!' They kiss again, then for a minute there's a special bit of hush between them, and Georgie bites her chewy pink lip. She blinks, wiping her streaming nose on her sleeve, then adds softly, 'I might even have a wedding dress in the cupboard, you know!' Meanwhile, Alan Blunt the Cunt carries on falling falling falling off the tower block, eyes full of tears like swelled-up clouds, and he starts really gaining speed and then he

Ten Storey Love Song

Acknowledgements

Thanks very much to Will Atkinson, Lisa Baker, Natalie Boxall, Lee Brackstone, Kate Burton, Byam Shaw School of Art, Jamie Byng, Angus Cargill, Pia Conaghan, *Dazed&Confused*, Sara Dennis/Middlesbrough Libraries, Greg Eden, Jon Elek, the fabulous Faber and Faber, family and friends, Helen Francis, Lydia Fulton, Tom Gillespie, Trevor Horwood, Laurence Johns/To Hell With Publishing/The Amuti Gallery, Lauren Laverne, the wonderful Carole Geoff David Andrew Milward, Andy Neil, Stephen Page, Rebecca Pearson, Michael Smith, Cathryn Summerhayes/WMA, Becky Thomas and Darren Wall.

Special thanks to Gavin Smith, Jim & Chris McGuinness, Paul McGee and Paul Costello, for starting the wheels on a magical trip. And for keeping them turning.

You must always be intoxicated. On wine, poetry or virtue, as you wish. But you must get drunk.

Charles Baudelaire (1821–67), poet and randy dandy

HARPER ● PERENNIAL

Originally published in Great Britain in 2009 by Faber & Faber Ltd.

HarperCollins books may be purchased for educational, business, or sales promotional use. For information please write: Special Markets Department, HarperCollins Publishers, 10 East 53rd Street, New York, NY 10022.

FIRST U.S. EDITION

Designed by Faber and Faber Ltd

Library of Congress Cataloging-in-Publication Data is available upon request.

ISBN 978-0-06-183448-6

09 10 11 12 13   RRD   10 9 8 7 6 5 4 3 2 1

Also by Richard Milward

Apples

Ten Storey Love Song

Paul McGee

ABOUT THE AUTHOR

RICHARD MILWARD was born in 1984 and recently graduated from Central St. Martins College with a fine arts degree. In 2007 his first novel, *Apples*, received huge critical acclaim. He lives in Middlesbrough, England, where he grew up.

"Heartbreaking, honest, and accurate . . . a tough, explicit, yet tender coming-of-age story." —*London Paper*

"The moment I started reading I was hooked. . . . Milward writes with ferocious, infectious energy [and] sharp, black wit." —*Mail on Sunday*

"A confident, no-holds-barred, and bizarrely optimistic story—a fairy tale with plenty of heart." —*Sunday Business Post* (Dublin)

"*Ten Storey Love Song* is an utterly absorbing novel. . . . Full of flawed and captivating characters, this is a truly riveting novel that sweeps along at a fast and very enjoyable pace."
—Ruth Atkins, *The Bookseller* (London)

"Milward has that rare gift of being able to capture and distill an entire generation in a single, simple sentence. Brilliant. Very, very funny and utterly original."
—Helen Walsh, author of *Once Upon a Time in England*

Praise for
Apples

"If this terrifyingly talented author really does have his finger on the pulse of today's youth, parents should probably just give up right now."
—*New York Times*

"A wonderful take on amoral youth. . . . *Apples* is unlike any other novel I've read. Who knows? We may have discovered our J. D. Salinger early."
—*The Financial Times* (London)

"Crass, graphic, funny, and unnerving. . . . A frighteningly recognizable glimpse into a particular experience of adolescence."
—*The Guardian* (London)

"In one breathless, drug-fueled rush of a paragraph, twenty-four-year-old arts graduate Richard Milward colors in the lives of a bunch of mavericks, misfits, and pill-popping cohorts living in a Middlesbrough tower block. . . . Sex, violence, and cracked poetry get mixed up in a gritty, urban, DayGlo, oddly beautiful kind of way."

—*Marie Claire* (London)

"Pay attention; the future looks like this. Richard Milward is a twenty-four-year-old from Middlesbrough, and his second novel is uncompromisingly set out in a single paragraph. The solid lump of prose looks a little daunting, but it leads the reader into a kind of drug-fueled *La bohème* set in a tower block. . . . Brash and loud, with startling flashes of pure poetry."

—*The Times* (London)

"'Precocious talent' is a much-abused phrase in the book world, but twenty-four-year-old Richard Milward is the real deal. His 2007 debut, *Apples*, was a raw, fearless, and funny tale of teenage love on a Midlands council estate, and with this follow-up, his distinctive voice has gained even more strength. Told in one unbroken paragraph (don't worry, you get used to it), *Ten Storey Love Song* charts the dysfunctional lives of the inhabitants of a tower block. A lot of sex and drugs are involved but nothing feels gratuitous; Milward's prose has a lyrical undertone and the all-important ring of truth. Highly recommended."

—*The London Paper*

"It's youthful, zany, and consistently funny. Middlesbrough, as depicted by Milward, is a hugely entertaining place to read about."

—*The Financial Times* (London)

"Milward is a major talent, and his love for his characters shines through any degrading obstacles he forces them to encounter. When writers are being churned out of creative fiction courses like salmon from fish farms, he possesses that scarcest quality: a highly original and engaging voice. He's also a novelist of great emotional power and deft skill."
—Irvine Welsh, *The Guardian* (London)

"The celebration of the everyday is overwhelmingly the pleasure of this book. Perhaps Milward's hero Irvine Welsh is the best point of comparison, but there is also a present-tense sense of motion, a wonder at simple things, and a total lack of embarrassment reminiscent of Updike's *Rabbit, Run*. The real marvel of Milward, though, more so than his casual reporting of filth and violence, is his ability to make you care."
—*Literary Review*

"The wunderkind of the latest wave of chemical-generation writing. . . . Milward's eye is at once unsparing, warm, and compassionate; here, he is wonderfully able to create a world where shambolic dysfunction and terrible violence coexist with flights into hedonism that have a quality of almost transcendent beauty."
—*Metro* (London)